THE UNEXPECTED WIFE

CAROLINE WARFIELD

SOUL MATE PUBLISHING

New York

THE UNEXPECTED WIFE

Copyright©2018

CAROLINE WARFIELD

Cover Design by Rae Monet, Inc.

Published in the United States of America by
Soul Mate Publishing
P.O. Box 24
Macedon, New York, 14502

ISBN: 978-1-68291-766-4

ebook ISBN: 978-1-68291-716-9

www.SoulMatePublishing.com

The unexpected wife.

<cjg>

BY CAROLINE WARFIELD

Dangerous Works
Dangerous Secrets
Dangerous Weakness
The Renegade Wife
The Reluctant Wife
The Unexpected Wife

To those who struggle

with addiction to opium

in all its forms

and to those who love them.

Chapter 1

London, February 1838

Crouched behind a dilapidated barrel smelling of fish and rot, Charles knew he didn't belong in the Isle of Dogs dressed like a dockside vagrant. *You're a duke for pity's sake*, he reminded himself repeatedly in the moonless night. *Have some dignity.* The coat his valet found in a ragman's hoard and the woolen britches with torn knees made dignity unlikely. His face, blackened with burnt cork, made it impossible.

The entire operation had ceased to be fun an hour earlier when the damp reached his marrow and the pains in his back outran the ache in his heart—an ache that had cried out for a distraction and driven him to the ludicrous adventure. Bent down and cramped, he struggled to remember why he had begged the inquiry agent to bring him along. Walter Stewart could bag their quarry on his own, as Charles knew well. Boredom and the malaise that had settled over him in the six months since his son's death made him stupid. There could be no other explanation.

Stewart had been certain Thorn had to pass the fishmongers' alley—if his information about the boy's intentions proved to be accurate. The docks lay steps to the right, the ship they had scouted anchored around the corner.

Where is the ignorant pup? Charles wondered. It had taken them three days to get word of his whereabouts after he disappeared into the urban underbelly, infuriating his father and sending his mother into a frenzy of worry, probably wondering if he were flat on his back in a drunken haze—or worse. *We're fools for sitting here on a frigid night waiting for a witless cluck who ought to be more careful about his associates.*

Charles might have given in to the temptation to leave, except he had known the boy from infancy and well-remembered the ruddy, happy, delightful child he had been before debauchery, drink, and poppy juice took him; except the boy's parents were family friends; except his father—Charles didn't want to contemplate the Duke of Sudbury. The duke not only wielded power in the opposition party, he loomed over Charles's boyhood, first as his guardian's closest friend and later as his mentor, leading him into a career in government. Charles alternately worshipped and feared the man. He didn't want to fail him.

The sound of shuffling feet alerted him. At that hour of night, only the desperate or foolish—the young marquess was most certainly one of those—braved the narrow alley. The young man who passed had dressed in black, his head hooded, but Charles recognized him.

A second boy who scampered after the first, running to keep up with him was unexpected. Unlike the first, he wore plain linsey-woolsey trousers and a rough shirt. The two appeared to be arguing. Charles waited until they passed as Stewart had advised and then pushed himself up, staggered, and steadied himself with one hand on the barrel.

My damn leg is numb. I'm too old for this. He limped out into the alley to see the two figures hurrying toward the waiting ship. The smaller boy tried to grab Thorn's shirt, but Thorn pushed the grasping hand away.

"Wait," Charles shouted. Both young men turned his way. Thorn took advantage of the interruption to send his companion reeling. The boy fell flat on his belly, and Thorn ran up the gangplank.

Charles staggered forward two steps and shouted again. "Wait." He tried to run but stumbled instead. *Where the hell is Stewart?*

He forgot about the inquiry agent when the boy pushed himself to all fours, giving Charles a view that drove all other thoughts away. Whoever chased Duke of Sudbury's heir onto that ship was no boy.

Hesitation earned him a violent attack from behind. He slipped to his knees and darkness descended over his puzzled observation. *The derriere encased in those trousers belongs to a woman.*

~ ~ ~

Hammers resounded in Charles's head with every heartbeat, echoing against his skull in some unholy sonata of agony. He had woken up in a bed not his own, but in a room he recognized nonetheless. It appeared that his uncle took him home. After what, he could not recall. *Another binge? Not whiskey. Not this much misery.*

His uncle, the Earl of Chadbourn, had been his guardian since he was ten years old, more of a father than his own had ever been. Discovery that the countess was his half-sister brought them even closer. He grew up in and out of the boisterous household with the earl's own brood and the countess's younger brothers. Charles's gratitude for that idyllic world warred with irritation over the earl's continued protective oversight, but this particular morning he suspected he ought to be grateful.

Pain left him momentarily weak, and he couldn't swallow his groans when he pushed himself up to sit on the edge of the bed. His tongue rasped against the roof of his mouth, dry as sand, but he detected no telltale sign of laudanum. Since his stomach appeared inclined to stay where it was, that seemed likely.

No laudanum. They didn't dose me with the god-forsaken devil's brew. He might have been relieved if it weren't for the pounding and confusion. *What the hell happened to me?*

One hand grasped the bedpost while he lurched to his feet and blinked at the light that filtered through drawn curtains. *Daylight? How late is it?*

He raised a shaking hand to his head and quickly found the source of his troubles. No amount of liquor could have caused the large knot on the back of his head. Someone or something had hit him hard.

The docks. I went to the docks.

He staggered to the mirror; red-rimmed eyes over a day's growth of beard stared mournfully back at him.

Sudbury's cub. The unruly princeling was— He struggled to remember, leaned on the washstand, and prodded his memory. It had been a lark. He had followed Thorn to the docks. The idiot quarreled with his father once too many times and thought to make his fortune by taking passage with a China Trader. *But— But what? Something else happened.*

Determined to confront his uncle, he pulled on his trousers and stuffed his soiled shirt into them, grateful someone had neglected to remove the thing. It wasn't good form to appear below stairs undressed, but he had run tame in the Earl of Chadbourn's house since he was ten. Neither his aunt nor his cousins were likely to faint at the sight. Charles padded out the door and down the stairs in his stocking feet.

A footman glanced up, eyebrows meeting his hairline. "Your Grace! May I—"

Charles ignored him. He followed the sound of voices to his uncle's study.

"They will manage, I assure you." The Duke of Sudbury's cold voice, unmistakable in its clipped tones, drew his attention. "The clipper I sent will reach Macao long before the tub they sailed on spews the two of them, wrinkled and travel weary, onto the docks."

Two of them. There was another. A boy. No—not a boy!

"If you're certain, I suppose they will be fine. I wish I could say the same for Charles," his uncle said.

Of course I will be fine. It's just a tap on the head. Does he think I'm an infant? Charles put up a hand to push the door open.

"He'll be right as rain as far as his head goes. I wish I could say the same for his spirit," the earl went on.

The hand stilled; his hearing sharpened.

"He sounded well enough last night when he insisted on trailing my son," the Duke of Sudbury said.

"Better yes. Not out of his mind with grief as right after Jonny's funeral. But last night? There was a desperate edge to him, a recklessness."

"There was no real danger. Dennison's men apologized for mistaking him for an intruder." Sudbury managed to convey just a soupçon of disgust. *Not above using a China trader to give his son rope, but too fastidious to actually respect them*, Charles thought.

Memory flooded back. He had accompanied Sudbury's paid inquiry agent to the docks to keep an eye on things. The duke wanted to allow his heir to believe his little escape had actual danger while paying the firm to protect the miscreant all the way to China. After months of defiance and debauchery, the duke hoped the experience would shake sense into the young Marquess of Glenaire.

A mental picture of the other stowaway formed. *Smaller, younger perhaps—and definitely not a boy.* Charles pushed the door open all the way.

"Tell me you didn't intend to allow your daughter to sail with them as well," he snapped without preamble.

His Uncle Will jumped to his feet and examined Charles as a nanny might a child who had fallen from a tree. The Duke of Sudbury, cool and composed, gazed back at him calmly.

"Of course not," the duke replied.

"Sit, sit," the earl said, falling back into his chair.

"Don't be a mother hen, Will," Charles grumbled. He sat anyway. Falling would not add to his dignity.

"I'm grateful you could confirm Zambak embarked. Her mother alternates between pride and panic over her as it is. I would not have wanted her to worry for weeks while we verified the girl's whereabouts."

"You aren't alarmed? A young lady on such a vessel? She's gone to China for heaven's sake." The duke's calm made Charles uneasy. It often did.

"My daughter is not just any young lady," the duke said with pride and exasperation he couldn't entirely suppress. "It is unlikely I could have stopped her. Glenaire may be weak, but he knows his duty well enough to have a care for his sister. I'm paying Dennison's captain to protect the boy. He will know to protect Zambak as well if he has to lock her in her cabin to do it. As to Macao—"

"Your clipper already sailed to arrive ahead of them."

"Three days ago."

"You knew? How did you— Never mind. How do you know anything?" Will said in frustration.

"So, the purpose of me skulking behind barrels was . . ." Charles raised a questioning brow.

"As I said, to confirm that they embarked and reassure their mother."

Will shook his head. "Richard, if my Emma tried that, I'd have her off that ship and locked in her room for a year." He handed Charles a glass of brandy. "As it is, the sooner I can have her safely married, the happier I will be."

"What now?" Charles asked, shooting his uncle a grateful glance.

"I didn't come here to discuss my wayward children," the duke said. I came here to bring you this." He retrieved a folded piece of vellum and offered it to Charles.

The fine paper and dramatic penmanship looked familiar, and the seal proclaimed the sender's identity. "The queen?" Charles gaped at it. The young queen had conveyed her condolences after the funeral, but he had no other dealings with her. She had come to the throne just a year before, and he had been too busy in the sickroom to even attend the coronation. Since then he had other things on his mind.

"The queen," he repeated. "What can she want from me?"

"Open it," Sudbury murmured.

Charles scanned the page, glanced back at his uncle's friend, and scanned it again. "China? Why me."

Sudbury leaned forward. "The situation is ugly. The Chinese have begun to resent rogue opium traders flaunting their laws."

"Rogue traders created by the East India Company," Charles muttered. Bile rose in his throat. Opium in the form of laudanum had destroyed his mother.

The earl leaned forward. "The traders have spiraled out of control since we ended the Company's monopoly. They've flooded China with contraband in outright violation of Chinese law."

"A necessary evil," Sudbury said.

"Necessary because China won't deal with us directly?" Charles demanded, not expecting an answer.

"That and they won't take anything but silver," his uncle said.

"The smugglers sell opium for silver, buy tea with the Chinese people's own coin, and sell the tea here for British sterling. Nasty," Charles muttered.

"Damned rum business, if you ask me," the earl said at the same time.

Sudbury waited for silence before continuing.

"Indeed. Yet the government depends on the revenue

from tea. Melbourne can't afford to let anything get in its way. And tea depends on the trade in contraband."

"Why don't the Chinese push back?" Charles asked.

"They have begun to. The situation has deteriorated so badly that the Jarratt & Martinson Company has begun to lobby for naval support to keep the Chinese off their back."

"Send the navy? Are they crying for war?"

The duke held up a hand. "Palmerston pushes to keep the government out of it, but Martinson himself has returned to London, spreading money and rumors around to make their point. Palmerston's man, Charles Elliot, in Macao has little authority, and no stomach for the trade."

"No stomach for opium, you mean," Charles fairly growled the loathsome word. "So the Prime Minister, Lord Melbourne, and his foreign minister—Palmerston—wish to avoid war while continuing to ignore the opium trade and profit from the tea. What has any of this to do with me?" Charles demanded.

"The queen needs independent eyes, someone on the ground who can give us an objective report on the players, the damages, and the long-term cost of the thing."

The queen does or Sudbury does? Charles looked back and forth between the two men. "Why me?" he repeated more forcefully.

Sudbury waited patiently, but said nothing.

I'm qualified. I spent enough damned time as the Assistant Secretary for War and the Colonies to pay my dues, but still . . . "There are others—men closer to the situation."

"That's just it. Men in the east are too close to the thing, and Palmerston's ministry . . ." the duke left his opinion unsaid.

"It's an opportunity to restart your career," Will added softly.

Charles tapped his lips with a bent finger. *It is that*, he thought. *Perhaps work is the very thing I need. Nothing keeps me here.* With his son Jonny gone and the estate in the capable hands of his cousin Fred, no one would miss him even if he chose not to come back.

He met Sudbury's ice blue eyes directly, refusing to surrender to the older man's manipulation too easily. "And this has nothing to do with your children . . ."

The duke stilled. He would never, Charles knew, do anything as common as shrug. Finally, he spoke. "Should you see them, news would be welcome."

Trust Sudbury to solve two problems with one blow. Charles looked down at the note in his hand. *Victoria R. Such a young woman; so much responsibility. Perhaps this is what I need.*

"I'll do it of course. How could I say no to the queen? But you knew that when you arranged this." He faced his uncle and his long-time mentor, resigned to his fate, and swallowed his brandy. *Solve two—no three—problems at once: reconnaissance for the queen, check on Sudbury's unruly offspring, and get the despondent nephew out of his malaise.*

The duke nodded. "Just so." Will glanced at the duke and away quickly, a furtive and uneasy glance.

"There's something else." Charles knew the two of them too well.

"No," Sudbury answered, chin up. Will stared at his lap, and the hairs on Charles's neck rose.

Chapter 2

Macao, September 1838

Nothing cluttered Superintendent Elliot's desk except the dispatch box that had been delivered that morning. No one looking at it would know it had been thoroughly searched, repacked, and placed in its habitual spot. For what Charles Elliot called "a slip of a girl," Lady Zambak Hayden was a highly skilled picker of locks. Neither the one securing the desk drawers nor the one on the dispatch case had given her the slightest difficulty.

Zambak rubbed her middle finger with her thumb, as if itching to take action while she considered her options. The information she sought had not been in the box. The superintendent's description of the British navy hovering around the mouth of the Pearl Delta while war junks patrolled and neither side took action would be laughable if the issues weren't so serious. A year earlier, the emperor's men turned a blind eye; no longer. For the second season, chests of opium piled up on Lintin Island just outside narrows while the war junks kept up the pretense that they could keep gunships from transporting it to Whampao just inside the narrows to be smuggled inland. Without silver from the smuggling, the tea traders, snug in their factories all the way upriver in Canton itself, couldn't pay their suppliers.

Where the devil is my brother in all this? Too much leisure will ruin him. Thorn had left with the other men at the start of trading season, off to the all-male bastion of Canton. *God only knows what manner of vice the bacon-brained nincompoop has gotten up to there while I cool my heels here.* Her hand fisted in frustration. For a moment, Elliot's desk lamp was in danger of being tossed against the wall.

Her shoulders sagged, and she stared back at the dispatch case. *How much does my father know? Most of it probably. Not much escapes Sudbury.* The duke would welcome information from another source, though, and she briefly considered reopening the case so she might take more extensive notes. She shook off the thought. *No. That will keep.*

For now, her brother Thorn mattered more. There had been nothing in the official papers about him. John Thornton Hayden, Lord Glenaire, her father's heir, The East India Company's newest and least competent clerk, had trundled off to Canton to take up his post. They quarreled before he left, and Thorn had accused her of being their father's spy. The accusation stung.

Someone has to keep an eye on the lack-wit, for the family's sake if not his own. Thorn will disgrace us all if he doesn't learn self-discipline.

She groaned. *Damn it Thorn, what happened to the happy boy of five years ago? The one who teased me out of doldrums, and kept the younger ones laughing?* She missed the boy buried in her sullen brother; she feared for him.

Zambak left the dispatch case undisturbed, cracked the door open, and, seeing no one, slipped out. There had to be information. Mrs. Elliot sent her pitying glances all through breakfast and had not been subtle about it. When sweetly pressed, the woman claimed she worried for Zambak so far from home—a patent lie. The woman had some sort of troubling information. If it wasn't Thorn, it came from England.

A thick missive addressed to Clara Elliot had accompanied the dispatch case, and Zambak turned her attention to locating it. It was not in the Elliot's office, and the only places left to search were the woman's private quarters.

A half hour, three detours to avoid perceptive servants, and one frustrating moment impressing the butler with her consequence later, she found what she wanted on the sewing desk in Mrs. Elliot's sitting room. An ear to the door detected no sound while she quietly scanned the precisely penned message.

She ignored the affectionate words from husband to wife, blushing hotly at one particularly intimate turn of phrase. She reread it twice, distracted by a view of marriage so different from her parents'. She forced her attention back to the matter at hand and found what she sought at the end of the lengthy billet-doux.

Wagner at the Company offices reports that Sudbury's heir continues to disappoint. Admittedly the lull has left all of them with little work, but the boy makes no pretense of employment. Wagner says young Glenaire's interest in Canton is limited to seeking directions to the flower boats and other dens of vice, the one subject about which he has made an extensive study. He should be sent home, but one does not challenge Sudbury. Thank goodness the daughter is all a lady should be—if one disregards the strange start that sent her to Macao in pursuit of her brother.

The paper dropped from Zambak's hands, and she leaned her head against the door. *Thorn may be ignored as he finds his way straight to hell while I'm all a lady should be.*

Rage so great her body shook seized her. A woman had sat on the throne for over a year, but the Duke of Sudbury's line of succession still passed over his eldest to land on a son with neither spine nor character. Behind the anger lay grief for the sweet boy of her childhood, the one who never let their parents hear of her adventures and never failed to make her laugh. Fear lapped at its heels. *What will become of him if I don't act?*

That fear had driven her to China—that and a desperate need to get out of London's marriage mart with its stifling expectations. So far she had succeeded at neither. Thorn had gone beyond her reach, and the narrow minds of the ladies of Macao surpassed those of London hostesses.

Canton. How can I get around the Chinese interdict against Western women there, find passage, and insert myself into the factories? The conundrum made her fingers itch.

~ ~ ~

A pink parasol bobbed up and down in Zambak's eyes, its fringe flying. Elliot's major domo—on Clara Elliot's orders, no doubt—insisted a servant follow her on her rambles, and that personage struggled to keep up with her long stride. The shading of "Lady Zam" constituted his sacred duty, and he worked mightily to carry it out. He gripped the base of the umbrella's long handle, bent at the top to cover her while keeping a respectful distance. Even with that canny device, he raised his arm above his shoulder to compensate for the difference in their heights.

What else has he been charged to do? Report back to the major domo? Does he know enough English to understand my words with the Irish smuggler over his odiferous little vessel? He appeared to cringe when I called the man a— She cut off the thought, wondering if the word had different meaning in Cantonese and glowered over her shoulder at him without breaking stride. He grinned back. More boy than man, a hint of European ancestry mixed with his very Chinese features.

"Bad man, Lady," he said, eyes twinkling.

He understood then. In the polyglot port of Macao everyone knew everything. She snapped forward and continued her climb up from the docks. If she didn't want the Elliots to hear about her efforts to convince someone to take her to Canton, she would have to bribe the boy and probably the major domo as well. She sped up and the parasol kept pace.

Frustration added length to her stride. Her effort to approach a ship captain earlier that day failed as readily as the last ones. They all liked the glint of her coin, but not one cared to risk his business smuggling a woman into Canton. The government decreed no Western woman could defile the factories of Canton, and the traders bowed to Chinese law in that at least. They might take opium up the coast, or sneak the contraband into Whampao, but they would not risk transporting a woman. She suspected they just preferred to keep their all-male bastion free of feminine interference.

The inevitable commercial street ran just above the port, winding around parallel to the shore. Zambak hurried along Rua dos Mercadores, as the Portuguese called it, and turned toward the place where it intersected with a major road, anxious to get to a more salubrious neighborhood. She skidded to a stop at the end, forcing the little servant to step sideways to avoid running into her. A peculiar group crossed in front of them, one never seen on the broad shore road lined with the mansions of wealthy traders, the carefully tended neighborhood of Superintendent Elliot and his wife.

A group of girls giggled and minced along, most of them barefoot, but some were wearing the tiny shoes of a well-bred Chinese girl or the raised horse slippers of the upper-class Manchu ladies. Many reflected Macao's mixed-race subculture. One or two appeared to descend from the black slaves of the Portuguese.

A white woman urged them forward. Of indeterminate age, but certainly older than Zambak, the woman dressed in plain clothes, the sort servants in her father's house might have dressed up with ribbons and frills to serve as

THE UNEXPECTED WIFE | 15

their Sunday raiment. She caught Zambak's eye and nodded before hurrying along behind her charges.

"How odd," Zambak murmured.

"Is very bad," her attendant asserted.

Diverted, Zambak asked, "How so?" In her experience, servants did not express opinions to their superiors unless requested, a situation that left her family uninformed more than once. Thorn would have benefited if servants had interfered years before.

"School for girls. Emperor not like." The little man shook his head.

"This is Macao. The emperor is far from here," she retorted. *A school for girls!* Her Aunt Georgiana would approve. Aunt Georgie sponsored a proper school for young women in Cambridgeshire, one that taught them history and politics as well as classical languages, to Zambak's everlasting gratitude.

Does this one teach subjects worth pursuing? Or is it one of those designed to keep women in their place—serving tea and stitching seat covers?

"Who is that woman?" she asked.

The little man shrugged. "American," he replied as if that explained everything.

A few of the wealthier American traders brought wives, but the ones she met looked nothing like the woman making her way down the road. Almost as tall as Zambak, she had a straight back and confident way about her but none of the airs the other women put on.

"Missionary," the attendant went on when she continued to puzzle over it.

Ah. American missionaries. Clara Elliot spoke of them occasionally, usually in disparaging tones. *The school probably teaches Bible and embroidery. Still . . .*

A broad avenue wound through the municipal park. A few yards in, Zambak darted into a space hidden between two hedges, forcing the servant—and the parasol—to follow. Her thumb rubbed the middle finger of her left hand through her gloves while she studied him closely.

To his credit, the boy did not shrink under her perusal.

"What is your name?" she asked at last.

"Filipe," he responded, driving her eyebrows upward. He shrugged. "My grandfather," he said in answer to her unasked question, eyes following the hand that reached into the pocket sewn into her skirt. They widened when she pulled out coins.

"So, Filipe, I did not visit the docks today. We visited churches, to see the sights."

One coin disappeared into his clothing. "Of course not. Churches only."

"Not even the major domo," she added sternly, drawing a cheeky grin.

"'Specially not old Hua." His delight in pulling one over on the major domo boded well for their relationship.

She held another coin between two fingers.

"That woman. Can you find out her name and direction?"

"If Lady Zam wishes, I can do," he said with a bow.

She smiled back. "I think you and I will deal well together."

Because lies with a bit of truth are easier to maintain, they set out to find a church while Zambak tallied her available resources in her mind. The funds the duke had put on account for her added up to much more than pin money. *Give father credit. He knew I'd need bribes.* She probably had enough to commandeer a ship if she could find someone to captain it.

A broad avenue took them through parks toward São Lázaro church, Macao's oldest, while a new plot coalesced in Zambak's mind. *If the smugglers won't take me to Canton, perhaps the missionaries will.* A smile spread from ear to ear.

Chapter 3

The HMS *Bridgetown* lay at anchor off Madras, its senior officers at ease in the captain's quarters with an excellent brandy and an amusing guest. The Duke of Murnane, well known from his time in the War Office, had been as generous and his brandy as excellent as his reputation led them to believe. His supply of racy gossip from England had been equally welcome.

Charles, for his part, sipped carefully, keeping his wits about him while he watched the navy men relax and their tongues loosen. He had unwound his cravat, removed his coat, and unbuttoned his waistcoat. After three days of pompous posturing and well-practiced nonsense from the East India Company, he much preferred these men. Whatever The Duke of Sudbury wanted from him—and he still couldn't be sure what the old fox actually intended—he'd find better intelligence for the queen among her navy in any case.

"You're telling me Maitland sailed with HMS *Wellesley* and the *Algerine* under orders not to fire a shot?" He didn't have to fake outraged amusement.

General disgust greeted the question and a quantity of well-chosen profanity. Captain McGuffin nodded dourly. "Aye. Nary a shot. Waste of a good voyage, and in the damned southern heat too." Charles met McGuffin during his early days in the War Department and knew him for a tough fighting man with no pretense. McGuffin had been temporarily invalided and spent time in the navy offices ashore until he worked his way back into a command. They'd shared a few memorable evenings together in that time, and unbent to the point McGuffin called him Murnane more often than Your Grace.

"D'ye think Elliot remembers what to do with a ship of the line?" the first mate asked to general laughter.

"Nah. Too much time dancing with ambassadors' daughters," another said, touching off a round of ribald comments about men who left the service for nancy jobs in diplomacy.

Charles opened another bottle, poured, and shook his head sympathetically even though he knew most of them would jump at a chance for Elliot's career. "Fools use the navy like a flag to wave, no? What is he trying to accomplish?"

"Near as we can tell, he wants to remind the Chinese who they're dealing with, though with that emperor a thousand miles away from the Pearl Delta and untouchable, I don't know who he hopes to impress. Palmerston doesn't want to piss off the viceroy in Canton."

McGuffin, swallowed a half glass of brandy in one gulp, screwed up his face while it burned its way down, and growled, "The Company danced to the emperor's tune these fifty years. The Chinese don't even recognize Her Majesty's government. Only let their merchants deal with our merchants." He spat the last word. "Time and past time we persuaded them otherwise."

"Force them to take our opium?" Charles's voice had an edge to it. He knew better than most how vile the stuff was.

"Opium, wool, cotton—hell, I don't care if we make 'em buy geegaws just so they show some respect."

Charles considered that respect had to travel two directions or it degraded into bullying. His view generally invited disdain; he kept it to himself.

"India, now, it's a fair English place these days," the first mate declared. "Canton is a cesspool of European merchant types trying to outdo each other. The pushy Americans are worse."

"We had some German Cit claiming to be a baron hanging around Madras a few months ago trying to cadge transportation to Macao. Rushing to see if he could cash in," another interjected.

"Drove Maitland mad. The admiral finally gave him passage on the *Algerine* just to shut him up," the first mate said. He leaned toward Charles. "The swindler claimed the trull with him was an English duchess."

The hair on the back of Charles's neck stood up. *Duchess.* A lump formed in his throat and went down hard before he asked. "Duchess? It takes balls to make that big a claim," he commented, a sharp edge cutting the humor from his voice.

"Maitland bought it," the first mate said in disgust. He opened his mouth to speak until a glare from the captain shut it.

"We get all sorts—" McGuffin began, but the flicker of sympathy in his eyes killed any doubt Charles harbored.

The hidden agenda. Damn Sudbury. "Let me speculate here," he said. "She claimed to be the Duchess of Murnane." *My wife.*

At his words, the first mate sank back in horror. "I didn't—"

A wave of a long-fingered hand stilled the man. "You wouldn't think it would you?" Charles told him. He turned his attention to McGuffin. "Julia?"

The captain stared at his drink. "So she claimed. I can't say that I ever met the duchess."

"That depends on when you were in London. She generally prefers aristocratic lovers when she can get them. Or land stewards. Or grooms. She has never been immune to navy men, though, so you might have," Charles ground out.

The world knows. The navy might as well. Julia. My wife. My unfaithful, lying, grasping, promiscuous wife. The woman who deserted her son for a lover, who found Jonny's illness disgusting. The chain around my neck. Julia has migrated to East Asia, and both Sudbury and my uncle—his partner in devilment—knew it. She must have run out of Italian counts.

The duke might not have known she headed for Macao, but he would have guessed she'd follow money where it took her, especially after Charles cut off her allowance three years prior. *Those damned interfering old nursemaids knew Julia would be here and sent me on a wild goose chase to confront the one person I least want to see. Ever.*

Charles wondered how quickly he could arrange passage back to England. Only one thing kept him from asking—the signature on his commission: Victoria R. He couldn't refuse a mission for the queen, and his meddlesome uncles knew it. He emptied a bottle into his own glass and began to drink in earnest. "So gentlemen, discerning men that I know you are, what is the best brothel in Madras?"

~ ~ ~

His binge through the stews of Madras changed nothing, the orgiastic bender earned him merely a sick head and self-disgust over cheap sex and third-rate liquor. Visions of the sad-eyed girl at the end would haunt him, in spite of the stack of gold coins he left in her pocket. The queen's commission still lay in his portmanteau. Little of use waited for him in London. Julia still lived.

Charles had never spent much energy considering her life or death before Jonny died. At thirty-three, death felt remote until he'd watched his son fade away and take the light from his life with him. That long final night while he sat next to the boy, and family fretted below stairs, one thought rose to the surface over and over: Why couldn't it be Julia instead of Jonny? If Julia died, he would at least be free. If she had rushed to their son's side, eager to play the grieving mother in the end, he might have choked her on the spot. She didn't come. After that he wished for his own death, but it hadn't come either.

Charles twisted his neck, impatient with the valet Lord Elphinstone had loaned him. It was another steamy morning in Madras, and the man fussed over his wilted cravat just as he had made a theatrical event out of shaving "His Grace sahib." Word came—twice—that the governor wished to speak to him, and Charles's patience ran out well before the man finally bowed and apologized for his obviously valiant effort to turn out the English duke in style.

Warnings from Sudbury and a snippet of gossip preyed on Charles's mind. Elphinstone, a canny Scot with the thinnest of titles, had gone from captain in the Royal Horse Guards to a member of the old king's privy council in four years. The queen—or those wanting to move him far from her, so gossip went—appointed him governor of Madras, but the position would not satisfy him for long. He bore careful handling.

"Don't underestimate the man's ambition or overestimate his skill," Sudbury had said. Charles might as well face him. He would face his own mess soon enough, God help him.

A footman bowed him into one of the smaller drawing rooms. A tall man in uniform stood in rigid contemplation of a seascape on the far wall. McGuffin.

"Your Grace! It is good to see you up and about," the governor rose to greet him. "Captain McGuffin told me you had a small shock."

Behind the man's back, the captain gave a discrete shake of his head. Whatever he told the man, it didn't include specifics.

"You were laid quite low—as any man would be—that some woman used your wife's name in such a way."

Charles swallowed the urge to set him straight. He'd had a lifetime of humiliation at that woman's hand; he didn't need more. Not this morning.

"One wondered, of course. The woman did not seem to be what she ought to be, but still. The Murnane diamonds…"

Every sense rose to alert. Julia had stolen the diamonds from his safe after seducing a former steward out of the combination. He believed them long gone. "She displayed diamonds?"

He hadn't thought the man could become more ill at ease, but Elphinstone managed. "Yes. A tiara and earbobs."

Charles had assumed she'd sold them all. The bracelet had turned up in Venice; the necklace he believed lost. *Trust Julia to flaunt the tiara.* "What makes you think they were the Murnane diamonds?"

"Lady Westervelt recognized them. Of course she claimed to recognize the, er, lady, so we might discount her word. When the woman sold them of course, one ought to have known. A tiara of that quality floating about Madras! It caused a stir."

Sold it! Charles would hunt it down even if it meant another month in the heat of Madras. In the meantime, he had business to conclude.

"If I may, Lord Elphinstone, I would like a private word with His Grace," McGuffin put in.

"Of course, War Department business I suppose," the governor replied, looking pained. He presented Charles with a stiff bow and dragged his feet to the door. "You will, of course, let me know if—that is, if anything of import impacts Madras."

Of course, you prancing fool. My mission has nothing to do with you.

The door closed, leaving blessed silence behind. Charles faced McGuffin with a raised brow.

"Nothing of import, Murnane, except to apologize. I just wanted to get that civilian out of our air."

A smile brought a lift to the side of Charles's mouth. "Apologize for what?"

"For letting uncomfortable subjects arise in your presence the other night and for—" He indicated the room at large, and Elphinstone in particular, with a single gesture.

"How did he get wind of any of it?" Charles asked.

McGuffin studied his feet and puffed out his cheeks, mulling over his words. "He sent me a not-so-carefully-worded message demanding to know what happened during your 'official visit' to the *Bridgetown*. I thought it best to come myself."

"And tell him a bit of the truth," Charles suggested.

"It's usually best to start with that."

"He's probably guessed the rest," Charles allowed.

"Yes, but too polite to do anything but protect your good name." McGuffin looked confident of that.

Charles had no response. The gossips of Madras would buzz in any case. At the end of the day, he would be judged "the poor duke," some version of a spousal monster, or a pathetic fool. It had been thus since he married her twelve years before. Only his own demeanor had ever saved his reputation, and he would not be in Madras long enough for it to make a difference.

They would probably conclude his true mission there had been to pursue her, and that at least would be helpful. Snooping visitors from London with the ear of the queen made colonial officials nervous.

"Those of us who know you, think well of you," McGuffin said, guessing his thoughts. "Tongues rattled in London as well, but no one judged you poorly for it. Did you know?"

"That she was here? No."

"I thought not. Bad luck."

Not luck at all. The duke and my uncle sent me into the fray deliberately.

He shook McGuffin's hand. Genuine gratitude added warmth to their good-byes.

Hands clasped behind his back, eyes blind to the exquisite patterns of the Persian carpet, Charles stood for a long time. He would always have to work for the respect of his peers as long as Julia ran wild. He could not rebuild his life as long as marriage tied him to her, either. Divorce was neither easy nor pretty, but it was the only route out of the wilderness his life had become.

The old men are right. It's time I deal with my wife once and for all. I'll divorce her, find some nice biddable girl to marry, install her in the country, and set up a real family for once. He would have no peace—and no career prospects—until he did. *I'll do it if I have to drag Julia to London by her hair—with or without her latest amour.*

Chapter 4

"Thy name is out of the ordinary, Zambak Hayden." It didn't sound like approval.

Zambak stiffened, unable to decide if the woman's outspoken comment and failure to use her title insulted or amused her. She had quite properly instructed Filipe to announce her as "The Lady Zambak Hayden," there being no other person to make an introduction.

"I am generally addressed as Lady Zambak, Mrs. Knighton," she said, holding the woman's eyes.

The direct gaze didn't falter. Few women stood tall enough to meet Zambak's eyes. "Among Friends we shun all titles, Zambak. Thee may call me Temperance."

"We aren't—" Zambak bit back a set down. *The woman must be a Quaker. They call themselves the Society of Friends.* "I am not one of your faith, and in my world, we do not shun titles, Mrs. Knighton."

Temperance smiled patiently, as she might have at a recalcitrant child. "My observation about thy name was forward, Zambak. I beg thy forbearance."

Temper never serves; Zambak held hers in check in spite of the woman's forward ways and her own long history of impertinent questions about her peculiar name. A proper rebuke would never endear her to the missionaries she intended to court.

"You are not the first to find my name curious, Mrs. Knighton. I am called Zambak after my mother. The Arabic word for Lily, her true name, was bestowed on her in Constantinople. Since I was born along the Barbary Coast, my father thought it amusing to name me Zambak." *And that is more than most people get from me on the subject, if this woman but knew it.*

"Is thy father often given to flights of fancy?"

The idea of the Duke of Sudbury succumbing to flights of fancy brought a laugh up from her depths. "Hardly. My name may have been his last impulsive act."

It brought an answering grin. "Perhaps he wished to bend thy character toward fortitude and strength, Zambak. My own wished a temperate daughter. We do not always turn out as they desire, do we?" the Knighton woman asked with a twinkle in her eye.

Shoulders relaxed, and the thumb of Zambak's left hand began to itch. *This might just work.*

The woman glanced back at her students, bent over their texts. "How may I help thee?" she asked.

"I hoped to learn more about your work," Zambak responded. *And find out if you can help me find a way to Canton.*

"It is as you see. Are thee a teacher?"

The thought startled. "No—that is, not yet. What is it you teach?"

"English first," Temperance said. "That they may might find employment far from the dens of evil in this city and others like it."

"You are training servants?"

"No Zambak. We teach these women that they are children of God, valuable and precious, that they are possessions of no man and may never be used for ill purposes."

Valuable and precious. Never mere possessions. I hadn't thought there were more important things to teach than history and economics. Perhaps I was wrong..

"How extraordinary. Women in England might benefit from your teaching, Mrs. Knighton." She squirrelled the thought away for another day. *Aunt Georgie would love this, but I have other more pressing needs.*

"All God's creatures are valuable in his sight. We teach them to read, which will prove useful in their lives, as will ciphering," Temperance explained.

Not embroidering then. Thoughts raced through Zambak. *What excuse do I have to grow closer to these people?* "Do you teach them about other lands?"

"We believe it useful for all to know the vast expanse of the Lord's world. We show them the globe and speak of our homelands, but many of them find it fanciful. Can thee teach of other lands, Zambak?" Temperance peered at her hopefully.

"I can." *Though what Mrs. Elliot will make of that, I can't say.*

In short order, days were chosen, and a schedule decided. Zambak would come to the school weekly to teach geography. They also agreed that she would teach politics and diplomacy.

"Thee might learn as well as teach, Zambak," Temperance suggested.

Yes, but perhaps not what you intend. "Is your husband engaged in the China trade, Mrs. Knighton?"

The knowing spark in Temperance's eyes this time took on a shrewd rather than merely intelligent gleam. "The trade brought us here and funds our work. My husband partners with Oliver and Company to bring furs and other useful items to exchange for tea." *This woman will not be easily fooled.*

Oliver and Company. A memory unfolded. "Mr. Daniel Oliver's company?"

"Yes. Does thee know him?"

"No, only by reputation." Daniel Oliver shunned the opium trade, refusing at all cost to touch the stuff. His company had become a reproach to the less scrupulous.

People called his factory in Canton "Zion's Quarter." Whether that denoted admiration or disdain depended on the speaker. Whatever else one said about Oliver's practices, he was his own man.

"Daniel is a man of great character."

"I would like to meet your Mr. Oliver some day," Zambak said. *I would like that very much indeed.*

~ ~ ~

The eastern sky faded from indigo to purple behind them as the *Bridgetown* swung around to approach its destination. Charles blinked against the sun now low in the sky, its golden fingers of light glinting off the sea in front of him and bathing roofs of the city while casting the fronts of eastern-facing buildings in shadow. Macao at last—close, but still not approachable. McGuffin estimated the *Bridgetown* could disembark late afternoon the next day. He leaned on the railing and wrestled with impatience. Sooner done; sooner over.

The tasks lying before him oppressed him as heavily on him as the humidity. The queen's commission would be the easiest. He spared it little thought. Dealing with Sudbury's stubborn children might prove more of a challenge, but not an insurmountable one. Even if he didn't maneuver them onto a ship home—something he had every confidence he could do—his report on their welfare should satisfy. That is, it would satisfy if he found them in good order. Time would tell. The great weight on his heart, the last of the three tasks, confronting Julia, made his stomach roil. Thoughts of Julia always made his stomach roil.

"It's a beauty." At McGuffin's voice, a welcome diversion, he pushed himself higher with both hands and turned to greet the speaker.

"In this light, yes."

"Cesspool, though, especially around the port side."

"All cities have stews," Charles said.

"True, but this one…" McGuffin trailed off.

"Explain." Charles stood upright, curious.

McGuffin shook his head. "Not so many slums as you might think. The Portuguese built churches and great homes. The China traders build bigger ones and better, strung along the shore like pearls. The world comes here: Americans, Germans, Dutch."

"English."

"Yes," McGuffin agreed, "but not our finest. Some try to maintain standards. You'll find Elliot is solid, but behind those fancy houses, anything goes on. Some go so far as to install their Chinese mistresses in them. Gives 'em ideas. Daniel Magniac married his. Forced to resign. About ruined his brothers. Crude manners. Crude dress. Crude practices. And those are just the natural perversions."

Charles could imagine the unnatural ones.

"The place swarms with mixed-blood products all vying for a place at the table, and there's plenty of money flowing to allow it. Madras and Calcutta are refined by comparison. Money rules here and not much else."

Charles gazed across the water at the city, closer now, shining in the sunset. "Opium?"

"Money—opium—same thing. It rules."

Something raw and long buried uncoiled in Charles. The boy who had watched his mother succumb to the siren song of laudanum, opium's respectable English façade, ached for her anew. "Opium corrupts all who touch it," he murmured.

"Like I said, cesspool."

"What of tea?" Charles asked, though he knew the answer.

"Britannia rules the waves. Tea rules Britannia. Worth a fortune back home, but they need the opium to get the tea, don't they?"

"Yes, and the Chinese want silver and nothing else for it. They hold us over a barrel." Sudbury told him the treasury relied on the tea tax for fully a tenth of its revenue. The tea trade had to continue at all cost.

McGuffin snorted. "We've made 'em want our Indian opium in spite of that emperor hidden away in his palace. We've taught 'em to crave it and pay silver for it. Opium for silver. Silver for tea."

"Is opium used in Macao?"

"It's China isn't it, or near enough?"

A flash of color in the shadows along the dock caught Charles's eyes. "Hand me your spyglass," he said.

"See something interesting?"

"What is a young lady doing along the docks?" Charles adjusted the telescope for a clearer picture.

"Meeting her lover most like—or husband, to be fair. I don't know why they bring their women out here," McGuffin said.

A gust of wind caught the young woman's bonnet and pushed it backward to rest against her back, swinging by its ribbons just as Charles brought it into focus. She pulled it back on quickly but not before Charles recognized her. The unmistakable white-blond hair of a Hayden brought a curse to Charles's lips. He swallowed it. McGuffin didn't need to know Lady Zambak Hayden prowled the docks. He'd bet a small fortune she wasn't there to meet a lover. *What is the hoyden up to now?*

"Hard to say," he said handing the telescope back. "How early did you say we will disembark?"

Sooner done; sooner over. He had to find Sudbury's headstrong daughter in the cesspool that was Macao and return her to her mother before some taint stuck so firmly she carried it back to London.

Chapter 5

Zambak hung the plain blue pinafore Temperance insisted she wear on its peg by the door and prepared to leave The Macao Ladies' Seminary. She suspected her new acquaintance wasn't so much worried that she might soil her dress as that the sight of Zambak's finery distracted the students; she found the pinafore business easy enough to accept if it helped ingratiate her to the missionaries.

"A blessing on thy day, Zambak," Temperance said as she tied her bonnet.

How does one respond to that? Nothing in her experience prepared her for this American woman's ways. "I wonder, Mrs. Knighton—"

"Temperance—"

"Would you perhaps care to take tea with me some day?" Most young women in London would leap for joy at an invitation from the Duke of Sudbury's daughter. This one frowned and appeared to be considering something. Zambak liked her better for it.

"I am not given to idleness, Zambak. Do thee wish guidance about teaching?"

Guidance? No one but the duke and duchess ever dared. That the woman knew she needed it didn't surprise her. The courage to say so startled her. "It would not hurt."

"Not this day, but perhaps soon," Temperance concluded.

"Which way, Lady Zam?" Filipe asked when she met him outside.

She thought for a moment, tempted to wander down to

the docks to see if any new—and more persuadable—ships had arrived. Tired of failure, she decided against it. "Home— the Elliots' home at least."

A blessing on thy day. Given to idleness. The words followed her. *What will you do today, Zamb?* If lucky, she would find Mrs. Elliot to be out, and there would be none of the never-ending round of calls from cronies and underlings, the incessant repetition of gossip that drove her mad. If lucky, she could retire to her room, sort through her notes, and record her observations in the journal she kept. She intended the journal as a report to her father in lieu of letters. Letters addressed to the Duke of Sudbury might go astray or be opened and resealed. She held on to the journal and her reports, often gleaned from her forays into Elliot's dispatches and augmented by overheard conversations, in hopes of finding a trusted courier for it.

Old Hua the major domo disabused her of hope as soon as she arrived.

"A guest awaits you, Lady Zam," he informed her, dismissing Filipe and gesturing toward the smaller drawing room. "Do you wish to freshen first?"

Do I? No. Sooner done; sooner over. She sighed. "Is Mrs. Elliot there?"

"The lady is out, I am so sorry to say. The guest asked for 'Lady Zambak Hayden.'"

Curious. She removed her gloves, holding both in one hand, but left her bonnet in place. "Very well, announce me." *I'll dismiss whoever it is quickly.*

The door swung open to reveal a sunny little room filled with exquisite porcelain vases full of flowers. A gilded teacart held a decanter of golden liquid and brandy glasses.

Not a lady then.

The man leaning one elbow on the mantle studied a particularly fine porcelain tea jar decorated, Chinese style, with swimming fish. His deep auburn hair raced from memory directly to her heart. Lean and whip strong, she knew he stood a half head shorter than she; she knew it because she knew the man. When he turned with the gracefulness of a dancer to frown at her, joy expanded in her chest only to collapse as his frown deepened.

"What the hell drove you to this misbegotten start, Zambak Hayden? You've outdone yourself this time." The Duke of Murnane, rigid with outrage, glared at her.

Zambak's chin rose as quickly as her spine lengthened and her heart froze. One thought consumed her. "Does my father expect you to beat me or merely drag me back?"

The duke clamped his jaw shut.

"Well, Charles? Isn't that why you have turned up here like some unexpected parcel?" No power on earth would make her look away.

He didn't flinch. "Do you honestly think your father needs to send a peer of the realm half way around the world just to collect his disobedient children? He could have you trussed up in a cell on any ship in Her Majesty's navy if he chose. The duke has more important things to do."

Of course. The fate of England always comes before his children. She often wondered whether Thorn would need to prove himself so desperately—or to defy their father—if the duke had shown him the attention he needed. She had puzzled over her father's reasons for not dragging her back since the day she arrived and found a clipper had arrived in Macao with his instructions to Elliot on her behalf and a line of credit in the bank before she and Thorn even disembarked. There had been no letter for Zambak and, she had been shocked to discover, no funds for Thorn.

"Are you here on England's behalf then or merely distracting yourself?" She strode into the room, removing her bonnet and passing it to the little chambermaid who had slipped in behind her to provide silent watch, a sop to convention so she would not be alone with a man. Hua left the door open a crack, no doubt with his ear to it.

"My mission isn't your concern." A stern expression she had never seen before transformed his once-familiar face. Their families were closer than most relatives, and she'd known him since infancy. He'd been a duke even then, as a boy of twelve, but never stuffy or arrogant like he was at present. Even at his son's funeral the year before, he had spared a moment to tease her.

She studied him for several moments, taking in the clenched fist and the unwavering line of his jaw. *Where did the funny, impulsive elf of my childhood go? Has Jonny's death stolen him away and left this sour old man in his place?* "Ever my father's disciple. Are you here to visit the emperor? Others have tried," she said at last.

"The queen—" He broke off and ran a hand behind his neck. "Look, Zambak, your father worries."

An unladylike snort accompanied her answer. "About disgrace to his title? He should look to my brother."

"Whatever you may think, he cares. What about your mother?"

"My mother probably cheers me on."

That brought a grin. He looked like the Charles she remembered at last. "Once she knew you were safe, she may have. That doesn't mean they don't worry."

"You may inform them I am well," she said, regretting the primness she heard in her own voice.

"Where have you been today?" *The sour old man returned.*

"I am unaware of any legitimate concern on your part," she replied with no regret about her tone at all.

"Only the concern of an old family friend. Where have you been?" he repeated.

"Teaching the women of Macao they need not bow to the tyranny of man."

His startled expression gave her every satisfaction she might have hoped for. She feared he might swallow his cravat. He schooled his expression while she remained poised and finally ground out, "Fascinating. You'll have ample time to tell me more."

"What do you mean?"

"Didn't the major domo tell you? I'm to be Superintendent Elliot's guest."

~ ~ ~

Buttons on the waistcoat worn by Elliot's junior secretary strained at their buttonholes, and his double chin threatened to cover his cravat when he gripped the arms of the superintendent's desk chair. Charles thought him rather young to be running to flesh; he would be corpulent at thirty-three, Charles's own age.

Is thirty-three young? It doesn't feel like it. He wondered if he was simply weary from the journey or if grief had aged him so much. Perhaps his confrontation with Zambak, utterly young and full of innocent zeal, left him feeling like an old man. *How old is the chit? Eleven—no twelve—years younger than I. Was I ever that naive?*

He gave the secretary a weary sigh. "Mr. Higgins, I merely asked how frequently dispatches are transmitted to Canton and—"

"If I could share the government's information with you, Your Grace, be assured I would, but with you here in no official capacity, I have no authority to provide details of the superintendent's whereabouts and travel, much less the transmission of sensitive reports. If you care to leave your message with me, I will see that it is delivered at the soonest possible moment."

Officious little worm. Charles clamped his jaw shut. He debated showing his commission. Victoria's signature would put a fire under the clerk. His reasons for holding back still made sense, however. If they knew he reported to the queen, they might bury him in falsehoods or clam up. He had come to gather information informally.

The missive in his hand merely announced his arrival as "part of my tour of the empire," begged the superintendent's hospitality, and congratulated him on his position. It would do. He handed it to Higgins, eyed the locked dispatch case on the corner of the desk, and left.

He stood in the hallway, grim in the knowledge he had just allowed a third-rate clerk to dismiss him, and at a loose end. He could swear the case had arrived that morning and longed to inspect the reports inside. Obviously Higgins had no intention of allowing it.

Having chosen the role of idle aristocrat, he would have to play it out. He had certainly done it before. *How do the idle rich spend their time in Macao? When I find out, that's where I'll find Julia.*

Zambak had disappeared above stairs after their confrontation. He tossed about for the best use of what remained of the afternoon, and found none. He had yet to speak to his supposed hostess. He went in search, hoping she had returned.

The major domo seemed to think obeisance for a duke required a bow so low his nose almost reached the floor. He rose with a gesture of abject apology. "Missy Elliot" it appeared had retreated upstairs, tired from her exertions. The man flicked a hand gesture, and another servant brought a folded message on a porcelain salver.

His face contorted under the force of rose scent pouring off the thing when he snapped it open. Waving it back and forth between two fingers helped, but he frowned as he read.

Your Grace,

My profoundest apologies that I was not able to greet you when you arrived. May I suggest we meet before dinner for a brief chat?

Respectfully
Clara Elliot

That door closed, Charles set off on foot to survey the city. If he didn't locate his wife's latest lair, he could at least get the big picture of the sprawling spectacle of Macao.

Dealing with Julia promised difficulty, and the Hayden children promised more. Only the queen's commission felt like a manageable goal. The commission came first; he planned to begin by finding his way into that dispatch box one way or another.

Chapter 6

Zambak paused at the drawing room, having arrived on time and properly dressed for dinner as Mrs. Elliot dictated. Conformance to small demands generally saved her unnecessary conflict better left for more important issues.

Higgins, eager for his nightly meal before toddling off to his boarding house, had arrived before her. Once she made it clear that she would suffer no familiarity soon after she met him—and quickly ascertained he would be no help with passage to Thorn—she had dismissed him as unimportant, and thus could ignore his sullen glance, quickly deflected, without effort.

Mrs. Elliot's worried frown gave her more concern. "I understand you met with our guest this afternoon," the woman began without preliminary.

"The redoubtable Mr. Hua saw to it all proprieties were met," Zambak responded.

"I have no doubt my dear. Still, a single man…"

Instead of exasperating her, the woman's discomfort shone light on a possibility. Zambak rubbed the middle finger of her left hand for control while she schooled her features to wide-eyed innocence. For once she wished she could blush at will like some of the more conniving debutants during the London season. The tiniest quiver added just enough meekness to her voice when she murmured, "It isn't the thing, I know, but he is an old family friend, and I didn't think I could deny the meeting."

At the play of emotion across her hostess's face, Zambak pulled her shoulders back and turned toward the window, suppressing a smirk. Her behavior hit its mark. *Clara Elliot wouldn't permit an unmarried girl in her charge to be discomforted by the close presence of an unmarried man. With any luck, she'll send him packing.*

The swish of silk from Mrs. Elliot's curtsey alerted her that the duke had joined them, and she managed her own curtsey with just a hint of mockery to remind him they would have dispensed with such nonsense at home. His blink of discomfort, quickly gone, rewarded her.

Even Higgins managed a tolerable bow. Charles's obvious distaste for him told her he had already met the man and didn't like what he found. Zambak pressed her lips together and dropped her eyes meekly, just avoiding a grin.

Mrs. Elliot's brows drew up in sharp line, and she wrung her hands. "I had hoped we might meet earlier, Your Grace," she said.

"My apologies, madam. My wandering took me farther than I anticipated, and I would not have wanted to delay dinner. Perhaps we might speak now? Or over dinner?"

Zambak puzzled over his "wandering," looking for a clue to his plans, but quickly chided herself. *What is it to me what Charles Murnane does? I won't let him get in my way. He can run home to my father and report whatever he likes.*

Mrs. Elliot did not appear comforted by the duke's response, and Zambak suspected she searched for a polite way to tell a duke he wasn't invited to stay in her home. At least, she hoped that was it.

Charles led their hostess in to dinner, and Higgins winged his arm toward Zambak who scowled when she put two fingers on it as she was expected to do, but she yanked it back as soon as they entered the room. Conversation over the various removes proceeded in fits and starts. The duke's efforts to bring up London or the political climate came to nothing. Zambak refused to assist him. *Let him employ his storied charm on this company; he didn't spare any for me today.*

She smiled into her soup and let him flounder. Clara Elliot, born in Haiti and married in the West Indies as well, cared little about her supposed homeland and tended toward complaisance about her four children's lack of knowledge about it as well, effectively blocking several lines of conversation.

Dialog picked up when Charles drew their hostess out about her many postings first as a navy wife and then as the wife of a diplomat. She droned on for a bit about their nomadic existence, following her husband from Jamaica to Guiana to Macao, and waxed passionate on climate and the discomforts of travel while showing much less interest in her husband's actual work, beyond the demands of entertaining as his hostess. It amused Zambak to watch Charles try to appear interested.

"What brings you to Macao, Your Grace?" the woman asked when they had run out of postings to describe.

"Visiting the outposts of the Empire, madam. Acquainting myself with bastions of British culture wherever I find them," the toad said glibly. She had known him far too long to swallow that one. *Whatever brought Charles here isn't idle curiosity.* Zambak said nothing and wondered why her hostess didn't find it odd that a duke had nothing else to do but sail about poking his nose in here and there. Zambak certainly would have.

The Elliot woman accepted his words at face value, however, and nodded sagely. The pause grew awkward. Zambak moved food about on her plate, one swift glance telling her he puzzled over what to try next.

Mrs. Elliot jumped into the breach. "It is good to have a gentleman for dinner," she said.

The strained smile Charles conjured up seemed to satisfy his hostess. "Isn't it unpleasant for you when the men desert

Macao for Canton for months every year?" he asked.

The woman chuckled. "I'm a navy wife, Your Grace. Needs must. We grow used to them being gone. Macao is a bit different, but not that much."

Zambak kept her ears sharp and her eyes focused on her dinner, hoping to avoid any attempt to involve her in conversation. She doubted he would recount their early confrontation, a conversation that gave neither of them credit, but when he spoke to her, alarms went off.

"How do you spend your days when the colony is so quiet, Lady Zambak?" the toad asked.

She wiped her mouth gently and put her serviette in her lap. "As ladies do," she replied in her best debutant lisp.

When she murmured nonsensical monosyllables in response to a more probing question, their hostess jumped in. "Lady Zambak spends many days sketching churches and other fine buildings." Zambak spared a glance from her intense study of her pudding and caught a suspicious glare from the duke. She ducked her eyes down again.

Mrs. Elliot rose to leave the men to their port after what felt like hours. Zambak stood as well, and Charles rose with them. He didn't appear prepared to endure a half hour of Higgins, and she feared he meant to follow her.

"I'll join you ladies for tea, if you do not mind," he said.

"Of course, Your Grace, if that is what you prefer," his hostess replied.

Zambak dropped a dramatically low curtsey in his general direction. Unless someone knew she had never curtseyed to him before tonight in her entire life, they might have taken her seriously. "I am afraid the excitement of company has left me weary," she said. "I will forego the tea and turn in early."

She made her escape, determined to avoid the man.

~ ~ ~

Mrs. Elliot opened her mouth to respond to Zambak's outrageous behavior, but the girl was gone before she could speak. The older woman's smile wavered when she took Charles's arm while Higgins followed looking mournful.

Charles clamped down his disappointment and prepared to play the ducal fool. *Hoist with my own petard. I'll have to endure another hour of insipid conversation.* It would be a few hours before the house settled down so that he could dig into Elliot's dispatches in any case. He resigned himself to his fate.

His frustrations had multiplied as soon as dinner got underway. The conversation yielded nothing of use, and Zambak acted the part of shy maiden so shamelessly he couldn't resist baiting her with that question about how she spent her time. *The scamp. Sketching churches indeed!* Not one word was said about the women of Macao or the tyranny of men. An imp prodded him to mention it in front of Clara Elliot, but he decided not to. She obviously had the woman bamboozled. He'd uncover the hoyden's mischief soon enough.

Now he teetered on the edge of an ebony chair, designed for European use but decorated *a la chinoise,* and searched for a way to avoid more tiresome chatter. Higgins glared into his tea, obviously piqued that he'd had to forgo port. Charles wondered idly if the household supplied the junior secretary with port when there were no male guests. He guessed not.

Mrs. Elliot fidgeted about as though trying to come to a point. Something about her manner put him on guard. He had assumed upon arrival he would receive an invitation to lodge with Elliot as Her Majesty's highest-ranking official in Macao. That would allow him to assess the man's performance, keep watch over Sudbury's wayward daughter, and find a way into the dispatch boxes.

When he thanked her for her hospitality, however, Mrs.

Elliot had been less enamored of that idea. Putting her cup down, she made a pointed observation about a single man in a home with unprotected women, one an innocent girl. What Zambak would make of "'innocent girl'" almost made him laugh out loud, but he hid his amusement under a sympathetic façade.

"I would assuredly not want to provide scandal or offend the young lady's sensibilities," he said. *As if the contrary chit's foolish starts aren't scandalous enough.* He paused searching for an argument that would allow him to stay.

Desire to outdo her neighbors might turn her in my favor. "Perhaps there is another family willing to host a peripatetic duke," he suggested. He peered at Mrs. Elliot over the exquisite porcelain teacup and forced a haughty and entirely ducal expression to his face.

Clara Elliot didn't bend that easily. His hopes died with her reply. "Most of the single men stay in the factories in Canton during tea season, of course, although some stay year round in the offices here. Mrs. Josie would be happy to accommodate you, I believe."

"Mrs. Josie?" he gulped. "I'm hardly just any single man. This woman—"

She appeared not to notice his dissatisfaction. "A widow of the captain of a China clipper," she went on. "Mrs. Josie opens her lovely—and entirely respectable—home to single men far from home. The meals, I'm given to understand, are first rate and the company excellent." *For a fee, no doubt." Clara Elliot knows how to hold her ground.* He almost admired her.

"Give me this estimable lady's direction. I'll seek her out in the morning," he said, bowing to the inevitable.

"Why, our Mr. Higgins can show you. He is quite content there."

Charles ground his teeth and glared at Higgins. *If the mushroom lives so contentedly with Mrs. Josie, why doesn't he make use of the first-rate meals and leave me in peace?* Seeing no way out, he beat a strategic retreat. He would not get to the dispatch boxes tonight.

Chapter 7

Unlike Canton, the Portuguese colony of Macao had no defined foreign quarter, but the various nationals tended to make their homes in clusters, avoiding the luxurious houses of the wealthy Chinese like so many grand dames lifting their skirts to avoid contact with street urchins. When Zambak left the following morning, she quickly walked well past the cluster of mansions belonging to English merchants that surrounded Clara Elliot's home.

Her satisfaction at having routed her father's spy the previous evening dissipated as soon as she turned off the quiet street in the direction of The Macao Ladies' Seminary and heard booted footsteps several paces behind her.

"He follows, Lady Zam," Filipe informed her. "The dook."

"Ignore him," she hissed, lengthening her stride.

Filipe had to run to keep up; the footsteps went faster. Zambak shook under the force of a frustrated sigh. The sneak would not give up, and she may as well face him. She stopped so abruptly the ever-present parasol dipped sideways, knocking her bonnet askew, and Filipe barely avoided running into her.

Charles had no such difficulty. He slid smoothly to her side and tipped his hat. "Why Lady Zambak, what a surprise."

"A delight, I vow," she ground out through clenched teeth. "I had no idea you had an interest in the merchant's quarter." *The damned man lay in wait for me!*

"All Macao interests me," he retorted. "Shall we explore it together?" He winged one arm.

She glared at it. "Do you plan to dog my every footstep?"

"I offer the protection of my presence, as a gentleman should."

"Gentleman or overbearing tale bearer?"

"As you wish." The tattler's eyes danced. His arm remained unwavering, awaiting her cooperation.

She took it with ill grace and continued her swift pace, pretending not to notice that Filipe's determined efforts to keep her shaded sent fringe flying into her unwanted escort's face until he spun around and spoke to Filipe. A coin passed between hands; Filipe and the parasol disappeared.

"You just bribed my servant," she snapped, walking on.

"I have no idea what you mean," he replied, easily keeping pace.

She rolled her eyes. *I'll have to increase the size of my bribes.* "It isn't proper for you to escort me without my servant to lend consequence," she said, glancing sideways.

"In Macao, the coolie takes the place of a maid?"

She nodded solemnly without breaking stride.

"Then it is well that he hasn't abandoned his post." He turned and gestured toward Filipe, now well out of earshot but gamely following. The boy grinned and waved. They had come to a road that wound down toward the docks. Charles seemed poised to turn that way and gazed at her thoughtfully when she led him in the other direction.

"You were at the docks two days ago."

How on earth— "My business is not your concern," she spat.

"I take it you have another destination in mind?" he asked. "Sketching churches, perhaps?"

They came upon one of Macao's many churches, the legacy of the Portuguese, and it tempted her sorely. She could sketch until she bored him silly, but the Knighton woman and the school expected her.

It could be interesting to see what he makes of Temperance Knighton.

She gave him a mysterious smile, declined to answer his question, and paraded him past shabbier stores and plainer buildings until they stopped in front of the simple whitewashed structure, a former warehouse that served as the school. A faded sign indicated its purpose. Her tormentor's obvious puzzlement gave her great satisfaction. She didn't hide her smirk.

"Thank you for your escort, Your Grace. This is where I leave you. I am expected."

Her gracious nod would have put any social climber in their place when she raised a languid hand to the knocker. Her performance quite pleased her until the door flew open and spoiled the effect before she could knock.

"Zambak, thee are a welcome sight. Maud has taken ill, and I must teach the ciphering as well as reading with the little ones under foot." Temperance rushed out but came to a halt when she realized Zambak had not come alone.

Charles raised one eyebrow, lips twitching. The dastard obviously expected an introduction.

"Forgive me. Thee brought a friend." Temperance looked from one to the other.

Zambak took a fortifying breath. "Mrs. Knighton, may I present His Grace, the Duke of Murnane," she pronounced.

Charles raised a hand to his hat brim to acknowledge the response he expected. It did not come. Temperance frowned at Zambak.

"Does thy friend have a name, Zambak? Thee knows . . ."

"Mrs. Knighton is of the Quaker faith, Charles. They don't believe in titles." She held her breath and her laughter in.

"I am pleased to make thy acquaintance, Charles. Thee may call me Temperance." The teacher stood so tall she looked down to meet the duke's eyes.

A smile, one full of the warmth he'd withheld from Zambak in his two days in Macao, stretched across his face. "I am pleased to make your acquaintance, Temperance," he said. "You may call me Charles. Zambak has spoken to me about your school." He flashed Zambak a smug look that wasn't lost on Temperance.

The lout isn't discomfited in the slightest!

"What has she told thee?" Temperance asked.

"That you teach women they need not bow to the tyranny of man," he answered.

Temperance's eyes widened, and Zambak feared her teasing had caused offence. That would not do. "How did you word it?" Zambak asked. "They are precious and no man's possession?"

"All of us are valuable in God's eyes," Temperance agreed with a nod, somewhat mollified but still studying Charles warily.

"That is so," he said, "and much better worded than my clumsy phrasing, Temperance. Pardon me, if I offended." He kept his face averted from Zambak and focused on the teacher, which was just as well. Zambak could feel heat burn up her neck to her cheeks.

"Thee are very kind, Charles. Now if thee will excuse us, Zambak and I have work to do."

Charles didn't move. "Did I understand you to say you are short-handed today?"

Zambak stiffened, terrified he would offer to help.

"I am." Temperance examined him with frank interest.

"Then I must not keep you. I would like to learn more about your work, however, and see your school. Perhaps tomorrow?"

Zambak feared Temperance would agree. *Charles can be damned charming. If he inserts himself into my efforts, he'll ruin everything.*

The invitation, when it came, was worse. "Would thee like to meet our supporters, Charles? Daniel Oliver has returned to Macao. I would invite thee to dine at our table so thee might meet him." Temperance smiled at Zambak and went on. "Thee wished to meet Daniel, Zambak. I hope it will please thee to dine with us and bring thy friend."

"I would be honored," Charles said. He and Temperance waited for Zambak's reply.

Great piles of cow slop. I finally get an introduction to meet Daniel Oliver, and Father's blasted spy plans to watch over my shoulder. Damn and double damn.

"I would be delighted," she told Temperance, wishing Charles to the devil all the while.

~ ~ ~

Mrs. Josie proved to be an excellent innkeeper— or hostess, as she preferred to pretend—and he quickly discovered she missed nothing and thrived on gossip. He spent thirty minutes over tea after he left Sudbury's willful daughter in Temperance's orbit. Mrs. Josie regaled him with every juicy tidbit she possessed about Macao society, but not one word about his wife.

He had expected to hear of Julia as soon as he landed, but had not. *Where Julia goes there will be gossip. If there isn't any, she can't be in Macao. If she diverted elsewhere, I need information.* He thought of the dispatches. She sailed with Maitland, and she would be giving the navy grief. Elliot would know.

Higgins had Elliot's dispatch case in hand for two days. Charles couldn't put off an inspection of the papers any longer, or the clerk, indolent though he may be, would begin to file and forward them. The dispatches should provide needed insight into Elliot's thinking and the state of Chinese response. He hoped word about his wife might speed up his other goal. Since Higgins guarded the dispatch case jealously, his inspection would have to wait until the respectable population of Macao slept.

After an hour spent tallying ships, guessing tonnage, and recording his statistics from a hill overlooking the port, he returned to the boarding house where he had to sidestep Higgins' efforts to draw him into billiards with another clerk. After dinner, he endured another hour of inane gossip from Mrs. Josie and made certain she saw him retire to his room at an early hour, taking particular care she witnessed him firmly close the door. The wait drove him mad; he coped by rewriting his notes.

When the house finally went dark after midnight, he dressed in unrelenting black, descended the stairs wearing dancing slippers to muffle sound, and escaped through a side door. The walk to the Elliots' took minutes; locating an unsecured window took only a few more. He passed an unlit lantern—one that could be lit but hooded—through the opening, lifted one leg over the sill, and climbed in after it.

Poorly done Hua. Any miscreant can just walk in. He would have to investigate security and see it improved as long as Zambak was in residence.

No servant stirred; no denizen of the house met him when he made his way out of what appeared to be a withdrawing room. He avoided the foyer and the marble staircase at the front of the house full of reflected moonlight from windows onto the landings and down into the entrance. Relying on instinct in the dark, he padded past the night porter asleep in his chair, sidestepped even more moonbeams pouring in a side window, and found his way to the study where he paused, every sense alert.

No sound emerged from the room, and the door remained firmly closed, yet he couldn't shake the instinct that something felt off. *Did Higgins return to get something done? Unlikely. An intruder? In the office?* He weighed his options.

Logic dictated that there was no one in the office, but Charles had long respected instinct over logic. If someone broke in, he needed to know why. If caught, he would have to claim he saw a break-in while passing by and came to investigate.

But if someone has legitimate reason to be there, I'll have to brazen it out. He lay a hand on the door and gently pushed; silent hinges gave.

Dim light across the floor confirmed instinct; someone else brought a hooded lantern. No lawful presence then. He pushed further, and a gray figure withdrew deep into the shadows on a hush of fabric and a hint of exotic fragrance, dousing the light. His whole body relaxed; he pulled the door behind him.

"A dark bandana. Brilliant touch. That hair of yours is a beacon," he whispered. "What the hell are you up to now?" He lit his lantern and hooded it before he held it high. Elliot's dispatch box lay open, and papers littered his desk, as they had not when he was there before. Wrapped to the chin in a dark dressing gown, Zambak glared from deep in the shadows. He reached for one of the papers; he could deal with her later.

"Wait!" she hissed. "I have them in order. Higgins will notice if you rearrange. You'll ruin everything."

How does she know how Higgins arranges the papers? Unless she does this regularly.

She stepped closer to papers filled with notes in some sort of cypher that lay flat on the table, held the dispatch case open with one hand, and pointed with the other. "See here? He arranges them by date before document type."

He followed where she pointed, acutely aware of her obvious familiarity with Elliot's files and even more aware of her smooth cheek next to his where she leaned over the table, and the exotic scent that moved with her—not sandalwood but some oriental mix: jasmine and a hint of cloves.

She turned to see if he followed, and her face came into focus in the lantern light. He remembered her as a child. *When did her face mature, her neck take on that graceful curve, and her lips . . .*

"Charles? Do you see?" she whispered, irritation sharpening the sound.

"Of course I see! Do you take me for an idiot?" He did see. Maintaining a neat organization made Elliot's papers easier to search without getting caught. Her efficiency irritated him almost as much as his own reactions. The last thing he needed was an entirely inappropriate attraction to his mentor's daughter twelve years his junior, even if she didn't have better sense than to be caught alone at night with a man clad in nothing but her dressing gown. "What I don't see is what you're doing with them. Get yourself to bed before I—"

"Before you what?" The question hung in the air for a moment before she went on. "And what are you doing here?"

"Apparently the same thing you are, spying on Her Majesty's Superintendent of Trade."

"Only Elliot? What about the so-called China traders, smugglers to a man, and the East India Company?"

"Not to mention the mysterious Chinese?" he retorted.

A faint smile played at her mouth. "Of course."

Laughter began deep in his soul and bubbled up until it threatened to overcome his ability to silence it. *Sudbury and the queen don't need an agent in China. They already have one, if only they paid attention.*

A dainty hand planted itself firmly across his lips, and eyes, pale blue but heated with a passion Sudbury's icy ones never held, met his. She moved her hand away slowly, her eyes still on his. They stood for a moment, so close they breathed the same air, watchful.

She moved first. "Get this done before we're discovered. We can talk later," she said.

He pulled out his notebook and began to scribble notes. "How long have you been doing this?" he whispered.

"Since I got here two months ago." Her tone suggested she found it a stupid question. She didn't pause in her work.

"You've kept it all on little pieces of paper?" he asked.

"I transpose it to a journal and burn the notes. I mean to report it to my father."

He had nothing to say to that. With Macao covered, he could go on to Whampao and Canton—if he could depend on her to behave sensibly.

She scribbled rapidly. He tried to keep up, but the nearness of warmth and woman distracted him. "You should be in London finding a husband," he muttered.

Her head darted up. "I will not be some man's brood mare," she growled. "I have better things to do."

Chapter 8

Charles stood in the shade of a camphor tree, running his long-fingered hands along the brim of his hat when she approached their agreed-upon rendezvous. Energy radiated off him as it had as long as she'd known him. Intense and full of life, he had led his cousins into boyhood misadventures and helped extricate them from real ones as an adult. He always entertained the younger set right down to the infants. The elders adored him—when they didn't worry for him. Zambak always had as well, but she was young and susceptible then.

The rogue didn't appear in the least discomforted for lack of sleep, unlike Zambak who had slept little and felt resentful. She lay on her bed until dawn reliving their encounter in the office. *Can I trust him? How far? Will he help me?* The questions had no answer but would not be silenced. Curiously, the memory of his slender form in tight black breeches climbing out the window cut up her peace as well, in the heat of the night.

"Why are you really here?" she demanded without preamble.

He flicked a glance at Filipe trotting up behind and said, "Why, idle curiosity, of course."

She seated herself on the bench nearby, dropped the bag she carried to her feet, and treated him to a scathing expression. "When pigs fly. What does my father want?"

He sank down next to her and put elbows to knees, peering sideways up at her. "What does he always want? Eyes and ears."

"On his children?"

"That too. He and Uncle Will ambushed me with a commission from the queen."

It rang true. Her father wanted as much intelligence as he could gather, and the Earl of Chadbourn worried about Charles, idle and grieving in London.

Watching with care that Filipe stood out of earshot, he went on, still leaning forward. He did not notice her abstraction. "I'm to be an objective observer of the impact of Palmerston's policies and Elliot's decisions. I'm to seek out a channel of direct communication between the British Empire and the so-called Celestial one."

"The holy grail of China relations," Zambak said sourly. "Others have tried."

"All have failed. Victoria cannot seem to grasp that," he agreed.

That won her attention. She studied him for long minutes and came to a decision. At least she had her trusted courier. She reached inside the bag and pulled out a journal covered with Chinese embroidery that, to a casual eye, looked like a diary in which a lady might record fashion or gossip.

"What is this?" he asked.

"Your report. I've been waiting for a trusted courier."

He looked from the book to her face and back, sat up, and took it from her, turning it over in his hands before opening it.

"The first part is simple chronology," she explained. "What I've gleaned about Chinese naval power is marked by the first ribbon."

"And tea prices and loads by the red one. What is black?"

"Opium. Dreadful stuff. And observations about those who deal in it."

"We agree on that at least," he murmured, examining the book. He allowed her to expound on her assessment of the entire seething mess.

"The Chinese do not want the opium,"' she reminded him in the end. "They ban it. The traders—smugglers the lot of them—go around their laws. Opium trade exploded after the crown ended the East India Company's monopoly, and the Company does little but wring their hands and fret over losses. Now the Chinese can no longer tolerate it. The smugglers are out of control, and we're destroying China from the inside."

He listened with every sign of respect, leaning his head toward her and nodding occasionally. He did not laugh.

"Will you deliver it to London?"

He didn't answer. He closed the book and tucked it in his coat before she could take it back. "You looked for something else last night," he said, his clear eyes waiting for an honest response.

She looked out across the park. There seemed no point in denying it. "Thorn. I am often forced to hunt for news of him from Mrs. Elliot's personal correspondence. What I do glean isn't good. He just can't avoid trouble," she said finally.

"He's why you came."

Her head snapped back to study him. "Yes. How did you know?"

"Guessed."

"He'll bring ruin on my family."

"And himself?" he asked. The compassion in his eyes made her throat contract.

"He's destroying himself." She swallowed hard and glared at Charles. "He is Father's heir—my family's hope for the future. He'll bring ruin on us all." She couldn't keep the bitterness from her voice.

"As I recall, the two of you shared a bond," Charles murmured.

"He was my champion, my partner, my—" She shook her head. "Not for a long while, not since his accident. He shut me out—he shut all of us out." She closed her eyes while visions of Thorn as a boy trailing after her squeezed her heart.

She pushed the hurt away and focused raging thoughts on her family name. After Thorn came Henry, just starting university—not Zambak; never the daughter. *Who knows how much harm Thorn might do before Henry can even try to set things straight. Father is healthy and vigorous but—* She opened her eyes to find Charles studying her.

"So you fled to Macao because of Thorn and the need to get away from London?" Charles asked, something suspiciously like compassion in his voice. One gloveless hand slipped over hers; she didn't pull away.

"London, yes: endless gossip, endless balls, endless obsession with marriage." Weariness threatened to lay her flat. Let him report that one to her mother. She'd made her position clear the night before; he didn't tease her with it. She glared at him until he removed his hand and looked away.

"I'll have to get to Canton and check on him," he replied.

"You do that," she spat. "You won't be marooned here in skirts with no way in."

Laughter did burst out then. "Is that what you've been trying to do? Get to Canton? Western women—"

"Are forbidden. No one knows that better than I."

He sobered, studying her until he rose and offered his hand. "We're expected at the Quakers' house."

She took it and stood next to him, with nothing left to say. *Cow shite. What good will dinner with Dan Oliver do me now? I can't ask for passage with Charles listening to every word.*

~ ~ ~

Family chatter made it difficult for Charles to question the famous China trader notorious for his opposition to opium smuggling as closely as he wished. The reverberation of laughter, the hum of conversation, and the sweet prattle of little ones crushed his soul. Warmth of affection overran warmth from the cheerful fire, and the heat in the Knightons' eyes when they looked at one another put him in mind of embers ready to burst into flame, subdued only by their quiet joy.

Everything I want. Everything I'll never have. He swallowed hard, tried to stretch some semblance of a smile across his face, and turned back to Oliver, but a small boy had taken the sea captain's attention. Charles's face felt tight and the upturn of his mouth artificial. *God, how I miss Jonny!*

Even more distracting, the youngest Knighton daughter, introduced to him as Blessing, snuggled into Zambak's lap. He watched her initial discomfort melt when the child popped a thumb in her mouth and leaned into her shoulder. A tender smile playing on Zambak's lips and a knife's edge of pain sliced through his heart when he remembered the feel of his son at that age, a warm little body curled in his arms, trusting and secure. Zambak unconsciously kissed the little one's head. *Whatever bone-headed idea she has about marriage, she will make a magnificent mother.*

"So the navy has withdrawn?" she asked Oliver, one hand absently caressing the child's back, pulling the conversation back to the topic of the tea factories in Canton and the opium operations at Whampao.

"For now, my lady, for now. Maitland gave Admiral Kuan some bottles of wine and a handshake before they scampered. Elliot seems relieved, and so are half the traders."

"What about the rest of the traders?" she asked.

"Hopping mad." Oliver's assessment of the situation in the Pearl Delta, carefully edited for the presence of children, sounded dire. Charles guessed what he didn't say. Jarratt and others hoped the navy would force the Chinese to accept the contraband or at least look the other way again.

"You think open conflict is likely, then?" Charles asked.

"You mean more than the dance they just did, all flag waving and circling? Yes. And worse." Oliver glanced apologetically at Temperance who bent to speak to her son, obviously stricken with hero worship for the great China trader. Oliver took a puff on his pipe. "Jarratt and his ilk are begging for it. They want to thrust your English sword down the Chinese throats."

"Daniel . . ." Temperance warned.

"Begging your pardon, Your Grace. None of them—ours or yours—respect Chinese laws." Oliver, an American of evangelical bent, didn't share the Quaker dislike for titles.

A swallow of the Knightons' ale, homemade and strong, cleared thickness in his throat. "I'm Charles here, Oliver, or Murnane if you wish. I appreciate your candor."

Oliver went on. "The brutes complain the Chinese don't respect your government, and call for the navy to teach them rough manners. War is an ugly thing."

"The war junks would be no match if we attack them," Zambak put in, her entire attention on the speaker.

"In the end, yes, but they'll do their share of harm in the meantime," Oliver said.

"Can it be avoided?"

Dan Oliver puffed silently for several moments. Charles knew the answer when it came would be carefully worded and circumspect. Even Temperance strained to listen, as she pretended to bustle about with meal preparation.

"Unlikely. The Chinese have become determined to enforce the anti-opium statutes among their people, as they ought. Innes, Jarratt, Dennison, Dean, and the rest defy the law." He glanced at the children. Charles could guess what he didn't say. The big traders had begun arming their ships and ran their opium almost to Canton itself. "The conflict will explode sooner or later, and we best be prepared," Oliver went on. He looked over at Aaron Knighton.

Temperance's hands stilled, and she leaned forward to take the baby from Zambak to balance her on one hip.

Aaron reached over and took his wife's free hand, a smile warming his face. "This day thee need only prepare dinner for our guests." Something tender and mysterious passed between them before Temperance called the company to table.

When violence explodes, will it reach Macao? Charles longed to ask Oliver, but he knew it best to postpone it until he could talk to the man privately. For now, dinner waited and the sight of Lady Zambak Hayden on a rough bench between two small children being asked to bow her head in prayer.

Prayer finished, an awkward silence ensued. Before more talk of war could cast a deeper pall on their gathering, Temperance said, "Daniel, I wish to thank thee for the funds to establish our clinic. How does the one in thy Canton warehouse fare?" She neatly turned the conversation away from war and on to her efforts to find space for a clinic in Macao. The captain obliged, an in-depth discussion of danger being inappropriate for the company. Charles determined to seek him out to find out more as soon as he could.

Chapter 9

Three times Thorn's name came to the tip of Zambak's tongue. Three times she bit it back, unwilling to disrupt the Knightons' peaceful meal and even less willing to air her family's troubles. She longed to drag Dan Oliver out and demand that he smuggle her into Canton, or to whatever godforsaken hole Thorn had crawled into. She no longer had any confidence that he kept to the Company's factory as he ought and Chinese law demanded.

Temperance served a plain meal, savory stew, and delectable bread. The fare would have horrified her mother's French chef, but Zambak found it delicious and satisfying. The ambience in the room, on the other hand, disquieted her; the entire evening left her confused. Open displays of affection, behavior utterly unfamiliar to her, passed between the Knightons: the touch of hand to back here, grasp of fingers there, warm glances in between. Her own parents lived in a perpetual cycle of vociferous conflict and passionate reconciliation. The Knightons' gentle accord turned her insides to jelly and unleashed a longing inside she couldn't name.

Sharing a bench with a six-year-old while Temperance held Blessing in her lap to feed her lay in equally unfamiliar territory. Children did not dine with the Duke and Duchess of Sudbury. Even in the Earl of Chadbourn's ramshackle household, there were limits. Charles's uncle preferred that his children know how to enter into conversation before they joined in family dinners. Even he didn't include them when there were guests. None of it felt comfortable, and Zambak loathed feeling ill at ease. Part of her wanted to bolt right back to Clara Elliot's formal dining room, but something about these people drew her in.

When Temperance suggested she tell the men about her teaching, she let herself be persuaded. By the time she described her lessons on Europe, the upheavals in the Ottoman Empire, and Russian nationalism, she relaxed into the story, strangeness forgotten. When she described Lai-min Lau's enthusiasm for her lesson on the Turkish harem and the education of women there—a topic Zambak knew well from her mother's stories—the general laughter held no disrespect.

"Lau? The hong?" Oliver asked.

"Correct," Temperance answered with a smile. "Her father deals in tea. She speaks of it proudly."

"Hong?" Zambak asked.

"Merchant," Oliver explained. "One of the honest ones. Good family. We buy their tea annually."

"Lai-min's father has also given us money for our clinic," Temperance put in.

Lai-min, one of the few upper-class Chinese girls in their school, spoke of her father with great pride. As Temperance predicted, Zambak learned as much as she taught, and language had been one of the unexpected bonuses. Still, Lai-min's English faltered, and Zambak's fledgling Cantonese could not always compensate.

Zambak made note of that. Her reports needed more information about tea, the beneficial part of the infernal triangle with silver and opium, to flesh them out. She had wondered before if tea wasn't the key to the entire mess.

"Lai-min learns quickly," Temperance said. "I have hopes for her."

"Are you drawing her to the faith?" Oliver asked.

"I am showing her how to listen to her inner light," Temperance answered with a sly smile.

A merchant who supports a free clinic must already know the light, Zambak thought. Daniel looked amused by Temperance's comment. Zambak knew the missionaries shared care for the poor but differed sharply on actual evangelization, Quakers being unwilling to dictate belief. She suspected Oliver knew it too.

"I think friend Daniel doesn't attend to the light as he ought," Aaron Knighton teased. The meal ended with good-natured laughter.

"Thee wished to see my wood working, Charles. Come and I will show thee my poor efforts," Aaron said, and the two men left through the rear door conversing amiably—and with obvious knowledge—about tools and woods.

What does Charles know about woodworking? He's a duke for pity sake. Father certainly has no interest in handcrafts. They act like old friends. Something about woodworking brought her brother to mind. She tucked it away for later.

She wondered if Charles had always been this comfortable with everyone he met regardless of his or her station. The few times Zambak encountered him at balls or formal dinners during her three miserable seasons, he displayed impeccable etiquette. On the other hand, he had never been pompous or aloof when she was growing up, although their interactions tended to be in informal settings among friends. She stared after the two men wondering if she knew him at all.

"It would be a great gift if thee would watch Blessing while I tidy up." Temperance's voice brought her back to the present. Zambak blinked twice at the sight of Daniel Oliver, wealthy merchant and ship's captain, dandling a baby on his knee. She sank into the chair next to him and reached for the little one, rescuing his cravat in the process. When Temperance turned toward the kitchen, Zambak had the opportunity she longed for.

"I was hoping for a private moment, Captain Oliver. I have a proposition for you."

He shifted uneasily. "A lady like yourself doesn't offer propositions to old sea captains, my lady."

She wouldn't allow the burning sensation that rose from her neck to heat her cheeks to deter her from her purpose. "If you accept my business, I will make it worth your while, sir. I need transportation to Canton."

He didn't hide his shock; she rushed on. "My brother serves with The East India Company there and can lend me consequence," she said without any hint that she found the idea absurd. *As if Thorn could lend anyone consequence, the lack wit.* "Perhaps you know him? Lord Glenaire? Or he may use his family name, John Thornton Hayden. I, I ah— need to see him."

Something troubled Oliver. His eyes had the strained expression of a man weighing his words. When he spoke, he didn't remind her that the Chinese forbad Western women from entering Canton. "When did you hear from him last, Lady Zambak?"

"When he left," she admitted. "That's the problem. I need to see him."

"December is upon us, my lady. The tea traders are concluding their business and beginning to drift back to Macao. Indeed, I concluded my own satisfactorily and early. Your brother may—"

"He may or may not be among them. There is something you aren't telling me."

"He may not be with the Company any longer," Oliver admitted.

Her heart raced, outpacing even her thoughts. *Resigned? Surely not dismissed. They wouldn't dismiss the Duke of Sudbury's heir, would they?* She opened her mouth to probe for information but shut it quickly.

Charles stalked across the room. His scowl would have reduced a weaker woman to pudding. Zambak lifted her chin and sat up straighter, the baby in her lap and her heated cheeks hindering her efforts to mimic the haughty glare learned at the feet of those dragon ladies of the *ton* who knew how to dismiss encroachment.

Charles flicked a glance between Oliver and Zambak.

"Would you have time tomorrow for a private word, Oliver? I have much to discuss with you." His eyes never left Zambak.

Much to discuss. The interfering sneak!

Chapter 10

The captain's quarters of the *Wild Swan*, Oliver and Company's flagship, reflected Dan Oliver himself: reliance on quality, honest workmanship, and no ostentation. Pleased that the captain's evangelical beliefs didn't extend to a ban on alcohol, Charles accepted a mug of rum, took a swig, and shuddered as it went down.

"Good sailor's rum, Murnane, same as my men."

"I admire your democracy in some ways, Oliver, but I might not extend it to beverages." He made a mental note to have a crate of the whisky his uncle obtained from a small distillery in Scotland sent to the man when he got back to London.

Oliver grinned at Charles's shudder of distaste. "You wanted a private word. It is yours to make," he said.

"You were choosing your words carefully last night," Charles said.

"Aaron and Temperance have good imaginations. They got my warning."

"So you think it will come to war?"

"You tell me. Will your queen—or your prime minister— step in to stop it? Money talks here, and the money wants the Chinese to back off," Oliver replied.

"And they won't."

Oliver nodded. "Not this time. They turned a blind eye for years, but the opium has infested their army, their regional government, and even—so rumors tell it—the Imperial court. This time they mean it, and it's about damned time." He shook his head. "Though it may be too late."

"Will Macao get caught in the crossfire?"

Oliver puffed on his pipe. "Might. Hard to say. I don't think they would attack the city outright—Portuguese get on with 'em too well—but I can't say for sure."

Charles ran a hand through his hair. *Half a dozen diplomatic officers have wives and families in Macao. God knows how many merchants do. Should Elliot be ordering them home? Will Zambak go if they order her to?* Oliver waited patiently, puffing on his ever-present pipe while Charles thought it through.

"When do you think Elliot will return?" Charles asked.

"Any day. He might have more ideas about the situation, but he sent the navy packing. Doesn't like the trade and isn't inclined to support the war mongers and opium smugglers." Oliver's voice held an obvious note of approval.

"You like him?"

"Well enough. He won't disobey orders though, no matter what his conscience tells him—and when he thinks it is time to act, well, he's a navy man at heart. If British interests are attacked, no telling what he'll do. Maitland left, but Elliot still has HMS *Reliance* under him. The captain reports to him, not Maitland."

"So the question is, 'what were his orders?'" Charles mused. Oliver had no answer to that. Charles could guess based on his knowledge of Palmerston, but he couldn't be sure. They drank in companionable silence for a while.

"Is that what you came for—to ask about Elliot?" Oliver studied him with somber attention.

Charles stared at the polished sheen of the floorboards; tempted to keep his biggest question to himself, but need outran fear of embarrassment. With an indrawn breath, he forced out the question. "I understand a woman and her protector sailed with Maitland. Would you know anything about that?"

"Might," Oliver replied warily.

"She presents herself as the Duchess of Murnane."

"Is she?" The American peered at him intently under lowered brows.

Charles met his gaze. "Perhaps. Probably. She never reached Macao."

"The German man with her—Baron something—fell overboard, dead drunk, one night off Lintin Island. Fell or was pushed. That's the story I heard in Canton."

"And the woman?"

Oliver watched Charles carefully, chewing the stem of his pipe, as if weighing what to say.

Charles didn't flinch. "Sorry you have to tell me things you would rather not, but I am unlikely to be shocked. I need to know."

Compassion softened the captain's voice. "The person telling the story was well into his cups, mind you, but he said Maitland tired of her whining—and attempts to whore herself to his officers—and put her ashore."

Charles closed his eyes and sighed. "It sounds like the right woman. What and where exactly is Lintin Island?"

Oliver rose, pulled out a drawer, and unfurled a map he drew from it. He jabbed one finger on a speck in Canton Bay. "Hunk of rock about thirty miles north east, at the head of the bay. They use it as a receiving station for the opium. The Chinese try to bottle it up there."

Thoughts jostled for position in Charles's nimble mind. He could easily reach Lintin. *If I catch her without a protector, will it be harder or easier to coerce her back to England? Will it make the divorce harder? Nothing will make it easier.*

"Are you sure there isn't anything else you want to ask me?" Charles looked up to see naked sympathy in Oliver's frank face.

Take me to Lintin, lay on the tip of his tongue. "Yes, one more thing, whatever Lady Zambak Hayden offers you, don't take her off this island."

Oliver's brows rose to his receding hairline and dropped back over amused eyes. "The lady can be very persuasive."

"Apparently not persuasive enough to convince anyone to take her to Canton."

"Canton?" Oliver laughed so hard he spilled his rum.

~ ~ ~

Sometimes, Zambak really did sketch churches. At least, she did it often enough to have sketches to show Clara Elliot. In the dim alcove of the interior of Santo Antonio, she sat on a small campstool and blinked up at a statue. Less flamboyant than the ones lining the high altar, the very simplicity attracted her—that and the subject. She added lines in swift strokes, attempting to capture the strength of the woman if not the quality of the statue.

Boot steps echoed off the walls of the cavernous church, breaking her concentration and sending a frisson of caution skittering up her neck. No priest made such noise. She turned, alert to see who invaded her quiet, hoping Filipe followed the man in. He did not.

Sunbeams through clear glass made islands of white light down the main aisle. The invader strode purposefully into one and out into the shadow. Zambak stared at his polished boots and firm legs encased in buckskin. He held his hat under one arm and moved with confidence toward her, stepping into another island of white. Light danced off auburn hair, and Zambak clamped her teeth shut. *Am I to have no peace from the man?* She turned her back to him and resumed her work.

"Aren't you expected at the school today?" Charles asked without greeting.

"How did you find me?" she demanded.

"That pink parasol's green fringe is unmistakable. Filipe is lounging under it. Shouldn't he be in here keeping an eye on you?"

She shot a baleful glance in his general direction and kept sketching. *Perhaps if I ignore him he'll leave me alone.*

He stood for several moments running the brim of his hat through his hands.

If he wants an answer, he will wait a long time.

When she refused to face him, he sat in a pew across from her with a sigh. "Who is it?" he asked.

"Who is who?" she asked. She gazed up at the statue's face. A few deft pencil strokes rendered the saint's stance determined rather than merely peaceful.

"The woman in the statue. It isn't the most interesting piece here," Charles observed.

"Catherine of Siena."

More moments passed with the scratch of her pencil the only sound. "Why her?" he asked. *Irritating man.*

"She interests me." Again, he waited. This time she went on. "She took a vow to remain a virgin but didn't retire to an abbey. She led a public life, commanded popes and the feuding houses of Italy, and she wrote the truth for men to hear."

"Formidable. A waste, though," he murmured.

She wheeled on him. "A waste? She changed the course of European history when she routed the pope from Avignon."

"Not her work. The vow."

"You think her virginity a waste? She owned the integrity of her own body and didn't bend to the will of some man. It enabled her to live her life on her own terms."

"On God's terms, I believe," he murmured softly.

"Good for God," Zambak snapped. "I admire her for it. Pity the Church of England—"

"Pity the Duke of Sudbury won't give his daughter that kind of freedom?" he asked.

She turned back to her work, showing him a shoulder rigid with outrage. *Typical male.* Again, the sound of pencil on paper, rapid this time in angry strokes, filled the air. She wondered, not for the first time, if Macao would provide her more freedom than London if she chose to live out her life there. *I could be my father's agent in China. I could . . .*

"Temperance Knighton has both children and work," he said. She kept eyes on her work. "A loving husband as well," he added.

"Aaron Knighton supports his wife—a rare and unusual man," she grumbled. He didn't reply, and she finished the sketch. "Why are you here? Have you nothing better to do?"

"Elliot is back. I thought you would want to know."

"Elliot? In Macao? Is Thorn with him?"

"Not that I heard. I don't know that the East India Company clerks return to Macao."

"Oliver told me Thorn may have left the Company," she said. His surprise gave her the satisfaction of having one piece of information he didn't.

"Elliot may have word, though," he replied.

"True enough." She rose in one fluid motion, bringing her drawing materials with her, and began to pack. "Then why are we here? Let's see what the man knows." She paused to make sure he heard the rest she had to say.

"You may have a commission from the queen, but my brother is my concern, Charles." He didn't argue. She was halfway out of the church before she realized he hadn't agreed, either.

~ ~ ~

What goes on behind that flawless face? I can almost hear the clockwork that drives her thinking. Charles realized with a shock how much she resembled her father whose formidable brain worked ceaselessly. In Zambak, however, long lashes, perfect complexion, and delicate features covered the unrelenting analysis. Men rarely, if ever, looked behind the dainty appearance to the tough mind. *Men see what they wish to see.*

He tipped his head to glance at her composed profile again while they strode purposefully toward the English neighborhood. Behind them, Filipe struggled to keep up, the ever-present sunshade folded under his arm and the campstool in his hand. She had declined Charles's arm and his offer to carry her drawing case, but the refusal owed more to distraction than churlishness. At the mention of Elliot's name, she had withdrawn into her calculations.

I would give a small fortune to peer into her thoughts. Their conversation disturbed him. *Virginity indeed!* Even the little queen was under pressure to marry, however, although Elizabeth never had. Parties had lined up to push various candidates closer to the throne. He wondered idly if Victoria would retain any pretense of power once she did. Put in that light, he sympathized with Zambak's desire to avoid being a dynastic pawn, but not her desire to avoid marriage altogether. *It would be such a waste.*

Her obsession with travel to the mainland worried him. News of Elliot's arrival came to the *Wild Swan* soon after Oliver stopped laughing, and he had set out to find her. He hoped the superintendent's return would put an end to her machinations, and it might if he brought positive news about Thorn. Charles would have to go drag the boy back to Macao if he hadn't returned, if only to keep Zambak from attempting such a folly.

Chapter 11

When they rounded the corner and climbed the steps to the Elliots' mansion, an agitated Hua opened the door to a chaotic scene. He did not take Charles's hat or Zambak's bonnet.

Luggage lay strewn across the foyer while servants carried parcels up the steps. In the midst, Clara Elliot lay weeping on her husband's shoulder, and his son stood by with wide eyes, while Higgins hung back, his expression pained.

"Mr. Elliot, show more care in your speech," Mrs. Elliot moaned while Elliot, a bluff man with military bearing in his middle years, patted her back awkwardly. Whatever news he brought had not been good.

When Charles laid a hand at the back of Zambak's waist, she didn't pull away. She studied the scene in front of them with troubled eyes. When his hand slipped to the curve of her hip, he couldn't tell if she felt comforted, but he did—too much so. He pulled his hand back.

"Sorry, Clara. You weren't meant to hear that," her husband soothed. His eyes met Charles's over his wife's back, a question clear on his face. He glared at Hua who hurried over.

"Most sorry, Your Grace. Family is not receiving," the old man said. At the mention Charles's title, Elliot stilled, causing his wife to stand and accept her husband's handkerchief. "You've caught us at a difficult moment, Your Grace," she said with a sniff. Higgins hurried over to whisper something to Elliot who said, "I'm afraid you have me at a disadvantage, Sir."

Charles inclined his head toward the man. "I merely escorted your guest back from her sketching expedition, Captain Elliot." He longed to stay and offer Zambak his support; he longed to pepper Elliot with questions. He could do neither without pushing himself into a private family moment, and etiquette left him with no way in. He had to leave. "Perhaps we can speak tomorrow," he suggested.

Zambak turned sharply toward him, and he raised his hand to touch her arm. "Perhaps…" she began.

He opened his mouth to tell her he could not stay, but Elliot spoke first. "Clara, dear, perhaps Lady Zambak could escort you above stairs."

Charles thought for a moment Zambak would refuse. Her shoulders sagged when she handed her drawing case and bonnet to Hua. "Of course," she murmured. Only Charles seemed to notice the fire in her eyes.

Mrs. Elliot leaned on Zambak's arm and allowed the younger woman to lead her upstairs.

"A moment if you please, Your Grace," Elliot said behind the departing ladies. "And then, yes, we can talk more tomorrow."

Zambak glared back over Clara Elliot's shoulder, pleading with him, but Charles forced himself to ignore her. *She'll be hopping mad tomorrow*, he thought. He smiled at the superintendent. "Of course, Captain Elliot. "I am—"

"I know who you are, Your Grace." Elliot led him to the now familiar study toward the back of the house, shut the door in Higgins' face, and got to the point. "I was not aware the government planned to send someone outside of channels. What do you have for me?"

Thoughts racing, Charles replied, "I am not here in an official capacity." That's true enough.

"Higgins told me you are making a tour of the Empire. Excuse me if I find it unlikely that a former Assistant Secretary for War and the Colonies stumbled by happenstance into Macao just as tensions spiked."

Charles scored the thought in Elliot's favor. *No fool, he.* He briefly debated opening up about his commission and decided against it. "I'm here for personal reasons, Elliot." True as well. Elliot waited, brows high, for more. "The Duke of Sudbury is a family friend." Another truth.

The superintendent relaxed a fraction. "His children? Well he ought to send someone. How he tolerated that girl's hare-brained pursuit of her brother, I do not know—no offense intended."

"None taken. The boy, I think, is a bigger concern," Charles said.

"Yes. Well. My instructions were to house the daughter. The young marquess took a position with the Company." He made a gesture as if to brush responsibility for Thorn off his hands. "A position I might say could have benefited a man who needed it more," he went on.

Charles nodded, his respect for Elliot rising. "I assume you hear from the Company. Any news of the boy?" Elliot's considering expression worried him. *I don't think I'm going to like this.*

"Scampered," Elliot told him. "Took a position with Jarratt. Didn't bother to resign."

"Jarratt?" Charles asked, but another voice interrupted before he could expand the thought.

"Who exactly is Jarratt?" Zambak stood at the open door, rigid with outrage while Higgins fluttered behind her.

Captain Elliot opened his mouth as if to issue a sharp reprimand but thought better of it. *Zambak Hayden is a formidable sight when she's determined to have her way— and she frequently is.* Charles bit back a smile.

"Mrs. Elliot's maid is caring for her, Captain," Zambak

said, addressing his unspoken concern. "I didn't abandon her." She stepped into the room and shut the door on Higgins's nose. "Who is Jarratt, Captain? You must know my brother is my concern."

Elliot's shoulders relaxed, but he looked like he had eaten something foul. "Pushing Scot. Principle of Jarratt, Martinson & Company. He and his partner have been agitating London for intervention. Probably thinks the boy gives him an in with the Duke of Sudbury."

"Then he doesn't know my father. Merely showing his son favor won't impress him," she said.

Something in Elliot's manner alerted Charles that there might be something else. "If he thinks blackmail would work, he's an even bigger fool," Charles added.

"Blackmail?" Alarm tightened Zambak's voice, and Charles cursed his loose tongue.

Elliot's cheeks took on a deep maroon, and he glared at Charles. "I don't know where you got such a fanciful notion! The young man works for Jarratt. That's all the information I have—that and the trader himself has returned to Macao." He eyed Charles balefully. "Perhaps that will satisfy your 'curiosity.' Now if I may excuse myself…"

Charles hadn't mentioned the commission. He didn't have to; Elliot already suspected. The temptation to ask about Julia lodged in his throat. It would keep as well. He'd heard quite enough about his wife for one day. He couldn't do much more with Zambak under foot; he escorted her to the door. "Satisfied?"

"Hardly!"

"Give me a day to learn what I can about Jarratt, Martinson & Company," he told her. The chit's expression didn't reassure him. He would have to act fast before she did her own snooping.

~ ~ ~

Zambak demanded assistance right after breakfast, and the Elliots' staff made a show of fetching bonnet, drawing case, and the ever-present Filipe.

The Elliots dined in their suite the night before, and Clara Elliot never came down to breakfast. Not that she would help; she had steadfastly insisted the information that caused her collapse could not be shared with "one of tender years." If Captain Elliot ate, he did so even earlier than the obscenely early hour Zambak had come down.

She finally found him locked with Higgins in his study, and briefly considered forcing her way in again but knew she would get no further information. She tied her bonnet with a yank and swept from the house and up the street while the coolie trotted along. *If no one will talk to me, perhaps someone at this Jarratt &Martinson firm will. Thank God the school doesn't expect me today.*

When they turned the corner toward her destination, Filipe spoke up. "Hua say the Viceroy very angry."

She stopped in her tracks. *Hua say... How can I have forgotten servant's gossip?* "What else does Mr. Hua say?"

Filipe shook his head sadly. "Much evil in Canton. Viceroy . . ."

Curiosity got the better of her. It had been obvious people were shielding her. "Spit it out, Filipe. What upset Mrs. Elliot?"

He dragged the toe of one foot across the path. "Hua say she heard Cap Elliot tell Higgins they hung a man."

She gasped. "Hung a man?"

Filipe apparently decided she would not collapse at the news. "Oh yes. Viceroy put cross in the foreign quarter—big marching ground in front of factories."

"They crucified him?" she asked in horror.

His face wrinkled up, considering the word.

"How did they execute him—kill him?" she prodded.

"Oh." Filipe grinned, gleefully grabbed his throat with both hands, and made gagging noises.

"They strangled him?"

"Strangled yes, but no finish him. English navy men very angry. They pulled down the pole, and Viceroy took him. Much fighting."

A riot. English jack tars rescuing a Chinese. Why? "Why did the Viceroy plan so public an execution? Why him?" she asked.

"Very bad man. Sells opium. Smoking parlor."

They can't stop the trade, and they are going after the low-level providers. Will the users be next? Do they mean to appeal to the smugglers' guilt? There isn't any. "Tell me what else Mr. Hua heard."

"Mr. Elliot leave again soon. He said, 'Enough is enough.' Wants English ships with guns out of the river."

Good for Elliot. Filipe blinked at her, eyes glittering. *What else does he know?* "Did he mention John Thornton Hayden? Or the Marquess of Glenaire?" She loathed the thought of servants gossiping about her brother but had to ask, and there was no telling how the servants might refer to him.

Filipe studied his feet and his toe in the dust moving side to side again.

She sighed, reached into her reticule, and held tight to a coin. "Tell me what you know now with no further greed, and I'll see what we can arrange going forward."

Filipe reached for the coin. She pulled it back. "My lord not at Canton." He shrugged. "Hua say he left with Mister Jarratt." He snatched the coin.

"And does Hua know where he is?"

"No Lady Zam. Ask the Taipan."

"What is Taipan?"

"Means great merchant, Mr. Jarratt."

"Where can I find this Taipan?

Filipe eagerly obliged, leading her to the prominent waterfront premises of Jarratt, Martinson & Company. With the name in gilded letters six inches high, there could be no mistake. A lady's entrance to the office raised eyebrows. The lady's title raised them higher. Her questions, however, obtained little besides closed mouths and shifty eyes.

"You know nothing about the Marquess of Glenaire? John Thornton Hayden?"

"Perhaps Mr. Jarratt can help you, my lady." The squirmy clerk volunteered no further information.

"Can you tell me where I might find this Mr. Jarratt who may have information about my brother?" She pressed through clenched teeth. An unmistakable snicker set her skin crawling, but she got the information she wanted.

Chapter 12

Jarratt's Chinese servants kept eyes averted and heads bowed. Zambak suspected Hua would greet a woman approaching a single man's establishment with cheeky disdain, even one who left a calling card proclaiming her to be of the highest social status. Filipe had certainly clucked his disapproval. He sat on a chair by the door outside the drawing room she was escorted into, glowering at one and all.

She didn't wait long. The man who entered carried her calling card. He sent his servants out with a gesture of his head and closed the door behind them. His frank assessment of her person made Zambak's skin crawl; the amusement in his eyes enraged her. She stood a little taller and glared back.

"I am William Jarratt," he said. "You wished to see me, my lady?"

The trace of Scotland in his voice didn't soften the obvious disrespect in his tone. Macao, she remembered, was not London. Niceties would have no place in this conversation.

"I understand you have employed my brother," she said.

"Right down to business. I like that," Jarratt smirked.

"My brother?" she prodded.

"Your sources of information are impressive. His lordship is indeed my employee." The note of triumph was unmistakable. The farmer's son from Dumfriesshire now employed the Duke of Sudbury's son; he didn't hide his glee.

"Where is he?"

One side of Jarratt's mouth tilted upward, and he took his time answering. She refused to pull her eyes from his, even if the gleam of power and brittle amusement made her stomach clench.

"Going about my business," he said at last. "He didn't mention that he required a sister to check on his welfare when he asked for employment."

"He approached you?" *Why would Thorn seek out this worm?*

"He begged," Jarratt replied, his eyes straying to her hem and meandering upward. "He seemed quite eager to leave the East India Company factory. So confining there, with the rules and restrictions. Always eager to avoid offending the Chinese they are."

Zambak began to regret going to see Jarratt. Her mind raced. Thorn wanted freedom; that in itself was not unusual. "Is he still in Canton?"

"Not that it's a woman's business, but he found my operation in Whampao more attractive."

Whampao. Down river from the port. The smugglers' gate to the mainland. If a man wanted opium, Whampao would be his goal.

Jarratt went on before she could think what to say next. "He has actually returned to Macao with me." Something in his manner set her nerves skittering.

"Where is he?" she demanded.

"Here as it happens. Resting. He will not wish to be disturbed."

"Here?" She kept outrage from her voice with great effort. "Kindly send word to him that his sister wishes to see him."

Jarratt stood with his hands behind his back. She very much feared the emotion lurking in the dark eyes that examined her so closely would turn out to be disdain. She raised her chin and met his piercing eyes with a glare of her own.

"I demand it!"

The side of Jarratt's mouth twitched, but he went to the door and had words with a waiting servant.

She steeled herself to ask one more question. "What exactly does my brother do for you, Mr. Jarratt?"

The boor's lips quivered as if suppressing laughter. "So inquisitive," he said.

"Well?" she demanded.

"I fear your brother finds the product more attractive than the work, although his contacts among the businessmen who sell our product directly to customers have been most helpful."

Oh God—Thorn dabbles in opium. A fist to her belly would have had less impact than Jarratt's words confirming her worst fears. She clamped her jaw shut, unwilling to give the brute satisfaction.

A scratch at the door took Jarratt's attention momentarily. "My servants have escorted your brother to my drawing room as you requested, your ladyship." He gestured to the door.

A silk-clad servant led her across the foyer. Filipe hopped to his feet and attempted to follow her. Jarratt, however, slipped between Zambak and the boy, blocking his way. Double doors opened on silent hinges, and Zambak stumbled forward, her heart pausing in its race before galloping off again.

Thorn lay sprawled across a settee, mouth agape. His unfocused eyes stared at the ceiling. *Escorted? They dragged him down here and dumped him!*

She leaned over her brother, caressed his cheek with one hand, and whispered, "Thorn?" A smile, painful in its sweetness, flitted briefly across his face. Memory of that smile peering out at her from his eight-year-old face when she helped him hide from his tutor so he could finish building one of his boats pulled at her heart. His voice echoed in her mind. "I'll build yachts one day, bigger and faster than Father's. See if I don't," he had proclaimed.

Just as quickly, his face went slack, and the eager young boy disappeared. She wheeled on Jarratt. "What have you done with him?"

"I? My dear lady, he does this to himself. Happily. I merely complied with your demand to see him. I did not think you wished to be above stairs in the home of a single man." Laughter lurked in his voice.

"I want him shipped back to London," she burst out. "My father—"

"I'm given to understand your father cares little what Lord Glenaire does. Foolish."

The sound of the heir's title on this man's lips sickened her. A groan from the settee tore her heart. "Don't think the duke will let you get away with encouraging his addiction," she spat.

"My dear girl, your father is thousands of miles away. He obviously had little control over his heir in England. He has less now. I am the one with influence here."

"What do you mean?"

"The young man is where he wishes to be, doing precisely what he loves best. I choose to permit it."

"And you could choose not to." She turned back to the settee and took her brother's hand, slack in hers.

"Exactly. You're bright as a penny just as I thought."

"How can I persuade you to send him home?" She turned back and sucked in breath. He had stepped closer to her. Too close.

"Persuade. Lovely word." Jarratt resumed his examination of her person. "I'm a merchant, Lady Zambak. Your brother's place as my employee is an asset. What do you propose to give me in return if I turn him over to you?"

"I have money. I could pay you to force him."

Laughter burst from him. "Money is a lovely thing. A man can't have too much. It isn't the only thing a man desires, however." His brows rose.

Zambak shuddered and took a step back, bumping her leg on the settee. "If you are unwilling to do business, I'll take my leave of you—and take my brother with me."

"I think not. The marquess as you see is in no condition to walk. He will recover his senses, be assured of that. He always has done so—at least he has so far. Come back tomorrow. Perhaps then he'll come with you willingly. Perhaps not."

"You could—"

Jarratt's face grew dark, amusement gone. "You have much to learn about business, my lady. I merely rejected your first offer," he replied.

"And I reject yours, Mr. Jarratt." She began to walk. Filipe's wide eyes in the door helped her restrain the impulse to run. The boy trotted after her to the outside door.

Jarratt's laughter followed them down the steps. She made it around the corner before the Elliots' superior breakfast revolted and found its way into the bushes. Even as she retched, one imperative seized her. *I have to get Thorn away from that man.*

~ ~ ~

After an hour with Elliot, Charles's worries and concerns mounted. The Chinese had dug in their feet and would not be moved. The traders, who had taken to running armed boats across the delta from Lintin to Whampao and even to the gates of Canton, wouldn't either. Elliot appeared to be on the brink of taking action, but it wouldn't take much to set off the whole tinderbox.

Zambak's absence worried him more. She didn't secure an interview with Elliot. When Charles inquired about, it the man seemed surprised she would want to. "Flighty thing," the superintendent called her.

She's about as far from flighty as I can imagine, but she has taken off—most likely looking for information on her own. He knew it wasn't her day for the school and dreaded to think where she might have gone. *I hoped she sought out Oliver. She'll be safe enough with him.* He strode toward his next target—William Jarratt—turned a corner, and heard a frantic voice call him.

"Yer Grace, come quick. Come quick. The lady." Filipe ran toward him. Behind the boy, Zambak leaned over a fence, holding her stomach.

"Zambak, what is it?"

She shook her head and wrinkled her brow. "Bad fish," she mumbled.

"You're as pale as a sheet." *Dear God! She's trembling. Lady Zambak Hayden does not tremble.*

"I just—" she began and swallowed back a sob.

He couldn't bear it. *She does not sob either.* He wouldn't have it. Searching frantically, his eyes hit upon a tall stand of boxwood between two houses. He pulled her into the secluded spot.

His hand, when it touched her cheek, trembled. "Zambak," he whispered. "What is it?"

She shook her head, but when she tried to speak, only a moan came out.

He laid a hand on her shoulder gently, a gesture of comfort. She leaned against him then and sobbed into his coat while his arms went around her, one hand rubbing circles on her back.

"Thorn. Oh God, Thorn," she cried. "My beautiful brother."

Behind her back, Filipe's face twisted into a mask of pity. "Mister Jarratt. Bad man."

The vehemence of Filipe's statement alarmed him even further. Torn between the urge to storm into Jarratt's house and the need to comfort, he glared at the servant. "Explain."

Before the boy could answer, Zambak pulled herself upright. He let his arms drop away, but one hand slid down her arm to hold her hand.

Filipe darted a glance at his mistress and back to Charles. "Lady Zam had questions," he mumbled.

Zambak pulled her hand away and straightened her spine. "Of course I had questions. No one would talk to me. You all treat me like a child to be protected from ugly news." She swallowed hard, and he feared for a moment she would cast up her accounts again.

He handed her his handkerchief and looked discreetly away while she removed any trace of her sick. "What happened Zambak?" he pressed.

"I had to know."

Charles glanced down the street. Elliot directed him to Jarratt's establishment; it should be just around the corner. *Did the little fool go there herself?*

"What about Thorn," he asked, searching her face.

"He—" She swallowed convulsively.

"Zambak Hayden, what have you done?" He took both her hands in his.

"I went looking for my brother. He lodges with William Jarratt."

Damn, damn, damn. "And?" He held her eyes, his thumbs gently rubbing both hands.

"He's ill."

"Ill?" Dread filled his heart.

"Opium can be a sickness, can't it?"

Something ugly formed in his throat. *I know better than anyone how true that is.* "Yes, very much so. Tell me what you saw." She did; he regretted it. Memories of his mother—

unresponsive, pupils dilated, skin gray—flooded him, but he shook them away. They wouldn't help.

"I have to get him away from here." The bleak desperation in her eyes and the way her voice cracked as if another sob threatened stretched his self-control to the limit.

"From Jarratt?" he asked through clenched teeth.

"Jarratt. Macao. China. I asked Jarratt for help. He refused. He said Thorn didn't wish it. He said Thorn begged him. He said—"

He went very still. "He's right."

She went rigid with outrage and shook off his hands. "Right?"

"He probably does wish it. Once under the control of the poppy, they crave more and more." He searched the blue of her eyes, darkened with emotion. He found the grief he expected, but instead of the frustration and determination he might also have anticipated, something there horrified him, something he never thought to see in Zambak Hayden: fear.

"Tell me what else happened? What made you cast up your accounts?" he demanded.

She looked down at his coat. "Nothing," she said. "Seeing Thorn upset me, and the sun was hot, and I realized this morning's fish must have turned." She stood back and laid a shaking hand on her belly. "I'm fine now. Truly."

Charles knew a bouncer when he heard one. He could see she withheld information again, but the stubborn set of her shoulders told him as clearly as any words that she would not be moved from her story.

"Nothing else?" he asked smoothly, retrieving his handkerchief and handing it to Filipe.

She glanced at Filipe, guilt all over her expression. "Nothing. Only Thorn matters. I will find a way to—"

"*We* will find a way to send him home where he belongs."

He expected her to object, but she didn't. She nodded, misery etched in every line of her face.

He didn't trust her pretense of acquiescence. The obstinate woman won't wait for help no matter what Jarratt said to upset her. She'll be off on her own as soon as I turn my back—Boudicca off to save her people. He wanted to drag her back to the Elliots' and lock her in her room until he could formulate a plan. He wanted to lock her in a cabin on the *Wild Swan*—Zambak and her wretched brother both—and pay Oliver to take them to London. He wanted—

Oh God, I want her. The embrace had been a mistake. He intended a brotherly gesture of comfort, but the feel of her curled against him unleashed a rage of feelings both protective and predatory.

She smoothed her skirt and tossed her head. "Well Charles—will you kindly move so I can be on my way."

The duchess had returned; he gave her a mock bow. "Certainly, Lady Zambak. I will be happy to escort you wherever you wish to go." He winged an arm for her to take and stood firmly in place until she took it with a tsk of irritation. She allowed him to lead her toward the Elliots' mansion.

Thorn deserves a thrashing, poor soul. Jarratt deserves worse. And Filipe? He and I are due for a little chat.

Chapter 13

He's going to pry until I spill my humiliation as disgracefully as I spewed my breakfast. Zambak walked in angry silence past several houses before she dug in her heels and forced him to stop. His tender care and the sensation of his arms around her tempted her to cling to him again, to sob her story out like some fragile flower of womanhood. She hated that feeling.

We will talk, Your Grace, but not about what happened at Jarratt's. "We do need a moment of private conversation," she said. "The public park is nearby." She almost laughed at his startled expression. She hoped he stayed uneasy, never sure what she would do next.

He let her select a secluded bench but turned to Filipe without sitting. "Your mistress will be safe with me," he said before handing the boy a coin and sending him to the apothecary for sugared ginger. "For the lady, mind. Make sure all of it comes back to her."

Filipe gave a cocky salute and took off at a run.

"Tell me everything Elliot told you," she said without preamble, determined not to give him room to interrogate her. "I gather the viceroy meant to make a point with the public execution."

He raised a brow. "You are well informed."

She made an impatient gesture with her hand. "How bad was it really?"

"As bad you might think. The Chinese have moved from blocking the wholesale dealers on their end—the illegal hongs—and begun to prosecute the lower-level suppliers.

The man brought up on charges ran an opium den near the European factories. Such blatant disregard for law will no longer be tolerated."

"But execution!"

He shrugged. "Elliot believes it may just be the beginning. The emperor is determined. Elliot applauds it. Does that surprise you?"

"Opium is vile," she said.

"No one knows that better than I."

Odd statement. She'd never known Charles to show signs of laudanum use, much less any other form of opium. "How so?" she asked, genuinely curious.

"Have you met my mother? She sometimes attends my uncle's holiday gatherings."

Zambak searched her memories. The image of a pale, nervous woman leaning on his uncle's arm came to her mind, the image of a perpetual invalid. "Laudanum?"

He nodded. "As you say, vile stuff. She determines to stop using it periodically. She always fails. Any problem or setback becomes an excuse to embrace narcotics again." He slumped forward, as if absorbed by the sight of his boots, and Zambak hesitated to interrupt his morose thoughts. "After she married her second husband, I hoped it would change, and she actually stayed away from it for several years, but when Douglas died, she took to it again with a vengeance." He breathed deeply and sat up straight. "And it is perfectly legal from any apothecary in England."

"Thorn as well. You may recall he broke his leg badly three years ago."

"He spent the summer in bed," Charles acknowledged.

She nodded. "They gave him laudanum for pain. It has been his constant companion ever since. He left university. He stopped seeing friends. He lost interest in sailing and even boat building. He wants—or wanted—to be a boat builder. Did you know that? He refused to tell Father, certain of disapproval." She sighed deeply. "I fear he has he moved on to worse."

"Smoking opium tar?"

"Temperance told me smoking ensnares users more deeply. Thank God that practice hasn't reached London."

"Yet," Charles responded bitterly. When he glanced over at her left hand, she stilled her fingers. "You're plotting something," he said, gesturing toward her hand.

"Thinking," she replied primly before her left thumb began to move again. "There has to be a way to bring a halt to this ugly business before it destroys China and our honor with it."

"Elliot hopes the Chinese will force the traders to back off. He hopes the government will continue to stay neutral."

"You need to get my report to London," she said, lost in thought. Her face lifted. "You said 'Elliot hopes.' What does he fear?"

"Shrewd question." The respect in Charles's expression warmed her heart more than his pity or protective gestures ever had. "He fears money rules in London. The government doesn't want to stop the trade entirely—the revenue from tea depends on supply, and the supply depends on the sale of opium."

"Yes, yes. We know that. Do you think the navy will return?"

"Jarratt's partner, Martinson, has reached London," he told her. "Bribery, lies, and pressure could force the government to send the navy back, this time with orders to attack."

At the mention of Jarratt, her stomach clenched, and a vile taste crept into her mouth. "What else?" she rasped.

Charles looked down. His sigh sounded deep and weary. "Elliot fears the Chinese response will eventually ensnare an English user or dealer. If they arrest someone or threaten violence, he may be forced to act."

If Thorn is as closely allied to the opium dens as Jarratt implied—and out of his senses from the narcotic—he could be—cow turds!

"Charles, I have to get to my brother. I can't leave him in Jarratt's circle."

The duke's eyes held hers until she felt him boring into her soul. He put out a comforting hand, and she gripped it to steady herself. "How exactly do you propose to do that, Zambak?" he asked.

"Jarratt said to come back. I'll go tomorrow. He implied Thorn might be well, might be willing to come with me."

"*We'll* go tomorrow," he corrected.

She stiffened in outrage for a moment before Jarratt's face leered at her in memory, and she sagged toward Charles. When he cupped her cheek with one hand and searched her face, she thought for a moment he meant to kiss her. *Absurd. Charles is a married man, and we're friends. Only friends.*

"We'll go together, Zambak. We will get Thorn help together."

Together. Relief flooded her. She had thought that accepting help made her weak, but the tenderness in the duke's eyes gave her strength.

~ ~ ~

With the men in Macao—however briefly—the women of the British enclave, starved for social life, demanded a formal dinner. Clara Elliot embraced the idea without question and sent invitations the day her husband arrived.

Party or not, revelations about Chinese actions lay like a dark cloud over the colony, and the mood in the Elliots' drawing room sank under its gloom that evening. Conversation took a ponderous tone, artificial cheer hardening ladies' faces. Fans flipped open, waved frantically, and snapped shut. Zambak thought they resembled nothing so much as nervous geese, frightened by a fox. The image of a fox made her scan the company again to confirm Jarratt's absence.

Either the Elliots don't wish for Jarratt's company, or Clara is afraid a single man will upset her seating arrangements at the dinner table. She wondered idly if she had missed another unmarried man in the room, being the only unattached woman present. Either way, the man's absence worried her.

On the heels of that thought, the drawing room door opened to admit a latecomer. Her stomach flipped over. *If they seat me next to Jarratt at table, I will be unable to eat, much less think clearly.*

The door opened fully, and Hua announced, "His Grace the Duke of Murnane," and Elliot greeted him warmly. Zambak's heart did a leap, and she let out the breath she didn't know she held. Sometime in the past week, her attitude toward Charles had shifted. *When did he become an ally and not an adversary?*

The duke's presence gave her confidence, but the memory of his arms around her, of his hand cupping her cheek, drove her temperature so high she feared her face must show it. The warmth in his smile chased her doldrums away in spite of the hint of sadness that had, she realized, lurked in his eyes as long as she'd known him.

When his welcoming expression drew her, she started toward him, but a shift in the conversation slowed her pace. Small whispers replaced the awkward cheer—gossip of some sort. Zambak had neither time nor patience for gossip. Charles and Elliot broke off what appeared to be an intense conversation as she approached. Charles took her outreached hand and bent over it, formal manners in place for the social situation.

"Lady Zambak, how delightful," he said. "May I say your gown is particularly becoming this evening?" His words sounded across a suddenly silent room.

Odd, that. Before she could puzzle it through, however, Hua announced dinner, and Elliot offered his arm to lead her in. Charles followed with Clara Elliot on his arm. Zambak hadn't given much thought to rank beyond what she took for granted daily, but this, her first formal dinner in Macao, brought home to her that she and Charles were the highest-ranking members of British society there.

A prickling up her neck brought the suspicion that rank might be disadvantageous in Macao, resented among all the self-made men and rising wealth. She wondered if that resentment caused the silence that greeted Charles. Upbringing came to the fore, and Zambak stood tall, taking her chair at the head next to their host with her most regal bearing. *No one could say the Duchess of Sudbury's daughter didn't know how to behave in society.* She glanced up and down the table daring the wives of merchants to criticize. One woman, caught frowning down at Charles, colored under Zambak's scrutiny.

After a pretty speech by Superintendent Elliot, conversation proceeded properly, each person dividing his or her time between the person to the left and to the right. Zambak, trained from childhood in the art of polite nothings, had no trouble. It took the entire first remove to pick apart the warm climate and its difference from London.

Halfway through the second course, Mrs. Dean, who had the place next to Charles, gave him what could only be described as a cut, refusing to turn back toward him when conversation shifted and keeping her eyes glued on Mr. Bunche on her left. Neither of those seated near Zambak dared such behavior. On the contrary, she had already grown weary of fawning references to her dear father and darling mama.

Not rank then. The women of Macao have taken Charles in dislike. When he caught her watching, Charles, ever the rogue, gave her a cheeky wink. He seemed utterly at ease in the face of the woman's rude behavior. Zambak swallowed her curiosity and set out to charm her companions.

Whether she succeeded or not, she couldn't say, but by the time the pudding arrived, she felt weary of the exercise. Elliot announced that "due to pressing business in the morning" the gentleman would keep their traditional port to a minimum and join the women in short order. She reined in her impulse to lean on the table and join them and trailed after the ladies, impatience making her fingers twitch.

Her store of meaningless prattle well exhausted, Zambak kept to a corner and tried to make herself inconspicuous. She failed. Mrs. Dean, the wind in her sails, charged directly at her and flounced into the seat beside Zambak. She opened with a breathless observation. "Our little society must be poor shakes compared to your normal fare, my lady."

Zambak murmured her demurral.

"It is our honor to have you among us. Your dear mother must be relieved to have you in the care of Clara Elliot." Speculation glittered behind the woman's façade. "One allows great surprise that the Elliots should be such a trusted part of your family's circle."

A fleeting temptation to set the woman straight disappeared under Zambak's determination not to embarrass the Elliots. It wasn't their fault her father had thrust her under their protection. She smiled and nodded, having frequently found that sufficient with people who enjoyed the sound of their own voices. The Dean woman's next question put her on alert.

"How well do you know His Grace?"

There was only one duke here. She mimicked wide-eyed innocence. "Do you mean Charles?" she asked sweetly, hoping to quash pretention. "Our families have been friends my entire life. I've known him since the cradle."

"Your parents know him well?" She looked like she had sucked something vile. "Your father approves of him?"

What the devil is this woman about? "Why yes. He loves him like a son." Zambak thought about her statement. It was true, insofar as her father displayed affection for any of them. "Whatever is the matter, Mrs. Dean?" she asked, feigning naiveté.

The woman wiggled in her chair, raising her bulk up somewhat, and leaned in to whisper, "With your dear mother not here, the attention of an older woman might be in order. I will speak to Clara on your behalf."

"I beg your pardon? I don't understand." She most certainly did not.

"Your parents may have been reluctant to soil your ears with certain facts about—about that man. It is to their credit that they have not. But here, far from home, I caution you, my lady. Do not find yourself alone with him."

She's warning me off Charles as if he were some sort of rutting rake? Cow slop. What in heaven gave her that idea? He may not be a saint but—

The return of the men cut off further speculation. Charles's eyes met hers from across the room, and he came toward her directly. Mrs. Dean gripped her hand—rather too hard— and murmured, "Remember my warning," before scurrying off without greeting the duke.

"What was that about?" he asked.

"I honestly have no idea," she replied.

His lips twitched in amusement, and for one moment, they were in perfect accord. The blue of his eyes seemed to deepen until it forced her to drop her eyes to her lap. His regard made her feel powerfully feminine.

Savor it, Zambak. Such moments are fleeting.

Chapter 14

Filipe trotted down the road to catch up with Charles and Zambak the next morning. "Lady Zam. You forget me?" he called, breathless.

"Not needed, Filipe. I can escort Lady Zambak," Charles told him. *I don't need another pair of prying eyes and big ears.*

"You may need me," the cheeky boy replied. *At least he left the blasted parasol behind.*

For the first time that morning, Zambak's tense expression softened, amusement crinkling the corners of her eyes. The sight made him wonder what passed between her and her servant. *I need to get the boy alone anyway.* He told Filipe to follow but stay out of earshot.

They turned back to their mission, Filipe trailing along behind them happily until he saw their destination. "Bad man," he muttered in front of Jarratt's house.

"So you warned us," Charles said, raising the knocker, Zambak rigid at his side. Filipe looked at the door and down at the steps. He sank down on the lowest one. "I'll wait," he said.

Charles thought Zambak might also bolt, but she stiffened her spine, thrust out a determined chin, and tossed a haughty glare at Jarratt's butler.

"Mr. Jarratt told Lady Zambak to return today. I trust he received my notice," Charles said, drawing a glare from Zambak. *Did she think we could arrive unannounced and find her brother on his feet? Of course I warned them.*

The servant didn't appear to be surprised. He escorted them into a large drawing room, one with the studied and slightly overblown sumptuousness of the nouveau riche—too much gilt, too many tassels, excessively applied velvet. Zambak's momentary hesitation at the door alerted him that the room was familiar. "What is it?"

"He isn't here."

"Is this where you saw him last?" He studied her carefully, or he might have missed the sick look, quickly suppressed. *Whatever happened in this room had been ugly.* She nodded, her deep frown leaving furrows in her brow. He reached for her hand, pulled her around to face him, and gave the hand a squeeze. "Courage," he said. "We'll know how he is momentarily."

A half hour later, Charles watched her pace the length of the room and feared they would not see her foolish brother at all. No word had come, nor had refreshments been offered. He had almost decided to summon the butler when the door opened.

The man who entered appeared to be approaching middle age, his lean face dry, wrinkled, and mottled; a faint bruise marring his chin. The newcomer's clothes hung on him as if they had been made for a much larger man. Charles realized with a jolt that he beheld Thorn Hayden, not some stranger fifteen years the boy's senior. Only the greasy white-blond hair that hung to his collar and the familiar ice-blue Hayden eyes, dull though they were and burdened with purple bags, identified him as the Marquess of Glenaire. *Dear God. No wonder his sister was horrified!*

"Come to cut up my peace, Zamb?" Thorn growled.

Zambak ignored his complaint. She rushed toward her brother, arms open to embrace him, but he brushed her away. "I'm not a baby to be cuddled!"

"He most certainly is not. He is a valued employee." The man who entered behind Thorn loomed over him, powerfully built and self-assured. Charles had no doubt who it was. "William Jarratt, I presume," he drawled like the vapid aristocrat he pretended to be.

Jarratt glanced down at him. "You are?"

Charles had long practice with men who thought their superior height intimidated him. He found, on the whole, his size gave him the benefit of surprise when needed. He stood, feet firmly planted and answered smoothly. "A family friend," he answered curtly.

"May I present His Grace, the Duke of Murnane," Zambak said. His name took immediate effect, but not in the way Charles expected. It neither impressed nor angered the man.

"Are you?" Jarratt drawled. "I heard you were in Macao, seeing the sights as it were. We have a mutual . . ." His lips twitched, and he watched Charles avidly. ". . . *acquaintance*," he concluded.

His odd reaction distracted Charles. *What in God's name?*

Zambak's outburst called him back. "Thorn Hayden, what has become of you? Mother would be horrified."

"Not a boy, Zamb. You heard him. I'm a valued employee. I don't take orders from women. Women don't need to push their nose into men's business. Women have their uses, but they are meant to stay out of men's affairs." His face twisted in an attempt at snide superiority; he achieved only childish petulance.

"Where did you learn that pile of cow slop, Thorn? Not at home, that's for certain," his sister spat back. The siblings glared at each other like two cats ready to spring, except it seemed to Charles "spring" might be beyond the young marquess's capability.

"Are you unwell, Thorn? You haven't been taking care of yourself." Charles modulated his voice to as mild a tone as he could manage.

The marquess blinked at Charles as if just noticing him and not liking what he saw. "Murnane? When did you come? If my father thinks he can force me home—"

"I'm not here to drag you home." He put a hand on Zambak's back to head off any outburst that contradicted him. He hoped she would catch his meaning. *I wasn't sent here for that, but it doesn't mean I won't try.* "Your father respects your decision to make your fortune on your own."

Thorn preened a bit. "Right. Making my own. Can't depend on the old man. Tries to run my life when I take his money."

"Quite. He who pays the bills always calls the shots." Charles glanced pointedly at Jarratt who studied the interaction intently. "You do not look well at all, though. Perhaps you should take better care of yourself." He caught Zambak's eyes then, silent messages passing between them.

"Charles is right, Thorn. To succeed you have to be able to give your whole self to the enterprise." If she had sucked on a lemon, her face could not be more sour. *Zambak Hayden is the world's worst liar.*

Thorn considered what his sister said. He pulled at his cravat and smoothed his jacket with one hand. "I have been a bit low, lately. I'll turn around, Zamb, don't you doubt it." He had begun to sway.

"I have friends here, Thorn, who could help. They understand this sickness and—" Anxiety gave Zambak's voice a breathless tone.

Charles assumed she meant the Quakers. He hadn't considered it, but he wouldn't be surprised if they understood opium and its remedies.

Thorn wasn't having his sister's help. "What sickness, Zamb? Ain't sick, just a bit low."

"Come with me," Zambak urged. "We can help you."

Thorn pulled his arm away when she tried to grab it, and rubbed his hands vigorously up and down as if his arms itched. "Don't need help from a woman. I don't hide in a woman's skirts." He looked over at Jarratt for confirmation. The boy had been coached, and coached well.

Zambak pulled back, leaning into Charles's arm. He took comfort in how well she fit. "Of course not. You're a man grown." Her voice cracked. "Why don't we at least take a walk? Some fresh air might do you good."

Thorn swayed again. "Don't need fresh air," he whined. "Don't need you, Zamb." He turned and took a step away. "I think I'll lie down now."

Zambak started to go after him but came to an abrupt halt when a large servant appeared in the doorway to lead Thorn away.

"You heard him, your ladyship," Jarratt said into the silence. "Your brother chooses to be here. He does not wish for your interference."

She spun on the man. "You could—" Whatever she meant to say, something in Jarratt's expression cut it off, and all color drained from her face.

Charles narrowed his eyes at Jarratt. The rotter had done something to frighten her, no small feat with this woman who dared much. She shrugged it off and stood a bit taller, justifying his belief in her great store of courage.

"I will see him tomorrow," she pronounced.

"Perhaps he will be receiving. Perhaps not," Jarratt retorted. "I, on the other hand, am 'at home' to the ladies of Macao frequently." He managed to give the word "ladies" a distasteful sound.

He nodded at Charles. "And visiting dignitaries as well," he said, amusement glittering in his eyes. "Perhaps you'll find something to amuse you in their company."

"Come away," Charles said to Zambak. "We'll talk." The hand she put on his arm trembled. *Jarratt will pay for this; he'll pay dearly if he hurts Zambak.*

They had almost reached the door when another voice interrupted. "Why, Charles, what a lovely surprise."

The hairs on the back of his neck rose. He knew that voice. It belonged to the woman he least wanted to see, and yet the one he had pursued across Southern Asia. Julia. His wife.

Chapter 15

Thorn disappeared from the upper landing. The burly servant's hold on her brother's elbow disturbed Zambak even more than his appearance had. She restrained herself from charging up the stairs with great willpower augmented by the duke's firm arm dragging her to the door. She almost missed the person who sauntered down the steps to caress the newel post at the bottom, but she felt Charles stiffen at the sound of the woman's voice.

Zambak turned to examine the lady—if she was a lady—through narrowed eyes and found her unfamiliar. Her excess of cosmetics and diaphanous, somewhat dated, gown gave her the aspect of a faded strumpet, but her eyes appeared sharp enough, and they cut like knives into Charles. "What a lovely surprise," the strumpet purred.

Charles tripped but caught himself when he turned to stare long and hard at the vision at the foot of the stairs. "Hello, Julia" he said at last, something thick in his throat muffling his words. "I heard you were in China."

Julia! Merciful angels. Is this harridan the famous Julia, the malicious beauty who abandoned her husband and son? The jezebel who betrayed him over and over? Zambak heard delicious whispers about the Duchess of Murnane now and then growing up and imagined a glamorous, but cold, woman who charmed men and led them to their doom. This sad creature bore no resemblance to her imagined siren. She did not even appear to be well.

"How good of you to come—or perhaps you didn't come to see me. Still an errand boy for the Duke of Sudbury?" She snaked a languid glance at Zambak, examining her head to toe as if she found her wanting.

Zambak shuddered under a furious temptation to slap the woman silly.

"Neither," Charles said with icy calm. "I am merely visiting parts of the empire. I heard of your intentions in Madras. Too late to turn back then."

"Wandering the world aimlessly, Charles? How unlike you," the woman smirked.

"I needed a distraction after Jonny died." If words could be constructed of ice shards, his were—cold, sharp, and intended to wound. The cruel tones cut into Zambak who had never heard him speak that way.

Julia's mouth clamped shut, the corners turned down. *Jonny. Her son. Dead.*

The two of them—husband and wife—held each other's eyes across the expanse of Jarratt's foyer. Zambak felt the tension, electric in the air around her. *Charles poured all his love into that boy. He held him when he died. Julia never came, not to the deathbed, not to the funeral. Did she even know before now?*

Zambak's mother had explained that the duchess couldn't bear that the boy had a defective heart and left as soon as he was born. Zambak wondered if she would have cared any more if Jonny had been healthy. Rage so raw it would have frightened her in any other man radiated from Charles's entire body.

Julia's gaze skittered away first. "Poor defective child is probably better off," she murmured, and Zambak found herself holding on to Charles's arm. This time she held him back.

"How touching," Jarratt said, pouring oily derision into his words. "A reunion in my foyer. Perhaps you two lovebirds would like a private room to catch up, although greeting one's wife with another woman on your arm isn't done, Your

Grace. At least not in your circles." Jarratt's avid eyes moved from his examination of Zambak's bosom to her iron grip on Charles's arm. "You really mustn't be so possessive, Lady Zambak. He isn't yours." The lout chuckled at his own wit.

Charles seemed to pull himself into the present, aware of her at his side. His eyes, when he turned to her, held an ocean of regret.

You aren't alone, Charles. The thought came unbidden, but it felt right. He had endured unbearable suffering, but he wasn't alone. He had Zambak.

"Take me home, Charles. I'll see Thorn tomorrow," she said. At that moment, Thorn's problems seemed far away, but she needed to distract him.

"Not alone, you won't." The flash of steel in his expression sent relief flooding her.

Charles faced Julia one more time. "We'll talk later," he said before he walked away, Zambak gripping his arm.

Julia's voice trailed after them. "Yes. We'll talk later. I'll make sure of it."

~ ~ ~

Is the sympathy of another person a boon or a burden? Walking away from Jarratt's house, Zambak held his arm, her hand warm and comforting. She did not complain about her problems with Thorn, scheme to drag the boy away, nor prod him about his own problems or the scene she had just witnessed. *God love this woman.* She stood steadfast and silent at his side, and he clung to her support, though his conscience shouted that he ought not.

They had moved from adversaries to allies, and he had counted it a success because it made it easier for him to protect her in spite of her determination to go her own way. He glanced over at her, and she smiled back, a smile of such sweetness that his heart contracted. *Not for me, Zambak. I don't deserve it.*

"Are you well?" he asked her.

"As can be. You?" Concern deepened her voice.

"As can be," he ground out.

She didn't intrude. She didn't say, "My, but that woman is horrid," nor ask, "How can you stand the witch?" Nor did she ask, "Have you always been a cuckold, too weak to control your own wife?" *Zambak Hayden, fiercely loyal, asks merely if I am well. Have we moved past allies? If so, what are we? We've become close. Too close.*

A married man—a soon-to-be-divorced man, if he had his way—had no right to court an innocent young woman. He had even less right to hold, to taste, or to touch, and at that moment Charles longed to do all three, to mine as much warmth and comfort as he could until the memory of his cold, conniving wife disappeared. A wise man would fear the wrath of the Duke of Sudbury at that thought. Charles feared the loss of his trust.

I have to put a distance between us before I do something completely inappropriate.

When they came to the crossroad, he searched the road behind them. Filipe grinned and waved. He could leave her here and do what needed doing.

"Filipe can see you back to the Elliots."

She searched his eyes but didn't argue. "I mean to visit Temperance. Her classes should be over. She can teach me more about opium sickness and its remedies."

"Excellent notion. Tell her everything." The influence of the steady Quaker woman had been good for Zambak. He hoped Temperance might strengthen her where Thorn is concerned.

The woman at his side nodded solemnly. "I mean to. Will you—" Whatever she meant to say, she thought better of it and sank back. She neither pried nor burdened him with an excess of sympathy. She watched Filipe come up, patted the arm she still held, and set off toward the ladies' seminary.

Watching her walk away he devoured her graceful form with his eyes and for a moment gave full rein to his longing. When she disappeared around a corner, he lowered a heavy door on his desire and locked it away where it belonged before setting about his business.

It took little more than an hour for Julia to appear in response to his summons. She came alone, with no maid or companion in sight, uphill toward the bench he had selected, one overlooking wharfs, far from the shady glade where he frequently met Zambak. While he waited, he reached a conclusion about the mystery of the Dean woman's odd behavior at dinner and the coldness of the other ladies. Julia had already spread malice about him.

She stormed up to him, breathing heavily and spewing outrage. "Really, Charles, is all this necessary?" She waved a hand to encompass the bench, the wharfs, the city itself. "It is just like you to demand to meet me in the least comfortable spot in Macao."

His weary gaze took in the battered feather on her bonnet, the frayed hem, and the discretely mended but obvious repair on her sleeve. Julia had come on hard times and, when she got wind of his arrival in Macao, set out to milk him. She would have to think again.

She huffed, dropped to the bench, and reeled on him so close he could smell the stink of rotten teeth and dyspepsia on her breath. Hard living showed in the rough skin of her complexion; its former beauty long eroded beyond recognition. No, Julia Wheatly, erstwhile Duchess of Murnane, was not doing well.

She looks sick. I shudder to consider what disease she may have contracted and from whom. If he had met any other woman in that state, he would not have been able to hold back compassion. For Julia he had none.

I once believed that I loved this creature. How could I have been so foolish? He had been duped. That his cousins had both pursued her offered no consolation. She made fools of all three of them.

He examined her closely in the several moments it took her to catch her breath. *She must need money badly to tolerate my demand she meet me here.* He watched her take one particularly deep breath and arrange her features into an expression meant to be coy. Julia managed only calculation. She stretched a hand to touch his sleeve. He pulled away.

"It must have been devilishly hard for you, losing your only son that way," she said.

"Our son." His jaw hurt from his clenched teeth.

Her painted brows shot up. "Of course. Our son."

"Fred took it hard as well." Her eyes widened and darted away. Charles had always known he didn't father Julia's child, but he loved him from the moment he held him for the first time. When his cousin and friend, Frederick Wheatly, had returned from India to become steward of the Murnane family seat, Eversham Hall, three years before, they had finally accepted what was plain to many others. Fred may have sired Jonny, but Charles was his father in every way that mattered.

She put on a smile meant to sparkle. "Fred came back? I'll posit a guess he is a wealthy nabob, rolling in Bengali jewels." She looked almost hopeful.

"Hardly. He has married and has four children. He and Clare manage Eversham Hall and the estate, and, of course, he is my heir now. His boy Arthur may be duke some day." *Arthur Charles Wheatly, two years old and brimming with health and life. God forgive how much I envy Fred.*

"But Charles, you could—" The hand she raised to gesture with fluttered to her lap under the force of his glare. "That is, if you truly need a legitimate heir, I—"

"Offering your body for money, Julia? Not the first time I suspect. What is it you want?"

Her tightly pursed lips trembled. "You've been so miserly," she ground out at last. "How am I supposed to live?"

"The solicitors notified you three years ago that no further allowance would be forthcoming from the Murnane estate."

"That was horrid of you. Darling Conte Giacomo dropped me the day the message arrived. I've struggled ever since."

"You must have run through the last of the Murnane jewels," he said. "The tiara in Madras cost me a small fortune."

She gave a shrug and sniffed. "It isn't as if you have a use for them." Her expression turned vulpine. "Unless you plan to offer them to Sudbury's chit in exchange for . . ."

His fisted hands ached from the effort to keep from throttling the tart. Before he could formulate a sufficient retort, she went on. Her mask slipped entirely, revealing the unbridled calculation beneath it. "A word here. A word there. How long before London knows Lady Zambak Hayden has engaged in an affair with a married man? The ladies of Macao already believe you are a seducer of innocents, and a violent abuser as well," she said, triumph giving force to her last words.

The suddenness of his movement stunned her. He gripped both her arms and put his face inches from hers, rage pouring from him. "Say what you want about me but stay away from Zambak. She has done nothing to you."

She blinked, but calculation returned quickly. "You do want her! What would Sudbury say about that?"

He dropped her arms as if they were hot iron and ran one hand across his neck.

"Alas, Charles you prove the rumors. A man who assaults his wife cannot be trusted with innocents." Her laugh, ragged and spiteful, ended in a coughing fit.

"Hurt her, and I will destroy you," he roared.

Her laugh had brittle desperation in it. "Too late for that," she said.

Something in that desperation struck him as significant. "Has Jarratt not been forthcoming with cash?" he asked.

"William Jarratt is a boor and a brute," she said, something thick in her throat deepening her voice. An expression of genuine disgust, quickly shuttered, skittered across her face, and she licked the side of her cracked lips. "For sufficient financial assistance, I could make the rumors go away."

Having seen Julia's state, Charles suspected the ladies of Macao would not be fooled for long in any case. If Zambak came to harm in the meantime, however, he wouldn't forgive himself, to say nothing of the hell he would face from her father.

"Let's keep this simple," he said. "You want money. You won't get a farthing to stop your vicious gossip. I want something more." He had her attention now. "Freedom. Come back to London with me, admit to the adultery the whole *haut ton* already knows about, and accept divorce with as little fuss as possible. I'll make a one-time settlement on you. One time. We'll be finished."

"How much?"

He quoted a staggering sum. She tried to hide her delight and opened her mouth, but he held up a hand to forestall her demand for more.

"No more. That is my only offer. Cooperate or I'll drag you back, let the scandal have full rein, and leave you with nothing after the divorce."

She sank against the bench, accepting the inevitable. "Why now? You've been too weak-willed to do it all these years. Why now?"

"Jonny." He closed his eyes, swallowed hard, and

lowered his voice. "I would never put Jonny through the ugliness of it. He's gone now."

"What of your uncle and all those loyal lapdog Wheatlys?" she chirped.

He brushed it aside. Will had urged him to divorce her for years, but she didn't need to know that. "That is the only offer you will get."

"I will need a small advance," she wheedled.

He dreaded what she might call "small." "No cash. I'll rent a modest dwelling for you—that and credit at the butcher and green grocer—until I can arrange to go back to London. I have a commission to fulfill first."

"Servants?" She raised her chin in a failed effort at contempt.

"One."

"Nip farthing as always," she sniffed. "How long until we leave?"

He considered his responsibilities. The report to the queen depended on Elliot's actions. His report to Sudbury depended on what he could do for Thorn. As to Zambak—that situation had become too complicated for him to consider with Julia in front of him. "It may be a few weeks," he told her at last. "I have work to complete."

"Don't take too long, Charles. I'll get bored. You don't like it when I get bored." She sauntered away, swaying her hips to a man with no interest in her withered charms.

He leaned his elbows on his knees. He had done it; he would end his farce of a marriage once and for all. That much gave him consolation.

His foolish heart brought Zambak to mind, and he laughed at himself. Even divorced, he had nothing to offer her but a tarnished title marred by the two generations before him and battered heart corrupted by Julia. *It will never happen. If I suggested it, her father would thrash me.*

Chapter 16

"Thee describe someone deep in the grasp of opium, Zambak. The narcotic has thy brother firmly in its clutches." Temperance squeezed Zambak's hand. "Did thee also observe tremors?"

Zambak nodded, blinking back tears. "And he rubbed his arms violently at the end."

"Some describe an itch nigh on to madness when the opium cannot be had." Temperance put a gentle finger under Zambak's chin and forced her to meet her eyes. "If you do what you wish, you must understand the terrible consequences. Pulling such a one as your brother from the pit in which he is mired will cause much suffering."

Zambak pulled away and sniffed, sitting upright. "Are you suggesting I leave him there?"

"I suggest no such thing. He will die without help." She studied Zambak closely. "I have seen strength in thee, and I believe thee have the courage to endure it, but it will take all thy skills and power to save thy brother. The effort will require all you can give it."

"Will you help me?"

"Tell me first, Zambak. Why does thee wish to undertake this trial?"

"He's my brother! He's my father's heir. He will be the Duke of Sudbury some day," she said, raising her chin. Describing Thorn's appearance dragged raw emotion to the surface. Pride demanded she reel it in. "My family's honor is at stake."

Temperance's face lost none of its intensity. "You wish to protect thy family's prestige. Only that?" she asked.

"Jarratt wants to manipulate my father in some way through Thorn," Zambak temporized. *And me too if he can.* She kept that thought to herself.

"Evil indeed. Will he succeed if thee do not act?"

"With my father? No. The duke is made of sterner stuff." She held herself very still, but visions of Thorn refused to dissipate.

"Then why?" Temperance prodded.

This woman is merciless. Zambak's heart threatened to burst open. "That man at Jarratt's isn't my brother Thorn," she cried. "My brother radiates health and joy. He skips through life with a laugh on his lips. He—" She broke then, sobbing into Temperance's waiting shoulder. Zambak had never been a watering pot; her inability to control weeping alarmed her.

"Tell me about thy brother, Zambak," Temperance whispered, still holding her.

Zambak took a shuddering breath. Her tears subsided, leaving her drained and grateful for the embrace of her friend. "Thorn brought light to our house. When my parents quarrel—which they often do—the entire household descends into gloom. Even as a small boy Thorn would make us laugh. He pulled our brothers and sisters together in the nursery and peppered us with funny stories until he made every one of us laugh." She warmed to her tale, describing pranks and mischief, until she grinned at the memory.

Smiling directly at Temperance, she said at last, "He also pokes holes in my nonsense when I get too bossy—never in a mean way, always with humor." She sobered. "At least he did once. For the past few years, since the laudanum took him, he lives like a shadow of that boy, lost in his own world." The respect she found in her friend's eyes stunned her.

"I will help thee, Zambak," Temperance murmured, "but thee must be prepared."

"For the pain? I can bear it."

"More than that. If thee restrain him, and force the opium from him, he may be well."

"That's what we want, isn't it?" Zambak asked, puzzled by Temperance's frown.

"In the end, he must choose. Only thy brother can decide if he wishes to remain free, and even then, he will struggle, perhaps for his entire life."

Zambak sobered, considering what she had been told. "You mean, my effort could be for nothing?"

"Perhaps. He may never be the laughing boy thee remember," Temperance concluded.

Zambak stiffened her spine. She could face the possibility of failure but not inaction in the face of the horror she saw. "So be it. We'll do our best."

Temperance nodded. "Thee are resolute. Thee will need to be. Come visit the new hospital. There is room there. Clean but secure. We will make thee welcome to bring thy brother, even against his will, and I will make space for thee to sleep nearby as well."

Zambak, blinked, startled. She hadn't considered the practical aspects of this. "You mean I'll have to care for him. Physically." She grimaced. She had ever hated the sickroom.

"Someone must wipe up his sick, soothe his aches, and watch over him so he does not harm himself. Would thee leave him to strangers?" Temperance asked.

At home we had servants—but no, Mother cared for each of us herself when we were ill. Another thought struck her. "Everyone in Macao will know." Zambak murmured, still considering. Temperance waited at that, and Zambak answered her friend's silent question. "I care not one whit about those people. I mind only for my parents' sake, but they can bear it. Better Thorn alive with our reputation in tatters than destroyed by this evil." She raised her chin and met Temperance's gaze. "I will do it. I can, and I will—if we can convince—or coerce—him to come."

Hours later Zambak waited in front of Mrs. Josie's boarding house. "That rude woman told me I could not wait inside." She stormed at Charles without preamble when he finally arrived. He hadn't told her the nature of his business, but his appearance suggested it hadn't gone well.

"Why are you here?" he demanded as if distressed to see her.

"I want to see Thorn again."

"Zambak—"

"I spoke with Temperance Knighton. We have a plan for treating him. Now I need to find a way to remove him from that house."

Charles took her hand in his. His smile, immensely sad, worried her. "By now your brother is back in the arms of Morpheus. There is no point in seeing him now. I'll check in at Jarratt's later tonight or tomorrow morning."

She began to protest, and he yanked on her arm. "No. You will not go there. I'll go and send word. We'll formulate a plan. I promise."

We. There it was again. She didn't have to do it alone; she had Charles, and she had Temperance. She flung her head back fighting surrender, jerked it down again, and frowned.

Cow shite. "Very well, my lord tyrant. I will wait."

It didn't matter. When she came down for breakfast the next morning, Hua greeted her with a missive in Charles's distinctive hand on a silver platter.

Unable to see Thorn. He returned to Whampao right after we left. We will talk later. C

~ ~ ~

Charles couldn't say for certain what drove him to the newly opened medical center that morning. The Knightons' description over dinner had impressed him, as had Daniel Oliver's support and that of the Lau family. He could easily have had a bank draft delivered, but something drove him to see the place for himself. Perhaps the need for something clean and good would rinse the distaste his confrontation with Julia still in his mouth. Perhaps a visit there would keep him from seeking comfort from Zambak. Whatever the reason, he found the facility impressive and the ever-competent Temperance a rock of strength.

"Thy contribution is most welcome, Charles, but thee do not need to do my work." A servant had called Temperance to the front before she could bathe the feverish and fretful child Charles took from her. He removed the cloth from her hand and urged her to go do what was needed.

"I have done more than my share of caring for a sick child, Temperance, and I'm good with children. I will manage this until you can send someone." Her grateful smile warmed him, and he turned to the crib, the only occupied one of the four in the room. He wondered how long before the people of Macao discovered this place and the beds filled.

"Now, little one, shall we make you more comfortable?"

Cool clothes did their work eventually, and the tiny girl, perhaps two years in age, grew less restless, but no less unhappy. When she began to whimper softly, he reached in and pulled her into one arm. With his free hand, he applied a fresh cloth to her head and picked up the cup of water at his elbow and began urging sips into the tiny mouth. It seemed to settle her.

Voices down the hall alerted him that Temperance approached, perhaps bringing someone to take over. He turned to the door with a welcoming smile and came face to face with a stunned Zambak Hayden.

"Charles! What on earth?" She examined his tiny companion, peered deeply at him, and seemed to probe his heart.

"It's a baby, Lady Zambak. Not an alien creature. Surely you've seen them before," he laughed. "I rather like them."

"I know. I mean, you've always been wonderful with the littlest ones, but here?"

Temperance laughed. "Charles came to contribute to our work and found himself lured into contributing more than money." She reached down and took the toddler from him. "Thank thee for taking her while I greeted my other guest. We have not yet hired sufficient servants to care for those we expect to heal."

"You are very welcome, Temperance," he said. "The little one and I managed fine." He rose, examined the wet stains on his coat, concluded they likely would dry without harm, and glanced up at Zambak. "What are you doing here?"

Only then did he notice her distress. "Is there a problem?" he demanded. *Has Jarratt bothered you? Or Julia?*

"Zambak has seen what facility we have so that she may care for her brother and witnessed an unpleasant scene—a victim of opium dependence," Temperance told him, bouncing the baby. "It is much to consider."

She may care for . . . She plans to do it herself? She must have read his thoughts, because she squared her shoulders, determination in every line of her body.

"What needs to be done will be done," she announced to them both.

Chapter 17

Bile rising in his throat, Charles studied the man who stood at ease across the Elliots' drawing room accepting the greetings of his fellows, accepting adulation as his due. Tall and powerfully built, Jarratt looked about the company as if he ruled it. He glared at Elliot with open disdain. Oliver nodded at Charles, followed his line of sight, and shook his head. The Americans' presence had been unexpected; they avoided Jarratt's court.

His walk home from the clinic with Zambak that morning had not gone well. She demanded to storm Jarratt's house and obtain her brother's return from Whampao. He hated how quickly she deflated when she realized the foolishness of that idea, but he had been momentarily relieved.

To distract her, he had described Elliot's plans to meet with the trader community and immediately regretted it when she rubbed her left middle finger with her thumb. He knew that gesture too well. "No. You will not confront Jarratt in front of all Macao," he had said.

"How can I? Women will be excluded," she responded bitterly before marching off, no doubt planning something worse.

Her prediction regarding the exclusion of women had been accurate. Mrs. Elliot and one or two of her cronies made their bows and quickly scurried away. When Jarratt made his grand entrance, Zambak took two steps toward him, caught Charles's warning glare, and turned her back to flee upstairs.

It occurred to him that, determined though she might be, she was afraid of Jarratt, and he wondered again what happened the day she visited him alone. *Not that it matters. Zambak Hayden won't let fear keep her from acting once she's made up her mind to do so.* He needed to have that talk with Filipe.

Elliot marched over to greet a gentleman Charles knew to be an aide to the Portuguese governor and raised a hand to bring the room to order. "Gentleman, I will be brief. The incident at Canton some days ago did none of us credit." Few heads nodded, notably Oliver's. Most faces remained blank; Jarratt looked on with a sneer.

"The bulk of you flout the Chinese law. With Maitland gone, you ignore my written warning to remove private gunboats from the river." None of the men looked impressed by this statement.

"As a result, the Chinese expelled Mr. Innes." Elliot nodded toward the irate-looking man in a rumpled suit near the door. "He merely returned here to Macao and continues to direct illicit operations." If a room full of powerful men could collectively shrug, this one would. Most of them knew they would do the same thing.

"Therefore," Elliot went on, "I have asked the governor to expel James Innes from Macao."

An electric reaction radiated through the room. Gasps and protests followed one upon the other, and several men spoke at once.

"My opium chests bear the mark of the East India Company!" Innes shouted. "I'm doing the bidding of the government, and you know it. You can't do this."

"I didn't. The governor did. The Portuguese wish to retain the good relations with the Chinese they have enjoyed for decades." Though the governor's deputy stood firm, his eyes darted nervously around the room.

"Her majesty's government won't like it, Elliot, if you start interfering." At the sound of Jarratt's voice, the room quieted. He stepped forward. "The Chinese don't understand free trade. Our opium boats are meeting resistance up and down the coast. Now the viceroy halted tea trading in Canton itself. The government must act to protect the tea. The Chinese must respect British interests. We have to force them to accept open trading."

His partner in London will do his best to see to it, even if he has to lie, cheat, and bribe to do it, Charles thought.

Elliot didn't shrink under Jarratt's thunderous glare. "Be that as it may, Mr. Jarratt, I'm superintendent for now, and we are at an impasse. Until the gunboats leave the river, the viceroy won't open the tea trade. James Innes is expelled from Macao. Unless you want to meet the same fate, I suggest you cooperate."

James Innes left the room on a string of curses. The sound of a slamming door echoed through the Elliots' quiet mansion. The man himself surveyed the room, peering at the traders one after another before continuing. "I have sent a message to Viceroy Teng telling him Her Majesty's representative respects his conditions. I will leave for Lintin and Whampao in two days on the *Reliance* offering my cooperation."

Jaws dropped, and men looked at one another, some ready to protest, but Jarratt gave Elliot a mocking bow, and the company quieted, watching for his lead. "Then I best see to my business," he sneered before sweeping from the room. The others followed him.

Oliver lagged behind. "I'm sending one of my ships to Whampao, if you have an interest," he told Charles while they watched Elliot see the Portuguese official out.

Charles considered his options. *I need to follow the Superintendent of Trade to Whampao for my report—and fetch Thorn Hayden. Perhaps it's time to be open with Elliot. Perhaps not, in which case, Oliver's offer has merit.* "Not going yourself?"

"I haven't decided," Oliver answered. "The missionary society may need me here, but I could use a clear head watching what the superintendent does."

Movement on the stairs, quickly gone, drew his attention. *Zambak no doubt.* The need to put distance between himself and the woman who had invaded his dreams added to his need to go.

"Let me speak with Elliot. If he won't take me, I'll accept your offer. I may need your assistance returning." *If I have Thorn in tow, I most definitely will.*

Observing Elliot's actions in Whampao might prove a sufficient end to his commission. When he returned, he could pack up Julia on the first ship for England. He would drag the Marquess of Glenaire out of Whampao and back to London by his cravat if he had to. *As to Zambak, I need to put as much distance between the lady and myself as I can. If she chooses to return home, she'll sail on a different ship.* His mind's determination didn't waver, but his heart protested mightily.

~ ~ ~

Charles leaned against the railing of Elliot's *Reliance* and watched the war junk carrying Viceroy Teng approach. Its low body and red sails, narrow ribbed and fan shaped, made it ideal for the formal procession of the ranking official enthroned under a gilded canopy on its quarterdeck. Charles judged it much less suitable for actual combat. The captain of the *Reliance* and some of its officers, similarly engaged along the rail, could make that assessment in more detail than he could.

The viceroy had responded to Elliot's request for direct communication with a message that contained a hint of agreement buried in the usual Chinese misdirection. It took four formal exchanges over two days to reach specifics. Elliot tempered his pride in what he clearly regarded as a major personal victory with no small amount of relief. "The emperor may not want direct communications with Her Majesty's government," the superintendent told him, "but Teng appears to be more pragmatic. Let's hope this unofficial meeting benefits us both."

Let's hope we conclude this business without open warfare, Charles thought as he watched Elliot being lowered in a skiff, back ramrod straight. *The man may lack imagination, but no one can question his courage.*

The junk approached close enough for Charles to watch Elliot brought aboard and to see the Chinese navy make what he suspected was a polite, but mid-level obeisance. The Chinese put even more stock in such etiquette than the British. At the approach of the viceroy, Elliot bowed roughly to the precisely correct level he would deploy before a visiting viscount—certainly not as low as the one he intended before Charles waved it away the day they met. *Had he mentioned he had a duke on board? Would the Chinese care?*

Elliot's interpreter stepped up to stand behind his left shoulder. A man stood in a similar position behind the viceroy. The learning of Chinese by the English had been forbidden, and a generation earlier such men were rare. Formal gestures, the tip of a head here, the flick of a hand there, told Charles nothing, no matter how intensely he watched. The officers next to him began to shift impatiently and drift away. A stiff wind had blown up the delta, and he heard an order to adjust the sails.

Elliot turned to depart just before laughter behind him broke his concentration. Jack tars helped a young man to his feet and pointed to the main mast. The young fellow appeared to overcome some reluctance before he started a slow climb. Charles turned back to the panorama across the water, but something about the boy tickled his consciousness. He strode across the deck to stand at the foot of a mast and looked up at the young sailor's rear end, a suspiciously familiar rear end. A surge of desire shot through him, quickly overrun by anger.

Is the entire crew blind? He looked around and found the second mate directing the men. "That young tar . . ." he began.

"Not one of ours," the mate said with disgust. "We take on hands from the port. That 'un claimed experience, but he don't know shit, begging Your Grace's pardon."

"I am certain he does not. That, ah, boy is no seaman. My valet disappeared three days ago. Took it into his head to go to sea apparently. I suggest you put him ashore in Whampao." *Or lock him in my cabin. Damn, damn, damn.*

Either Charles or a man he hired had followed Zambak for two days whenever she left the house. He cornered the ever-present Filipe on the second day, but the miscreant suddenly lost his understanding of English when Charles tried to question him about Zambak's behavior over Jarratt and her brother. Even money didn't move him. Charles suspected the boy had fallen half in love with the obstinate woman.

Before departure that morning, he determined to make sure she stayed put at the Elliots'. When he got near their house, however, a familiar green morning dress under the ubiquitous pink parasol with its garish green fringe had bobbed along in the distance on its way toward The Macao Ladies' Seminary with Filipe hopping along behind, and he had assumed she was behaving. He had been wrong.

She made a fool out of me. Who was under that damned parasol? It certainly was not Zambak.

"As you wish, Your Grace," the mate said, amusement lurking in his eyes, bringing him back to the problem at hand.

"Never mind, Mr. Johnson. The miscreant still has time on his contract. I will confront him now, and certainly reimburse any wages."

"None paid. Do as you desire, Your Grace." Amusement gave way to speculative assessment, but Johnson wisely chose not to voice it. He bowed and walked away, leaving Charles the center of attention at the foot of the mast.

Damn and double damn. Now I'll have to carry on this little farce.

He stared up at the figure that had reached the top of the mast and was clinging to it in away no experienced seaman ever would. Ice blue eyes met his, a spark of triumph in them. He slammed his fist into the mast, and she looked away. *Is she holding on even tighter?*

"Don't worry, yer grace," a passing tar told him with a gap-toothed grin. "'e'll make it down. They always do—one way or t'other."

An hour later his quarry still clung to the mast, the company had lost interest, and Elliot called him to his cabin. He had to go below. *I hope she climbs down on her own. I shudder to think what 't'other' may be.*

"What did Teng have to say?" the duke asked without preamble upon entering the captain's cabin.

The superintendent's well-pleased smile broadened. "We'll sail in a flotilla ordering the gunboats gone, clear the smugglers out of Whampao harbor together. Once done, he will open Canton to trade."

"For now."

Elliot sobered. "For now. Jarratt and his cronies won't take it well, of course. God only knows what mischief they'll get up to in London. I can only await changes to my orders, if any. For now, they are to keep the peace and the tea flowing. I am doing that." His anxious expression begged reassurance.

"Voices in parliament opposed to allowing opium smuggling have been loud for a year. Voices demanding an opening of free trade are louder, and Martinson will fan those flames."

Elliot nodded morosely, his air of triumph gone. "One season at a time. Getting tea to London may tilt it either way. For now, it feels good to act."

Whatever else I have to report to the queen, I'll make certain this man gets credit for the knife's edge he has to walk. They may leave him spinning in the wind.

"Lost in thought, Your Grace? Did you have something to say?" Elliot asked, a hint of challenge in his manner.

"You've done more than most men could, Elliot. Let's both hope you can keep the peace going forward." Charles rose to leave. "I'll leave you to your reports."

"One more thing, Your Grace. A trifle. My officers tell me they accidently took on your reneging servant. Do try to keep him out of their way."

"Put us ashore in Whampao. We'll return on one of Oliver's vessels." *With luck there will be three of us. What am I going to do with a woman on this ship in the meantime?*

Chapter 18

Cow shite. Where was the sneak hiding? Zambak met the duke's glare without flinching when he appeared in front of her the moment her feet reached the deck. They gave way beneath her, but she pulled herself up before she fell. Charles, she observed, made no effort to assist. She blinked into the setting sun behind him.

Have I ever seen him so angry? Let him be. I thought we were allies, and he knows I have to get to Thorn. He should be supporting me.

"Mr. Jones, your effort to run from your contract has failed," Charles spat through clenched teeth.

Jones? What is Charles playing at? She could think of nothing to say, and he was drawing uncomfortable attention.

"You lied to these officers about your freedom and your non-existent seamanship," he roared.

She lifted a defiant chin but said nothing, confused by his words. *What does he mean, "freedom"?*

"You will stay in my employ until you can buy your way out of our contract, or I'll have the bailiffs on you. Do you understand me?"

She did not.

"Get below to my cabin and make yourself presentable."

How in God's name does he propose I do that on this ship? And what will Elliot do to me if Charles tells him? She stood her ground, furrowed her brow, and tried to make sense of it.

"Move it, sir," he roared again.

Sir—he's keeping up the charade! Understanding flooded her with relief. She took one tentative step and wobbled. *Not good. Not good at all.*

"Very well, Jones." He took a predatory step toward her. She stumbled backward, but he caught her and threw her over one shoulder to the cheers of the crew. He spun on his heels with ease and began to climb down toward the officers' quarters. She attempted to wiggle away, but he held her more tightly. For one built on such graceful lines, Charles possessed hidden reserves of strength.

"Put me down," she ground out when they were out of sight.

"Would you rather I had one of the crew carry you? That would put a period to your little disguise." He dumped her into a small cabin, smaller than her dressing room at Mountview. "As it is, they all think you're my catamite."

"Catamite?"

"Sexual partner. Male." He threw the words at her and took satisfaction from the way her face burned. "You will do nothing to disabuse them of that idea if you want to disembark in Whampao."

He stood a foot from her, and his breath felt warm on her face, chest heaving. His breathlessness owed more to rage than exertion, she thought, and a tremor of excitement ran through her, pricking down her spine and doing odd things low in her belly. *At least he didn't uncover my disguise to the crew.* A tremulous smile played at the corner of her mouth.

When his eyes dropped to her mouth, darting lower for a second before rising to her face again, something intense and hot, something she didn't recognize, had replaced the anger. Her mouth went dry, forcing her to lick her lips and drawing a moan from Charles.

"Stop that now, Zambak Hayden." The anger returned, and he stepped back, bumping into a wall in the confined space. He yanked out a haversack and pulled out a shirt, a rumpled waistcoat, and some soap.

"I'll have to borrow a jacket from the ensign. Get that soot off your face and change into this clean shirt. You have four hours to turn yourself into some semblance of a sensible valet before we land. Keep those—" he gestured toward her chest "—whatever you used. And do something with—" He yanked off the kerchief with which she had covered her hair. At the sight of her close-cropped curls, his jaw dropped, momentarily silenced.

"I could hardly keep all that hair hidden, could I?" she grumbled, running her fingers through what remained.

He seemed transfixed for a moment before mumbling, "At least one less thing to worry about." He shook his head as if to clear it and sidled by her to the door.

"You'll march off this vessel as Mr. Jones, understood?" She nodded.

He slammed the door on his way out. She stared at it, more shaken than she liked. *What just happened?* She pulled the filthy shirt over her head and poured water into a bowl next to the narrow bunk—the very narrow bunk—and began scrubbing her face. The scent of sandalwood filled her senses while Charles and his behavior ricocheted through her mind. She refused to regret doing what had to be done, but his reaction gave her pause. One word brought fire to her cheeks. *Catamite! How can I show my face on deck?* She put on his shirt and buttoned it carefully.

I'm not, that's how. Once we disembark, and we find Thorn, I'll find another way back. Charles will help me. Now that we're here, I know he will.

~ ~ ~

Charles rejected his initial instinct to expose her to Elliot and tie her up if he had to. Delightful as the image was, it died at the thought of the biddies in Macao. They would eat her alive if Elliot brought her back in boys' clothes trussed like a goose. Her parents expected him to protect her, not expose her to scandal. Besides, she would only try again; better she do it in his company. They set out in the grim silence that had come down between them as soon as they disembarked.

I just hope I get through it with some shred of honor intact. After a sleepless night on the floor of his cabin while she slept in his bunk, an arm's length away, he wasn't sure he could. Sudbury's rebellious daughter had become a siren, calling him to the rocks. He had been celibate too long; it was his only explanation. If he gave into impulse—and if, God help him, she permitted it—not only would he violate an innocent, he would destroy lifelong friendships in the process.

He directed their search to one of the smaller warehouses, unwilling to confront Jarratt's company directly. With the directions for the handful of opium dens that might cater to a foreigner, he set out down the rabbit warren of lanes and narrow closes that made up Whampao with Zambak—the scamp now reveling in her role as Mr. Jones—dogging his steps. Her presence necessitated even sharper attention to his surroundings and the ever-present threats. Her nearness distracted him when he could least afford it, his body humming with awareness, and all his senses bending toward her. He forced himself forward and refused to look back.

"They think we are ugly," she whispered over his left shoulder. She astounded him with her unexpected—and highly useful—command of Cantonese. *Opportunities provided by Temperance Knighton's students and talent inherited from her mother, a noted linguist, no doubt.*

A group of well-dressed women followed by a rather large bodyguard crossed their path. Their tiny stature, bent posture, mincing steps, and swaying gait all gave him confidence in Zambak's disguise. Chinese despised Western women for their height, big feet, and what they considered mannish mannerisms. From them, at least, she hid her gender well.

Turning down a particularly seedy alley toward the third establishment on his list, Charles found a Westerner leaning against the wall. Dressed like a warehouseman and dead sober, he assumed the man to be the agent of one of the smuggling operations.

"Lookin' for some 'un?" the man demanded.

English then. Or a Scot, if I'm hearing right.

"Exploring opportunity," Charles answered.

"This un's Jarratt & Martinson business. Look elsewhere. There's plenty o' Chinee to be had."

Jarratt. Wouldn't Thorn most likely gravitate to that company's clientele? Judging from agitation behind him, he suspected Zambak had the same thought. He needed to act before she exploded.

They brushed past the guard. Charles expected opposition, but the man pulled away at the last moment. In the smoky darkness, the stink of unwashed bodies mixed with the odor of narcotic assailed his nose. Zambak huddled against him, in no hurry to move away.

A Chinese gentleman in blue silk made a deep bow. "Welcome, Sirs. You wish try our product?" His eyes darted between Charles and Zambak plastered to his side. "Finest in Whampao," he said. "Best Indian." The heavily accented English was clear enough. They had come to the right place.

"We're looking for a friend," he said.

The man looked confused, and Charles wasn't sure whether it was an act or not. Zambak moved a step away but held on to his upper arm with one hand. Their eyes began to adjust to the gloom.

"Friend," Charles repeated. Zambak translated the word absently, her eyes scanning the room.

"Many friends here," the man said gesturing widely.

Couches and berths lined the area he could see, filled with recumbent figures. Some dressed in Chinese clothing; some in Western. Some sucked on pipes; others held pipes in slack hands and lay back with vacant eyes.

"Charles—there!" Zambak darted away, forcing him to follow her at a run.

John Thornton Hayden lay on his back on a filthy coverlet and stared back at them with unfocused eyes. His brow furrowed as if he tried to pull up a memory, while his sister caressed his cheek.

"Thorn, what have you done to yourself," Zambak crooned.

"Zamb? How did you get to Canton—no, Whampao. Forgot." He began to giggle.

"You are coming with us," Charles told him, slipping an arm under bony shoulders. The boy's wasted body made no resistance.

"Charles? They have dukes in Whampao? Jarratt will be surprised." He laughed again but allowed them to pull him to a seated position and then to his feet. He swayed a bit, but they steadied him between them. He pulled one arm away and reached back to pick up his still-burning opium pipe. He tucked it in a torn coat pocket. "Paid for it," he mumbled.

The proprietor danced around them, protesting and urging them to "Stay. Enjoy much happy . . ."

They reached the door—Thorn's right arm over Charles's shoulders, and Zambak with an arm around his waist—where Charles paused. He took a furtive glance outside and, seeing no one, led them out.

"I say!" Thorn blinked at the sunlight, painful to his enlarged pupils.

"Close your eyes, and we'll lead you," Charles told him.

"Better to stay," Thorn objected and dragged his feet, slowing their progress.

They made it to the first turn before Jarratt's guard

appeared in front of them and two more bullyboys came out from dark corners behind them. "Mr. Jarratt don't like folk interfering in his trade," said the guard who had obviously gone for reinforcements.

Clarity and calm took over, casting two things in sharp resolution: the men would not hurt the young marquess as he was one of Jarratt's assets. And he had led Zambak into danger. Blood red rage took over.

He shoved Thorn into the man in front and spun to confront the men behind only to see Zambak land a neatly directed kick in the privates of one of them, sending him reeling to the ground, where she kicked him again for good measure. The second attacker turned on her with a roar, a lethal-looking weapon in hand. The knife in Charles's sleeve stopped him in his tracks. The thug bent at the waist, dropped to his knees, and crumpled over top of his fellow, pinning him to the ground.

Charles pushed Zambak behind him and turned to face the first man, but Thorn leaned on wobbly knees into the man's shoulder. The attacker held him with one arm and pointed a gun at Charles and Zambak with the other. The brute appeared indecisive, and Thorn's hand on his cheek didn't help him any.

"You can take me back to Ping's. I'm comfortable there," the boy mumbled.

"We have no quarrel with Mr. Jarratt's business," Charles put in, preventing Zambak from pushing forward with his free hand. "We merely want to visit with the marquess. Old friends."

The guard looked down at Thorn. "You know these men, m'lord?"

Thorn peered over with unfocused eyes. "Charles, did father send you? Not my friend then. Father's."

The guard appeared to come to a decision. "I'll have the knife," he said. "We'll see what Mr. Jarratt has to say."

Chapter 19

With the threat of William Jarratt in front of her, Zambak was sorely tempted to run. Whampao's dozens of closes, alleys, dark alcoves, and hidden lanes offered no end of hiding places and opportunities to escape. At least they would if Charles hadn't clamped his fist onto her wrist and allowed the ugly bruiser with a gun to push them forward.

Escape would still be more tempting if said bruiser didn't have a beefy arm around her brother, half dragging him along. Desire to stay as close as possible to Thorn warred with her urge to avoid Jarratt at almost any cost—especially while dressed in trousers. Almost. Their guard and the Chinese around them saw her as she intended, as the duke's servant. She wouldn't fool their master.

"Jarratt will recognize me," she hissed at Charles who greeted that obvious observation with a disgusted snort.

He gripped her hand more tightly. "We have to brazen this out."

With Thorn's complaints increasing, the guard led them to one of the open-fronted warehouses along the docks where casks of opium overshadowed bags of rice in the lower floor, and offices lay above. Pushing through the jumble, he ordered them into an empty room.

Charles planted both feet and stood arms akimbo. "We demand to see your superior. Tell him the Duke of Murnane demands it." The brute shoved him backward, hefted Thorn over one shoulder, and shut the door. Zambak heard the lock tumble and collapsed onto a wooden bench, the only furnishing in the room. "How will we get to him now?" she wondered out loud.

"Retrieving your worthless brother is the least of our problems," Charles said over his shoulder while he rattled the wooden grill covering the only window, and ran fingers along the frame. "It will take a miracle for me to get you back to Elliots' with your reputation intact."

"Do you think I care about that? Let the gossips talk?" she shouted back. "Maybe my parents will give up attempting to marry me off."

Charles ran his hand along the wall, circling from one end and the other, scanning for weaknesses. "So you plan to explain to Jarratt what you're doing in Whampao, and the devil take the consequences?"

"Jarratt? No, I—" The trembling that shook her body overtook her voice. Charles loomed in front of her before she saw him approach, dropping to his knees and taking her hands.

"It's Jarratt that worries you, isn't it? What happened, Zambak?"

She moved her head from side to side with deliberate slowness. *I will not talk about Jarratt with Charles, I can't.* She refused to face him. "Only the most ancient of threats," she mumbled. His hands squeezed hers until they hurt. She hastened to add, "He didn't touch me or threaten, not really. He just— He has Thorn and he implied—" She shuddered to silence. She couldn't say it.

He gave up after a wait and heaved a bitter sigh. "Listen to me. There is no way out of here. Use that magnificent mind of yours. Can you explain why Lady Zambak Hayden wanders the back streets of Whampao dressed as a man?"

To fetch my brother, of course. Jarratt will know that. He'll remind me of his vile "offer" in front of Charles. "No," she mumbled.

"Then we carry on with the charade. You are my valet, Horace Jones. I came here determined to check on Thorn, and I can now see him for the hopeless mess he is. You say as little as possible. Whatever he thinks he knows, we'll make certain he doubts his eyes." He pulled her to her feet and wiped the smudge on her face with his sleeve.

"Do I have to be Horace?" she asked, using all her strength to respond to his determination with humor.

He put one knuckle under her chin and tipped her head up. "That's my girl. Shall we settle on James?" She let his confident smile sink deep into her chest. Their eyes held, and her breath sped up, but the door opened before she could consider why.

Jarratt rushed in with a great show of concern. As always, he approached with flawless grooming, expensive tailoring, and perfect fashion—much too perfect, the result of acquired deliberation and not instinctive good taste. He bowed to the duke with the same calculation.

"Your Grace! We meet again. My profound apologies. Whampao is not, I fear, safe for unsuspecting Westerners."

"So Elliot led me to believe. One wishes to experience places for oneself, you know. I have explored many foreign ports in my travels. I had hoped, of course, to check in on the Marquess of Glenaire again. He seemed much more interested in my company today than the last time we spoke."

Charles can adopt a haughty posture in the blink of an eye, and drop it just as quickly. Zambak hung back behind him, praying to avoid notice.

Charles continued on attack. "In any case, I worried about the Chinese. I didn't expect to be attacked by Englishmen. Am I to understand the ruffians are—or perhaps were—your employees?"

English? Jarratt? Judging from the sour pursing of lips, he doesn't like being called one. Scottish to the bone.

Jarratt's faux-humble expression and folded hands fooled no one. "The man mistook you for a rival. The trade, here, I fear, can be rather ruthless. A gentleman like yourself wouldn't sully his hands in it."

His geniality wears thin. Zambak wondered how long it would be before the mask slipped entirely.

Charles made a show of preening as if he couldn't decide whether Jarratt had complimented his gentlemanly instincts or his sense of adventure. "Apology accepted. Now if I may see the young man, he and I will be on our way."

The guard stood behind Jarratt, blocking the doorway to the little room. His master's smile showed firmly clenched teeth. "Ah yes. My man told me you removed one of my associates from an establishment under my protection," he said, "He was unaware of your connection. I can only apologize for the misunderstanding. As I told the lady in Macao, the young man has chosen to remain under contract to me and, regretfully, will stay here."

"You allow your associates to fraternize with the Chinese?" Charles demanded.

"We find the relaxed atmosphere of Whampao to be more conducive to business than the artificial enclaves of Canton. If some of my associates indulge a bit . . ." He shrugged broadly. "What can one do? The boy has shown a particular interest in—"

"The young marquess smoked opium. In filth and degradation. I know this family. They will not be happy." Charles packed the words with aristocratic superiority, confident in its power to demand obedience.

Jarratt's head shot up. His eyes flicked between the duke and Zambak. When he glanced back momentarily, she could not mistake the spark of recognition. Her stomach tightened, but she kept herself still with great effort. The trader twisted his head to the side and upward as if considering something.

"The family's power does not hold sway in Canton and

Macao. Marquess he may be, but he sought employment with me. He appears to know his own mind." Jarratt looked directly at Zambak and went on, "As I told his sister when she came to visit me."

A stiffening of Charles's back told her the sally hit home, but to his credit, neither his posture nor his voice betrayed any concern. "Yes, the sister. Hoydenish creature. Sudbury wisely referred her to the protection of the Superintendent of Trade and the refining influence of his good wife."

Zambak bit the inside of her cheek to remain quiet when Jarratt sneered. "She might dare anything. Even the streets of Macao are not safe, even for a duke's . . ." He gestured toward Zambak. "Servant is it?"

"My valet knows how to handle himself," Charles said smoothly. "As one of your men discovered. Elliot will, of course, want the young marquess cared for, and my valet will be at his service."

If that move stymied Jarratt, it didn't last long. "Elliot also prefers to avoid scandal. Macao can be particularly vicious." *Julia!* The thought hung in the air between them.

"My dear Mr. Jarratt, I'm well experienced in dampening gossip," Charles drawled. "Bring the boy, and I'll be on my way."

Jarratt glared at Zambak. Charles took a step in front of her. "The superintendent will be happy to learn of your cooperation," he said.

"The superintendent is an old woman," Jarratt muttered. Zambak had seen a similar expression on her father's face when he planned six moves out in chess. Charles, she remembered, could outrun most men at chess, even her father on occasion. She hoped he had a plan, because her ideas had led them into a dead end, and her confidence that they could get her brother out of Whampao had eroded completely.

~ ~ ~

Charles raised Elliot's name to force Jarratt to release them. The smuggler anticipated the weakness in that move and countered with a smirk. "Do you sail with your, ah, valet on Elliot's ships? One understands some parts of the navy look the other way from irregular relations, but Elliot is an intolerant sod, isn't he?"

Charles would bet his boots that Jarratt recognized Zambak. *He expects his hints at sodomy will force me to admit to her disguise. He'll expose her to Elliot and all of Macao if I do. If I don't—*

Jarratt jumped into the silence when Charles hesitated. The sly grin widened, "What does the fair Julia think of your 'valet'? She struck me as a tolerant woman, given how freely she shares her favors. That must make life simpler for you."

Charles swallowed familiar anger; he'd heard worse about his wife, but never from a snake as vile as Jarratt. He put the problem of Julia aside for another time.

"Are you considering passage with Oliver? He's not bloody likely to look the other way." Jarratt went on, eyes glittering.

Caught between the need to protect Zambak and fear she would balk if he failed to obtain Thorn's release, Charles changed tack. She wouldn't hold her peace about their main objective much longer. "I'm certain Daniel Oliver will welcome us. My valet will help me with the marquess. He'll need care when we see him to Macao." *An unconscious chaperone would be better than none.*

"Did I not make myself clear? I have a contract. The boy might buy his way out of it I suppose." The shrewd eyes sharpened. "Perhaps you could ask him in the morning if he is sober." He brightened, pretending to a sudden idea. "That might just do the trick. May I offer you and your servant my hospitality for the night?" He drawled the word *servant*.

Charles had been backed into a corner. When they were shown to a single room with one comfortable bed, the trap snapped shut, making Jarratt's intentions clear. The worm would not harm Zambak, at least not physically. Any designs he may have on her person had their roots in desire for power, not lust. He would not waste his opportunity on something as short-lived as rape. *He means to ruin her and Thorn as well and use it as leverage over their father for political influence in London. I have to get them out of here.*

"How will we get to Thorn?" Zambak asked.

"It would be a damned sight easier if I didn't have to deal with you, my lady," he said, holding his temper by a thread.

"I'm sorry, Charles. I've botched this," she murmured. "I should never have involved you." The fingers of her left hand rubbed together vigorously.

"You should have stayed put and left it to me," he retorted, somewhat mollified. "Your disguise complicates everything. I won't abandon him, Zambak—not entirely." He ran his hand through his hair, untangling thick knots with his fingers.

"We can't leave him. We—"

"Not we. I. I will get you back to Macao and Thorn someplace he can sober up. I don't promise to do it at the same time." She looked ready to argue, but he stared her down.

The door opened, interrupting them. A Chinese servant brought a tray of food, placed it on the tiny table by the window, and bowed out without a word. Charles tried the door. It opened easily, and he pulled it shut. *A test?* "We could walk out," he said.

"Not without my brother." She had steel in her voice.

He briefly considered throwing her over his shoulder as he had on the *Reliance* and carrying her down the wharf until he found Oliver's premises. She would not make it easy, and the likelihood that Jarratt had men watching made it unappealing.

He opened the door again. The bruiser waved from his chair at the end of the hallway and asked if he might help them. Charles pulled the door shut, dragged one of the chairs over, and wedged it under the handle. When he walked past the table, delicious smells bombarded him. One porcelain bowl held rice; the other, bits of meat and vegetables in a savory sauce.

"We'll think better on a full stomach." He moved the table so that one of them could sit on the bed now that the other chair had taken on guard duty.

"We again?" Zambak grunted.

He glowered at her and ladled food onto one of the two plates they'd been given. "There is no fork or spoon," he said, mystified.

Zambak lifted two sticks from the tray and waved them in front of him. "Allow me to show you how the Chinese eat," she said. She proceeded to manipulate the articles into a scoop and carry food into her mouth. *Where did she learn that skill?*

"Lai-min Lau taught me," she said, answering his unspoken question.

Several spills and missteps later, Charles managed the thing with some success. *Hunger is a great motivator.* "Jarratt sent these on purpose," he grumbled.

"Probably," she responded cheerfully. "Do you suppose he is watching?"

"Watching, listening, or both. I'm afraid he plans to expose you publicly in the morning, and then put it about we spent the night together."

She wrinkled her nose. "I thought he meant to put it about you have an unnatural relationship with your valet."

"It isn't me he wishes to disgrace, at least not entirely," he replied with exaggerated patience. *The simpleton hasn't even the sense to worry for her reputation. Except Zambak isn't simple; she's devious and too damned intelligent. If it weren't for her brother, she'd be enjoying this.*

Charles carried the tray to the hallway, waved to Jarratt's spy, and put it on the floor. The man still sat at the end of the hall. *If I have to guess, that is where they put Thorn. At least he doesn't appear to have his ear to our door.*

He joined her in searching for a peephole and found none, even when he pulled the bed from the wall. The bed, table, and two chairs made up the only furnishings. No pictures decorated the walls.

"Spartan accommodations indeed, but at least his spies aren't watching us," she said at last.

"Listening perhaps?" he suggested. She put a finger to her lips and tiptoed toward the bed with mock seriousness. He stifled a laugh.

The window, loose in its frame, opened onto a back alley. If she could handle the final drop, he could hand her down. He leaned on the frame, visions of her alone in the lawless smuggler's enclave at night in his mind, and rejected that idea. He leaned out farther so he could see to his left. Four windows stood between his and the end of the building, one of them opening on Thorn's room. The sound of footsteps below made him pull back inside.

"Zamb—" he began and lost track of his thought at the sight of her asleep on the bed. She had sat down on the edge and fallen over. He knelt to remove her boots and pulled her legs up onto the bed.

"Charles?" she said without opening her eyes, the sound muffled. "We'll get Thorn in the morning." She turned to her side.

He watched her steady breathing, pulled back the hand that itched to touch her, and forced his eyes back to the window. He sat on the far side of the bed and studied it while he explored possibilities. He could raise the window, stand on the sill, and swing himself up and onto the roof. It wouldn't be the first time he performed that stunt. From there, it was a short crawl across the roof to the farthest window, the one most likely to open up onto Thorn, where he would swing down, drag the self-centered fool out, and drop him to the ground. It would be easy enough.

If shattering the other window didn't cut me too badly.

If Thorn made no sound.

If the fall didn't kill the boy.

If I didn't have Zambak to protect.

If I didn't have Zambak.

She lay curled to her side breathing evenly, the cropped hair around her head like a nimbus, and his heart turned over. Asleep, the tough outer shell she used to keep the world at bay evaporated; vulnerable and relaxed, her feminine curves called out to his least honorable instincts.

He hesitated, grateful for Jarratt's pointed reminder about his marriage, but he couldn't take his eyes from her, and finally gave in to temptation. Lying under the thin blanket, he justified himself on the grounds that the night grew cold. *Surely the Almighty won't begrudge us the warmth.* He wrapped himself around her and felt her relax into his arms still sleeping.

Heaven and hell in one embrace. The exquisite torture of Zambak curled against him and the need to protect her kept him sleepless until dawn sifted through the windows, and she began to wake up. Long lashes blinked over pale blue eyes, while he kept himself perfectly still. He had waited too long to move.

"Charles?" she asked, confused to see his face close to hers.

His erection, hard and painful, had to be obvious to her. He swallowed, frozen in place, and found no answer to her unspoken question. When puzzlement gave way to joy and her mouth curved into a contented smile, her tempting lips lay inches from his. She raised a hand and pushed a lock of hair back from his forehead, and the last of his self-control crumbled; he leaned toward her.

The door rattled, shaken by unseen hands on the handle, and he jerked away. Charles couldn't be certain whether he felt relieved or frustrated. "Both," he muttered, sitting up and ruffling his hair, and willing his unruly body to behave.

Zambak flopped onto her back and covered her eyes with one arm. "Bother," she grumbled.

Neither had time to ponder what had just happened. Thorn stood in the hall dressed for travel, Jarratt's servants on either side of him. "Mr. Jarratt doesn't like to wait," the bruiser told them as if it explained everything. He urged them to follow, and they did, still in yesterday's clothing, rumpled, and unkempt.

"There has been excitement in Canton over night. Business demands that I visit the factories before I can return you to Macao," Jarratt told them, adding slyly, "And you may hear the same from any you approach." He stood at the front of his wharf, impeccable as always, and did not explain the nature of the "excitement."

He led them out toward the docks with Thorn staggering at their side. The marquess either failed to recognize his sister through her disguise or, judging from his smirk, had been coached to ignore it.

The bustle of ships readying sail—the large ships to return to Macao and the smaller craft to go upriver to Canton—seemed to confirm Jarratt's prediction. Charles scanned the anchored fleet looking for the *Wild Swan* or barring that the *Reliance*, hoping for a friendly face, and praying Jarratt would back down from a public confrontation if he found one.

"What's going on?" Zambak hissed from behind him. "I can't make out what the Chinese are saying, but their eyes shift from side to side. Something made them nervous."

"Elliot has ordered the traders out of Whampao," he guessed, but he didn't elaborate. He had more immediate concerns. "We'll leave you here, Jarratt," he said. "Elliot must be here still. I'll have to throw us on his mercy."

"You wish to stay in Whampao while you search? It won't be safe for you—or your valet," he added pointedly. "I'm afraid the superintendent finished his little circus with the viceroy, and gunboats are ordered out of the Pearl Delta. All foreigners are pulling out while Elliot lurks off shore on the *Reliance*."

"Oliver and Company doesn't employ gunboats," Charles responded. We'll wait."

"Oliver and Company doesn't have dealings in Whampao. You won't find the mission set here."

True enough normally, but Dan said he wanted to observe Elliot's action. He must— He looked around frantically. Only one small ship, blessedly nearby, flew the American flag. As if conjured by the wish, Dan Oliver's voice called from the deck. "Your Grace! I expected you yesterday. You almost missed us."

"Oliver, thank God," Charles responded. The ship across from them wasn't the *Wild Swan*, but a smaller vessel. American seamen swarmed the deck preparing to sail. Jarratt looked like he'd swallowed something vile.

Oliver's eyes narrowed at the figure behind Charles. *No fool, he.* "My valet came with me," Charles told him, praying he said nothing about the woman. "And I've brought an extra passenger." He indicated Thorn with a shrug of his shoulder, keeping his eyes averted from Jarratt. "I presume you have room for all of us." *I hope to Hell you do.* He also hoped they planned to return to Macao, but given the vessel appeared to be one suited for upriver travel, he feared not.

Oliver peered at Jarratt who looked ready to object and shrewdly asked no awkward questions. "Of course. Come aboard, quickly though."

Charles took Thorn by the arm before Jarratt could speak and gestured Zambak toward the gangplank.

"See here," Thorn mumbled. "I don't know . . ."

Jarratt turned to his guards but stopped when several of the American seamen moved down the gangplank, and one reached over to assist the swaying marquess. A fight with the Americans did not appear to suit Jarratt's plans.

"As you wish, Murnane. We will settle my associate's contract soon. I never leave business unconcluded," he growled, staring right at Zambak, who stood poised to bolt up the gangplank.

"You may be sure of it, Mr. Jarratt. We will most certainly settle." Charles turned his back to the man and followed Zambak and her brother.

Chapter 20

"Sorry, m'lady." Oliver leaned back in his chair, the ever-present pipe in one hand. "We can't take you and your brother directly back to Macao. The good Lord knows I wish I could." He glanced around the tiny cabin that served as his command post, everywhere he could but not directly at Zambak. Once she climbed aboard his ship, he had not been able to contain his horror at the sight of a woman in trousers and waistcoat. There would be no pretense on the vessel.

"Captain Oliver," she objected, "my brother is just emerging from an opium sleep. My understanding is that shortly he will—"

"Aye th'boy will need the drug, and that's for certain."

"I'm supposed to deliver him to the Lau medical center. Temperance—Mrs. Knighton—expects us. We plan to—"

"I know. I spoke to our mutual friend. Can't be helped. I have to transport medical supplies to the clinic at Zion's Quarter first. We'll find help for you there."

"We don't have much time. Without the opium, Thorn will be difficult to handle."

Oliver's customary compassion warmed her, but his eyes skittered away quickly, fixing on Charles who sat with his head down, hands folded in front of him, a picture of exhaustion. She suspected he hadn't slept since he found her on the *Reliance*.

"I sent a man to fetch a bit of opium tar, enough to begin weaning th'lad without throwing him into crisis, at least until we can get him to Canton."

Zambak's brewing frustration came to a boil. "Canton? We're no closer to our goal than we were with Jarratt! We ought to have stayed and—"

Charles shot upright. "Don't talk idiocy, Zambak!" He looked nervously at Oliver, leaned forward, dropped his voice, and folded back into formal address. "Lady Zambak, Jarratt means you and your brother harm—or rather your father harm. He means to bend Sudbury's influence through the two of you. It's vital that we extricate both of you from his sphere."

"We? I have no say in it. You mean 'vital to Her Majesty's government,' and our needs don't matter. Keep the Marquess of Glenaire and Lady Zambak Hayden wrapped in cotton wool for the sake of queen and country. That's it, isn't it, your 'commission'?" Rigid with outrage, she glared at Charles. "I will not be used as a political pawn! Not by my father, not by Jarratt, not by the government, and not by you."

"Don't be ridiculous. Jarratt is—"

"—only the latest in a long line," she said suddenly weary. "Someone always wants a piece of Sudbury's heir or, barring that, the daughter. They always have plans to exploit us for gain." She tapped the captain's desk with the middle finger of her left hand.

Charles looked toward Oliver, his hands making an apologetic gesture. "We've had a difficult few days," he explained.

"Don't apologize for me, Charles. I know I sound like a sullen child." She straightened up. *An embarrassing excess of emotion solves nothing.* "Needs must when the devil drives, Captain Oliver. Canton it is. Will my brother be made secure at this clinic of yours while we deal with his illness?"

"Dr. Peters has some knowledge, m'lady. He'll see to the boy."

"I will care for my brother, myself, Captain. What promises to be a most unpleasant task is entirely my responsibility. I'll be grateful for the mission's hospitality, however, and certainly see to it you are reimbursed for any costs."

Oliver tipped his head to one side and looked at her fully at that. His approval slipped under her guard. The respect of this man, not easily given, mattered to her. She looked down at her clothes and back at the American. "I apologize if my appearance offends your sensibilities, but I have none other at the moment."

"Perhaps it's for the best," Oliver said with reluctance. "I can't think how we would smuggle an English woman into Canton otherwise. You'll be needing a hat as it is." He rubbed his chin. "Though how we'll find women's clothing in Canton—Western clothing, that is—I don't know."

Zambak felt a smile tease the edges of her lips. She rose, and the men did as well. *Rather as if we just chatted over tea in my mother's house. How does one curtsey in trousers?* "If you will direct me to this seaman sent to fetch the demonic substance, I'll check in on my brother." *Cow shite. I hope I can manage the thing.* Fear for Thorn dogged her steps.

~ ~ ~

Canton at last. I ought to have come here straight away. I might have avoided— Charles squashed the thought as Oliver's seamen rowed them closer and closer to shore. Regrets were pointless; there had been other fish to fry. Now, with Julia under his protection in Macao and the Hayden offspring where the missionaries would keep the two of them confined, he was free to learn what he could for the queen and positioned to do so thoroughly.

As it unfolded, darkening twilight covered Zambak's entrance into the foreign compound. The sailor's cap Oliver insisted on helped as well. Her silvery hair would have gleamed in the moonlight and drawn attention. In the shadows, she easily passed for a common seaman. Charles watched Thorn shake off his sister's embrace and sifted through their earlier argument.

Her attack on his motives, if she actually believed what she said, set their relationship back where it had been upon his arrival: she, the put-upon daughter; he, the father's spy. *It's best if she believes it. Thorn certainly does.* He told himself to be grateful that she put a wall between them. Even if he sorted out the mess that was his marriage, no good could come of his growing attraction. He had her report; he would add what he gleaned in Canton and embark for London as soon as he could manage the thing.

Their boat butted against a pier, and unseen hands tied it up. Oliver alighted first, helping both Zambak and a hostile Thorn get out. Charles followed, jumping on to the pier and taking a moment to savor the sight. An open ground, one the traders called the exercise yard, spread in either direction. Beyond it, buildings lay tooth by jowl the length of the waterfront, their backs to the city, each one flying the flag of its nation. Union Jacks fluttered over the East Indian Company factory and the smaller consulate building next door.

Oliver motioned him toward a building at the far-left end, past a massive flagpole flying the stars and stripes. Thorn spun his head around as if looking for an escape somewhere along the dark parade ground and, finding none, slouched forward. Charles couldn't hear all his complaints, but he made out the word "Jarratt."

He didn't envy Zambak the task she set for herself, but he admired her for it. Her chances for success were few. Even if she did manage to see him through the hell, Charles suspected Thorn would try to bolt back to Jarratt or whoever would supply him with opium as soon as he got free of her. It would be up to Charles to prevent it.

Light flowed out across the stone pavement when a door to the American's factory opened. It drew them in, the warmth of the welcome matching the warmth of the private quarters. The competent young men who made up Oliver's Canton staff, Americans all, asked no questions nor did they show any surprise when ordered to escort an unknown man obviously under the influence of opium to a room near the clinic on the lower floor and lock him in. Charles suspected Thorn might be known by reputation in Canton.

"A moment if you will, my lady," Oliver said when Zambak attempted to follow. "Hezekiah will see your brother settled." He cut off her protest. "I know you wish to follow, but he's had a bit of the poppy, and that ought to see him through the night. Go see him settled. Come back when you are satisfied. I need a word."

Someone showed Charles to a private room, as tidy as it was tiny, with the same cheerful acquiescence. Not the largest of the Canton factories, Oliver's had been dubbed "Zion's Quarter," for his refusal to deal in narcotics. Since it doubled as a supply depot for American missionaries, included a printing house for their newspapers, and housed a clinic run by some of them, the name fit. Warm water, clean clothing, and bread appeared. The place ran as smoothly as his uncle's manor at Chadbourn Park, for all its air of democracy.

An hour later he sat in eager anticipation over a savory dinner, chatting gratefully with his host.

"The lady has joined us!" Oliver beamed.

Charles turned around to see Zambak enter, scrubbed and gowned, and he gasped for breath. She wore Chinese clothing, a wonder in pale blue silk that enhanced the blue of her eyes. The wide sleeves of the jacket and the hem that came to her hips were outlined in darker blue while an underskirt in the same blue fell in folds beneath it to a hem also outlined in the darker blue. Chinese women lacked her height, so the skirt failed to cover her ankles, for which Charles breathed a prayer of thanks when he eagerly examined them. The entire jacket had been elaborately embroidered with pink and yellow flowers, a masterwork.

"How on earth did you find this treasure, Captain Oliver?" Zambak asked. "I've never worn anything this lovely." Since her usual wardrobe, from the finest modiste in London, had been augmented by trips to Paris, the compliment was enormous, perhaps more than Oliver realized. The dress suited her.

Oliver beamed. "I fear William Bradshaw, my factor, will have to find another gift for his wife." He indicated the other man at table.

The factor smiled. "May I say the clothing becomes you, my lady, and you are welcome. I'm glad we could help in your need. I'll find another for Maud."

Zambak held out a hand to the man. "I'm grateful, and you must be as well since we've avoided scandalizing that shy young gentleman who is watching over my brother." If she missed wearing trousers, she gave no sign.

Bradshaw chuckled. "Unfortunately, you won't be able to go about outside, but you will brighten Zion's Quarter."

"Not go outside at all? Will they arrest me?"

"More likely me for transporting a woman here," Oliver grumbled. "Sit please. Bradshaw has much to tell you both."

Charles lifted a questioning brow and followed Dan Oliver's lead, tucking into dinner.

Bradshaw, a raw-boned New Englander, wasted no words. "The emperor means it this time. He has appointed a high commissioner to end opium use entirely. Lin Zexu's reputation is one of absolute integrity and unbending opposition to crime. They are going after the trade from the top down. Chasing out the gunboats from Whampao and Lintin was just the start."

"That being the top?" Zambak asked.

"Yes, my lady."

"Explain please," Charles said. "What does it mean for the Chinese?"

"Those who buy, sell, or use the stuff are subject to execution," Bradshaw told him.

"Surely not!" Zambak's horror reverberated around the table.

"Chinese laws tend to be harsher on paper than in actual practice. They've never enforced the laws before, not like this, so it is hard to say, but it is likely they will at least make an example of some."

"What of foreigners who smoke opium?" Zambak asked, her voice just above a whisper. She didn't have to spell out the reasons for her concern.

"They've never gone after foreigners before either. However, our contacts, the hongs—the merchant companies—our equivalent on the Chinese side—tell us the special commissioner is known for rigid law enforcement." Bradshaw made no attempt to hide his worries.

"Don't high commissioners sit in Peking and issue edicts from there, only to have them be ignored here?" Charles asked.

"Not this one. Reports of his approach have thrown the hong community into panic." Bradshaw leaned forward and gestured with his fork for emphasis. "A message sent *en route* arrived yesterday. It named names."

"Names?" Charles asked, acutely aware that the opportunity to see the commissioner's arrival would provide unexpected value to his report.

"Fifty-four Chinese merchants known to have traded in opium. The worst of it is, the list was accurate. The Chinese community is frightened, and the opium traders are scurrying to shore up their relationships."

"That explains Jarratt's urgency to come here," Charles murmured.

"An end to the opium trade would be a good thing," Zambak said.

"A blessing," Oliver agreed. "If it can be done without exploding into war."

Zambak caught Charles's eyes, and he knew she shared his thoughts. *We have to stay. I can't walk away from the opportunity to observe this high official before it's too late. I just pray I can get the Haydens out of Canton in one piece when I'm finished.*

Chapter 21

Lovely as it was, Zambak found the jacket of the elaborate clothing Bradshaw gave her to be impractical in a sickroom. A heavy shirt tied at the waist and covered with a canvas apron suited her better. She retained the silk skirt as a sop to the sensibilities of the men who seemed determined to protect her from their own ogling.

Alexander Peters, Boston physician and practical man, agreed with her decision. She had been drawn to the missionary doctor quickly. Tall and gaunt, his fundamental kindness lightened what might otherwise have been an off-putting austerity, and his professional expertise boosted her flagging confidence.

Thorn slept much of the night thanks to the opium they'd given him in a tincture the night before. His moaning, filtering through the wall to the tiny cell she occupied next to his, had awoken her before dawn however, and the war had begun.

His first words to her in the morning had been to demand his pipe. When she refused, he called her selfish and turned his back to the wall.

By midmorning, she no longer had time to consider it, though nursing had so far proved to be less repulsive as she expected. "Just a wee bit, Zamb," Thorn begged. "Take the edge off." He rubbed his legs to soothe the ache.

"Walk with me, Thorn. Doctor Peters says—"

"I'm weary of your Peters, Zamb! Damned chapelgoer. Probably begrudge a man good whisky too," he complained.

But he walked. So far Thorn had been more cooperative than she anticipated as well.

"Walking feels good, Zamb. Why don't we walk outside? I can show you around the parade grounds," he said. "I feel better. Truly."

"We can't, Thorn," she said. "I'm confined to the factory. Oliver doesn't want me seen." Her brother laughed at that.

"No women in Canton. You still can't obey the rules—I should have warned them that ordering you not to do something just incites you to do it." His laughter sounded sincere. Still, he never could fool her for long. *He'll try to scamper back to his friends as soon as he is well enough. He's holding on for that.*

Thorn took four more laps of his ten-by-ten room before he sank the bed and yawned spasmodically. "Need sleep, Zamb. Just a bit. Enough to get me rest."

When she laid a hand on his back, he jerked away. Her hand came away wet. What horrified her more than the profuse sweating, which Peters had warned her to expect, were the protruding bones of his back. Thorn had become as devoid of flesh as any starving wretch might be.

"Sit for a while. I'll fetch a clean shirt." She picked up the empty water pitcher. "More water as well." The clinic had supplied her with a half dozen Chinese cotton shirts, neatly folded on the little dresser in her room.

"Just a few drops of poppy juice in it, Zamb. Peters won't know," Thorn pleaded.

She didn't answer him. It had already become hard to say no. Sticking to her determination would take every ounce of strength she had. She forced herself to remember Temperance's words, "He will die without help." *This is the only way. The only way.*

Zambak locked the door behind her. She hadn't taken two steps before the door handle rattled and her brother tried to open it. Her heart almost broke in two. *We have caged him like an animal. You couldn't stand it, Zambak. How can expect your brother to endure it?* She stood in the hallway, one arm tight against her stomach, until she heard him return to his cot. She forced herself to repeat, *This is the only way. The only way.*

To her left the hallway led to the clinic, tempting her to go that way and ask about the wisdom of using small amounts of the narcotic. Dr. Peters forbade her to enter the clinic, however. "As much as I would be proud to show you our work," he had said, "we can't risk our patients reporting that we're harboring a western woman here." *I'm as much contraband as the opium.* Left to her own devices, she might defy that edict outright, but she couldn't put the doctor's work at risk. She turned to the factory's kitchen instead and rinsed out the pitcher, burdened by the sympathetic gaze of the cook's helpers.

"We'll bring midday luncheon soon, my lady," one of them said. "Soup only, as you asked."

With a shirt under her arm and the pitcher in one hand, she struggled with the key, but managed to unlock the door. She turned the handle, but before she opened the door fully, Thorn pulled it wide, his gaze fixated on the pitcher.

"Did you bring it?" he demanded. He didn't mean the water.

"Of course. Sit, and I'll bring you some." She kept her voice steady, relieved when he sat. She set the pitcher on a tiny table in the corner and locked the door, putting the key in her pocket. His eyes, she noticed, followed the key.

If he tries to take it from me, can I stop him? Unlocking the door with her hands burdened had been unwise. He didn't overpower her, but he easily might do when he became more frantic, as she feared he would.

"Did you bring it?" he asked again. She handed him a cup of the liquid. He spat it out. "That's just water!"

"Water is what you need." She gave him another, which he gulped down. After the second cup, he began to shiver.

"Let me change your shirt," she suggested.

He said nothing. When she lifted the soaked shirt and pulled it up over his head, he yelped. "It hurts! You have no idea how badly. I ache all over."

She held the filthy shirt between two fingers and dropped it in the corner before reaching for a soft towel. She attempted to dry his damp skin; he reacted as if she were torturing him.

"I hurt," he moaned. "You hate me. You've always hated me."

"I love you too much to let you destroy yourself, Thorn. The opium will kill you. You must know that." She handed him a clean shirt. He twisted it in his hands without attempting to put it on.

"Laudanum would help. If you love me as you say give me just a bit of it. Medicine isn't it? Can't hurt."

"It already did you harm, can't you see that?"

Demanding turned to begging and, when that failed, anger.

"You think you're high and mighty because you're older, but you're a girl Zambak, just a damned girl. You hate me because I'm Father's heir and you are not!" he shouted.

"I don't hate you," she snapped back. She resented him, though, or at least resented that gender excluded her from inheriting. They both knew it. Once he might have sympathized. Not now.

"I'm the heir," he repeated. "I give the orders! When I inherit—"

"Keep it up, and you'll never be Duke of Sudbury. You won't live long enough!" she shouted back. When his face crumpled and he sank back onto the cot, guilt tormented her.

He can't help it; that's the poppy talking. She slipped his arm into the clean shirt. He didn't complain. He didn't react at all until she finished, and he rolled over to stare at the wall.

So the day went. He accepted water but rejected soup after three swallows. Zambak had difficulty finishing her bowl, anxiety roiling her stomach. Complaints continued in waves interspersed with sullen silence.

Once he leapt up from the bed and paced while frantically rubbing himself everywhere he could reach. "My skin! It crawls." He allowed her to rub the lotion Dr. Peters had supplied onto him, but its effects lasted an hour or less.

The doctor himself stopped by in the afternoon to see how she managed. "You mustn't wear yourself out," he advised. "This will be a long process."

Thorn threw insults at him during the entire visit. "If you want my sister, think again. I won't let some third-rate quack sniff up her skirts!" He snarled at the man's back when he left, leaving Zambak with a red face. Her sympathy for her brother eroded hourly.

Late in the afternoon, Thorn sank into fitful sleep, and Zambak slid down the wall to sit on the floor, her head on her knees. A gentle tap startled her. She glanced quickly over at Thorn. He thrashed a bit but didn't awaken. She opened the door to find Charles. He looked over her shoulder at the sleeping form of her brother.

"How are you?" *You, not him*, she noticed.

"Tired," she admitted. "Glad for a respite."

He nodded. "Can you leave him for a while?"

Peters suggested she do that. He recommended she not wear herself out by constant attendance. She glanced at Thorn. "Yes. Do you need me?" she asked.

"Lin Zexu arrives. His retinue has been sighted. The city is in an uproar. I thought you might like to see."

She locked the door behind her, untied her apron, and strode toward her room. "Let me change into my jacket."

She came out to find him leaning against the wall, an amused smile on his face. "Dressing up for an audience, my lady?"

"I can hardly greet—but you aren't actually suggesting I greet him, are you? Do you plan to?"

"Formally greet the high commissioner? Good God, no. Not today in any case. Oliver thinks we might see the retinue from the roof." He winged his left arm at her.

She took it with her right grudgingly. "Will I be expected to hide behind you?"

"Perhaps there's some sort of potted plant you can peer through," he answered in kind.

His teasing soothed her resentment. As they climbed the stairs, Zambak lay her free hand on his arm. "Thank you, Charles," she murmured.

"For what?"

"Remembering me. Knowing I would hate to miss this."

"History, Zambak. How often do we witness it?" He opened the door to the upper terrace where Oliver handed her the telescope he had been using. She focused the sight expertly and trained it to the outskirts of Canton where Oliver pointed. A gilded palanquin swayed toward the city. She counted twenty bearers carrying the commissioner's chair or holding tall poles with red pennants flowing in the wind. Armed men in elaborate uniforms marched before and behind. A drummer led, and two men holding signs on high poles led the entire entourage.

She handed the telescope back. "The man does know how to make an entrance," she said. "One hopes he can wield actual power as effectively."

~ ~ ~

"He means to intimidate, of course," Zambak commented over dinner that night, good beef and potatoes supplied from the Chinese hinterland and served on porcelain plates in a willow pattern. Charles had seen such designs before on plates made in England. He suspected they were made in China for the American import trade and shipped by the barrelful on Oliver's ships.

The silk clothing flattered her still, and her voice sounded firm, but Charles didn't like the dark shadows around her eyes. She had come reluctantly, leaving Thorn weeping with a Chinese orderly to see to his needs, but she didn't argue when Peters and Charles insisted she join them and eat. He suspected the opportunity to discuss what she'd seen had drawn her as much as the food.

"Intimidate? Isn't that what men in power do?" Bradshaw replied. Charles said nothing, happy to watch Zambak take the lead.

"Those that understand real power and know how to wield it use intimidation with precision. His entrance—as much as the list of names—announced an end to business as usual. He will follow it with quick action. You may count on it," she replied.

"He already has. We heard in the clinic that he demanded several of the hong leaders appear before him in the morning," Dr. Peters told her.

She nodded sagely. "That would be a classic first move. Make them account for their behavior."

"You have a shrewd mind for politics for one so young and far from home, Lady Zambak," Oliver observed. Charles had no doubt the captain meant "for a woman."

"My father has been a force in the Foreign Office since before I was born," she replied. "I grew up with it."

Charles cleared his throat and spoke up. "Lady Zambak learned international relations in the nursery and at the dinner table. Her mother is an ambassador's daughter nurtured in the great capitals of Europe. Her diplomatic dinners entertain visitors—official and otherwise—from the four corners of the globe. Her aunt—"

Zambak raised a hand to stop him. "These gentlemen aren't interested in my childhood," she said. He differed.

Bradshaw looked baffled, Peters impressed, and Oliver astounded.

"What about your aunt?" Bradshaw asked.

Zambak bit back a laugh, her cheek between her teeth, before answering. "I fear my father's sister has some rather strong opinions about the education of young women. My Latin is excellent, my Greek merely passible, and I have three other languages not counting my attempts to master Cantonese." She ticked history, geography, and philosophy off on her fingers.

They stare at her as if she were some sort of exotic creature—which she certainly is. At least they see it. The Elliots and their ilk never will.

"Lin Zexu. What do you know of his past?" Zambak asked, turning the subject. Charles listened to her lead them through everything they knew about the man and the workings of the court. In short order, he had to request pen and paper to record the answers.

"A scholar?" she asked.

"The normal route up the bureaucracy in China," Peters told her. It had become clear quickly that of the three he was the expert. "To succeed in government, a man has to prove he deeply understands the writings of Confucius, that he can write and speak well, and that he is a man of culture."

"Does military experience matter?" she asked, tapping her left fingers as she sorted through the information. Charles had little need to engage in the questioning. She did it for him, leaving him free to absorb the answers and observe the men around the table. *God's teeth, but she is magnificent*!

"Military's more difficult to say," Oliver replied.

Peters shrugged. "Hard to know how big a part it plays in a man's career. Some. The ruling class took control by military force two hundred years ago, but they haven't been tested since."

"What else do we know about the commissioner and opium?" she asked.

Bradshaw laughed ruefully. "They say that, as Governor of Huguang, he managed to rid the province of opium."

"Interesting. Where is Huguang?" Zambak asked.

"North," he answered, "One province north I think."

"Not on the coast," she murmured. "Do we know how he did it?"

The three of them looked at one another. "We've heard nothing, except that he uses threat of punishment."

"That alone wouldn't work."

"You sound sure of that," Charles said, curious but less skeptical than Oliver.

"You've seen Thorn. He won't give up the poison easily. Threats aren't enough."

Peters nodded. "Yes. She's correct. The poor wretches chained to opium sell everything, betray everything, and risk everything for more of it. Threats aren't enough."

Zambak frowned deeply at the doctor's description. *She must wonder what Thorn would betray—or what he already had.* "Which leaves us wondering how he did it," she said.

"I suspect we'll find out soon enough," Oliver replied.

"True. He won't hesitate now. I would like to meet this man," she said.

All four men shifted in their seats. Charles took breath to forbid it but knew better. She would likely have no opportunity, and if she did, he would have difficulty stopping her.

"Never fear, gentlemen," she said with a sigh. "As much as I loathe the restrictions, I will not put Zion's Quarter in danger. I'll remain your one act of rebellion." She stood then, and they scrambled to their feet. "I will leave you gentlemen to your port." She paused, peered at the missionaries, and wrinkled up her nose. "Or whatever after-dinner treat you indulge in. I best get back to my patient."

"I'll check in on you later," Peters said.

When the others sat back down, Charles took his leave, stuffed his notes in his coat, and hurried after her.

She glanced over at his approach. "Did you get most of it down?"

"Yes. Invaluable intelligence. I'll transcribe it."

"Add it to the journal along with your observations about Whampao and Jarratt. You do still have it, don't you? I meant you to hand carry it."

"Of course. The journal is yours, though."

She stopped and turned to him. "What happened to 'ours'?" she asked.

Charles felt his heart skip a beat. "Ours," he repeated. "Partners?"

"Separate reports would be foolish at this point, don't you think?" She said over her shoulder as she turned a corner, forcing him to follow her downstairs. "Though, of course you'll have to summarize for your formal report to Her Majesty."

"We have to summarize."

She gave him a rueful smile. "Victoria doesn't actually approve of independent women. Ironic, isn't it? The journal goes to my father. You will leave Thorn out, of course."

"Zambak, one thing. I can't leave here now, not with the current developments."

"What of Julia?" she asked.

Julia. Ever the fly in my ointment. "I provided for her until we can return to London."

"Will she stay out of trouble?"

"Possibly. We have an agreement." *Probably not. She probably already has a lover. She may have savaged Zambak's reputation.* He studied the woman in front of him, realizing how little this proud young woman cared about that. Zambak herself has given them all plenty of fuel for that fire. "If she hasn't kept it, I can't do anything about the situation until we get to Macao and survey the damage," he said in answer to her question.

They had reached the door to Thorn's room, and loud cries met them. Zambak lifted her chin in the "duchess" manner he knew so well. "We're in agreement. In any case, I have to see Thorn through the worst of this, and he can't be moved. We stay in Canton for now."

The dread he saw in her eyes made him long to protect her from what she faced behind that door but knew she wouldn't welcome it. She faced what she had to with valor. He watched her go about her business, torn between relief that she would remain inside the compound where he could protect her and an overwhelming urge to get her and her brother on the first ship leaving China before war exploded around them.

Chapter 22

The nightmares began that night. At least, the screaming did. She found Thorn on his cot backed up into the corner of the wall, a blanket over his head, screaming. When she tried to pull the blanket away, he knocked her to the floor shouting, "Help!"

She scooted away to press her back to the door, unable to stop shaking. No one came to her aid, and it seemed an eternity before Thorn returned to his corner, rocking back and forth and mewling like an injured animal. Terror gave way to shame—she let her younger brother terrify her.

She felt her shoulders relax. "It's me, Thorn. Zambak. You are going to be well." She pitched her voice to its most calm, stripping it of the fear he'd engendered. He didn't respond. Several heartbeats passed, and she said the words again. The crying out ceased, but he remained huddled, knees to chin, in the corner. For a brief moment, he reminded her of the blond little boy who slept on his cot in the nursery. Though only two years older, she used to slip out from under the covers to check on him when he had eaten too many sweets and gone to bed with a bellyache.

She tried again after a half hour. "Zamb?" he whispered, voice quivering. "You have to help me."

She went to him then. When she sat on the bed, he latched on to her as a drowning man might grab his rescuer to pull them both under. "They're keeping me prisoner, Zamb. I want to go . . ." Her heart heard "home," but she suspected he meant some place else.

"You need to stay until you are well, Thorn. You will feel better, I promise."

"But I hurt so badly!"

"Let me fetch some water." She extricated herself from his grip.

"No," he roared. "I need my laudanum. You know I need it. You know."

"It's destroying you, Thorn."

"You don't know how badly it hurts. I hurt, and you lecture. You don't understand."

She struggled to formulate soft words, some platitude to calm him, but couldn't.

"You hate me. You've always hated me. Jealous, aren't you? You want me dead."

Dead is what he will be if he won't help himself. The family mausoleum on their father's estate came to her mind. It struck her that the grave would be larger than the little room they struggled in. She sank to the floor and dropped her head, holding it with both hands, horrified by her thoughts. *You brought him here to save him, not to let him destroy himself.*

He rocked back and forth before spewing more poison. "You're just a woman. Women are only good for one thing." He spelled out the last statement in words so degrading her stomach tried to rebel. When he pushed up from the cot and started toward her, she scrambled away, reaching for the key in her pocket, but he fell back down, fisting his hair in both hands and yowling horribly.

"Lady Zambak, are you well?" Dr. Peters asked through the door.

Heart pounding, she opened to admit him. "I think so. My brother had a nightmare. He . . ." She meant to say he was better but knew it for a lie. Her shoulders sank. "I don't know what to do," she admitted.

"Let's walk," the physician suggested. "Come, my lord, let's see if we can make you feel better."

"Won't work," Thorn mumbled, but he didn't fight them. Peters led him to the hall. He and Zambak took turns walking him up and down, pushing him when he would stop, and pulling him forward when he stopped to holler. After what might have been an hour—she couldn't tell—she helped him into a clean shirt and rubbed lotion on to arms covered with scratches from his frantic itching. Thorn collapsed on his cot, rolled toward the wall, and fell into fitful sleep.

"You've done what you can, my lady," Peters whispered. "Save your strength for tomorrow." He locked the room behind them.

"Thank you. I was at my wit's end."

"Try reading tomorrow," the physician suggested.

"I beg your pardon?"

"Poetry might help." Peters smiled ruefully. "Like music, they say it hath charms that soothe a savage breast," he quoted. "My wife uses it with unruly children."

"Congreve." She smiled. "Where might I find his poetry in Canton?"

"You didn't know? Dan keeps a library on the upper floor next to his office. He will happily give you access."

"Thank you. It may not help Thorn, but it will calm my nerves while I sit with him."

"All to the good, my lady, all to the good."

Zambak sat in the sun on the upper terrace late in the afternoon, tipped her head back, and let the sun warm her face. She wished poetry might heal her heart. A book of Wordsworth's poems lay unread in her lap.

The sickness Temperance warned her about had set in early that morning. She cleaned the first mess herself, and the second as well, before asking for help. As Thorn's stomach rebelled in every direction, the day had been interminable.

She grabbed at Peter's emphatic order she take time to clean up and rest, leaving her heaving brother to the kindness of strangers.

"Zambak?" Charles's voice, close by, felt like a caress. She opened her eyes to see him kneeling at her side and smiled. "A friendly face," she murmured.

He touched her cheek with a tenderness that sent echoing tremors deep inside, and she longed to fall into his embrace. She knew that would be a bad idea, but she no longer remembered why.

"Is it horrible?" he asked. "Peters told me he sent you here."

"As bad as you can imagine," she replied, sitting upright and forcing him to pull his hand back. "Do you need me?"

He paused at the question. "Yes," he answered at last, "I believe I do." Their eyes caught for a moment, but Charles looked away and pulled a chair next to hers. "I need the resources of that analytical engine in your head."

~ ~ ~

He had her attention, to his great relief. *Anything to take her mind off the sickroom.*

"The commissioner issued four edicts. You were entirely right about his probable actions. At least we now have some idea what worked in the provinces, how he undoubtedly expects to fix the problem here."

"Four?"

"He appears to be a systematic thinker. The first edict requires teachers to eradicate opium smoking among their students. He expects them to organize students into groups of five for mutual support and, one supposes, supervision."

"Yes. Save the young first," she said deep in thought. "I assume punishment will occur for those who fail?"

"That's the interesting thing. Those addicted to smoking are given eighteen months to free themselves from it." Her bleak expression told him more than anything else had how things went with Thorn.

"What are the other three?" she asked.

"The second was addressed to the "gentlemen, soldiers, merchants, and peasants" of Canton and its province. He's trying to shame them and appeal to honor and patriotism. He tells them the situation is not hopeless. He seems to believe that even someone dependent for many years can free themselves from the need for opium."

"And again, they have time to correct their lives?"

"To remove the poison from their bodies, yes. The third edict attacks sailors on the coastal patrol boats, accusing them of collaboration and corruption as well as smoking opium themselves. There appears to be less mercy for them."

She nodded, obviously in agreement with the commissioner on the third point. "He's attacking corruption on all levels. What is the fourth?"

"It is similar to the one for schools. He addresses the rural villages, demanding of the elders what he ordered for the teachers. Households are to be grouped in fives as well."

Zambak's brows drew together, and her left hand moved in a familiar gesture. "That's all?"

"For now." He could almost see the machinery in her mind working, measuring each word, arranging and rearranging facts.

"Nothing about foreigners?" she asked after a while.

"Not yet."

She nodded. "It will come. You're correct. He is systematic and thorough. I would add *determined*. He means to attack the problem on every level. The traders have come up against a formidable enemy. Do you think Elliot is up for it?"

He held her level gaze. "Do you?"

She didn't answer. They both knew it to be unlikely. They sat in companionable silence for several minutes. He wished he might know her thoughts.

His own centered on the woman in front of him, not where they ought—on his commission. Fate had dropped them there at a crucial moment. He turned his responsibilities over and over his mind. He tried to convince himself that he had fulfilled and exceeded expectations with the providential opportunity to judge the new commissioner and Chinese intentions now that he knew about the edicts. It ought to be enough to reinvigorate his career—once the scandal of divorce died down—if he managed to avoid bringing even greater scandal home from China.

Unconvincing line of thought. Too much more intelligence lies waiting to be gathered, and Zambak must know it as well. He still believed any future he could envision that included her was hopeless, but her respect had come to mean the world to him.

Zambak, lost in her own thoughts, seemed unaware how closely he studied her. Her strong profile and the gentle slope of her neck held him fixated until she shook her head to clear it. "Thorn needs me. I can't abandon him now, even if he hates me for the rest of his life. If what you say is true, Doctor Peters may need my assistance as well. The users will seek help where it can be found. Zion's Quarter will be overrun with people trying to free themselves from opium."

He stood with her. "They aren't your concern." Her weariness worried him.

"Aren't they?" she asked, thumb worrying her middle finger. "There's more at stake here than my need to impress my father, isn't there?" Her eyes when she raised them to his had strength beneath the sorrow.

"Stay a moment, Zambak, if you will. I have decisions to make. I could use your ideas."

Chapter 23

Bundled against the late winter wind, Charles set out the next morning toward the British consulate and the offices of the Superintendent of Trade with a long, determined stride. The most brilliant diplomatic mind in Canton, held prisoner by her gender in the American factory at Zion's Quarter, agreed he ought to approach Elliot before he carried out the plan she called "audacious, but correct."

The foreign quarter consisted of the factories with their offices, living quarters, and warehouses abutting one another in an unbroken line, a fortress of commerce, each roof flying the flag of its country and often the banner of a trading company. Their rear faced the city proper, but they fronted along a wide parade ground that separated the factories from their ships anchored in the Pearl River. The open ground gave the young men plenty of room for exercise and a release from the pressures of business. The flower boats bobbing in the water around the foreign ships served a similar, though less virtuous, purpose.

He crossed the entire length quickly. Before he could do anything, he wanted to speak to the superintendent; circumstances frustrated his plans, and he cursed himself for not acting sooner.

"Superintendent Elliot did indeed stop in Canton, Your Grace," Elliot's useless deputy told him. "He left soon after to patrol for gunboats and return to Macao."

"I presume he has been informed of the high commissioner's edicts," Charles said.

"Yes, Your Grace. We sent word as soon as we heard. The dispatch will reach him when he arrives in Macao."

A vision of Higgins filing the papers away, oblivious to their importance, struck him. *These dolts see no urgency about threats from the Chinese. It's all routine paperwork to them.*

"Did the superintendent make an effort to contact Commissioner Lin directly as he did Viceroy Teng?" *Give Elliot credit for enforcing the law so far.*

"Alas, he left before Lin arrived."

The dispatch and the renewed suspension of next year's tea trade will drive Elliot back to Canton, but how long will it take for him to get them?

Elliot's absence left Charles in a quandary. He wondered how the Chinese would react to a message from a traveling duke if the superintendent had not communicated directly with Lin. His title and connections would mean nothing to the Chinese. He needed to survey the city, something Dan Oliver advised against. The Canton system required foreigners to stay inside the quarter.

"Tell me, does the government have a means of travel through the city?"

The deputy sneered. "The damned Chinese, begging Your Grace's pardon, don't believe our government exists." Charles raised a questioning brow, but the man hurried on, "As good as. No government equals theirs. We can't arrange a thing. All communication and any travel has to be between merchants: our firms talk to their merchants, the hongs, and the hongs are running scared."

Sick of inaction and frustrated with constraints on all sides, Charles returned to Zion's Quarter determined to explore the city of Canton one way or another. That Zambak agreed with him confirmed the importance. He barged into Dan Oliver's office to find Dan and Bradshaw deep in conversation with two Chinese gentlemen. A young interpreter appeared to struggle with a particularly knotty exchange.

"My apologies gentlemen. I'll return when your meeting is concluded." Oliver and Bradshaw stood and bowed deeply. The interpreter, who had been standing, followed their lead.

Odd that, coming from the Americans. I thought they ignored such formality. The two Chinese gentlemen studied the proceedings with serious expressions; Charles assumed the show of respect was for their benefit.

"We were just finishing, Your Grace. Feel free to stay while we say our farewells," Oliver told him.

"I presume your visitors are merchants."

After a glance at Oliver, the interpreter made introductions. The Messrs. Kwan, apparently father and son, bowed. After a moment, Charles returned it. He could think of no gain in arrogance. They left soon after.

"What was all that bowing about?" he demanded.

"The Chinese put more stock in it than even you British," Oliver replied. "I didn't think it would hurt to have them take you seriously."

Charles grunted. *He was probably right.* "Did your meeting go well?"

"They came to reassure us that the new commissioner's edicts would not impact our business. Traders that shun opium have naught to fear—at least that is what they told us."

"You don't appear convinced."

"It's true to a point. Some of the other American traders have announced they're abandoning trade in the stuff, God be praised. Trying to cover themselves and keep their hong relationships strong. We're walking a knife's edge here. If your British troublemakers push us into war, we'll all go down together."

The sense of time running out drove Charles to blurt out his most urgent thought. "I need to see the city. I want a tour."

Oliver scowled at the abrupt change of subject. "As if I don't have enough trouble."

Bradshaw leaned across the desk. "You know foreigners aren't free to roam the city," he said.

"But your hong partners could arrange it, couldn't they?" He looked from one to the other. They didn't deny it. "Listen, Oliver. I can return to London with the same set of facts everyone else is feeding the government, or I can try to educate the queen. I can make certain she knows exactly who these people are, how this world works, and the impact of our actions on the lives of the Chinese. I can't do that running tame inside this building."

Oliver continued to frown. "I'm harboring a woman as it is. You'll bring the authorities down on us."

"That isn't my intent." *I don't want the authorities coming down on these people, and I certainly don't want Zambak in the middle.* "If you won't help me, the East India Company will. I ought to have more leverage there."

Oliver looked so relieved Charles regretted putting him on the spot. "I should have thought of that in the first place, Dan. You've been nothing but kind since the day I met you." He rose to leave.

"Keep our name out of it if you can."

He nodded in agreement but made no promises. "Audacious, but correct," Zambak had said. One way or another, he would inspect Canton from the lowest slums to Lin Zeux's headquarters before they left.

~ ~ ~

Within days, the impact of the edicts began to be felt inside the clinic. On the occasions she encountered Dr. Peters, his exhaustion and perpetually worried frown made him unapproachable for anything other than sympathy. No servants came to help her under the circumstances.

Thorn, improved, albeit slowly, and his rebellious stomach and bowels settled down, for which Zambak thanked the angels and saints. The urge to plan his funeral and the images of his grave that haunted her subsided.

That morning she found him looking pale and wan but lying peacefully on his cot. He accepted porridge without complaint. "Nursery fare," he called it with a ghost of a smile. "Do you remember Mrs. Hildegard, Zamb?"

"'Eat your porridge young man, if you want—'" Zambak began, quoting their old nanny.

"'—to grow strong like your sire.'" Thorn finished, perfectly mimicking the old woman.

"Oh dear, I've turned into a nanny!" Zambak said with mock horror.

"Always were," he retorted. It was an old joke, and they laughed together. That small moment of sibling accord sent her hopes soaring.

His stomach didn't revolt, but he complained a half hour later that the porridge sat hard in his guts. He clutched his waist in gesture that had become all too familiar to Zambak, and he lashed out in a series of complaints about her dictatorial ways that owed nothing to humor.

Soon, patients desperate to free themselves from opium overran the public rooms and spilled into the downstairs staff quarters. Zambak passed Chinese patients and their families on her way to and from Thorn's room. She moved her own things above stairs to make room for two more pathetic souls eager to comply with Lin's edicts.

She couldn't wall herself off from their suffering; before long, her activity flowed over to rooms besides Thorn's. His continued improvement meant she could ease her vigil. Peters caught her ministering to a man who had scratched his arms bloody from the devilish itching.

"Lady Zambak, Dan will be horrified, to say nothing of what His Grace might think."

She glanced over her shoulder and went on rubbing ointment on the ragged, foul-smelling man in front of her. "Dan Oliver fears retribution when the authorities discover I'm here, those authorities that created this crisis. With any luck, they will be too busy to take notice of one woman tucked away in Zion's Quarter."

"But . . ."

She stood to face the physician. "You need my help."

Dark eyes under the shock of black hair liberally sprinkled with gray reflected the doctor's frown. "It isn't—"

"Fitting? Proper? Not much about my situation or my brother's is proper, Dr. Peters, but we do what must be done. To ignore all this suffering is impossible. You can't do it. Don't ask me to."

The respect that overtook his expression and his sharp nod soothed her soul, though they did little for the ache forming in her back. "Very well. When you finish here, patients two doors down need similar treatment." He didn't wait for a reply.

She followed him into the hall to find Thorn leaning against the doorframe to his spare quarters. She had quit locking the door when he calmed, but this was the first time he had ventured to the hall. The pained expression on his face, all too familiar, sprang from a new cause.

"You're acting like a servant. When did you lower yourself to consort with the dregs?" he demanded.

"When you sank into the sewer," she snapped. "You begrudge these people the same care you got?"

"Care was it? You've kept me prisoner here. I see no other doors have locks. You show those peasants more consideration than you showed me."

"These men are desperate to rid themselves of opium. You had no will to renounce it."

"No one chooses to leave the embrace of the beloved," he murmured.

His choice of words made her sick. She swallowed bile, but the acid taste remained. "They do when the alternative is death."

He snorted. "The emperor making noises again? All bluster. Jarratt said—"

"Not this time, Thorn. The new high commissioner assigned to eradicate the opium trade takes his calling seriously."

"He's threatening those who smoke?" Thorn's outrage left her cold. He couldn't admit his own degradation.

"Yes, and those who sell it to them, too. He has gone after the owners of opium dens, the hong merchants who deal in it."

"Not the China traders, I'll bet," her brother murmured, lost in thought.

"Not yet, but pay heed. No one who uses opium will be safe, Thorn. No one." She glared at him, arms akimbo.

"Nonsense. Your commissioner wouldn't dare touch me, much less Jarratt, Dean, or the rest. Free trade. He can't interfere with free trade," he growled.

"Open your eyes!" She grabbed him by the arm to pull him toward the clinic door. "Look at the suffering Jarratt's "free trade" has wrought. The Chinese are right to demand we obey their laws."

He yanked himself free and swayed on his feet. Instead of arguing the point, he turned on her. "Your behavior ain't right, Zambak. If word gets back to London you are here, your chances are dead. No man will have you." He left her staring after him when he disappeared into his cubicle.

A rustle of cloth alerted her to Charles who watched the conversation from the foot of the stairs. He dressed entirely in black, and he carried a Chinese robe in a green so dark it almost looked black thrown over his shoulder. He wore a bowl-shaped hat.

"He's right, you know," he said.

"About being above the law?" she demanded.

"About ruining your chances for a good marriage."

She rolled her eyes. "You know how little I care about that."

"I didn't say dynastic marriage—I said good. You have seen what Temperance and Aaron have—or my uncle and aunt." He wandered closer and leaned one elbow on the wall next to her. "Don't you wish for it? You ought to, Zambak."

The warmth in his eyes pulled her in, driving the breath from her body. *Charles wants what they have for himself. This gentle man, locked in union to the hellish Julia, wants domestic peace above all else.* For the space of a heartbeat, she longed for it as well, but knew it for the impossible desire it was. "I, Charles? I want to own my life, to not be a pawn in some political chess game. In the unlikely event a choice like the one you describe arises then, yes. I might take it. I have little hope that it will."

His eyes lit with a fire that burned into her. "Sometimes life surprises us with unexpected gifts," he said, studying her. His intensity burned deep into her heart and radiated through her. When he leaned closer, she realized he meant to kiss her. His desire didn't frighten her; it filled her with wonder. Her own yearning to accept him, however, shot terror straight to her core.

Good God, Zambak. You're lusting after a married man! She pulled away.

Stricken, his face flushed red, and he stood straighter. "Zambak, I—"

"What have you done to your face?" she asked. She didn't know if he meant to apologize or express disappointment. She couldn't bear either of them and was grateful when he let her turn the subject.

"Walnut juice."

She felt her lips twitch into a smile. *He always finds a way to amuse me.* She loved that about him.

She reached out to the robe he had thrown over his shoulder and rubbed the silk between her fingers, refusing to meet his eyes. "Lovely," she murmured, "And dark. No one looking close will mistake you for Chinese, however. Neither that hat you wear nor walnut juice will fool them for long. Is that why you are here? With Oliver and Elliot gone to Macao you found someone willing to guide you into the city?"

"I assumed you would want to know. It took little enough pressure at the East India Company factory to produce a guide."

"And an interpreter?"

"One and the same," he said, cupping her cheek with one hand and drawing her face to his. "I wish it were you."

"I do too. Your life may depend on it." She forced a smile, suddenly fearful for him and determined not to beg him to stay. She had urged him to go; she couldn't stop him now. "Be careful, Charles. I'll be waiting to hear what you discover." Any information he gathered would enhance their report; a month before that would have been her greatest priority. Zambak didn't know when her hopes had shifted, but she understood deep inside her soul that the man had taken priority over the mission.

Chapter 24

Charles pushed away from the wall. He needed to speak to Peters before he took to the streets. "The high commissioner contacted the clinic—directly," he told her. "I need to know the details."

"Peters never mentioned it!" Her mood shot off in a new direction. One moment she gazed at him with emotion he didn't dare name. The next her hackles rose, and she growled at him. He could almost hear the words in her head: *No matter what I say or do I'm only a woman to these men, never a colleague.* He found her passion delightful to see but feared she would explode with the resentment that shook her.

"From appearances both you and he have your hands full here," he soothed. "He probably forgot." An unladylike snort met that lame attempt. "Actually, your work may be precisely the cause of the contact. Lin wishes to know how best to help the poor wretches give up their opium."

She trailed after him until he stopped at the clinic door to say good-bye; the fire in her eyes stopped him. He shook his head as she followed him into the clinic, past a disapproving assistant, past numerous Chinese witnesses, directly into Dr. Peter's office. The poor man looked utterly spent, but not so much he couldn't frown up at Zambak for disobeying the rules.

Charles spoke before the physician could object to her presence. "We understand you've heard from Commissioner Lin. What does the man want?"

"Miracles," he replied, running a hand through his disordered hair. He gestured to pieces of paper covered in formal Chinese script. "My lady, you know—"

Her expression stopped him mid sentence. "What miracles?" She gestured toward the pile of paper.

"I had one of my servants read it out loud. Sometimes things get lost between spoken and written Chinese. My reading had been accurate enough, though."

"You read Chinese?" Zambak couldn't keep the awe from her voice. "Learning spoken Cantonese dialect has been difficult, but . . ." She reached for the missive and pulled her hand back. Charles wondered how long it would take her to learn to decipher the characters if someone would read it out loud to her.

Peters acknowledged his skills. "It is frowned upon by the Chinese who view their written language as some treasure to preserve, but yes. It has proven useful in our mission efforts, and the Chinese choose to ignore our efforts."

"Lin must know if he contacted you. What's in his message?" Charles demanded.

"As I said, he asked for miracles. He wants advice on treating addicts."

"Give the man credit for compassion," Charles said.

"And thorough strategic thinking. He attacks the problem on every level," Zambak added, impressed. "What did you tell him?"

"Nothing yet. I fear 'fluids, isolation, and skin potions' will not meet his expectations."

"You will add your observations about the length and course of the treatment and that sort of thing. Help set his expectations," she told him.

"His interest in your work is important Peters. When Oliver returns, he will want a full report—Elliot as well," Charles told him. He quickly outlined his planned foray into the city, listened while Peters suggested ways to avoid being more conspicuous than he had to be, and accepted the physician's instructions about how to gauge the mood of the crowds and recognize signs of trouble.

Some of it puzzled him. "Chains?"

"Particularly among the higher classes. If you see a wealthy merchant with chain around his neck, he's a marked man. Avoid him."

Charles absorbed what he could and returned his attention to the papers strewn on Peter's desk. "This contact is stunning. He reached out to a foreign entity."

"Not Her Majesty's government," Peters observed.

"No, but vital all the same." His words were directed at Peters, but his eyes were on Zambak. "I'll leave you two to discuss it. I'll want to know more when I return."

Grateful for shadows cast by narrow walls and, for once in his life, his slight frame, Charles slipped out of Hog Lane and followed his guide through winding streets and narrow tradesmen's alleys outside the city walls to the gate of to the Old City, tunnel like in its thickness. He rated the walls strong but not impregnable. Direct bombardment would bring down the brick eventually, but direct bombardment would not be his first choice. When they reached the main gate to the old city the guard balked briefly until silver coins, discretely passed, did their work.

Unlike the grimy settlement he passed through between the walls and the foreign quarter, Canton proper reflected money and quality. Behind its enclosure, the city huddled under low roofs; most structures, even those clearly the opulent homes of the hongs, did not reach the height of the massive walls. They skirted the Yuen-hua Academy, reputed to be the headquarters of the new high commissioner.

A few impressive towers dotted the skyline, however. His guide pointed out the Flower Pagoda of the Temple of the Six Banyan Trees rising nine stories from its base and beautifully painted. Even taller, the minaret of the Huaisheng

Mosque astonished him. He had not expected a Muslim edifice in Canton. It was, his guide informed him, a beacon for ships. *A lighthouse?*

While they walked the streets, he counted eight main gates and two water gates along a stream leading down to the Pearl. They made their way north moving uphill to face yet another massive tower the guide called the Five Story Pagoda. When they came to the open field in front of it, the guide pulled back. The pagoda appeared to be a massive guard tower perched on the northern hill overlooking the city.

"Forbidden, Your Grace. We cannot go close."

"This whole benighted expedition is 'forbidden.'" The guard tower fascinated him, positioned as it was in the northern wall and provisioned with troops.

"Heaven smiles so far, your worship. In the open ground too many soldiers."

The man had a point. However well his disguise worked so far, out in the open it might be harder. Yet, the sun dipped low in the West, putting his approach in shadow. Bowed head, submissive gait—it might work. He took several steps forward only to stop when a unit of troops came barreling down the hill in the direction of the river.

People scattered in front of them like geese. "Where are they going?" he demanded.

"The boats, your worthiness."

"Boats?"

"Commissioner Lin has ordered destruction of opium warehouses.

His mind reeled. *Chinese or western warehouses?* An attack on foreign property, inevitable though it may be, would constitute an escalation. *How far will he go? What resistance will the merchants put up?* He turned to his companion but found only empty space. The man had evaporated into the gathering mist.

Alone in the growing dark, Charles had neither map nor interpreter in a city swarming with soldiers bent on destroying Western goods. He knew one thing; the factories—his only safety—lay to the south and west, toward the setting sun. He had no choice. He followed the troops.

Chapter 25

Dawn crept across the windowsill in the upper dining room when Zambak leaned on it, straining to see the city beyond its walls. Charles had not returned. She prowled the halls most of the night before collapsing into restless sleep until she awoke with a start, unable to shake feelings of dread.

Peeking out to make sure the corridor was empty, she invaded his room, only to find it undisturbed. She picked up the miniature of his son Jonny from the dresser, hugged it to her breast, and collapsed onto his unused bed breathing in the scent of sandalwood and Charles, admiring the orderly arrangement—as neat and pragmatic as the man himself—and storing away what she learned about him in the treasure trove of memory. Try as she might, she couldn't escape the realization she behaved like a lovesick schoolgirl.

Dawn brought a painful admission. *You want him, you ninnyhammer. You yearn for a married man—and he's lost in Canton.*

Hunger drove her out to seek her breakfast and hope for word of the man. There was none. News of unrest in the city overnight increased her anxiety; Lin had begun to seek out and seize opium stores. Reduced to watching and waiting, she seethed with frustration. As the sun rose higher, she watched a steady trickle of Chinese moving toward the clinic doors from an upstairs window. Not one wore a deep green gown; not one had the telltale bearing of an English duke.

She leaned her forehead against the window and squeezed her eyes shut, but the muffled sound of a drum forced them wide, and she stood up straight. A small party of official-looking men in formal court garb strode down the lane from the city gate, one carrying a document case.

Another communication? She and Peters had worked out a response about the treatment of opium sickness and dispatched it late in the previous afternoon. She would not have expected a reply so soon. She set out for the clinic at a run.

Zambak watched Peters bow to the commissioner's messengers through the open door before she pulled back into the corridor. It was one thing to walk freely through the Chinese patients in the clinic—she'd been treating the poor wretches who came for their help after all—but quite another to parade herself in front of government officials. She owed Peters and Oliver that much discretion. She waited impatiently—one ear cocked to the conversation beyond the door—pulled at the sleeves of her embroidered jacket, and smoothed the pleats in her skirt several times before the party departed.

Peters greeted her explosion into the clinic with a sardonic eyebrow and a weary gesture to follow him to his office. He called for Jian-bo, his most trusted assistant.

"Lady Zambak, kindly sit. You will want to hear this."

She did, avidly watching when he opened the long narrow box and pulled out a long scroll, laying it across his desk.

"A request for more information? Looks a bit wordy for that." Something in his expression struck her as midway between amusement and exasperation.

He pulled out a second scroll and lay it next to the first. The second contained not Chinese symbols, but English words. "Not even close. What you see here, my lady, is a formal letter to a sovereign."

"What sovereign?" she asked, eyes wide.

"Yours." He waited while she absorbed that information, too polite to mention that her jaw gaped.

"It's a letter to Victoria?" She squeaked out at last, too stunned to remember to use the woman's title.

"Aye. And he's asked my help to make certain the English is clear and 'respectful.' The commissioner wishes to be seen as the renowned scholar that he is."

"From the looks of this, he needs help," she replied, fingering the English document. "The attempt is hardly readable. How shall we go about this?"

Peters sighed heavily but didn't question her assumption of participation. Someone with knowledge of the queen and the English court could only help the process. He suggested they read through the current English version and then have Jian-bo read it to them, while the two of them discussed wording of the translation.

Trouble surfaced almost immediately. "He's implying the emperor speaks for all mankind," she mused.

"He believes he does. The emperor believes he has the mandate of heaven to do so."

Zambak asked his assistant to read the first few lines. "'His heart is the heart of both heaven and earth.' Heart or mind?" she asked.

"The court translator wrote heart," Peters replied. "Move on to the next."

"Dear God! Does he actually mean to say the kings of England have been respectful and obedient? That would be an enormous surprise to the queen, I can tell you that!" Zambak didn't know whether to laugh or rise up on outrage on behalf of England itself.

"Obedient or perhaps submissive. They've expected what few representatives have made it to the Celestial Court to kowtow to the emperor with unpleasant results."

"Kowtow? Doesn't that mean bow? He would expect a foreign ruler to bow?"

"Bow nose-to-carpet actually. On their knees. I doubt if they expect it literally. They assume it figuratively."

Outrage on behalf of womankind outran patriotism. "Victoria won't accept lectures from Melbourne—or my father. A moral tirade from a Chinese commissioner? She wouldn't take it from the emperor himself! As to the government and Palmerston . . ."

"The concept of parliament would be lost on Lin, I fear. Let's go through the meat of the thing."

The heart of the letter dealt with law and an expectation of rule by law. However much she might object to the tone and its underlying assumptions about power, she couldn't disagree with the commissioner's insistence that the law be obeyed. She couldn't fault him for destroying contraband. Revenue agents in her country destroyed smugglers stores— when they found them. People died in those raids.

Thinking about Lin's edicts distracted her. *Where the devil is Charles? The damned idiot probably threw himself into the operation just to watch it unfold!*

Peter's voice pulled her back. "He seems to labor under the belief that the rulers of England, Scotland, and Ireland understand the evils of opium and refuse to allow it in their own 'kingdoms,' and assumes that your queen will, therefore, support his efforts to enforce the law in his own country."

"He has no idea," she said, pinching the bridge of her nose at the thought of the political complexities Lin glossed over: revenue from tea, rival political parties, the waning influence of the East India Company, the opium plantations in India, lobbying by merchant groups, limitations surrounding the little queen herself.

"More than many Chinese, actually," Peter's countered. "He's made an effort to learn, but yes, he doesn't understand the constraints on Elliot's authority nor the nature of your government. His moral points are correct however."

"He says the opium traders are—what does he call them? Rogues? Scoundrels? Pirates?"

"Barbarians."

She thought of Jarratt. "I might agree with him on that one. He assumes opium is forbidden in the United Kingdom. Alas, it is not."

"No, nor in the United States. He would believe us to be mindless reprobates if he knew that."

"On some level, he would be right, at least about opium. Poppy juice is vile, and we allow it in every apothecary in the country. Even gin is more regulated. People give it to infants!" Thorn's pain and his struggles overrode her misgivings about Lin's worldview. "What shall we do with this thing?"

"Clean up his English. Make sure we send him a translation as exact as we can make it."

"We can't clear up his incorrect assumptions though, can we?" It wasn't a question.

"No, we cannot," he replied.

"The queen will be outraged!"

"If she ever sees it. How would he have it delivered? Via Elliot? A military attaché? Your government would likely bury it."

"The fundamental demand is that the government cooperate in forcing the traders to turn over their opium stocks," she said. "But of course the traders see it as taking their property and violating free trade."

"His men are destroying whatever they get their hands on, but they can't get to the ships and won't enter the factories. What will Elliot do?" he asked.

"He forced the gunboats out of the river. Elliot might cooperate. He hates the stuff." She doubted her words, even as she said them.

"Elliot walks a fine line, and the English traders have friends in London."

"And a never-ending supply of opium from India, which Lin appears to understand quite well. Reread that passage, Jian-bo. I want to be sure of his meaning," she said.

The servant reread a lengthy passage that revealed Lin's obvious knowledge about poppy cultivation and the regions of India in which it took place. Zambak repeated his "suggestion" that the queen order her subjects to eradicate the growth of poppy plants and "hoe the fields under to plant the five grains in its stead."

"Good, but alas futile, advice. Thorough as always," she murmured. "Kill it at its source. The East India Company will laugh into its exquisite special reserve port over that."

"Perhaps," Peters responded. "As I said, our task is to translate it as written. That is what the commissioner demanded. Do you wish to help or not?"

She nodded and leaned forward. "You may be right. The queen will never see this."

He shrugged. "What would you do with it if you were Lin?"

"He may be uninformed, but he's no fool. He knows to go around the officials on the ground." She considered the commissioner's options for a moment. "He'll publish it—make it an open letter and attempt to shame all of the traders into compliance."

"It won't work. It will merely escalate the conflict." He sighed. "We could refuse to help," he said, but she knew he would not. *How could we refuse a direct request from the highest official in Canton?* They set to work.

Hours later, she rose bleary eyed from the clear, pompous, and ultimately fruitless document they created. Peters planned to review, rewrite, and send the translation the next morning. She left sick at heart over escalating tensions.

No word had come from Charles the entire day, and fear sat like a stone in her belly.

A brief interview with her brother did little to improve her mood. He continued to see himself as a victim and complained about everything from the food to the overworked servants.

"I'm bored here. The missionaries don't hold with rum, and none of them will call me a skiff to the flower boats."

Mention of the flower boats sent a prickle of unease up her neck. On his feet, he could get up to mischief, and she had no excuse to keep him locked in. She had to get him out of Canton before trouble escalated, but she had no idea where Charles was.

I need to find a way to keep him busy—to keep both of us busy.

Chapter 26

Twelve hours hiding behind a tanner's workshop waiting for the cover of darkness gave Charles ample time to contemplate the folly of his actions. He couldn't regret them, however, even though he couldn't even understand the snatches of conversation that floated back to him.

The soldiers he followed had led him far upriver from the factories to a massive warehouse, a beehive of activity. The sight alone had been worth his risk. Workers with dogcarts and sledges brought opium chests by the dozen, handing them over to officials. Charles watched those officials seal each one and mark it, a hedge against corruption he assumed. The quantity—and the monetary value—of the confiscated contraband staggered. The chests and workers appeared to come from the Chinese hongs. No obvious sign a Western firm had handed over opium stores showed itself, but he could not be certain.

The activity had been so frantic, no one bothered to notice the odd man in the dark robe of a wealthy merchant. When he had seen enough, Charles meandered backward, ready to slip into the shadows of city streets. He didn't dare walk along the open waterfront even though that would have been the most direct route back to the foreign factories.

A shout called his attention back to a scene of horror. A man pulling a sledge had attempted to remove one ball of opium tar—a small fortune for a poor man—and slide it into his garments. The man still gripped the substance in his hand when soldiers knocked him to his knees and lopped off his head. The lull had been brief; the lesson, obvious. Work continued unabated.

Even the summary execution of a thief hadn't compared to the sight of troops dragging two merchants with chains around their neck to their doom two hours later. They marched with ceremony and panache that would not have been out of place at a coronation. He knew he would struggle to describe the crowd that followed once he got to pen and paper. He didn't understand the mob's shouts, but he suspected they demanded death to the perpetrators. Yet the mood belied the sort of blood lust that might accompany a public execution. Their eyes held fear and perhaps great sorrow. Many of these people welcomed the effort to stamp out opium even as the rapid flow of events alarmed them. The troops had carried out their mission swiftly and ruthlessly.

An encounter with a lone soldier in a narrow lane, a knife fight that left both Charles and the soldier bruised and bleeding, convinced him stumbling around in the deep of night was a bad idea. He crawled into the foul-smelling alley, tore strips from his black shirt, and bound the slice down his arm as best he could. He slept little and that fitfully while he waited for morning. Dawn had come sharp and—by the time he roused—bright, so bright it seemed prudent to remain hidden and wait for the shadows of dusk.

Why do costumes and derring-do always sound more amusing at the beginning? You're too old for this nonsense. As he shifted his back for comfort, he doubted Zambak would be impressed. She would probably chide him for being a damned fool—unless, of course, she found the information he brought back as fascinating as he did. *Zambak. Did I really tell her I wished she could come with me? She would have come without hesitation if she could have. That alone tells me my wits have gone begging.*

It had been equally unwise to allow himself sensual images of her in the night, but they had kept him warm and focused on return like a lodestone. When the sun dipped behind the Five Story Pagoda, he pulled the black hat down on his head, shook out his robes, and prepared to appear meek.

Following the soldiers the previous night had another benefit. He had not been challenged when they went out the city gates. The harbor settlements outside the walls, a jumble of lanes lined with unpleasant businesses like the tanner's, repulsive food shops, and dark hovels—what in London might have been seedy gin shops—lay between Charles and the factories, but no walls and no guards.

He reached the doors of the clinic at Zion's Quarter just before full dark when they were locking up for the night. With Peters nowhere in sight, Charles brushed off the attendants except to ask them to order a bath. He needed to get out of his filth and find Zambak while his observations were fresh in his mind.

~ ~ ~

Two days. Fifty-two hours. Zambak felt minutes pass with excruciating slowness while she sat in the dark hugging Charles's pillow to her chest. Even anxiety over Thorn or dread that the actions of the army would spill over into the factories couldn't push aside her fear for him. It had been two days—fifty-two hours—since he disappeared into the night, and they had heard nothing since.

Alone as the shadows of his room turned to full dark, cold truths haunted her. The reports she'd gathered for her father had to be weighed against her childish and impulsive behavior. She had worried her parents, she had complicated the Elliots' lives and career, and her actions did little to change her brother, still bent on self-destruction. Worst of all, she feared she led Charles to take risks he shouldn't have.

One other thing took shape and came into focus so sharply she couldn't turn away. She loved Charles Wheatly, heart and soul. A desperate laugh—half sob, half hysteria—escaped her at the thought. She finally fulfilled her mother's fondest wish and found a man she could respect and love—one that offered little hope of a respectable future. She had no idea what to do with the thought. As it turned out she had little time to consider it.

"Who is here?" Charles demanded. He stood outlined in the light from oil lamps in the corridor behind him. Caught between love and fury over the fear he caused, she flung herself from the chair.

"Thank God!" She didn't know whether she would hug him or slap him until she threw herself into his arms and was being kissed senseless.

He pulled his lips from hers and kissed his way down her neck. "What is this foolishness?" he asked against a tender spot beneath her right ear. His gentle hands began to roam.

She captured his mouth again, invading before he could object. "Where have you been?" she asked between moans of pleasure. "Don't ever frighten me like that again."

He shifted and pulled her closer, kissed her more deeply. She felt one of his hands, warm against her skin, slip under her lose jacket.

Zambak melted against him, but reality intruded as the initial heat subsided. "You stink!" She pulled back a few inches, his arms still holding her, and wrinkled her nose.

"I slept behind a tannery last night, in an alley ridden with some dubious substances. I meant to clean up before reporting to you."

She pulled away reluctantly, one hand clinging to his, and picked up a candle from his bedside to light it from one of the oil lamps in the hall. She looked him up and down with disgust, put the candle down, and began undoing the heavy robe. "Let's get you undressed," she said, setting words to action.

"Lady Zambak Hayden, how inappropriate—and how utterly delightful," he said, allowing her to have her way with him. The outer robe hit the floor, and she kicked it to the corner. She began undoing the fasteners on his shirt, but he brushed her hands aside and pulled it over his head. "I've ordered a bath. Will you help me with that too?"

Heat surged through her at the image he conjured. Her face burned momentarily, but the sight of the seeping bandage on his arm sent ice water through her. "My God, Charles, you're hurt!"

"It probably needs to be looked at, but I wanted to clean up first."

She unwound the filthy strip of cloth, cringing at the seeping wound running almost the length of his upper arm. "Cow slop! This can't wait. You spent the night in filth." She punched his shoulder then.

"Ow! What was that for?"

"Stupidity. This could fester, and I'll have to fear for you all over again." She grabbed a towel from his washstand, wet it in the basin, and dabbed at the cut with one hand. "This will need more thorough cleaning—and whiskey, liberally applied."

When the other hand absently rubbed his naked chest, he took it in his and kissed her fingers. "I'm sorry," he murmured. "I would never want to cause you pain."

She felt his kiss on the back of her neck where she bent over the wound just before she heard a familiar—and entirely unwelcome—voice say, "Murnane, damn it. I told you not to venture out. Are you trying to put our entire enterprise in trouble with the commissioner."

Zambak went still. Charles held her close, his back to Oliver, blocking her from view. "Daniel! I didn't know you were back."

"Arrived two hours ago. All hell's breaking out, and I hear I have a wayward duke loose in the city, which as you were informed is strictly illegal. First I have to deal with a damned woman pushing her way in against the law and now—"

She took a shuddering breath; something had alerted Oliver. She dipped her forehead against Charles's chest and left a swift kiss before she stepped into the open. Charles turned to face him as well. "If the 'damned woman' has caused you trouble, Captain Oliver, I apologize. It wasn't my intent," Zambak said head high.

Oliver went pale, eyes wide before he tore them away to glare at the duke's bare chest. "The reason I sought you out, Your Grace," he ground out, "is to bring you news and a warning. Your wife has been busy in Macao."

His wife. Cow shite. What have I done? She raised her chin and stiffened her back. "I'm certain His Grace will want a full report, Captain. However, you interrupted my attempt to clean his nasty wound. Perhaps when it is properly dressed he can join you in your office." She held Oliver's eyes until she forced him to turn away.

"Perhaps, Lady Zambak. May I can send someone from the clinic to assist you?" the American asked, staring at the wall behind her.

"That would be excellent. A bath has already been ordered, and the orderly will undoubtedly assist His Grace."

"Undoubtedly," Oliver said through stiff lips. He studied Charles for a moment. "The lady is correct. You will join me in my office once the effects of your little 'adventure' have been removed. We can discuss the speed with which you and the lady will want to return to Macao." He spun on his heels and strode toward the clinic.

"Zambak—" Charles reached out a hand, but she stepped away before he could touch her.

"Hush. He's right. We've outstayed our welcome. As it happens, Thorn is able to travel, and I fear what mischief he'll create if he's here much longer." She met his eyes then, and the pain in them almost made her knees buckle.

This will not do. "Excuse my foolishness of moments ago," she said. "Someone I counted as a friend gave me a fright. Apparently, you took it for something else." She forced a haughty sneer. "If you think you can have a piece of Sudbury's brat, think again. I'm no man's for the taking. The orderly can finish this."

She left, proud of the control that kept her from running, with her chin up and her tears in check. *Well, that should put a period to dalliance.*

She stumbled toward her room and closed the door. *But why do we have to avoid it? I never plan to marry anyway.* Frustration and confusion mingled as the tears began to flow. Between hiccupping sobs, she remembered the passion with which he chided her about Temperance and Aaron and ruthlessly squelched the niggling thought that it might not be marriage per se she desired, but he would never settle for less.

Chapter 27

Julia. Always Julia.

Charles choked on anger, willed his body to still, and told himself Oliver couldn't have seen much of what happened with Zambak. It didn't matter; she'd been alone with a half-dressed man. Oliver raged across his cramped office, knocking over a pile of ledgers in the process, and refused to meet the duke's eyes. Their host didn't need to bring up the scene in the bedroom; he had plenty of other cause for anger.

"You will leave in the morning," he demanded, "before Commissioner Lin discovers I've been harboring two people who are—by his light—felons: a man who entered the city without official permission and a woman whose very presence in the factory compound is anathema." Oliver paced across a worn carpet and gesticulated with uncharacteristic ferocity. "Elliot himself would agree on that last one. A lady does not belong in a compound of men."

Being lashed with the truth didn't take the sting from the lashing. Charles curled both hands into fists and glared at Bradshaw who stood, grim and disapproving, while his superior went on. "We've worked for years to build up a reputation of respect for Chinese law and you—the two of you—ignore all warnings, act on impulse, and threaten to undo it in a matter of weeks."

A bath and clean clothes had removed all taint of the tanner's alley, but tactile memory of Zambak's hands and lips moving over his body would not go easily. That and Oliver's words made it increasingly difficult for Charles to remain still.

He clung to one thought while he waited for the irate merchant to wind down. "What news of my wife, Oliver?" he asked through tight lips, giving it voice. "You sought me out to tell me earlier."

"Did you hear anything I said? Is your damned report to your everlasting queen so important you can trample on a man's livelihood?"

Charles dipped his head and breathed in. "I regret any problems my exploration caused you. We will, of course, leave Oliver and Company in peace as soon as you can arrange passage. Pray God we manage it before the commissioner gets wind of my activity." *Or threatens Zambak who ought to have had the sense to remain hidden.*

Oliver huffed mightily and threw himself into his chair, reaching for his pipe. "Thank the Good Lord Lin doesn't know the lady interfered with his ill-advised letter to Victoria. Tomorrow's tide, Murnane. I have a packet leaving then, bound for Macao."

Charles jerked a nod in response and repeated his question, "My wife?" and waited in grim anticipation. He had allowed Zambak Hayden and his commission to distract him with a pathetic few days of adventure, and now he would pay. *You knew the damned slattern would never settle meekly where you put her. Julia drives a knife into your life whenever it teeters on happiness.*

The misery in Oliver's face took on softer lines than the rage over his business, but profound unhappiness remained. "I received a note from Aaron Knighton. She has taken up with Jarratt's nephew. He parades her around Macao on his arm while she regales the respectable ladies with tales of her abusive husband." He looked at Charles directly for the first time. "We can acquit you of that at least," he said.

It sounded grudging to Charles's ears. "Don't trouble your conscience over it. She's a convincing liar," he snapped. *And Jarratt can be creative in revenge.*

"Convincing enough with some, I fear, but not with me," he insisted. "Her hints about Lady Zambak's behavior are vague, but effective in some quarters. Unfortunately, her presence here with you confirms the worst to the ladies of Macao even if your wife keeps silent."

They glared at one another across the battered desk. "I want you gone, Your Grace," Oliver said at last. He clamped his teeth down on his pipe.

"That gives us one thing on which we can agree. Tomorrow you said?"

The captain nodded.

Something Oliver said came back to him. "Before I pack, I need to record my findings. What's this about a letter to the queen?"

"Lin asked Peters to assist in translating an open letter to your sovereign. Lady Zambak inserted herself into that effort as well."

Of course she did. That and my findings need to be compared and recorded before rumormongering, lies, and accusations distract us beyond the point we can retrieve what we've learned. The combined determination of Oliver and Bradshaw made it unlikely he would see her alone in the confines of Oliver and Company's factory.

"Mr. Bradshaw," he said stiffly. "I have need of an interview with the lady. There being no females present, would you kindly sit with us to lend propriety?" Charles thought of barn doors slamming shut after horses that had already bolted and felt a bit foolish. The look on Bradshaw's face, seemed to indicate that he, at least, approved of the request to chaperone.

I'll owe him an apology as well. The "wayward duke" went missing on his watch. The man's forbidding countenance held him back. They reached the dining area in silence; Bradshaw took the first seat he came to and leaned his elbows on the table, hands clasped.

Charles twisted the side of his mouth and pursed his lips, wondering if it would be more effective to lean on his title or speak man to man. The American had never stopped Your-Gracing him, a fact he found irritating. Before the duke could decide, Bradshaw glanced beyond him, and his face brightened as if lit from within. He rose respectfully, causing Charles to turn toward the door.

Zambak held the summons to meet between two fingers, tapping it on her hip, drawing his eyes to her feminine curves. A heavy Manchu skirt disguised her body, but Charles had ever possessed a good imagination, now augmented by his exploration of her curves. He quickly pushed images aside under the force of her shuttered ice blue eyes. When she turned attention to Bradshaw, the smile on her face reached those eyes and warmed them considerably.

"Mr. Bradshaw, this is a pleasant surprise." She reached out a hand. "The new dress surpasses even the other two. Be reassured, I will reimburse you as soon as I reach my funds in Macao—and please tell me you also bought one for Mrs. Bradshaw. Such beauty will bring her great joy."

The damned American assured her his new gift for his wife lay secure in his sea trunk, and Charles tried not to hate him for the glow on Zambak's face. "Touching," he snapped, "but Lady Zambak and I have business to conduct, business for her majesty's government. All due respect, but I invited you along to protect Lady Zambak's reputation, not to listen to our conversation."

Bradshaw's bow held more mockery than respect, but he moved to the far end of the room, leaned into the kitchen door, and spoke to servants before sitting and staring into steaming coffee with rigid concentration.

"My reputation?" Zambak hissed, taking a seat.

"One of us needs to concern ourselves with it," he responded. He cut off whatever retort she planned with one hand. "We don't have time. You need to hear—and record—what I learned while it's fresh." He laid her journal on the table.

She flipped the journal to the first blank page, waiting.

"I understand you've been busy as well," Charles said., "Shall we start with this letter to Victoria?"

~ ~ ~

Zambak had long grown royally sick of her everlasting reputation. Everyone seemed to care about it more than she did. *Why can't they all—my mother, Sudbury, Charles, and even Dan Oliver—just accept that I don't care if I ever make a so-called respectable marriage and leave my reputation to me? I thought I abandoned the damned thing when I left London.*

"The letter, Zambak?"

This, at least, ought to impress him. She pulled a rolled paper from her sleeve, feeling rather like the cat in the cream. She had the duke's total attention, but she tilted her body to make sure William Bradshaw didn't see or ask awkward questions, and felt her mouth quirk into a sly grin.

Charles glanced from the paper to her face and back, eyes wide, and took what she offered, unrolling it across the table. "You made a copy," he murmured. "Of course you did—brilliant woman that you are."

Her insides warmed under his praise. Whatever else lay between them, that moment of shared partnership gave her strength. She would carry it with her.

Charles read the letter in silence while she examined him. He may have cleaned up, but even the remains of his walnut stain didn't disguise the dark patches under his eyes nor the underlying pallor. She longed to check his bandages, but she knew he wouldn't permit that. They best conclude their business quickly so he could seek his rest.

He reached the end with a shaking head. "I've never seen so much wisdom and ignorance in a single document before."

"There is much you and I might agree with," she commented.

"And more, he simply doesn't understand or at least woefully underestimates. Do you have any idea how he plans to send this?"

"Peters and I think he will publish it as an open letter and perhaps send it to Elliot."

"She'll never receive it," Charles declared. "Palmerston will see it suppressed in England—if it gets that far."

Zambak's mouth curled into a smile of feigned innocence. She waved the letter in front of him, rolled it back up, and tucked it into her sleeve. "Perhaps I will have tea with Her Majesty when we return, being of an age as we are and sharing some history."

Charles didn't try to control his amusement. "Lady Zambak Hayden causes an international incident. I can see the broadsheets now."

She shook her head, suddenly serious. "Victoria is too wise to overturn apple carts. She needs to know this, though, and not have all her information filtered by men. They all try to marginalize her and act as if decisions about her marriage ought to be her primary concern."

His eyes bore into hers until she broke eye contact. "Tell me about your little adventure. What did you see?" She could hear the note of resentment in her voice and refused to regret it. He already knew she longed to prowl Canton at his side. She picked up the pen and raised a brow. "Begin at the beginning."

He did. Watchtowers and fortified buildings, wealthy homes and temples came to life in the words she recorded. She no longer thought of the journal as hers alone. By the time he described the troops pouring out of the Five Story Pagoda, she had no thought for anything but his story.

"Again, Charles. How much opium did you see being delivered?"

He estimated tons.

"A king's ransom in one warehouse! It has to be a tempting target for corrupt officials," she observed.

"Perhaps, but so far Lin does not appear to be one. In any case, it is still a small fraction of what exists."

"We're hearing in the clinic that he demanded the western traders turn over their stores," she told him.

Neither voiced the thought they shared: would Elliot support that edict?

"One more thing," he said. "When night fell, I watched the lighthouse minaret flash a signal."

"For the boats?"

"The Five Story Pagoda repeated it and then flashed a slightly different one. The Chinese have a sophisticated signaling system."

She noted it, impressed. "What else happened?" she asked. "I want to know all of it." He rushed through the end of his story, making light of his abandonment and the attack. When he finished, she read what she recorded out loud, "An alert soldier saw through the Duke of Murnane's disguise and attempted to arrest him for violating the ban on Westerners inside the city walls. His Grace fought off his attacker but suffered a severe knife wound in the process."

"That detail is hardly necessary," he complained.

"I wrote what I wrote," she retorted, closing the book. A brief moment of accord passed between them before she asked softly, "What now, Charles? If we're to have any hope of impacting policy regarding opium, we need to deliver this as soon as can be. You must see that."

He opened his mouth, but she raised a silencing hand. "Don't argue," she said. "There's more. I need to get Thorn out of here before he sinks back into the vice, or gets caught up in Lin's nets."

"Don't assume you know what I think. I agree with you. We've seen enough. Also—" he cleared his throat.

What now? A sick feeling pooled in her stomach at his expression.

"Oliver wants us gone. Between us, we've done damage to his hard-won reputation as a respecter of Chinese law. Now that he knows you refused to stay hidden"—she sputtered, but he rushed on—"and he discovered my little foray into the city, he is furious with us. He has a packet ready to sail to Macao on the morning tide. The two of us are to be on it."

"And Thorn," she said, relieved to have the matter settled.

"And Thorn," he agreed.

"Back to corsets and Clara Elliot for me," she sighed. Something in his expression alerted her. She sat up straight. *There has to be more.*

"Mrs. Elliot may be unhappy with you," he said choosing his words too carefully for her peace of mind.

"She'll frown on my little escapade, I am certain," she responded.

"At least that. Perhaps more. Julia has been fanning the flames, dropping hints about the two of us, I suspect, while garnering pity for herself as an abused wife."

"That's what Dan came to tell you? I thought you had an agreement with her." Zambak frowned ferociously. *Is there no end to that woman's mischief?*

"She lives to betray—and I suspect Jarratt made her a better offer. He likes his revenge served cold."

"We need to remove ourselves from Macao as well, don't we?"

"Yes. I'll arrange passage to London for you and your brother as soon as we arrive there," he promised.

"What about you?"

"Julia and I will sail separately."

Separately. A dozen arguments leapt to mind, but a mask of stone had come over his face. Her heart sank to her shoes; the wall he built between them could not be breached.

Chapter 28

Darkness lay over the harbor when Charles rolled the blood-stained silk robe, tied it with cords, and strapped it to his kit bag. He had come to Canton with little. He would take that and the robe out. A sleepless night with only his throbbing arm to distract him from thoughts of Zambak left him wrung out.

He found his *faux* valet—Mr. Jones—a sullen-looking Thorn, and a sternly disapproving William Bradshaw at the harbor entrance to the factory. Zambak would leave the same way she had come, as Jones, a sailor's cap pulled over her hair. They would try to maintain the pretense at least until they passed the Chinese fortresses where the river narrowed.

She cropped her hair again. It won't endear her to Clara Elliot. I'll have to lock her in my cabin.

Bradshaw hefted a battered sea chest. Charles assumed it contained Zambak's treasured Manchu dresses.

At a pointed look from Bradshaw, Thorn picked up his kit bag. "Don't you have servants to carry luggage?" he grumbled.

"Normally," Bradshaw muttered.

"What do you mean?" Charles asked.

"The Chinese servants disappeared overnight," Zambak told him, her mouth set in grim lines. "A rather ominous sign, I think."

Thorn growled something insulting. Bradshaw caught Charles's eyes, the two men in silent agreement. The sooner he got the Hayden siblings out of Canton, the better. There seemed no reason for further speech.

The four of them trudged toward the docks in the dawning light only to encounter a knot of seamen in a heated discussion, the captain of the Oliver and Company packet among them.

"Problem, Captain?" Bradshaw asked.

"You could say. The Chinese have blocked the river. No ships in or out."

The surly faces in the crowd of men left little doubt about the seriousness of the situation. "We could run it, if Elliot hadn't forced the armed vessels back to Macao," an American said angrily.

"Have they given a reason?" Charles asked.

"Not to us," another—obviously English—said, spitting on the ground. "Dirt under their feet we are. Someone needs to teach these heathens some respect."

"Mr. Bradshaw, I suggest Mr. Jones accompany Lord Glenaire back to Oliver and Company. Perhaps you and I can find more information at the consulate or the East India Company premises."

Bradshaw nodded. "Dan headed over there earlier," he replied. "I'll go with you."

You might have told me that sooner. Charles swallowed his retort.

"I'm not going to be sent back to Zion's Quarter like some choir boy. I'm going to the Company factory," Thorn insisted, turning on his heels in that direction.

"Jones!" Charles snapped. "You will wait for me at Oliver's factory." He glared at Zambak who too obviously looked prepared to follow her brother. *The fewer people who notice her wandering about the better.*

"His lordship may have need of me, Your Grace," she responded.

He heard muttering among the seamen. "Damned titles and strutting aristocrats . . ."

"You will escort me to Zion's Quarter, Mr. Jones, and I'll brook no opposition," he repeated through clenched teeth. As badly as he wanted to search out Dan Oliver, he wanted Zambak off the parade ground more. Thorn strode halfway across the open space while they stood their ground: Charles determined and Zambak defiant.

"We'll lose him," she hissed.

"Better him than you," he retorted under his breath. "Captain, I will thank you to see my luggage stowed aboard until we can sail. Mr. Bradshaw, you will let me know what you discover, will you not? And please escort Lord Glenaire back to the factory." Neither American looked pleased to be ordered about by an English duke, but they didn't argue.

Stepping away, he addressed Zambak in a furious whisper. "You cannot parade your female self around outside. You know that—and that disguise of yours fools few. We're in enough trouble."

"We need to keep Thorn in hand," she stormed back.

"I can't handle both of you at once if you're going to be defiant. Move quickly before we entertain the waterfront with the image of a duke taking his valet by the arm."

"If I go back to Zion's Quarter, will you go after Thorn?"

"That's what I intended, damn it Zambak. Of course it is. Use that magnificent mind of yours for a moment."

She took several steps before she gave in. "Yes. Do it," she answered in clipped tones.

When he reached the Company headquarters, he found the Marquess of Glenaire to be the least of his problems, even when he found him in conversation with Jarratt's Canton manager.

"No one's going anywhere, your lordship," Charles heard the man growl. "Not into the city. Not onto the boats."

Charles gave the boy a hard look. "Follow me. We'll get to the bottom of this," he said, turning on his best ducal voice. "They can't force us to stay here." He wished he believed that, but Thorn at least accepted his tone of authority and followed him.

"You're right. The Company ought to accept—" Charles ignored the rant about privilege that followed, making a bee line for Oliver and the other senior officials.

Dan Oliver paled at the sight of him. "I hoped you got out before the blockade," he said. "Bradshaw tells me otherwise. Where is . . .?

"My valet? Back at Zion's Quarter." Oliver's shoulders sagged in relief. "What has happened?" Charles went on.

Jarratt's minion had followed him. "Lin demands we turn over our opium," he said.

"We knew that," Charles answered. "What has changed?"

"We're under siege," Oliver told him.

"The servants have all disappeared, the river has been blockaded, and supplies have been cut off until we submit and hand over all our opium," the East India Company man explained.

"How long can we hold out?"

Oliver glanced at Thorn. "That depends on how careful we are.

"You have no opium, Dan. Doesn't Lin make an exception?" Charles asked.

"So far, no," the American said, "but individual demands are reaching each factory. I need to get back to Zion's Quarter. Your "valet" may be there when demands arrive." He studied Charles, waiting for his meaning to sink in.

Lin may attack Oliver for Zambak's presence. Worse he may demand— Charles shuddered to think what the high commissioner could demand.

~ ~ ~

Zambak listened to Peters read the decree in flat tones. She had reverted to the Manchu dress rather than watch the Americans squirm uncomfortably over a woman in breeches, and scurried to Dan Oliver's private office to find them about to start without her.

"The High Commissioner holds Oliver and Company in great 'esteem' for want of a better word," Peters translated, while Dan, Bradshaw, and their troublesome guests crowded around the captain's desk.

"But?" Oliver prodded.

"Friendship with, . . . hmm" With no Chinese staff remaining, Peters had no help. He murmured the Chinese word out loud.

"Barbarians, I believe," Zambak put in.

"Yes. Barbarians, I suppose. He says we allowed friendship with barbarians to cloud our vision. He calls on Hong—he means merchant—Oliver to reject lawlessness and expel lawbreakers from his premises." The doctor's expression sagged even as his pallor deepened.

"What is it, Peters? What does he want?" Charles demanded.

"He asks Dan to hand over the English lawbreakers that he shelters so that he can . . ." He scanned the message once again and then twice. "Judge—or perhaps correct—their behavior."

Zambak spoke over thickness gathering in her throat. "What is the punishment for westerners who violate the ban on entering the city walls?"

"Banishment," Oliver said.

She took a relieved breath. "And the presence of a woman?"

"More complicated. No one has tried it. I would have expected him to call me on the carpet for allowing it. The crime would be mine in his eyes, I should think," Dan Oliver told her.

"Do they execute women?" she asked, looking from Peters to Bradshaw and back to Oliver.

Peters shrugged. "I haven't heard of it happening, but that doesn't mean they wouldn't."

"The logical thing then, is for me to obey the summons while His Grace remains here," Zambak said.

"No!" Charles shouted.

"My lady—" Oliver began at the same time.

"Did you hear me? There is risk," Peter's said. "We can't let a woman put herself in that position."

"I am willing to take that risk. Besides, I will learn a great deal if I go. It is my life and my decision to make."

"Zambak Hayden, you cannot——" Charles began.

"You have no right to order me, Charles. My decision. I will go. We owe it to Oliver and Company to help them redeem themselves in the commissioner's eyes."

Silent communication passed between Oliver and his colleagues. "It will certainly help us if it goes well," Dan Oliver said. "Are you certain, my lady?" Peters watched anxiously; Bradshaw studied the floor.

"Certain," she reiterated.

"Then I go too." Charles glared at her; she glared back, equally determined. *Stubborn man.*

"Your Grace! There is no guarantee that banishment is the only—" Peters sputtered.

"I need no guarantee. She isn't going alone."

"Charles, isn't it better if one of us stays back?" she said, as sweetly as she could muster.

His stormy blue eyes bore into hers. "You aren't going alone. It is my life and my decision to make."

He's thrown my words back in my face. Cow shite. She had no argument to dissuade him. They would face the commissioner together.

Chapter 29

Lin's messenger, as it turned out, waited for Oliver and Company's reply at the front gate. Within an hour, he returned with an escort and what Peters assured them amounted to promises of safety for the woman. Charles kept his skepticism to himself. Zambak dressed as a Manchu lady but could do little with her hair. The white blond, entirely un-Chinese curls, blessedly short, responded to Canton's air with unruly enthusiasm, flying about her head. Charles dressed as an English gentleman ought, albeit, given the choices available in such a place, with considerably less grandeur than he might have worn to greet the Duke of Sudbury. Peters, Oliver, and Bradshaw watched them go, unable to disguise the concern in their eyes.

Charles positioned himself just behind Zambak's left shoulder, marching in step. He didn't understand her greeting to their escort, but the gentleman in court dress responded. The two large, armed guards on either side did not. He expected to be led to the Five Story Pagoda or other garrisoned building, so when they were taken instead to the compound of Yuen-hua Academy—which he had assumed to be merely Lin's residence—he wondered again about the man who had summoned them.

He can whack off heads in a schoolyard as well as a parade ground, he reminded himself.

After marching them through a sunny courtyard lined with cypress and dotted with artfully placed sculpture, their guard brought them what appeared to be an academic assembly room hastily repurposed into an audience chamber of sorts. A group stood between them and the dais, three well-dressed gentlemen with chains ominously around their necks. He tilted his head forward to listen to Zambak's whispered translations. "They are waiting for—" A glower from their escort silenced her, and she bowed her head respectfully. Charles would have laughed if the stakes had been less high. *Theater, remember. She said theater.*

After several excruciating moments, a door opened up behind him, and a man came down the middle of the room surrounded by an honor guard, his pace stately and somber. Commissioner Lin Zexu appeared to be of middling height, only an inch or two taller than Charles, but he exuded confidence and power beyond his size. He had the gently rotund shape of a jovial grandfather, but no one would mistake his expression for anything other than sober. The men in front of them dropped to their knees when he mounted the dais and touched their foreheads to the carpeted floor, once, twice—three times. Witnessing the famous Chinese kowtow for the first time, Charles wondered in a panic if they were meant to do the same thing, but Lin's attention appeared to be entirely on the men in front of him. "Opium den operators," Zambak hissed.

Lin made short work of the trial, if that is what it was, barking a reprimand, and—judging from what appeared to be desperate begging—passing sentence. Guards dragged them out the door. One wept openly.

Lin raised his eyes, and Charles felt it cut through him. After a second's hesitation, Zambak dropped to her knees and made a perfect imitation of the kowtow she had witnessed. *Theater.* Charles made a spilt-second decision to stay erect. Instead, he gave Lin a perfect court bow, exactly as he might to the queen. He wondered whether the brief flicker of surprise that crossed Lin's face owed more to her obeisance or his refusal. With a hand gesture, the commissioner summoned an official to stand behind him. He then barked an order, and the man, apparently a translator, said in heavily accented English, "The lady may rise."

She stood, head bowed. "The High Commissioner wishes the names of those who flout our laws," the translator pronounced. Charles didn't wait for Zambak. "I am His Grace Charles Emery Wheatly, the Duke of Murnane. This woman is Lady Zambak Hayden, daughter of His Grace, the Duke of Sudbury." It was almost perfectly correct, insofar as a duke could introduce himself.

Her lips twitched. *She probably wants to tell me not to lay it on so thick.*

"Duke is a high official?" the translator asked.

This time she was ahead of him. "Second only to the Queen, my lord," she said in English and then went on in Cantonese.

Lin wrinkled his brow and conferred with his translator, puzzling Charles. "Official proceedings take place in Mandarin as is proper. The High Commissioner orders that we speak English or Mandarin. The lady's common Cantonese will not do," the translator said smugly.

Zambak bowed her head.

Lin spoke again. "Does this English duke know barbarians are forbidden inside the city walls?" He glared at Charles while his minion translated.

Charles breathed in. "I have been informed of that belatedly. I apologize that my curiosity and desire to learn about your ways drove me to break the rules. I understand that the commissioner, a man of great learning, often wishes to gather information about our ways as well." He looked directly at Lin, whose eyes glittered, though whether with amusement or anger, Charles could not say.

"The commissioner asks if there are no books in your country."

Charles smiled at that. "My private library has ten thousand volumes. What few I have about China were written by Englishmen. How accurate can they possibly be?"

The translator earnestly murmured in the great man's ear. *Amused this time, no question.* Charles felt like he had successfully negotiated through trial by ordeal.

"Why does a big-footed western woman dare pollute Canton?" the translator demanded.

Zambak waited until Lin indicated with a gesture that she should answer for herself. "My beloved brother became a slave of the opium poppy. My desire was merely to find him and free him. In doing so, I was caught up in activity that brought me here. Intruding on Canton was never my intent."

Again, a flurry of talk on the dais. Lin sat upright and made a pronouncement. "The High Commissioner has been told that the lady assisted in the clinic of Doctor Peters with the poor souls who wish to free themselves from opium. Is this true?"

"Yes, my lord," Zambak said, head high now.

"The Commissioner says further that your presence is an insult and against the law."

"I regret—"

The interpreter cut her off. "You will not speak! You have broken our law, but the Mandate of Heaven can be merciful in its justice. Commissioner Lin permits the merchant Daniel Oliver to expel you from Canton and transport you to Macao where you belong."

Zambak bowed murmuring thanks.

"As to the duke," he went on speaking only to Zambak. "We are merciful to fools as well. He may go with you." She bowed again, and this time Charles did as well.

"Thank God," he breathed. He took a step backward, assuming they were dismissed and prepared to back out of the room as they might in the queen's presence.

"One more thing. The commissioner wishes to know how it is the lady speaks Cantonese."

"I listen, my lord," she replied. "I listen, watch, and learn. It is a gift I share with my esteemed mother."

Good point. It never hurts to invoke one's honored parents.

The commissioner spoke directly to the translator who said something to their escort in rapid Chinese, Lin made a dismissive gesture, and they did indeed back out. When they got to the outer courtyard, however, the escort pulled Zambak aside, separating her from Charles. When he tried to follow, the guards pulled him back. "What is it?" he called.

"The commissioner wishes to speak with me," she said over her shoulder, looking bemused. She disappeared into a side door, leaving him in the sunny courtyard, alone except for a guard brandishing a vicious-looking sword.

"What do we do now? Wait?" The guard responded with a fierce glare. "Wait. Right." He stared helplessly at the door through which she disappeared.

Chapter 30

Lin at his ease gave a very different impression than Lin in command. He rested on a divan in a sunny room filled with flowers and the odor of cinnamon and nutmeg. He had not changed his robes, yet his appearance shifted subtly from stiff to comfortable. As Zambak entered the room, servants brought tea and almond cakes and bowed to the commissioner. Here, in what Zambak could only guess were private quarters, there was no kowtow. No translator appeared, and her escort withdrew to a far corner.

No theater then.

"Sit, lady, and try the tea. It is my personal blend. Very fine," Lin said in perfect Cantonese.

Zambak followed the lead of his servants and bowed at the waist before accepting a porcelain cup, so thin as to be translucent and without handles in the Chinese style. She sniffed scents of jasmine and undercurrents she could not identify. He had not lied. The exquisite taste teased her palette gently, lingered, and satisfied.

"My mother would be delighted with this blend, my lord," she said.

He nodded, obviously pleased but, she thought, not so easily flattered. "Tell me about your mother," he requested. She did, relating the Duchess of Sudbury's childhood as an ambassador's daughter and wife of a powerful force in the Foreign Ministry. She did not exaggerate in her description of diplomatic dinners at Sudbury House in London.

"The Duchess, your mother—she is a member of the court?" he asked.

How does his idea of court differ from ours? she wondered. She answered him truthfully in spite of qualms he might not understand the impact of politics on the queen.

"She served our previous queen, my lord, but Queen Victoria prefers to have ladies of the Whig party serve her." *Much to Mama's relief. She respected Queen Adelaide but has no desire to pamper Victoria nor cater to her whims.*

Lin frowned, but nodded sagely. "There are always factions. Your father is not in power?"

Papa claims he belongs to the Party of Good Sense but can't escape nominal identification with the Conservatives. It doesn't stop him from sticking his spoon in when the Whigs are in power. How to explain all that to Lin? Better not to. "I believe my father prefers to exercise his influence behind the scenes."

"Wise man." She thought his respect might be sincere.

The breadth of Lin's conversation astonished her. His questions ranged from cotton manufactories to the government in Calcutta to the state of English roads and railroad development, confirming the rumors he read European books and newspapers.

Zambak sat as she had been trained to do, upright, back not touching the chair back, and nibbled almond biscuits with well-learned ladylike manners while replying with the force of a mind some considered unfeminine. Lin didn't object. His questions became more pointed, and her responses and opinions sharpened.

They came at last to what Zambak suspected was his true goal in this meeting. "What is the power of your superintendent of trade?" he asked.

She answered as truthfully as she could. Elliot had been appointed by Palmerston, the foreign minister, to insure the free flow of tea back to England. She explained, patiently, the chain of command from Elliot to the foreign minister to the prime minister. She hesitated. In Lin's world, the prime minister then reported to the queen who held all power. The letter to Victoria made it painfully clear the high commissioner didn't and couldn't understand the differences.

"And so he has command over these opium smugglers?"

Less than he would like. Lin must know he had been able to order the gunboats from the river, but his power to do so was tenuous. "Not directly," she answered, "But somewhat."

He shook his head back and forth. "Poor policy," he said. "What do you think of this man?"

For a moment, being asked for such opinion by the great man left her stunned. He deserved an honest answer.

"He is a man of conscience, my lord. A former naval officer who knows his duty. He was sent to supervise the tea trade but has no sympathy with the opium smugglers. He urges the government to stop them."

"Urges, but has no power to act." He held her eyes, this man of action, his opinion of a man who could not act in the face of evil all too clear without speaking. She made no reply.

"You may return to the Oliver factory now. Do not leave it, even to visit the other westerners. We will send documents of safe passage to Macao for you, this duke of yours, and your brother."

Zambak stood and bowed, hands at her waist, as she had seen others do. "Thank you for your kindness, my lord," she said, and then she looked up at him again. "If I may be so bold, one other thing about Charles Elliot."

He waited patiently for her to speak.

"He considers it his primary duty to protect English interests here. If he thinks England or the trade in tea is threatened, he will act."

Black eyes met ice blue. He understood. She bowed again and withdrew.

And God help us if Elliot does act, she thought, backing to the door.

~ ~ ~

Lin's promised safe passage did not arrive the next day or the one after that. Trapped in Oliver and Company's premises and anxious to get back to Macao to deal with Julia, Charles prowled the upper floors until Oliver told him to stay out of the offices so he could get work done.

Thorn's presence didn't help. When the lack of servants and embargo on incoming supplies made life in any of the factories uncomfortable, he had been lured back by the promise of safe passage to Macao. He sat in the dining area as bored and frustrated as Charles. He considered learning to make his own tea, there being no Chinese servants, but had not yet done so.

Even Thorn's presence couldn't banish the visions of Zambak—some real, some imagined, some wildly erotic— that haunted him in his enforced inactivity. The two of them hadn't spoken since they returned to the factory and she gave him a summary of her odd interview before disappearing downstairs and leaving him to record it in their journal. She had moved back into a cubbyhole near the clinic, far from the guest corridor, avoiding him as much as she could. Pacing failed to banish his unruly thoughts, and he eventually gave in to the need to check on her. He thought perhaps reality would push the worst erotic images aside.

When Charles went below stairs, he found Zambak covered in a stained apron assisting an opium patient in the throws of cramps and upset. That put period to romantic imagery but filled him with respect and warmth, which were in their own way worse.

She looked up from where she held a basin over which the man heaved. "Charles! Make yourself useful. There is clean water over there. Dampen a rag for me." She indicated the dresser with her head. "Have we heard from the high commissioner?"

"No, I just came to check on you," he replied, doing as she asked.

She wiped her patient's face and laid him back on his cot shaking uncontrollably. "Bored, Charles? We could use your help. You're the one with sickroom experience."

"Not like this," he sighed. "So much human misery."

"Better to alleviate what I can than to sit and wait," she told him.

"True enough. Work might help your irritable brother as well," he added, taking the basin from her. "Where do I empty this?"

She told him, but he paused in the doorway. "Do you think Lin really intends to give us passage documents?"

"He's a man of his word, so yes. He will use the timing to his advantage, however," she replied.

"While punishing a felon who trespassed," he muttered as he wandered off with the foul-smelling basin.

Charles worked in the clinic for almost four hours after Zambak left to speak to her brother. When asked, Peters had plenty of tasks to assign to a willing duke; they became increasingly unpleasant as the good doctor came to believe in that willingness. Charles had a particular affinity for the children, even fretful ones, and Peters seemed happy to turn them over to him to free up orderlies to deal with the flood of opium patients who continued to beg for help.

A clock ticking toward execution is a great motivator, Charles thought, watching another fall weeping through the door.

One small girl burned with fever, the result of an operation to remove a tooth abscess. The clinic deemed her unready to return home, and her mother, burdened with six other children, left her in their care. Charles worked steadily with cool, wet cloths to keep the fever down. Checking his watch, he prepared another tisane of willow bark, slid an arm behind the child, and began the tedious task of coaxing, cajoling, and convincing her to down it all. Ignorance of Cantonese words posed a difficulty, but he found tone of voice—augmented by funny faces—to be a universal language for children.

He laid her back, leaned over, and bumped his nose to hers, eliciting enough of a giggle to warm his heart. When he reached over to put the empty cup on a table, he sucked in a breath. Zambak, standing primly in the doorway, her apron over her arm, studied him gravely. Her eyes hazy with moisture gave his heart a pang.

"What is it?" he asked.

"Oliver has called for us."

He stood and pulled down the sleeves of his shirt. "Safe passage at last?"

She shook her head. Her eyes followed his hands when he fastened the neck. "Something else I think. It doesn't sound good."

He buttoned his waistcoat and slipped into his coat. "Whatever it is, let us face it together." The flare of something in her eyes warmed him, though he couldn't be certain what he saw.

~ ~ ~

I ogled him like a common trollop. The thought echoed all the way up the stairs to the door to Oliver's office. The sight of the duke's gentleness with the child squeezed her heart until warmth spread through her body and robbed her of speech. When he rose, she couldn't take her eyes off his hands and the expanse of skin revealed by his rolled-up shirtsleeves or the place where his shirt opened at the neck. The memory sent the heat soaring. Now she felt one of those hands against the small of her back urging her forward.

How will I concentrate on what Oliver has to say? She needn't have worried. What he had to say drove all other concerns aside. The trader didn't mince words. He sat back in his captain's chair behind the worn wooden desk and spat it out. "Lin wants Dean. No promise of safety. In fact, a request for a guarantee of his safety has been summarily refused."

"I beg your pardon? Why?" she demanded. "He treated us well enough." They took seats across from him.

"Your crimes didn't rise to the level of opium smuggling. They've all had a week to turn over their opium stores, and they have either ignored the edict or, as in the case of Dean, outright refused."

"He means to execute him," she whispered. Memory of the summary execution of the men in the audience hall for opium related offences distressed her. *If Lin executes an Englishman . . .*

"What response has been made?" Charles asked.

"Dean's company sent back an insulting message," Oliver told them, disgust filling his words. He waved his ever-present pipe when he gestured.

"That won't help!" Zambak said.

"No, it will not. The East India Company has sent a request to negotiate." Oliver shrugged. "Lin doesn't seem to be in a conciliatory mood."

"He wants to make an example of one of them. It was bound to come to down to Dean or Jarratt." She rubbed her middle finger with her left thumb, staring down at the desk. The silence that met her comment alerted her. She glanced up. "What?" she demanded at the looks on their faces.

"Why do you say that?" Oliver appeared genuinely interested.

"Jarratt or Dean? They are the worst of the lot." She looked from face to face finding no disagreement, though she doubted the Americans would have given voice to it.

"What did you mean about Lin?" Bradshaw asked.

"Lin does not act according to 'mood.' His commission is to eradicate the opium and the trade in it. He takes action, yes, but not impulsively. He lays out a strategy and follows it inexorably forward. He wants the opium stores. He will get them one way or the other. At least he believes so. He would execute Dean and then ask for another."

Oliver sank back in his well-worn desk chair and sighed deeply. "Two more American firms have publicly renounced the trade and turned over their stores. The Scots and English are relying on your navy to protect their 'assets' and force opium down the Chinese throats."

Shame washed through her, shame for her country. She caught Charles's eyes.

"Have you no influence, Your Grace?" Bradshaw asked.

"Some, but in England, not here. There the lady's father has even more. The anti-opium forces need ammunition, however, and we're no help here. We need to get our reports to London before it's too late."

The bleak cloud in his eyes told Zambak he believed it was already too late. *He's probably right, but we have to try.*

"What of you, Dan? Are you still in danger of his wrath?" she asked.

"I think not. Turning you over apparently put us back in his good graces." Oliver colored up at that. They all knew the decision to comply had been Zambak's. Not one of the men would have turned her over.

"That and the clinic," she replied. "He knows the value of what Alexander Peters does."

"Still no word about safe passage, though, and it grows more urgent every day." Burdened with misery, Charles's voice sounded harsh.

"I suspect he will wait until the matter with Dean is settled before he lets even one ship out," Oliver said.

The weight growing in Zambak's chest threatened to flatten her. She reached out a hand toward Charles for strength, caught herself, and pulled it back.

"He will not be moved from his purpose," she said.

"What about Elliot?" Charles asked. "Have you heard any word?"

"Still at Whampao last I heard—or perhaps Macao." Oliver paused and chewed the stem of his pipe before he continued. "I believe Commissioner Lin may have sent a message to him."

Charles rolled his eyes before shooting her a worried glance. "Rook to Queen Four. Your move, Captain Elliot."

Chapter 31

"Come quickly! You have to see this." After three days of uneasy waiting, Bradshaw's rare appearance in the clinic received instant attention. Charles laid the sleeping child he had been rocking on her cot, followed without question, and ran up the stairs after Zambak. Thorn, torn from his concentration on paperwork Zambak had given him to complete, joined them. Elliot had come.

They met Oliver on the roof. A pinnace, small but under sail, had been allowed inside the blockade. Though intended merely as a ferry between ship and shore, this one had been fitted with mast and pole; the Union Jack flapped above it. Even from their vantage point at a distance and high above the harbor, it spoke of Britain's might.

Oliver handed his spyglass to Zambak who expertly focused it. "Dear God!" she gasped and handed it to Charles.

The figure of a man came into focus. Elliot, erect at the bow, sailed into Canton in his full dress navy uniform, decorations gleaming in the sun, his expression grim. The power of empire had arrived, and he made sure everyone knew it.

"Well. The man has courage, I'll give him that," Oliver said.

"That he does. Pray God he has wisdom as well," Charles answered.

"Queen takes rook, I think," Zambak said. "I hope he has an end game planned. He'll go to the consulate first."

Charles handed the telescope to Zambak. "I don't want

to miss this. I'll meet him there." She failed to meet his eyes. "Zambak—"

He followed her to the stairs, ran the last few steps, and pulled her to face him. "Don't even think about it. Lin ordered you to stay inside." She looked ready to object, but they both knew Charles hadn't been included in that particular demand.

"As always, you are free, and I am not," she said raising her chin defiantly. "Go quickly. Miss nothing."

At a loss how to respond, he groped for words, but she caught him off guard, covering his mouth with a kiss as passionate as it was brief. "For luck. Be careful, Charles. Come back and tell me what you learn."

Chapter 32

The irritating man has been gone for over three hours. How long does it take Elliot to perform his act in this drama?

Zambak could not resist glancing at the clock in the corner of the clinic whenever she passed through the main room. She managed—just—to keep from darting out every few moments to check. Their beds were now full, and all hands needed.

And blast you, Commissioner Lin, for taking our Chinese helpers when we needed them most. She paused at the thought, damp rag in a hand that hovered above a patient. *Perhaps, given his general attitude toward Oliver and Company, he might make an exception for the clinic?*

She made a mental note to ask Dan Oliver—whenever he and Charles returned—and went back to her work, mulling the impact of such a request on Dan's already strained relationship with the other traders.

Moments later she decided to check on Thorn—and the time. She had put him to work transcribing Peter's notes and editing the doctor's articles for *The Chinese Repository*, the missionary journal. His restlessness hadn't abated, but work addressed his boredom. His pride in drafting a particularly complex report gave her hope.

She found him outside the office, staring at a man who had been carried to the clinic by his frantic family on a stretcher. The patient had gone into convulsions just as they arrived, and one of the orderlies had taken over his care. She spoke briefly with the family, who conceded they would allow his sister, a slip of a girl fourteen or so, to help with his care. She spoke to the girl with as much confidence as she could muster, but the wide eyes looked no less frightened when she followed the orderly and the now-resting patient down the hall.

"Did I do that?" Thorn rasped.

"Convulse? A few times," she murmured.

"Wouldn't it be better to allow him to continue using the opium?" he said.

"Then he will cease to live long before he actually dies, but die he will even without Lin's threats. No. It isn't an option." Her eyes bore into him.

"You have no idea . . ." he began.

"You forget—I watched. I have every idea, and some you choose to ignore, like the impact of watching a loved one throw his life away. I planned your funeral while I watched you. Twice. Did you know that?"

He blinked at her but didn't respond to her comment. She studied him closely, noting that his color had improved in recent days, which was not to say he looked healthy. He had put on a few pounds, though, and for that she was grateful. Watching the family scurry to the door, his ashen complexion paled further.

One of the seamen drafted as orderlies ran up and whispered to Peters. "They're back, my lady," the doctor told her.

She tossed her apron before he finished his sentence and ran for the stairs. She was half way up before she realized Thorn had followed.

"Do you think he'll let us go now?" he asked.

"Now? Maybe. Maybe not."

She skittered into the doorway of Oliver's office. "Well?"

~ ~ ~

It took all Charles's self control to keep from pulling her into his arms and swinging her around in front of all of them. They had won.

"Elliot called all merchants sailing under the Union Jack and ordered them to give up their stores," Oliver said.

Zambak's eyes widened. Charles saw the moment she caught the problem. "Will they do it?" she asked.

"They'll make a show of it. Jarratt has so much stored at Lin-tin Island and Whampao, even a quarter would impress the commissioner's men."

"Of course, and if they attempt to use what they hold back, we'll be right back where we are. I assume Elliot just wants to break the blockade and get tea flowing back to England for this year with as little fuss as possible."

"That and save Dean's worthless hide," Oliver spat. "Most of them have enough silver for this year's trade. They will lay low with their stockpiles of opium until they need more."

"So, is it over?" Thorn asked.

"Not quite." Oliver glanced up at Charles. "Elliot refused to hand Dean over."

Charles breathed in for strength and explained the rest. "Lin sent back a renewed demand for Dean. Elliot refused again. He quoted 'extraterritoriality.'"

"He's demanding the right to deal with our own citizens and denying they are subject to local law." Zambak wasn't asking a question; she understood the concept well.

"Correct," Charles said. "The entire company cheered. He essentially promised to shield them all from Chinese law." He watched her face. The analytical engine that was her mind spun rapidly. "What are you thinking?"

"Elliot has found a stable platform he can stand on. Opium bothered his conscience, but protecting Englishmen is his birthright and his duty as a naval officer. He won't be moved on this any more than Lin will be moved on ending the opium trade."

Dan sighed. "I feared as much. No negotiating those two positions. Between clerks and jack tars all over the delta, there is bound to be more of this. Sooner or later, Lin will have an English lawbreaker in his court, and it will blow up in our faces."

"Has Lin responded again?" she asked.

"Yes. We waited for it. That's what took so long. He informed Elliot he had already judged two of her majesty's subjects—one of them a duke—and chosen to be merciful," Charles told her.

"Oh dear."

"Indeed. Elliot was fit to be tied. When we submitted to Chinese law, we undermined his sense of rightness in the world. I'm afraid we're *persona non grata* at the moment, particularly because Lin sent along safe passage documents specifically for 'the Lady Zambak, her brother, and the Duke of Murnane.' Elliot demanded to know what we told the commissioner."

She ignored that last part. "Do you have them?"

He pulled a sheaf of paper from his coat and feared for a moment she would throw herself in his arms. The effort to control the urge appeared to push her into full duchess mode.

"Well, Captain Oliver, it appears you will be free of your troublesome guests soon after all. How quickly can you arrange passage?" she asked, chin high.

Oliver ignored her haughty tone of voice. "Done, my lady. You have two hours to prepare."

Not that we have much to pack . . .

"We're leaving? Thank God," Thorn burst out. "But poor Dean."

"I suspect that when the opium flows into his warehouse, the commissioner will forget about Dean," Oliver said, and Zambak agreed.

"Lin will have a fortune stored. He'll probably share the profits with the emperor in Peking, but still—" Thorn whistled.

Zambak wheeled on her brother. "He'll do no such thing! He is a man of integrity. Mark my words. He'll destroy the lot."

"Not one man—present company excepted—who attended Elliot's meeting believes that," Charles said.

"They judge him by their own greed and malleable ethics. They are wrong. Elliot understands that much at least. I hope," she replied.

"He probably does," Charles said, "but I'm not sure it matters in the end."

Charles followed Zambak and her brother down the stairs closely enough to overhear Thorn say, "Zamb, I hope you are right about Lin. Opium is harming people." Charles wondered if the boy really believed that. *If he does, how long will he remember it?*

~ ~ ~

They left Canton on Oliver's river packet, *Swan's Journey*, under cover of darkness, endured a few tense moments while a Chinese captain scanned their safe-passage documents with ill-concealed disdain, and sailed downriver away from the blockade. They employed no river pilot, but the American crew knew the route well.

Her brother grumbled at being kept from sleep and wandered below to seek a bed. The adventure of it zinged through Zambak's veins; she hurried to the bow to watch their progress, Charles and the captain at her side.

"We aren't out of the woods yet, my lady," the captain murmured. With Lin's explicit mention of "the Lady Zambak," they had dropped all pretense of her disguise as the duke's valet. Dressed as a Manchu lady, she gripped the rail with a white-knuckled ferocity that unmasked her studied calm for the lie it was and stared forward. She felt a warm hand cover one of hers, and her grip relaxed. Charles stood next to her looking determinedly out at the river. Neither moved to face the other.

"We still have to sail between the cannon from the Chinese forts where the river narrows, I believe. Jarratt called them 'children's peashooters.' Was he right?" she asked.

"They aren't up to Her Majesty's ordnance, but no. I wouldn't call them toys. Chinese cannon can do serious damage. Normally they ignore our passage, but these aren't normal times. You might want to go below while we pass, my lady," the captain said.

"Not on your life. I wouldn't miss this." *And I damned well don't want to be trapped below decks if we're attacked.*

The American looked troubled.

"I promise not to get in your way should there be trouble, Captain. I can handle myself," she said, addressing his unspoken concerns. "And His Grace is more than able to manage both of us in a crisis," she added as an afterthought, drawing a glower from Charles.

"I'll leave you then," the man said with a casual salute before returning to the quarterdeck, leaving the two of them alone at the bow.

She turned back to the railing, eyes fixed on the river ahead and the banks slipping slowly by. A full moon illuminated trees and cast exotic-shaped shadows on both sides; the smell of jasmine filled the air. When Charles turned back along with her, his body shifted closer so that their shoulders touched, and his warmth burned down her side.

Moments passed in peace before his arm reached around her side and his hand covered hers where it held the railing. Moments more before her head drifted to his shoulder. When she felt his kiss on her head, she turned into his shoulder, and he pulled her closer. She breathed in sandalwood and Charles, and allowed her blood to heat.

"You're safe," he murmured.

I doubt it, Charles. Oh how I doubt it. She loved him. She knew that, if she knew little else. Her ideas about marriage left her confused, and what she knew about the wreck of his confused her more. In that moment, however, with his arm pulling her closer until she clung to him shoulder to toes she understood with perfect clarity.

Zambak raised her head so that her lips reached his ear. "Perhaps we should go below decks," she said against his skin.

He didn't pretend to misunderstand her meaning. He kissed her mouth, a salute as brief as it was sweet. "Not a good idea, Zambak. Not wise at all."

She returned his kiss open mouthed, refusing to accept his restraint. He responded with all the passion she might wish, sliding his arm lower to hold her flush against him and cupping her bottom with the other to pull her against his growing erection. He ran kisses up her cheek to repeat in her ear. "Not wise at all."

Charles lifted his head, looked around the deck, and led her into the shadow of a dingy anchored to the railing. When he knelt on the deck, she slid down beside him, and they tumbled to the floor, lying on their sides face to face locked in embrace, his arm cradling her head. One hand gently held her cheek, his thumb under her chin rubbing her mouth before his renewed kisses grew more possessive, and hers became more frantic. Her hands wandered, tugged his shirt loose, and moved to the waist of his trousers, eager to explore.

An iron grip on her wrist brought her to an abrupt halt. Charles yanked his mouth from hers, withdrew a few inches, and touched her forehead with his. "We have to stop this," he said, breathing heavily.

Zambak couldn't accept that. She sought his mouth again and wiggled up against him, eliciting a groan. He rolled to his knees and pulled her up then, tugging her silk jacket back into place.

"Don't go honorable and protective on me, Charles. I know what I want," she sputtered, grabbing his lapels and snuggling her nose into his shoulder.

"That fills me with more joy than I can explain, Zambak," he said. He stood, pulling her with him, and turned her outward to face the shore while he put his arms around her waist to hold her loosely from behind. "You aren't so naïve that you can't tell how badly I want you," he whispered in her ear.

Smug and filled with triumph, she spoke without thinking. "I know. I fear I've tumbled entirely in love with you, Charles. It is new and precious and—" She sank her head back against him. She felt safe in his arms, yet frustrated. When she wriggled free to face him, he held her at arms length, one hand on each arm.

"You don't understand what you're suggesting," he said.

"Perhaps not entirely, but I'm eager to find out. We can manage this thing between us. I know we can. For now—"

"For now, nothing. Listen to me, dear one."

Dear one. She felt her smile fill her down to her toes. She sank back on her heels and studied his face, grave in the moonlight.

"You've told me over and over again you do not wish to marry," he reminded her.

"Maybe I was wrong. I don't wish marriage as dictated by rank and land and the rest. Or maybe I don't need marriage. There's Julia in any case and—and I'm jumping ahead."

He smiled then and loosed his grip, taking a step away. "You certainly are, and I'm making a mull of it." He reached out a hand to cup her cheek. "Lady Zambak Hayden, I find that I have also tumbled into this maelstrom. I love your brilliant mind and unbounded courage. Your lovely body drives me mad, as you will have noticed. But—"

She growled deep in her throat. *Always a "but."* She put a finger to his lips, but he shook his head, and removed his hand from her face.

"Listen to me. You may not believe in marriage, but you deserve no less than my total commitment. I am a married man, who can't make his addresses with any honor."

"I thought you and Julia had an agreement," she reminded him.

"We do. But Julia's word is always questionable, making any agreement equally questionable. Divorce is tedious and difficult at best, ugly and scandal-ridden at worst. When it's done, she will have shredded my good name."

"I know you. I know better. I don't care." She didn't. She couldn't believe he'd think otherwise.

His smile held infinite sadness. "Your father will care, and your mother wants more for you than a man twelve years your senior with an ugly past."

"Piffle. Even if that is true—and I doubt it, because they know you. They know what you're made of—I am of age. They will have to accept it, because I will defy whatever they might do to stop me."

"Yes, you would," he replied with a sigh. "You defy them in many things, and it seems to fall to me to keep you out of trouble."

He reached over and took her right hand between both of his. "Very well, Lady Zambak Hayden, will you—"

She tried to throw herself into his arms, but he held her back. "Wait. Listen to what I'm asking. Will you wait for me to be free? Will you wait as long as it takes to extricate myself from my joke of a marriage so I can come to you honorably and make my offer?"

She sank back, subdued. "I don't want to wait." Stony features looked implacably back for a long moment until she gave in. "But I will if you give me no choice, because I promise you this, Charles: there is no other man but you and never will be. I love you."

His eyes bore into hers. "I won't hold you to it, Zambak, but I love you for saying it." He kissed her then—a fierce caress that battered her soul with the enormity of his feelings—stepped away and bowed. "Now I will join the crew on the quarterdeck for both our sakes, since you will not go below."

He left her in the moonlight, cold and alone, but with hope firmly set in her heart.

Chapter 33

Sudbury will have me horsewhipped. A sudden vision of Zambak taking on her father if he attempted such a thing brought a smile to his lips. Sword drawn or cannons blazing, she would take on an army to get what she wanted.

From the quarterdeck, he devoured her with his eyes, astounded he had the good sense to walk away before they entertained the crew any further than they did. He forced himself to scan the banks in a pretense of watching for the Chinese forts. Soon enough, they sailed into the narrows, and the forts came into view just as the sky lightened.

When the ship drew even with the guns, Zambak glanced back at the quarterdeck but didn't budge from her vigil at the bow. The ship moved forward unmolested.

Are they allowing all traffic, trusting in the blockade up river, or did they somehow get word to allow this particular vessel to pass? He examined the fort and its exotic architecture. Lights flashed from the top—signal towers again. Lin's one advantage would be his communication system. Charles pulled a folded paper from his coat and noted the observation. Lin's navy must have signaled ahead to allow passage. *Swan's Journey* sailed peacefully on toward Macao.

They reached their destination when the sun lay low in the west. Charles, weary and ill at ease in the new reality between them, went to alert Zambak where she dozed in a chair fixed in a corner of the deck. Her eyes fluttered open and gleamed with love for him, visible to the world. His heart flipped over while he kept his body between her and the eyes of the crew, cleared the thickening from his throat, and looked past her to the sea.

"We're nearing Macao, my lady. You may want to prepare," he said for all to hear.

Hurt flitted across her face followed quickly by understanding. He could only hope she would follow his lead. There had been enough gossip already.

Thorn came out on deck, blinking at the setting sun. "At last! I thought we'd bob about all night." He glowered at the sight of Charles offering his hand to Zambak to help her rise. "The sooner we get you to Mrs. Elliot's supervision, the better, dear sister," he said.

Zambak stared back sourly but refused to answer him, to Charles's relief. The last thing he needed was sibling bickering.

The three of them disembarked in silence and plodded uphill toward the Elliot house. When they drew within sight of it, Zambak said, "Hopefully we won't have to stay here much longer, Thorn."

The boy drew back in outrage. "You can't expect me to stay under the Elliots' care like some schoolboy," he frowned. "Though I suppose Jarratt & Martinson won't take me back either. Not after weeks at Zion's Quarter." Crestfallen, he bowed his head. Charles almost missed the words he whispered next. "Not worth much to anyone."

Zambak opened her mouth to object, but Charles cut her off. "Let me introduce you to Mrs. Josie. Her place caters to young gentlemen like yourself." That appeared to mollify the young man but aggravate his sister.

"Zambak, I'm afraid I'll have to leave you here for a while. My first priority is to find passage for you and Glenaire back to England."

When she planted her feet and stood arms akimbo on a public street, he knew he'd made a tactical error.

"And when do you plan to join us?" she asked.

"I told you before, Julia and I will sail separately."

Before Zambak could protest, her brother spoke up. "Quite right, Zamb. Charles knows what's up. You will have my protection."

She rolled her eyes at him. Charles, however, viewed the boy with dawning respect. *Perhaps we can make something of him after all.* "Can we talk about it later?" he asked. He didn't have to wait for an answer. They had reached their destination.

The door swung open, and old Hua bowed profusely, moving back and gesturing them in. "Welcome back, Your Grace, Lady Zambak, and, er, gentleman."

Thorn stiffened, and Zambak spoke for him. "You may announce my brother, John Thornton Hayden, Marquess of Glenaire." Hua bowed again, drawing a nod from Thorn, but they were spared further comment.

Clara Elliot bustled in, obviously summoned by a footman. She skidded to a stop, horror marked on every feature. "Lady Zambak," she sputtered, studying the Manchu gown, "You will be relieved to know your good English dresses are all well cared for and waiting for you."

Zambak started to speak, took a breath and, Charles suspected, changed her tack. "Thank you, Mrs. Elliot. I appreciate your care."

Clara Elliot ignored her; she had moved on to glower at Charles. "You, Sir, will wish to stay away. I have children here, and they are to be spared scandal."

Julia has been thorough, he thought morosely. "Whatever you may have heard, Mrs. Elliot, I would urge you to view with skepticism."

The lady pulled herself up to her full height—even at that she stood well below Charles's slight frame, coming merely to his cravat. "I am well able to judge ladies' gossip—even tittle-tattle as ugly as what flew through the European community this month—but my husband himself told me the lady chased after you dressed as a man. A man!" Her chin wobbled in outrage.

"You may rest easy. The lady will leave you as soon as I can arrange passage home for her with her brother," Charles replied through tight lips.

He bowed respectfully to Zambak. "I will leave you to recover from your ordeal, Lady Zambak," he said. He bobbed his head to Clara Elliot. "Mrs. Elliot," he said, then spun away and left before he lost his temper, determined to find the true source of his problems and shake her until her teeth bounced in her head.

After a moment, he heard Thorn follow.

"I'm not blind," the young marquess told him as he rushed to his side. Charles ignored him. "I see the way you look at her."

Charles clamped his jaw shut, reined in his boiling temper, and walked steadily on. *Julia, the Elliot woman, Thorn—they all have damned prurient imaginations.* In his heart, he feared they were accurate.

"What are your intentions toward my sister?" Thorn demanded when Charles refused to speak.

He stopped so suddenly Thorn ran into him and had to step back. "Honorable, damn it. You've known me since you wore dresses. You ought to know better."

"How can a married man gape at her the way you do and call himself 'honorable.'? What can you possibly intend that won't ruin her?"

Charles began to count backward in his head to slow his heart and calm his words. Her brother deserved an answer. "Walk with me," he said at last. "There are things you should know. Julia and I haven't lived as husband and wife since the first six months of our marriage." Keeping detail to a minimum, he outlined Julia's behavior, her spite, and their agreement. "I hope there will come a time when I can make my addresses to your sister honorably," he admitted, "and in the meantime, she has my respect and protection."

"Father won't like it," Thorn muttered.

"Probably not. Zambak seems to think he doesn't have a say."

Thorn grinned. "That sounds like my sister." He sobered quickly. "The horrid old woman you just spoke to is already reacting to scandal. I suspect all of Macao already thinks Zambak is ruined. It'll get back to London, and my parents will have six kinds of fits. I should probably call you out, since my father isn't here to do it himself."

"Your job, my young lord, is to show the world your sister's virtue, maintain the façade of respectability, and whatever you do, don't cause talk on your own before I can get you on a boat for home."

They had reached Mrs. Josie's boarding house and entered the foyer, causing a bell to ring. At the sound, his hostess hurried from her parlor. Her eyes opened wide at the sight of him.

"You! I'm surprised you have the nerve to show your face. That woman came here. She spoke to me herself of what she has endured at your hand!"

"Is my coin insufficient for you, Ma'am?" Charles asked coldly. "My companion the Marquess of Glenaire seeks rooms as well. Shall we go elsewhere?" The harridan didn't miss his emphasis on "marquess" nor the mention of coin. Her eyes sharpened.

"Of course, the baggage has been lying low since Jarratt's nephew dropped her flat—called her a poxy trull in front of Mrs. Dennison, he did." She watched him speculatively. "Nine-day wonder if you ask me," she mused. "I'll expect full payment for the weeks you were gone and half again as much for my trouble with her and keeping your things."

He let her talk until she finally assumed a benign expression. "I won't raise your rent, but I expect the same for his lordship here."

Charles chose not to point out he paid in advance before he left. He had enough conflict on his hands. *The nephew humiliated her in public? Julia must have shown her colors early—or the Jarratts were finished using her to get back at me.* He completed the transaction quickly and led Thorn to the stairs.

"Tell him the rules. No late hours. No women." Mrs. Josie eyed him carefully. "And no opium pipes. I run a clean establishment."

The rules. I just hope Thorn pays attention.

~ ~ ~

Zambak slept far into the following morning, grateful for a comfortable bed and soft nightclothes. Her awakening, when it came, was sudden and rude. A troop of workers herded in by Clara Elliot and ordered to "set the poor girl to rights" were followed by a hastily delivered tray of tea and biscuits that made Zambak long for the hearty breakfasts spread out for the men in Zion's Quarter.

After enduring the attention of three maids and a hairdresser, Zambak stood trussed in a corset and gown, her cropped hair ruthlessly coifed, and stared out her bedroom window at the jasmine blooming in the garden below. She rubbed her middle finger with her left thumb and considered her few options.

If I sit here like the fine lady I'm expected to be, smiling over tea at the harpies while I wait for Charles, I will go mad. If I charge out to confront Julia, I'll look a fool.

There was nothing for it. She had become accustomed to being useful. Hard work, Peters had taught her, filled many a hollow space in the heart. She smiled as she considered

Temperance's reaction to finding a clinic volunteer on her doorstep. The thumb stilled. *At this hour, Temperance will be there.*

She strode to the door and flung it open on a welcome sight. Filipe sat cross-legged on the floor staring up at her door. When it opened, he broke into a smile that lifted her heart.

"Fetch my cloak and bonnet, Filipe. We're going to visit Miss Temperance." He leapt to do as she bid. "Welcome back, Lady," he shouted as he ran. She scribbled a note for Mrs. Elliot and left.

Temperance found her hanging her cloak and bonnet on a peg and donning a smock. "Zambak! Thee have returned." Her sharp eyes and swift examination brought a flush to Zambak's face. "What are thee doing with that smock."

"Preparing to work." Temperance's skeptical expression brought a wan smile. "I spent time with Dr. Peters, Temperance."

"Thy brother?"

"Yes. The ordeal was as horrible as you predicted, but we came out the other side, he to lick his wounds, and me? I was able to help the clinic. They are flooded with poor souls eager to escape the opium—and the high commissioner's threats."

"We as well. We would welcome thy new-found skills," Temperance said thoughtfully. "Where is thy brother now?"

"Charles—His Grace—took him to board at Mrs. Josie's."

At mention of Charles, Temperance sobered. "Vile stories fly through the city Zambak. Thee should be warned."

"From his wife?"

Temperance shrugged. "I have not met the woman, but I understand she is the source. Thee know I do not countenance gossip, but I believe she means thee harm."

"She means Charles harm for some reason," Zambak replied, her eyes skittering away from her friend's deep concern. *She can see right through to my heart. She knows he is lodged there.*

To her relief, Temperance didn't probe. A mischievous expression came over her instead. "It is pushing of me, and I beg thy forgiveness, but temptation wracks me. Did thee really come back dressed in Chinese clothing?"

Zambak grinned then and put an arm around her friend's waist. "Yes! I will show you some day. I have had such adventures! Give me work to do, and I will tell you them."

Chapter 34

The men at Josie's boarding house got a late start as well. Thorn, in particular, slept half the day away. Charles was forced to endure a lecture on strict meal schedules and warm their hostess's greedy palm in order to get the spoiled princeling fed and settled. It took most of the rest of the day for Charles to deal with his financial affairs. As much as he distrusted the restless set to the boy's posture, he couldn't keep an eye on him all the time. He had other fish to fry.

The sun sank well past midday when he finally set out toward the little house he had rented for his wife. As he turned off the main thoroughfare, the sight of a pink parasol bobbing along from the direction of the mission brought a pang.

At least one of the Hayden offspring contributes to the world's store of good. She certainly contributes to mine.

The temptation to follow her came over him, but he forced his footsteps to turn toward his wife, anger rising at every step. *Twelve years of Julia's lying, deceit, and cruelty is enough. She will not turn it on Zambak, who is worth twenty of her.*

He strode purposefully to the door, shoved it open, and went in expecting her servant to challenge him. None did. No one did. The house stood silent and cold, late afternoon shadows casting it in darkness. *The bitch must have moved out.*

His nose wrinkled at a foul stench. *Trust Julia to leave food to rot.* He wandered the lower floor looking for the source and found the kitchen bare, its cupboard empty but for a liter of flour, stale biscuits, and a few dried apples. A moldy rag, dried in its filth lay over a sink, was ugly but insufficient to account for the smell.

He came around to the front stairs. *Can the odor be upstairs?* Climbing upward, the stench worsened. He gagged at the top of the stairs.

He found her lying in her filth in the larger of the two bedrooms in soiled nightclothes covered with a thin—and equally soiled—sheet. A bowl with the congealed remains of some sort of porridge lay on the table next to her bed. It appeared to have been there several days. A brown bottle, cap off, with dried remains around the rim sat next to it.

He picked up the bottle. Even surrounded by the foul odor, he recognized the smell: laudanum. He grimaced as memories of his mother's daily struggles flooded him. Blinking them away, he studied the labored breathing of what was left of his wife. Vomit and excrement smattered the bed. Julia, yellow and sunken, had lost even more weight since their last encounter. Her once-glorious hair hung in oily ropes around her. Poppy dependence might account for some of the devastation, but he suspected something else was killing her.

He knew she had been ill, saw it in her desperation when they met. He assumed syphilis or some other venereal disease, but none of those would cause the rapid horror. As he stared, she gasped, an explosion of air, and blinked her eyes open.

"Who?" The momentary panic subsided to blank despair. "Charles. Come to gloat?" Her words came out in a ragged croak.

Too disoriented to speak, he searched the room and found a small wooden chair. He pulled it next to the bed, back toward Julia, and straddled it.

"What is it?" he asked. "Not syphilis."

She almost choked on an ugly laugh. "You would think that." She licked her chapped lips and peered at him as if struggling to focus. "I have a cancer in my belly," she said at last. "The navy doctor assured me it would kill me. He didn't mention it would be this fast." Her face twisted in a spasm. "Or this painful."

"Where is the servant I hired?"

"Hugo sent her away after she spilled wine on him."

"Hugo Jarratt? The nephew?"

"He refused to hire another. I did everything he asked." She breathed shallowly with great effort for a while. "All I got were a few coins and one miserly bottle of laudanum." She turned her face away.

Charles went cold. "What did he ask?"

He thought the response was a muffled laugh. "Why, to savage the uppity Lady Zambak, of course. She'll not be making a respectable marriage, that one," she said, still turned toward the wall.

Ah, think again, Julia. Perhaps not respectable, but marriage most certainly.

"And you of course," she went on, turning as if she had gathered strength. "Jarratt would rather keep you from any position in government if he can, or hurt you at least. He seems to have taken offence that you removed the marquess from his control." Spite gleamed in her eyes.

"Why you, Julia? Why do you hate me?"

"I don't hate you, Charles. I merely despise you. So easy to bamboozle. So easy to—" a cough took the rest.

And the adoration of just one man would never be enough for you. You thrive—or used to thrive—on keeping us competing in circles. He surged to his feet, convinced the harpy had fallen asleep, and stood with his hands fisted as he considered his options, unable to leave and yet unable to act.

"You cheated me." He almost missed the whispered words.

Rage surged up. *How in God's name did I cheat her?* He turned to leave.

"You'll get your freedom, and I'll see none of that lovely money."

He stopped dead. *Freedom. The only thing I ever wanted from her.* He turned back and loomed over the bed.

Her eyes flickered open, suddenly sharp. "Laudanum. You owe me that much. The pain—you have no idea." Her face twisted as if to demonstrate. *Is she faking?* With Julia he could never be sure.

When she began to shake, he reached instinctively to cover her but pulled his hand back, repulsed by the dirt. He watched long and hard, but this time she didn't wake up.

She would soon be gone, and he would be free of her. He told himself to walk away and be grateful, but his feet would not move. Finally, he let out a string of curses, none of which woke the woman on the bed.

I can't leave her alone like this. She is still my wife. His analytical mind began to take stock of what needed to be done. *Zambak would know what to do. The valiant Zambak who had swallowed her pride to learn from Dr. Peters and who even now— No! Lady Zambak Hayden will have nothing to do with this hellhole. Julia is my damned responsibility and mine alone.*

Lists swirled in his head as he walked to the door; he would be back.

~ ~ ~

Three days of no word from Charles or her brother left Zambak dejected. She made daily trips to the mission—both the clinic and the school—grateful to be useful and grateful to avoid the ladies who found excuses to pay calls on Clara Elliot hoping for a tidbit about the now-notorious Lady Zambak Hayden.

She trudged home late on the fourth day, the ever-eager Filipe trotting at her heels, and braced herself for another scold from Clara. Old Hua bowed her in. "Ladies in parlor, Lady Zam. Missy Elliot say you come when home."

Damn. Dare I claim headache? She handed cloak and bonnet to Filipe.

Too late. Clara Elliot stood in the parlor door, "Who is it Hua? Ah! Lady Zambak. We have visitors." Her eyes defied Zambak to walk away.

She almost did, but breeding and manners propelled her forward. Mother would approve at least. "Face them down," she would say. *How much harm will a few moments do?*

Four pairs of glittering eyes met hers: Mildred Dennison's beneath a bonnet festooned with feathers like those on a Roman centurion's helmet; her cronies, Lucy Ingram and Eunice McIlroy, flanked her.

Mrs. Dean—Alice, she remembered—crouched in the corner. Zambak caught fear beneath a veneer of resentment. *The woman's husband is still in Canton and still under indictment, albeit under protection in Elliot's headquarters. She must hate me. At least that one has reason. I'm here, and her husband isn't.*

A pregnant silence lasted as long as it took Clara Elliot to pour Zambak's tea. When it broke, she reevaluated her mother's question about how much harm. The women could do a great deal in very few moments.

"You have had such an adventure, Lady Zambak," Mildred Dennison exclaimed breathlessly. "Trapped with all the *men* in Canton." The emphasis on men was unmistakable.

"Did you really meet the evil Lin Zeux? What did you do to convince him to let you go?" Ingram's wife broke in. She dropped her voice to a whisper. "Were you . . . tortured?"

Zambak set her teacup carefully down lest she throw the delicate porcelain into the hearth. "Commissioner Lin, a man of great character, treated me with respect and consideration despite the fact that my presence in Canton violated his country's laws and his own sense of propriety," she responded. "He required only that I leave forthwith and arranged for me to do so."

Disappointment flickered in the woman's eyes, but Mrs. McIlroy spoke before she could object. "Surely you don't condone that pagan? He has trapped our men inside the foreign compound, starving them into submission."

Zambak thought of the young clerks frolicking over leapfrog and cricket on the parade ground and their amusement at being forced to learn to cook rice and eggs. *Hardly starving. Hardly miserable.*

"Pagan he may be and of a culture known for cruelty, but the commissioner wishes only to enforce Chinese law. He asks merely that we obey."

"But we are British!" Mildred exclaimed as if that explained everything.

Zambak sighed. "Captain Elliot is doing his best to spare Mrs. Dean's husband the harshness of Chinese law. He has determined none of Her Majesty's subjects will be judged by any law but our own."

"See? I told you, Alice. My Charles will take care of your husband. He will." Clara Elliot's chin shook with pride.

Mildred Dennison sniffed. "He sent the *Lorne* on dispatch to Madras, and I just hope he's calling for the navy. They could break through that blockade. Our own husbands' ships are prepared to assist. Why doesn't he use them, Clara? I ask you? We could smash the Chinese."

Yes. Three dense perimeters of Chinese war junks, and our navy could smash them like twigs—Jarratt & Martinson gunships as well. Elliot may not have authority to declare war per se, but he can command any firepower he chooses.

"Captain Elliot wishes to avoid war, Mrs. Dennison. Shouldn't that be our best desire? Bloodshed will benefit none of us," Zambak said sweetly. She hid her anger under a practiced sip of tea, graceful and contrived. *Mother would be proud.*

"What does His Grace have to say about the matter?" Lucy Ingram asked, her glittering eyes examining Zambak as if looking for any sign of debauchery or ruin.

We come to the real issue. Politics be damned. Are you sleeping with the duke? That's what they came for.

Again, she set the cup down carefully. This time she whispered conspiratorially. "I shouldn't be telling you this," she whispered, drawing all of them to lean forward, eager to hear of scandal. "His Grace has come at the queen's bidding to report on conditions here." It was known among the men by now, so it did no harm to say. "He will be returning to London as soon as he can arrange it."

"Yes," Eunice McIlroy cooed, "but what does he have to say to the matter. Surely he confided in you."

Pillow talk do you mean? Alas no. She chose to lie. "I have no idea. A powerful man like the Duke of Murnane would not confide a confidential report in a mere girl." *Cow slop, every word of it. I hope she chokes on her curiosity.*

"Do you know his duchess is in Macao?" Mrs. Dennison asked. All eyes darted to Zambak.

"I have been at the mission the better part of four days," she responded. "Even there, rumors abound. I hope the woman is well."

Eyes slid to one another in some mysterious communication. *Who will be first with the deliciously poisoned knives?*

"We thought so at first, so charming she was on the arm of Hugo Jarratt, that delightful young man," Alice began. "We're lucky to have him here in Macao during our troubles. Such a kind young man."

"He found her alone in a pokey little house—abandoned with one meager servant, he said. Not well done of the duke,

I must say," the Dennison woman added, picking up the thread of a well-rehearsed conversation.

"She looked wan and pale, however, so one wondered," Eunice piped up. "And then when she said, well . . ." The woman had the grace to blush at her own tittle-tattle.

"What exactly did she say?" Zambak asked.

"What were her exact words, Mildred? Something about recovering from the duke's last *visit*?" The woman gave the word a salacious tone and didn't meet Zambak's eyes.

"Something like that," her friend responded. "She blushed prettily and turned the subject from such a delicate admission. Men can be such beasts."

Some men. Not Charles. Zambak bared her teeth. "Ladies, I know you are far from London these many years." *And not one of you social-climbing spiders would move in the same circles as the Duke of Murnane if you were.* "So, there may be much you do not know." She peered in each face one by one, holding their attention, daring them to push themselves forward. "Throughout the *ton*, His Grace has a reputation for absolute propriety and honor." She paused while three of them swallowed hard and eyes widened, some eager, some wary.

"The duchess does not enjoy such a reputation. Her behavior has been a byword my entire life—so much so that even as a young girl I heard of it. Mothers present her as an example to their daughters of what they must not become. I would warn you against believing a word she said, or"—she paused again for effect—"repeating it. The Duke of Murnane has endured much from her with great forbearance."

Eunice McIlroy blinked. Mrs. Dean blushed. The Ingram woman looked down, but Mildred Dennison didn't back away. "Be that as it may, Lady Zambak, she seemed quite distressed that you of all people had gone off with her husband under questionable circumstances. We heard you actually dressed as a man."

"And came back dressed as a Chinese," Eunice squeaked, darting glances at her fellows and wringing her hands.

"No wife would put up with that," Mrs. Dennison spat. "No matter what did—or did not—go on while you were gone. You must see that."

"I see a great deal, Mrs. Dennison, and you are much mistaken in your views of the Duke of Murnane. He continues to be a man of honor." *Damn him anyway. I have all the disgrace and none of the pleasure.* She stared the woman down, generations of ducal breeding lending her a finely honed ability to rout any encroaching mushroom who dared attack.

In the silence that followed, Zambak rose before they could regroup for another attack, like a pack of jealous terriers eager to enforce the will of the pack on a superior animal.

"If your curiosity is quite satisfied, I'll take my leave. I am weary from my labor today, and there are those who will appreciate it tomorrow. I bid you farewell."

The door didn't quite close behind her before the whispers began.

Chapter 35

Servants may be eager for work and still shrink from a house that smells of death. Rank and money eventually overcame scruples, however, and Charles directed his newly acquired army to set up a bath in the cleaner of the two bedrooms first. A plaintive cry from the other room told him their efforts had awoken Julia. *Still among the living.* He ignored it.

Only when the tub steamed with water, and the scent of jasmine and lavender pushed against the house's stench, did he enter the other room, swallowing a gag. He had changed into clothing generally consigned to the bottom of a trunk and only pulled out when he had the need to crouch behind barrels or fade into neighborhoods in which rank would be a hazard, a self indulgence he vowed to outgrow.

Striding into the room, he yanked the sheet from his wife with one swift movement and ripped her nightgown neck to hem before slipping it from her skeletal shoulders and lifting her from the bed.

"Designs on my body, Charles?" she whined.

He ignored her, carrying her toward the waiting tub.

She weighs no more than a newborn kitten, he thought. *Jonny, sick as he was, weighed more than this at eight.* Memories of Jonny gave him strength to endure it. Whatever else Julia may have done, she was Jonny's mother.

"You are hurting me. The women of Macao already believe you're a monster," she shrieked.

He overcame the urge to drop her into the water, laying her tenderly down instead, in spite of her sharp cry.

"Let the warmth help, Julia. You'll feel better."

"Why should I believe you? You want me to suffer." She sank into a whimper.

Do I? Probably—to my shame—but it won't be at my hand. He didn't answer her. He placed a rolled towel on the tub's rim and laid her head against it. Two little half-Portuguese maids with scarves tied across their noses peered back at him.

"Let her soak for a while first," he instructed them in Portuguese. "Take care she doesn't slip under the water. Before it cools, clean her thoroughly."

The girls looked dubious, but they bobbed down in a semblance of obeisance and ogled the tub.

"When you are finished, put her in a clean night rail." He pointed to a package on the nearby table, and the narrow cot nearby. "You may sit her on that bed until we are finished." They blinked at him; he hoped they understood.

He met more servants in the larger room. Once the bedding, Julia's clothing, and the mattress had been dragged to the yard and burned, work proceeded with a bit more alacrity. Two men hauled more water upstairs to clean the larger bedroom and hallway, scrubbing from ceiling to floor at the duke's orders.

A cook had been more difficult to hire, and that only on condition he would not have to go above stairs for any reason. Once the worst of the burning cleared the air, Charles noticed two small boys buzzing around the kitchen, climbing up to wipe shelves clean, and carrying in the supplies Charles requested. He had given the man full rein to buy what he needed, explaining that the primary need would be broth and plenty of it. A flock of chickens, not long for this world, squawked in cages in the corner of the kitchen, and in short order, water boiled on the rickety stove.

Taking stairs two at a time to check on progress, the duke found Julia in a thin gown shivering on the cot while both girls stood by helplessly doing nothing. He cursed himself for a fool, ordered them to dispose of the now-fetid water, and went back down to scrub his hands and forearms with a lye soap until he rubbed them almost raw. Once satisfied, he pulled a coverlet from the pile of clean linen on the cart he had waiting in front of the tiny house and sent two men to carry the new mattress up.

Julia made no protest—and showed no gratitude—when he wrapped her on the coverlet and laid her back on the cot. The bath had exhausted her. As he started to leave, a trickle of red caught his attention, and he glanced around the room but found nothing to help. His over-zealous little maids had removed all linen and probably planned to burn them as well. He removed a handkerchief from his shirt and wiped the dribble of blood and spittle from the corner of Julia's mouth. A flicker of a sneer rapidly disappeared as she began to rock in pain.

Laudanum. It had proven harder to find than servants. *A sea of opium tar, and I can't find a simple tincture of the stuff.* He ran an agitated hand through his hair. It would have to wait.

Three hours later, more coin and the promise of escape from the house induced three of the temporary workers to build a laundry behind the house. Julia had soiled herself again before he could move her into the newly cleaned room, and at the rate he was going, he would empty Macao of bed linen in a week.

With Julia back in the larger, newly scrubbed room, he attempted to negotiate with two little maids in a mixture of Portuguese, English, and his few words of Cantonese. He expected to spend most of his time there but needed someone to stay with her when he went out.

"Will you sit with the lady?" Two heads nodded vigorously.

"Will you give her water and broth?" More nods.

"Do you think you can take turns?" That question elicited confused looks. He was eventually able to convey the concept, but the girls looked so nervous about being alone with a dying woman doubted they would carry it out.

"Do you have another sister?" He asked. Their enthusiastic "Yes!

His attempts to convey the concept of round-the-clock care were interrupted by loud knocking on the door. When no kitchen staff bothered to answer and no major domo magically appeared to greet guests properly, he flew down the steps and yanked the door open.

A bright smile and two sparking black eyes looked up at him. Filipe bent double, bobbed up, and pronounced, "'r Grace, I have found you! Honor to your house." Charles had no response to that, but it didn't matter. The boy rattled on. "The Lady Zam wishes to know are you well?"

"As you see, I am," Charles said, swallowing a laugh. "But—"

"The lady wishes to tell you that you are a—" The boy scrunched up his brow, trying to remember the exact words. "Pathetic excuse for partner. Don't communicate. Typical man, she say."

She could have called me worse. He opened his mouth to respond.

Filipe got there first. "She wishes to know, do you need help making arrangements. Lady Zam goes to England. Filipe wishes to come. Good servant! Can—"

The boy drew breath to expound on his virtues, but Charles cut him off. "Tell Lady Zambak that I have as yet not had time to make arrangements. Tell her my own affairs are complicated and will take time. Besides, most of the British shipping is tied up at Canton except for the few anchored off Hong Kong Island waiting for trade to resume."

Filipe rocked up on his toes. "No problem 'r Grace. English merchants here. Here now. Cap Elliot brings all from Canton. No more tea trade. All boats to Hong Kong, Macao—some in harbor this morning."

Elliot pulled the tea traders out? Is he trying to pressure Lin? Charles doubted the commissioner cared about the tea, but the hong merchants did and, he suspected, the emperor might.

Filipe lost interest in the traders swiftly. He peered behind Charles at the Chinese girl on the stairs. "New servants 'r Grace? I can help." He slipped behind Charles before the duke could stop him and quickly fell into animated conversation with the cook.

God help me. Zambak will get an earful. Charles stood at his door and ran a hand over the back of his neck. He needed to find laudanum. He needed to change his clothes. He needed to talk to Elliot. His hand fell to his waist.

I need Zambak, but I can't have her. Not like this.

~ ~ ~

Zambak studied the tiny woman who appeared to have a poker up her back, lips so tight they might crack, and stone cold brown eyes. *This must be the famous Mrs. Josie.*

"I run a respectable boarding house," the woman repeated, rigid with indignation. "Young women are not permitted. Respectable ones do not knock on my door."

Zambak called up aristocratic arrogance, the product of eight hundred years of breeding. "My dear lady, do you know who I am?"

"I've heard about you. The Duchess of Murnane made certain of that," Mrs. Josie spat, unimpressed.

The left side of Zambak's mouth quirked; she respected a woman with backbone. She changed tactics.

"I appreciate your delicate position, Madam. I'm here to see my brother, however. The Marquess of Glenaire?" *And Charles, the wretch, if he is here. He dumped me at the Elliots' and disappeared.* She had Filipe scouring Macao for the pair of them when neither saw fit to communicate for three days. Now she couldn't find Filipe either.

"The Marquess is out I fear, Lady Zambak," the landlady replied. "Mr. Hugo Jarratt called this morning, and the two of them went out. Right happy, the marquess looked."

Zambak groaned inwardly. *How could Charles let that happen? He promised to keep him out of trouble until we can get him on a ship.*

"His lordship has been lonely here with most of the men trapped in Canton and that duke off about his own business." Mrs. Josie's sniff at the end managed to convey her conviction the duke's "business" involved no end of foul debauchery.

Where the hell has Charles been? She tossed around for a way to ask if the landlady knew where he could be found.

Both women spun around at the sound of raucous conversation at the boarding house gate. Several young men—clerks by the look of them, and more than one slightly foxed—argued over something that made Zambak pay attention.

"I say he didn't. I don't care what Oliver, that old grandmother, reported."

"Oliver swears he had every ball of opium tar smashed, buried in salt and lime, turned into sludge and dumped into the sea?" That one seemed to revel in the description.

"Twenty thousand chests of opium? Impossible. It would take an army."

"Old Lin has an army, you lack wit. He can do what he pleases. Oliver doesn't lie."

"Doesn't mean he wasn't bamboozled. He's in Lin's pocket. No one would destroy over twenty million pounds in opium."

"Lin would," Zambak said from the porch, pitching her voice to the fools coming through the gate. "He is a man of honor."

The dregs of Macao's trading company clerks, sweating in English wool in an attempt to appear respectable merchants rather than the smugglers they assuredly were, gaped back at her.

"I say, aren't you the tru—er, lady who met Lin?"

The men eyed Zambak in open speculation, the same questions the more circumspect ladies had the day before naked in their eyes. *What did you give him to let you go? Were you tortured? Raped? Or did you give your favors freely to escape punishment?*

She clamped her jaw tight and glared back.

Paying customers on her doorstep overrode any other consideration for Mrs. Josie. She stepped forward to welcome them. "Gentlemen! So many of you at once. Cook will be *aux anges*! Come in and tell me what you need after your horrid ordeal. Did those savages starve you?" She clucked like a mother hen, ushering them past Zambak. "Have the Chinese given up?"

"Ought to." One of the men sneered. "Elliot made us give up a lot of opium—some firms turned in half of what they have—to meet Lin's demands. He pulled us all out. Threatening to stop trade completely—all a hum, of course. Getting back at Lin."

Elliot pulled them all out? Zambak's left thumb twitched as facts fell into place, and she turned them over in her mind one by one.

"Good thing the company made other plans," one said proudly. "The rest of you will have to catch up."

"What plans?" she asked, suddenly alert.

One snickered and nudged the man who spoke. "Works for Jarratt & Martinson. Always six steps ahead."

The first preened. "We are. Soon as Lin claimed he would destroy the opium, the price dropped in India. Old Jarratt himself has been in Manila buying cheap and setting out for the coastal routes. We're already starting full bore up the coast in Fukien."

Of course they are. They'll make a fortune. She had never doubted they would. "Do I understand Captain Elliot is back?"

They glanced around until one answered her. "First boat in. Probably ran home to the missus."

She set out for the Elliot mansion without a backward glance.

Chapter 36

From the house he rented for Julia in the respectable, but crowded, neighborhood near São Lourenço, Charles had to walk downhill toward the harbor. Opium was no more legal in Macao than any other part of China, but the Portuguese authorities preferred not to know when and where it could be found. Stores near the house held nothing so very British as laudanum, and while Charles sniffed at various suspicious local remedies, he found nothing he dared purchase. He promised Julia laudanum, and he planned to deliver it.

He had sent Filipe back to Zambak with a stern warning to "look after your mistress and tell her I said to stay away." He hinted that he and he alone had power over any future removal of servants from Macao and prayed the boy paid attention. The boy promised to go as soon as he helped carry in supplies for the kitchen.

Charles now had two choices. He could scour the streets along the port, a haven for contraband on any continent, or go hat in hand to one of the English trading firms and beg. He preferred the former.

Filipe hadn't lied about the fleet. From the top of the hill, Charles caught sight of a horizon bristling with masts off shore and the gigs, launches, and dinghies crowding the docks. Men disembarked and scurried to offices, or trudged upward toward him, undoubtedly seeking homes, rented rooms, and rest. Two caught his eye, and the hair on his neck began to rise. Thorn Hayden walked up from the commercial strip with a well-dressed merchant.

The other man, sharp eyed, caught sight of Charles approaching, and amusement gleamed in his eyes. The resemblance to his uncle was unmistakable. *Hugo Jarratt. Damn. Sudbury's heir twists in the wind to these men.*

"I say, Charles." The young marquess had the grace to blush.

"I thought I asked you to stay put," Charles thundered without preamble.

Thorn dug in his heels. "You can't expect me to sit all day in Mrs. Josie's parlor staring at her bric-a-brac!"

"I should think not," Jarratt chuckled, drawing a grateful glance from the marquess who took a step close to him.

"You might find a way to make yourself useful," Charles replied, though how exactly the boy might do it escaped him.

"I have been given the impression you objected to Lord Glenaire's gainful employment with our firm," Jarratt interjected. "But we haven't been introduced, have we?" He made no attempt to acknowledge the duke's rank.

"I know who you are," Charles growled. "And yes, I object. You seem to have a strange set of behavior standards for your employees."

Jarratt studied Thorn, making no effort to hide his amusement. "Only our most valuable ones." The marquess, oblivious to the undercurrent, preened.

Jarratt did bow then, a simple inclination of the head. "This is where I take your leave, my lord," he said to his companion. "You obviously have things to discuss with your—tutor is it?" He walked back down toward Jarratt & Martinson premises, chuckling while Thorn turned beet red.

"Damn it, Charles, you act like my nanny. You have no authority over me. My father—"

"Your father told me to watch over you, and I intend to do so. What did Jarratt want from you, anyway?" He examined the boy carefully but found no signs of opium.

"Nothing. He just came to check if I needed anything."

"Did you?" Charles demanded.

The question took the marquess off guard. He stuttered, shifty eyed, "No. Well, yes. Bored you know. I need work, but Hugo says you won't let them hire me. No one wants to hire me. We went to tea. That's all it was. Tea."

"Did he offer you opium?" *Truth, Thorn. Tell me the truth.*

"Don't be daft, Charles. It's all hidden!"

Hidden not gone.

The marquess babbled on. "Anyway, I promised my sister. It's just . . ."

"Laudanum, Thorn? Did he give you laudanum?" Shame flooded Charles; he hoped the answer was yes so he could take it to Julia.

Thorn refused to meet his eyes. "His firm keeps a supply. For staff, in case they need it." He looked up sharply at that. "Only if needed. Carefully guarded. Only goes to trusted employees."

"Do you have it?"

"What? No! I told him about the pain—you don't know Charles. You don't understand the pain—and he offered." The boy lied poorly.

"You know where it leads, Thorn. You've been to that hell." *Give it to me.*

A belligerent chin stuck out. "But the path lies through heaven. You don't know that part, do you?" Thorn said, a smug expression, ugly across his face, as if having one up on a duke made him important.

I hope I never find out. Torn between a desire to send Thorn to demand laudanum for Julia and a drive to keep him far away, Charles froze in thought. As much as he loathed the idea, he would have to chase down Jarratt's blasted nephew.

The marquess turned the subject before he could. "You know Elliot is back? Lin's been subdued for now. The companies are trading up the coast, out of the line of fire.

Old Elliot will be so busy keeping the Portuguese pacified he won't have much energy left to watch. You going to tell him?" His words had the pattern of a well-coached argument.

I have no time for Elliot. I have to get this lost boy on a ship home with his tempting sister before it all crashes down, put my own damned affairs in order, and leave this pestilential place once and for all.

"He knows. Neither Lin nor Elliot are the fools the traders take them for. They are engaged in a dangerous chess game, though, and I intend to make sure we aren't caught in the middle. Get yourself back to Josie's until you hear from me about passage. It won't be long now." At least, he hoped not. He swung away and headed after his quarry, certain his words would have no impact on the marquess.

With the traders returned, and—from the looks of it—HMS *Lorne* back from Madras, he could board a ship with Zambak and her brother and leave. At least, he could if he left Julia to die alone. The servants he hired would strip the house and disappear as soon as he did.

He could leave. But he wouldn't.

~ ~ ~

Charles Elliot had little to say to Zambak when she hurried into his parlor, bonnet askew, to ask a dozen questions. He waffled between exasperation and astonishment at them, but managed to convey three things: Macao's safety remained secure, he would handle Lin, and he needed to spend time with his wife.

Effectively dismissed, Zambak sought out Temperance to apologize for neglecting her duty and to ask for her assistance. She wondered fleetingly where Filipe had gotten to and why he hadn't returned, but her brother's earlier absence worried her more. She begged her friend to go with her to Mrs. Josie's boarding house.

"I do not see why thee need my protection, Zambak."

"Not protection, Temperance. Respectability. The duchess and the gossips between them have convinced the proprietor I'm a woman of easy virtue. You are the most respectable woman I know."

"Thee are not that, Zambak. Thee are a lady of character."

Her friend's staunch defense warmed Zambak's heart, or would have if honesty didn't force her to admit how close she was to embracing easy virtue, at least in her own heart. "Will you come if I help you finish here?" she begged.

Temperance accepted help readily and finally went reluctantly when Zambak's fears for her brother overcame her friend's disgust with "false stories and outward judgment."

In the shabby front foyer of the boarding house, Mrs. Josie's face softened slightly at the sight of the well-known Quaker missionary on her doorstep. She glowered from Zambak to Temperance and back before stepping aside with a reluctant sigh.

"You'll find the marquess in the back parlor. He has been there for hours—ever since Hugo Jarratt left. Quiet as a mouse he is. I wish all my boarders behaved as well. You can have ten minutes, mind you, and only if Mrs. Knighton chaperones." She swept back into her office and left them to find their way down the dim hallway.

Cow shite. Jarratt. Fear crept up her neck, fear confirmed as soon as she found her brother smiling blankly at a potted fern from a chair in the corner. He leaned back against blue silk upholstery worn thin by others before him and grinned like a booby.

"Thy brother found his oblivion, Zambak," Temperance whispered. A brown bottle hanging from his pocket confirmed it.

Zambak yanked the laudanum from her brother's side and stuffed it in her reticule.

"Zamb? Best give it back. B'longs to J&M. Only let trusted employees have it," Thorn slurred. "Trusted. Only

most esteemed colleagues. Hugo said so. Great gun is Hugo."
He stirred slightly.

Zambak knelt at her brother's feet and grasped his hands.
"Do you know why the Jarratts court you, Thorn?"

"You think they just want to cozy up to the title, don't
you?" he answered, shaking off her hold. "Hugo likes me—
respects me. Says I have the right sort of views. Will do well
in Asia. Hugo says so."

She shook her head sadly, wishing she could confirm
Hugo's "respect." Her brother badly needed it. She swallowed
and tried to force her voice to sound calmer than she felt. "I
wish they were merely imposing mushrooms. They are far
worse than that."

Her brother screwed up his face in confusion. "I don't
think . . ."

"Listen to me, Thorn. Hugo's uncle has been sending
thousands of pounds to London where Martinson has
established himself. They're filling the papers with reports
of Chinese treachery."

"Chinese are treacherous," Thorn nodded agreeably.

"False stories, Thorn. They are trying to buy public
opinion. They are bribing ministers and MPs—they want
support for intervention to keep the opium trade expanding,
and they want to use you to pressure Father to stay out of
their way. They will stop at nothing."

"Silly Zambak. No one can make our father do anything.
The great Duke of Sudbury listens to no one." He closed his
eyes, repeating "no one" over and over until Zambak thought
he had fallen asleep. She stood up just as his eyes snapped
open. "Doesn't care about me, you know. Father doesn't.
Told Hugo so." He rolled to his side and shut her out.

*Oh, but he does. Rather desperately. He just can't seem
to show you.* She stepped back and knew her heart must be
in her eyes when Temperance's arm came around her waist.

"I warned thee, Zambak. Some will sell their immortal soul for poppy juice. Thee cannot fix him. He must fix himself."

"I can't. But I can fix Hugo Jarratt."

Temperance ran to catch up. Her long stride kept her even with Zambak, but she could not convince her friend to stand down. They strode side by side into the Jarratt & Martinson premises where Zambak demanded to see the proprietor's nephew. The clerks were no more prepared to assist her than the last time she invaded the male bastion, but she made her voice heard, and it drew her quarry from his cave.

"This is indeed an honor, ladies. May I show you into my office? We can speak more comfortably there," Hugo said with a raised brow. He had his uncle's dark hair, great bulk, and knowing eyes. Unlike the elder Jarratt, he showed so much sign of dissipation that Zambak suspected his vices would kill him eventually. The thought gave her devilish satisfaction.

She checked to see if Temperance would follow her into the private office, gave a sharp nod, and responded to his gesture directing her there. His pointed gaze sent clerks running back to their work.

Hugo moved behind his desk, but Zambak didn't pause. She waved the laudanum bottle under his nose. "You have no business giving this to my brother."

"Brother? We haven't been properly introduced"— he smirked—"but I deduce you mean the Marquess of Glenaire."

At the sound of the heir's title she had coveted since she was old enough to know what it meant, the title so tarnished by her feckless brother, Zambak's stomach clenched. "I do indeed mean Lord John Thornton Hayden, Marquess of Glenaire, eldest son and heir to the Duke of Sudbury. My father can and will ruin you if you harm his son, and harm him you have." She glared across the gleaming desk at the man behind it, her body rigid.

"I fear you're mistaken about me, my lady. Did you ask your brother where he got the poppy juice? Not that you can believe the word of one in its grip."

Her right hand fisted in fury. "You're lying." She felt Temperance's hand on her wrist and let her arm go slack but didn't step away.

"We do keep medicinal laudanum for staff, but of course, your brother is no longer our employee." His eyes watched her avidly.

"I'm surprised you can allow employees to disappear into a laudanum bottle with all the business you are conducting in—Fukien Province, is it?"

"I see you are as well informed as your reputation suggests, my lady." His grin broadened. "Of course, most of Macao knows and admires our business prowess. Elliot probably knows, too, but the spineless bureaucrat won't admit it."

"Elliot and Lin no doubt know. Neither is a fool."

The genial mask slipped. "Neither understands trade and its drivers, madam. Money drives trade, not politics. We go where it can be made. Governments can be bent in the service of trade, make no mistake. The future lies in money, and money lies in Asia. You and your landed relics will fade away. The future belongs to the man who knows where to find coin and how to accumulate it."

That's it then. The hatred of the self-made man for inherited wealth and tradition. They want power at all cost and be damned to honor, grace, and duty. She realized then why she admired Lin. They had more in common than the surface showed. *There has to be a middle road.*

"Hate us if you will, but stay away from my brother," she spat.

"Come away, Zambak. This man will not help thee," Temperance said.

"Wise words. Listen to your friend, Lady Zambak."

Temperance tugged at her arm; she let her shoulders sag, prepared to leave. Jarratt's voice pulled her back.

"Interestingly, one other person came today to ask about the product. Someone you may know. He had similar wrong-headed ideas."

"I beg your pardon." He had her perplexed now.

"The Duke of Murnane bought three bottles today. I refused at first, but of course, when he begged . . ." He let his voice trail away.

"I don't believe you," she said through lips that hardly moved. *Why would Charles want laudanum? He despises the stuff.*

An elaborate shrug answered her. "Who can explain a man's predilections? According to his duchess, his are—well perhaps best not described here. We might offend our missionary friend. But then, you may already know about that. Perhaps he accommodated your brother."

Temperance's audible gasp appeared to delight him. "You know, of course, Mrs. Knighton, this lady followed the duke to Whampao and Canton dressed as a man. If one were of a lascivious imagination, one might—"

His fierce hatred stopped her in her tracks when her slap echoed through his office. She stepped back. She ought to run, or at least walk away with what dignity she had left, but one more thing ate at her.

"Where is he?" she demanded.

"I beg your pardon?" He glowered down at her.

"The Duke of Murnane. You said he came here. Do you know where he is?" She almost choked on the words. She hated having to ask. *Where the devil had Filipe gone anyway? I sent him to find answers.*

The corners of Jarratt's eyes narrowed, his expression sly, his eyes cold. "My dear lady, don't you know? Your lover is with his wife, the lovely Julia. How she tolerates his odious attentions, I don't know."

His laughter followed her to the street.

Chapter 37

Zambak shivered under the coverlet Temperance wrapped around her, clutching a cup of strong tea in a sturdy cup. She rocked in the well-worn chair in the Knightons' practical kitchen, having sent word to the Elliots that she would stay the night there. Blessing, the youngest Knighton, crawled into her lap, and she welcomed the warmth.

In spite of the warm June evening, shock and frustration left her cold, and she seemed unable to silence the ugly words echoing in her head. No one could give her direction to Julia's house, and Temperance convinced her that scouring the neighborhoods this close to night would not be wise.

Filipe, dirty and apologetic, found her there long after dark. He bowed until she wanted to shake him and force him to talk. "Sorry, Lady Zam. Much help needed. Filipe worked hard."

"Worked where? I needed you!"

"His Grace, little house need much work. Sick lady very bad. His Grace gone much, needs help."

"Sick lady?" Her mind raced. *Julia has fallen ill*? She struggled to recall the woman's appearance when they met in Jarratt's foyer, but her mind had been on Thorn and Jarratt's vile suggestions. She leaned out of the chair to grab both his arms. "Tell me everything."

He did, rattling on about loose chickens, fetching water, lazy carpenters, and maids who appeared to be not only celestial, but virtuous. The maids, she suspected, had been his chief interest.

"But the lady?" she demanded.

"Very sick. Bad luck house. Servants paid much to stay," Filipe said.

"Chinese fear closeness to death, Zambak," Temperance explained. "Charles must have a difficult time obtaining help. You are very brave, Filipe."

"Yes, Filipe has no fear. Others?" He shrugged.

Zambak threw back the coverlet. "You must take me to this house," she said.

"I forgot. His Grace say, 'tell Lady Zam stay away.'" He smiled back, satisfied he had done his duty. "I stay until His Grace come back, and then I go search for Lady Zam."

"I don't care what the wretch said. Take me to the house."

Temperance objected strongly. "Thee are not a fool Zambak Hayden. Thee will not wander streets at dark. Morning is soon enough to seek Charles and offer your help."

Offer help? Why didn't he ask for it in the first place? He knows I can manage the thing. I will throttle him for keeping this from me. He hasn't contacted me once since we got back.

Filipe and Temperance between them managed to keep her inside, but she set out soon after dawn, stiff from a sleepless night sharing a bed with two little girls and fortified with sweet thick porridge. A sleepy-eyed Filipe led the way, the pink parasol nowhere in evidence.

Doubt ate at her, planted in the offices of Jarratt & Martinson. In spite of Filipe's lurid tales of the sick house, one thought kept resurfacing. *He put Julia ahead of me.* Jealousy knows no reason; guilt—the sure knowledge that she loved another woman's husband—fed jealousy. *He shut me out and went to Julia when she needed him. What about my need? What about his promise to look after Thorn?* Jealousy fed anger. Anger sped her steps until Filipe had to skip to keep up.

Pounding on the door brought no response. "Cook say not his job to answer door," Filipe muttered. She pounded again. Filipe peered into a window. "Coming," he said.

A tiny girl answered, the maid no doubt. She stared up at Zambak, speechless, noticed Filipe at her side, and giggled.

"Where is your master?" Zambak demanded. Filipe whispered in the girl's ear. She giggled and pointed upstairs. Zambak pushed past her. She reached the foot of the stairs before Charles appeared at the top.

"I told you to tell her to stay away, Filipe," he said.

"How dare you order my servant," Zambak shouted, pounding up the steps. "You have no right. You—"

He had her in his embrace before she cleared the top step, his mouth on hers sending ripples of heat to her belly. She vaguely heard giggles from below disappear toward the kitchen. When he pushed her up against the wall and began to kiss his way across her ear and down her neck, coherent thought fled.

He wrenched his mouth away but pinned her to the wall with one elbow on either side of her head, his forearms holding her in place, his body pressed shoulder to knees against her, leaving no doubt his need was as great as hers.

"Dear God, Zambak. You shouldn't be here. I don't want you here, but I'm overjoyed to see you."

She pushed at his shoulders, and he moved back a few inches, still close enough for her to feel his breath on her cheek. "You miserable contradictory man! You want me, and you don't. Make up your mind."

"My mind isn't the problem," he said ruefully. "It knows this is no place for you."

"Oh? Are we still under the impression I belong on a silk cushion, decorative in my idleness?" she said acidly.

"What? No. Damn it, Zambak. That isn't want I meant."

She recalled her earlier anger and poked him with a pointed finger. "You chose Julia's needs over mine. You promised to get us passage and to keep Thorn out of trouble, and you've done neither. You chose her over me." Tears threatened, infuriating her further. Lady Zambak Hayden did not, would not, become a watering pot.

"You don't understand."

"No, I don't. Enlighten me."

His head sank back for a moment on a long breath before he stood upright, took her by the hand, and led her to the door of a dingy bedroom. The skeletal body of the Duchess of Murnane lay under a clean coverlet, her rasping breath agitating the cloth.

"The death rattle," Zambak murmured. She had come to know it too well in the clinics.

"She's dying, Zambak, and she's my wife. I can't turn my back on her. I have to finish this."

When Julia died, he would be free. The temptation to rejoice curdled in her heart at the sight of the woman on the bed, dying painfully and, but for the generous heart of the husband she abused and abandoned, alone.

Zambak knew this man, his capacity for love, his forgiving heart, and his powerful drive to care for those under his responsibility. She understood the guilt that wracked him—not over his treatment of Julia, never that, but over his desire to be free at the cost of her life. He may hate what she had done, but he wouldn't abandon the woman, not even for Zambak. This was his penance, and he would suffer it to the end. Alone.

Her shoulders slumped. *He doesn't want me here.* "What about Thorn?" It was a half-hearted attempt to seize a scrap of his attention.

"What of him?"

"Did you give him laudanum?" She glanced at the brown bottle on a side table.

"No! Did Jarratt tell you that?" She nodded, and he seemed to realize the import of that. "Can I at least convince you to stay away from them? Promise me, Zambak? Let me finish this."

When she didn't answer, he pulled her to his chest, rubbing circles on her back. She felt kisses on her hair and over her ear. "Please," he begged. "Give me time. Just stay with the Elliots, and I'll get us out of here."

Us. The word gave her hope, but she made no promises.

A moan pulled his attention away. He bent to give his wife a sip of water. Zambak watched it dribble from the corner of her mouth and him gently wipe it away. She left without another word.

~ ~ ~

After a stop at her bank, Zambak returned to her sunny room in the Elliots' mansion that afternoon to wait, as Charles asked. She spent the afternoon sorting her belongings behind a locked door. In her privileged upbringing, a lady left packing to her servants. Not so this time.

She pulled her smaller traveling trunk from her dressing room and lifted the false bottom. Charles still had her first journal, but she had another, and it fit easily under the board, along with the few pieces of jewelry she had sewn into her breeches when she left London. A wad of the currency from her account went into the hollow space; a second one remained in the reticule she planned to keep close.

She left the breeches and most of her English dresses out, choosing instead to squeeze both sets of Manchu costume in over the false bottom, followed by the bare minimum in personal linen and practical clothing. If needed, she could dress in her Chinese finery on the voyage home.

Won't that just please my mother? She smiled to herself at the looks of horror she planned to provoke. She closed the trunk and lifted it by both handles. She could manage it herself if she needed to; she shoved it under her bed.

She left the larger of her trunks open in the dressing room. If they left in an orderly fashion, she might have servants pack the rest of her belongings. A tension in the air suggested she might have to move too fast, however.

No word came from Charles that day or in the ones that followed, and Zambak spent more time at Temperance's small home, returning to the mansion to sleep most nights or to change her clothes. Filipe followed her some days and disappeared others. When he came back, he never had messages, and she gave up asking. Clara Elliot, preoccupied with her own fears, did not stand in her way. The sense of rising tension left the British community stewing in the summer heat.

Temperance spent her mornings at the school, before she and Zambak worked side by side in the missionary clinic every afternoon. Opium-recovery patients continued to make heavy demands on their resources, and the Portuguese authorities were of little help.

After one such afternoon, they returned to the Knightons' home to find Aaron entertaining a guest. Dan Oliver leaned toward Temperance's husband in earnest conversation.

"Dan! Thee are welcome as always, but thy face tells me thee do not bring equally welcome news," Temperance said, giving voice to Zambak's thought.

"How bad is it?" Zambak demanded.

"We don't know yet, but it isn't good," he said.

"Then tell us simply," Temperance told him, "and be done with it."

He chewed his pipe for a moment, drawing a scowl from Temperance. "Trying to decide where to start," he said. "Do you know the *Lorne* has returned, Lady Zambak?"

"No one has said so outright, but I've heard snatches of conversation." *And read Elliot's dispatches all week.* "I am given to understand it is anchored off Hong Kong Island along with the *Reliance* watching the situation."

"Watching the war junks that are watching them, yes. Just like last year," Oliver agreed. "Boring work for fighting men. Some of your jack tars went on ashore along the coast for a bit of leave. They caused some mischief."

"How much mischief?" Zambak asked.

"A man is dead. They burnt down a temple—caused a riot." His ferocious frown conveyed his opinion about the matter.

"Shameful behavior," Temperance said. "They will be punished?"

Dan took a few more puffs, choosing his words, his eyes on Zambak. "That's the crux of the problem. The dead man is Chinese. Lin wants them turned over. Chinese law is harsh on matters of murder."

"And Captain Elliot refuses," Zambak finished for him. *Of course he does.* The hopeless inevitability of the crisis made her sick.

"He has them in custody and has promised a trial." His eyes caught hers.

He knows. For killing a foreigner? They'll get a slap on the wrist. "We have another standoff," she murmured.

"This time in Macao. Rumors down river are that Commissioner Lin is coming to consult with the Portuguese governor. He wants the murderer."

Zambak caught a tender exchange between the Knightons. Their entire life lay in Macao, their work as well as their precious children. Aaron took his wife in his arms. "Will there be room on thy ship, Dan?"

"If it comes to that, yes. But Aaron, it is the British Lin wants, not us."

Temperance took Zambak by the hand. "Perhaps thee ought to warn Charles."

Her heart leapt. An excuse to see him would have driven her there even if fear didn't. She glanced out the window. "I best go quickly before dark."

Light shown in the kitchen but nowhere else when she arrived at the little house. She wasn't surprised when no one answered the door. She went to the rear of the house, side stepped the laundry tubs, and picked up a handful of pebbles. It took her three attempts to hit the window where she believed Julia lay.

The damned man has it closed against a draft. *Isn't he hot in there?*

She hit the window a second time before it came open and a familiar auburn head peered out. She devoured the sight. He looked exhausted and, when he recognized her, panicked.

"Zambak! What is it? Are you well? Is it Thorn?"

"No, I—" She realized with a jolt that she had pushed the marquess from her mind. Helpless to change him, she had simply avoided the problem.

"What is it?"

She told him, eliciting a string of curses. "Lin is coming here?"

"Yes. Elliot will keep his prisoners off shore, but the Portuguese will do whatever the commissioner asks. Civilians should be safe." More hope than belief lay in that last statement.

"What were you doing at the Knightons'? I told you to stay with Elliot. You'll be safest there." He flicked a glance back over his shoulder and turned back to her. "Be ready to leave."

"I am." She smiled up at him.

"Good girl. I'll check on Thorn and make sure he's ready as well."

"Can you evacuate Julia?"

"Not without increasing her misery or hastening her death." The pause that followed bristled with unspoken wishes and unspeakable thoughts.

"No, you can't," she said. "I will wait with you."

"It may not come to that. We don't know that the city is in danger."

"Yet."

"If it is, go home. Be safe. Do what Elliot tells you when the time comes," he insisted. She stood her ground, watching him above her leaning both hands on the window frame. "Did you hear me, Zambak?" he asked, his voice cracking.

"Yes," she replied softly. "Be safe yourself, Charles. I love you."

Chapter 38

Charles sank to the floor, his back to the wall under the window, his head cradled on arms folded across his knees. *How much more of this can I endure?*

"Charles?" the voice sounded stronger than usual.

As long as I have to. "Yes, Julia?"

"That was Sudbury's chit, wasn't it?" his patient whined.

"Yes." He didn't move from where he sat, weary to his marrow.

"No better than she should be," Julia mumbled, attempting to sniff and failing. He couldn't work up any more rage.

"Charles?"

"Yes."

"Talk to me please. I hate the silence and the dark." *She hasn't spoken in two days. Why now?* Zambak's presence, he realized, disturbed her.

"What would you have me say?" he asked from his corner in the growing darkness.

"Tell me about my son. Tell me about Jonny." Her voice sounded thinner and farther away.

"No. Not again. Not tonight." *I can't bear it.*

"Rand then. What happened to your gullible cousin? Did he really marry a red Indian?"

Visions of Rand Wheatly and his family snug in their cabin in Upper Canada cheered him. "He married a woman of great courage and strength. A woman of character. He has become quite wealthy. Did you know that? They call him a timber baron."

"*Nouveau riche*," she mumbled dismissively. "Stupid farm boy." He let her drift back to sleep before going down to fetch Filipe.

He had failed his son, though doctors assured him he could do nothing. He was failing Zambak. He could at least try to salvage her brother.

~ ~ ~

"Two days, Your Grace. He left to stay with Mr. Jarratt two days ago. You never came back." Mrs. Josie stood palm out. He greased it with coins, ran upstairs, threw the last of his belongings into a haversack, and fetched Zambak's journal from under the floorboard. It was one more thing he could do: deliver their reports to her father. At least he could if he could get free of the dunghill that kept him in Macao.

The Murnane tiara came next to hand, shooting beams of light from his hand. He tried to envision it in Zambak's hair and failed. Emeralds would compliment her white blond hair far better. He briefly considered leaving it, but diamonds make useful bribes should it come to that. He reached deeper beneath the boards and pulled out two sleek percussion pistols and a bag of shot. There was no time to obtain a proper box. He added them to his haversack and set out to find Thorn.

He found him readily enough on the steps of William Jarratt's flamboyant mansion perched like a bird of prey uphill from the Elliots'. The marquess and the trader's nephew dressed in evening clothes and, looking as if they planned an evening in one of London's finer hotels, emerged from the house as he approached. Charles doubted very much they would seek anything respectable. Thorn's clothing hung loosely on him, and Charles concluded the boy had stopped eating again, living instead on laudanum. In the lamplight, his sallow skin testified to dissipation.

He bit back frustration and forced cheer into his words. A verbal battle with Hugo would be pointless. "Stepping out, gentlemen?" he asked sweetly. Too sweetly.

Thorn blinked twice, slow to gather his thoughts.

Jarratt had no such problem. He eyed Charles with the intensity of a fencer planning his killing blow and said, "There are delights to be sampled in Macao, Murnane. Care to join us?"

"Alas, no. I have responsibilities. I would like a word with the Marquess of Glenaire, however. A private word." He hoped the title might penetrate the haze around Thorn.

Jarratt glanced at the boy and back at Charles. "Yes. One recalls the duchess is ill. Pity that."

Bile rose in Charles's throat, and he fisted his hands to keep from attacking the man who left Julia in her filth in a deserted house to die. "Thorn, a word, please," he said.

Zambak's brother looked at his supposed friend, and the brute nodded. "I'll step away so you can have a little— family is it?—talk." He sauntered toward a waiting carriage, leaving Charles alone with Thorn on the porch. Hugo leaned against the carriage door and watched them through hooded eyes.

"Do you have any idea what's happening here?" Charles hissed.

"Quiet evening," Thorn responded, looking confused.

"Do you know about the murder?" Charles asked. He outlined Lin's demands.

"Hugo says Elliot won't give in. Send in the navy first. Hugo says Lin is a, a—" Thorn scrunched up his forehead. "A paper dragon."

Charles bit down hard, frustration with the fool wreaking havoc with his self-control. Thorn, oblivious, went on cheerfully. "When the navy comes, we can expand trade. We'll all be rich. Even my father will be impressed." He patted Charles on the arm.

Charles shook him off and leaned in until is face was inches from Thorn's. "Listen to me carefully, Thorn. Lin is no paper dragon. He will enforce Chinese justice. He may not be able to do it forever, but he can, and he will make life hell for the British in Macao and the entire Pearl Delta while he's doing it. He is on his way to Macao, and the Portuguese will bow to his wishes. They have to if they want to retain their city."

"Hugo says—" Thorn looked confused.

"Be quiet and listen. No matter what the minions of Jarratt & Martinson tell you, remember this. Your sister is here. Whatever comes down on the city, she will be in danger. Do you hear me?"

Thorn's eyes widened, and he said nothing.

"Do you hear me?" Charles repeated. Thorn nodded. "Your sister will need your protection."

"But you—"

Charles overrode him. "I may not be able to help her when the time comes. I pray she stays close to Elliot, but you know Zambak as well as I do. She may put herself in danger. If I can't get to her, she will be alone. You have an obligation—a duty—to protect her. Do you hear me?" Desperation gave his words force.

Thorn looked toward Hugo Jarratt as if the man could help him sort out a confusing puzzle.

"Coming, Glenaire?" Hugo called. "Delights await."

The powerful longing in Thorns eyes drove out all other thought, and Charles knew with certainty where they were going. Having reintroduced him to laudanum, the Jarratts planned to bury him in opium smoking next. Darkness seeped into his soul.

"I have to go, Charles. Can't wait the horses." Thorn brushed passed him and hurried to the carriage with more animation than he had shown about anything else. Thorn, he could see with black despair, would be lost to them.

Chapter 39

Word came from Zhuhai just beyond the gates, brought by breathless runners to Charles Elliot's door, that the commissioner had paused in his journey. That same morning, placards appeared across the city declaring in Chinese and Portuguese that, if Commissioner Lin were to hear that a Chinese citizen had murdered a foreigner, he would without hesitation order the murderer's execution. His meaning was not lost on the Chinese and mixed-race residents of Macao—nor on the foreign community.

Zambak haunted the lower rooms while men came and went, their loud voices echoing from Elliot's study, and Clara Elliot fluttered about the place as if nothing unusual was happening. She kept busy in part by adding to her journals what she gleaned from *The Chinese Repository* and from nightly forays to pry open dispatch boxes. There was little enough of it. One detail appalled her. Elliot thought removing the British from Canton removed them from use as hostages again. It never occurred to him Lin would move on Macao.

Elliot held the guilty sailors in the brig of the HMS *Fort William* anchored off Kowloon and prepared to put them on trial. Lin pretended not to hear his petitions and sent further demands that they be handed over to Chinese justice.

The day following the appearance of placards, frightened Macao hong officials huddled with their foreign counterparts. Word filtered to the Elliot mansion quickly. Commissioner Lin sent a formal edict reminding them that the prohibitions present in Canton applied to merchants in Macao as well, and the penalty for disobedience remained the same—death. He subtly made clear that he knew full well the extent to which the "treacherous barbarians" had held back opium and were plying their trade from Macao.

When several traders came to talk to Elliot, he stood in the door and told them to "stop the nonsense until this blows over."

Zambak, sitting quietly in the shadow of a potted palm near his office, heard Elliot's angry outburst when another petition came back unopened. "He can't seize the property of British subjects with impunity, and he will not get custody of members of Her Majesty's navy."

Replies from the Portuguese couldn't have been clearer. They could not help and would not try. They meant to hold on to their colonial outpost and the British be damned.

Zambak did not believe Lin's wrath would blow over— or bend. They defied him, and he singled out the British to pay. Two more American firms had signed bonds demanded by Lin and publicly renounced the opium trade—the sincerity of which actions Zambak begged to doubt. Elliot had ordered the British not to sign, and the merchants had happily complied. Now Lin approached their doorstep. Elliot, she knew from the dispatches, had finally sent for the navy.

Filipe came twice daily, only to run back to Charles with missives from Zambak in which political events mixed with desperate declarations of the heart. When asked about the situation in the little house, Filipe just shook his head sadly. No change.

Three days after the edict, lightning shattered a massive tree in the Portuguese compound, and rain pounded the roofs of the city. As if in harmony, the political storm broke. Charles Elliot, wary of Lin's intent and tired of waiting for the navy, suggested the British community take to their ships rather than risk a blockade like that at Canton. All his petitions for an audience had been refused.

Lucy Ingram rushed in, dripping rain to spew terror and hugs all over Clara Elliot, who struggled to calm her own children before announcing she would be first to board her husband's ship.

"It will take a day or more, Captain Elliot," Clara declared. "I can't just drag them out in their socks."

Zambak carried her small trunk down and placed it discretely next to the growing pile of Elliot luggage. She left her larger trunk to the mercies of servants and sought her bonnet. She would at least say good-bye to her missionary friends and perhaps glean some more sanely parsed information from Dan Oliver.

She tripped running down the front walk, righted herself, and darted down the street. Unlike the eerie quiet of the previous several days, frantic activity now swirled around her. She turned toward the missionary compound, and a decision solidified.

I'll go to that blasted house when I'm done and send Filipe after my trunk. I will stay with Charles as long as it takes—whether he wants me or not. I won't leave without him.

When she reached the Rua dos Mercadores, crowds confronted her. Clerks and secretaries in British-style clothing walked toward the docks, and others went about their business, but the bulk of the seething mass tended north toward the Border Gate on the causeway connecting Macao to the rest of China. Small patrols of Portuguese soldiers made a show of keeping order.

He's coming. She stopped in her tracks. *How can I turn my back on the arrival of the commissioner to Macao?* After everything she had done so far, she refused to leave without seeing this act in the drama. She fleetingly considered a return to the Elliots' to change to Chinese dress and swiftly rejected it. Within moments, Zambak had scribbled two notes and, with the help of a few small coins, dispatched one to the American mission compound and another to the little house near São Lourenço.

Lin Zexu would come down the causeway with his retinue in full display. She didn't plan to miss it.

~ ~ ~

Deep in the night death lurked, its sound as familiar as its face. Charles alternately paced and sank into stolid waiting. What could be said had been said; what could not be reconciled had been endured. Selfish to the end, Julia neither begged forgiveness nor forgave him for the indebtedness his tenderness and care thrust on her. She took his ministrations with resentment and paid him back by clinging to life as long as possible.

As her breathing grew shallower and shallower, each breath further from the last, Jonny's last hours came to him, and he wept—not for the woman on the bed, but for the wreck that had been his marriage and for the boy, the one good thing that had come from it. He wept until he couldn't and knew in his heart he had finally let go of his son and all that tied him to the past.

She took a shuddering breath, and he murmured, "Try to find peace, Julia, if you can. You won't find it here." He rose to pace again, but silence spoke to him more loudly than words. There had been no other breath. He waited momentarily, and hearing no other, placed his hand over her eyes to make sure they closed and consigned her to God's mercy. He pulled the sheet up over her head.

He stood, a hollow shell, staring down at the bed until a voice brought him back to the world. "'r Grace? I talk now?"

Filipe hopped from one foot to the other in the doorway, casting wary glances at the bed. He had burst into the room the evening before and been summarily thrown out. Charles vaguely remembered one or two attempts to interrupt him later. He had turned them away.

"Yes. Talk now. What's so important?"

"Lady Zam sent note."

Lady Zam. Emotion flooded into his emptiness, a torrent of yearning and desire, a bone-deep need to see, to touch, to possess. *I have to tell her. I need—* The boy's words penetrated him finally. "What note?"

"You didn't want, so Filipe read it," the boy went on, proud of the accomplishment. "I fetched her trunk, but she not come."

"What do you mean 'come'? Where?"

"Come here. She say to fetch trunk and meet here. I do, but no Lady Zam."

He cursed in three languages—two of which the grinning boy seemed to understand. "Why isn't she at Elliots'?" he demanded.

"Missy Elliot say Lady Zam is in her room, but I looked. Dresses everywhere. No Lady Zam. Missy Elliot say 'Foolish girl will have to meet us at the dock. Go find her.'"

"Did you?" Charles ran an agitated hand through his hair. "Of course you didn't. Otherwise, you wouldn't be dancing in the doorway. Where is this message from Lady Zambak?"

Filipe dug around in his grimy shirt and pulled out a much re-folded paper.

Charles

Not to worry. Lin has begun his formal entry—you know his penchant for show—I will just watch a bit, duck into Knightons' to say good-bye, and join you. The entire British community is packing to leave. Be ready.

I won't leave without you, you stubborn man.
Zamb
P.S. Have Filipe fetch the trunk that is by the clock in Elliots' foyer. I will join him at your house.

"See. My name," Filipe said proudly, pointing.

"Did you look for her at the mission school?"

"Last night only. Not there. Not at house of mission lady." He sobered. "'r Grace, streets very bad last night. Gangs. Soldiers. Very bad."

Charles crumbled the note and considered the possibilities, some of them unthinkable. "Either she returned to the Knightons' late and stayed there, or she returned to Elliot's when things got dangerous," he said, groping for his packed haversack behind the foot of Julia's bed. *Or Lin has her.* He shoved several uglier thoughts aside, loaded both pistols, and shoved them into his belt.

He bolted to the door only to be brought up short by the sight of her trunk next to his front door. He flipped it open, hoping for a clue that might help him locate her but found only her neat and practical collection of traveling clothes. He smiled at the Manchu fabrics, reached under, and easily sprung the false bottom.

I need to teach her better subterfuge. He whistled at the wad of money. Trust a Hayden. He returned a fourth of it and split the rest between his boot and haversack. He left her trinkets. The real treasure, her journals and notes, he put with the one in his haversack.

The situation is moving in too many directions at once. "Filipe, take this blasted thing back to Elliots'. No! Better. Get it on Elliot's own ship, HMS *Reliance*. Failing that, get it on any vessel of Her Majesty's navy but not—and this is important—on a merchant ship. Am I clear?"

He handed the servant bank notes and hoped he didn't

drop the trunk in the harbor and disappear onto the mainland. He couldn't worry about it. He started out the door.

"Where meet?" Filipe asked from behind him.

"Pardon?"

"After I take trunk. Where meet?"

"Stay with the trunk. We'll find you."

Chapter 40

Night terrors never bedeviled Zambak Hayden; at least they didn't until a city in chaos left her confused, lost, and utterly alone.

There had been other westerners in the throng along the road toward the sea when Lin's entourage came, banners flying and drums beating, to the Lin Fung Temple, and the great man himself stood to address them. She had been too far to hear his words, but she could guess them, and the unease that built around her confirmed her fears. The western barbarians would not be permitted to flout Chinese justice.

She had edged away then, forced toward the coast and the fishing shacks along it. She moved confidently enough at first and quickly realized crowds made it impossible to go directly across toward the mission compound. Prudence dictated she get herself back to the Elliots' mansion instead.

I can send word to Charles from there, she had thought. It would be hours before she realized how futile that might be.

Crowds and the need for caution slowed her significantly. Once she bought rice to eat. When she tried to hire a messenger, the scoundrel fled with her reticule and most of her money. She hoarded what little she had in her shoe after that, fearing a greater emergency. By nightfall, she had begun to limp and was still far from her destination.

A few kind looks came her way, but the local people mostly gave her wide berth. In the end, it was Portuguese soldiers that spooked her. She was not so innocent she did not recognize the lust in the eyes of the tall man who tried to maneuver her toward a dark alley. She didn't miss the second one who circled around to her other side, outlined against light streaming from the door of a cook shop. She looked around frantically for help; only the blank faces of the Chinese met hers, the faces of people who found it prudent to stay out of the affairs of westerners in troubled times.

Zambak darted between the two men, overturned the vegetable cart an elderly gentleman nearby attempted to unpack for the night to stop them, and fled. Sounds assaulted her from every side, and shadows nipped at her heels. She ran until the breath left her body and collapsed against the wall of a Buddhist shrine on an unfamiliar street, feeling like a fool for giving in to blind panic, and waited for the area to shut down for the night. It took hours.

Now she pulled her knees up and assessed her situation with deliberate calm.

Think Zambak. Think. Where are you?

A shaft of moonlight illuminated the street along which the temple sat. She rose to her knees and peered around the wall. Row after row of low Chinese-style buildings lined the road, shuttered now. She pulled back once when two men came down the road, but neither looked her way. They appeared to be collecting waste. Only the sound of small animals burrowing broke the quiet.

She examined the street again, building by building. Chancing a glance up, she finally saw it, the outline of a larger temple some streets over rising above the roofline. She sank back and dropped her elbows to her knees, her head to her hands.

A proliferation of temples here. I must have circled back toward Lin Fung where I started. I can use that as a starting point and find my way if I can figure out which direction it is. She couldn't.

She breathed heavily, determined to brave daylight when it came, until something—an intensification of the darkness where she sat perhaps—made her scalp prickle.

"Found you," the disembodied voice declared, and her heart stopped.

~ ~ ~

Charles walked, ran, and, in some cases, elbowed his way to the missionary clinic only to find it closed and Temperance's school as well. Moments later he pounded on the door to their house.

"Charles, thee are welcome," Temperance said, opening and inviting him in. "Have thee word of Zambak?" Her worried frown didn't bode well.

"I was hoping you did. The impulsive chit sent a note and disappeared. I wouldn't put it past her to demand an audience with the commissioner."

Dan Oliver sat in the rocker, pipe between his teeth. "Aaron and I looked for her in the crowd by the Lin Fung temple with no success. The old fox is holding court up there, and the Portuguese went hat in hand to kowtow."

Temperance pressed a cup of tea into his hand; he realized it was shaking. "Have thee eaten, Charles?"

"Not since yesterday. Maybe the day before, I don't know."

"Thee must eat. I have oat porridge this morning, but perhaps cold ham? Thee must eat." She studied him with the eyes of a skilled nurse—or mother.

"She—my wife—died, and I haven't been able to. Now I don't have time," he said.

Aaron Knighton spoke from the corner. "We regret thy loss, Charles, and the burdens thee have carried."

Temperance gripped his arm, a moment of comfort, quickly gone. "Eat now. Thee will think better what must be done." A steaming bowl appeared in front of him. He wolfed it down while Dan described the situation in the city. He realized halfway through that the American's words were carefully chosen and spoken with deliberate calm. He glanced around as he ate; Aaron had shuttered their windows and locked them down with iron bars.

"What are you avoiding?" he demanded.

"Just waiting for you to fortify yourself. You can't stay here," Oliver told him.

He shrugged. "We need to leave. How is that new?"

"Warnings came last night—some Portuguese official who preferred not to be named sent word to McIlroy. Lin plans to surround every British household tonight."

"Hold us hostage in our houses?" Ruthless even for Lin Zexu. It horrified him.

"At very least. The evacuation has turned into a rout," Dan said.

Charles glanced around at the shuttered windows, the food stocks piled on Temperance's dry sink, and her children at her skirts. "If I stay here, I put you in danger," he said.

Dan shrugged. "Probably. Maybe even if you don't. These stubborn fools insist on staying in any case."

"We are not British, Daniel," Temperance said. "And our calling is here."

"Lin may distinguish between Yank and Englishman, but the rabble won't if unleashed," Dan said sternly.

She shook her head. "We have friends here. We will stay."

Charles pushed to his feet. "Thank you for feeding me, Temperance. I'll remove one hazard from your home at least."

"Wait! Where are you going? You have a few hours at best." Dan rose with him.

"I have to find Zambak first," Charles said.

"You'll find her faster with help. I already sent for some of my crew. See, here." He spread paper on the table and sketched out a crude map of Macao on its peninsula, the port on the lee side and the other facing the sea. They agreed to begin at the northern Border Gate and fan out. Dan's third mate and another seaman, both Chinese, would take the sea approach where the fishing boats tied up and go around to the port. Dan and Aaron would come down the other side, scour the area near the seminary, and search the commercial area around the harbor. Charles insisted on beginning at Lin Fung Temple and searching down the center of Macao.

"Meet us in the harbor, Charles. Promise us. If we do not find her, the final place to look will be on the boats. The lady will not thank thee if thee lag behind," Aaron said with the conviction of a married man who knew his woman's needs, and the need of two souls to protect one another.

"Don't wait for me," he replied, hafting his haversack and reaching for the door.

Dan started to object, but Charles waved a staying hand. "I will go to the harbor, but if we get lost in the confusion, I'll look for Elliot's vessels for preference. If I can't find them, I'll take what I can—and yes, I'll search for her on the boats."

His grim determination kept his fears at bay when he made his way toward the Lin Fung Temple.

Chapter 41

Sun beat down on Charles where he lay, parched and hungry, on the deck of the *Reliance* two days later. Elliot commanded rationing of food and water throughout the floating city that lay at anchor at the mouth of the Pearl River between Macao, Hong Kong Island, and Kowloon. War junks prevented them from going ashore for supplies, and Elliot chose not to risk outright confrontation with women and children aboard, at least not until reinforcements arrived.

"Water, 'r Grace." Filipe stooped over him, a half cup of liquid in his hand.

"Give it to the children." Charles didn't care if he lived or died.

"Cap Elliot say 'tell 's Grace not to be idiot.' Drink."

Idiot? They had sent word to every ship in the godforsaken refugee fleet after Oliver and Aaron hustled him onto the *Reliance* to no avail. Zambak had not made it to the boats, and Elliot refused to put Charles ashore. He considered stealing a dinghy in an insane moment the night before and would have if he had any idea where to look. He could only pray that Lin had her and that the commissioner chose to be merciful. It seemed unlikely.

He dragged himself to his knees and took the cup Filipe offered. The boy jumped up and stared at the bridge. "Something happening, 'r Grace," he said.

Another damned message? The officers sent dispatches back and forth like old women exchanging gossip at a tea party. Charles glanced up idly. Something in the posture of the officers was different, and he sharpened his gaze. He stood to investigate as a cheer went up from the nearest merchant ship and began to spread.

He sprinted to the bridge. The first officer grinned and handed him the spyglass. Three ships approached from the southwest, the Union Jack flapping from their masts and cannon bristling from their sides. The navy had arrived, or enough of it to give Elliot a show of force.

God help the city. A fully armed frigate sailed into view accompanied by two other ships. Charles focused closely. He made out the *Hyacinth* close behind the *Volage*. He handed the telescope to the second mate. When he got it back, the HMS *Bridgetown* came into view. *McGuffin! Thank God for the sight of a friend.*

Late that afternoon, two seamen rowed Charles and Filipe, sitting on Zambak's trunk and happily bearing the haversack, to the *Bridgetown*. The duke left, happy to escape the miserable women and children in Clara Elliot's care. Elliot for his part appeared equally relieved to be rid of his troublesome guest.

McGuffin grinned down as he scrambled up the rope ladder and landed on the deck with a graceful leap, Filipe stumbling up behind him. The captain made an ostentatious bow.

"Welcome aboard my little kingdom, Your Grace," he said, managing to be welcoming while reminding Charles that aboard ship titles mattered little. The captain ruled. He clapped Charles on the back. "Rumor has it conditions have not been great. I have an interesting bottle of rum in my cabin that may ease the pain."

Charles doubted rum would ease what caused his anguish, but there would be time enough to explain that to McGuffin.

A cry stopped them halfway across the deck. "Ahoy *Bridgetown*!"

"More guests? Did you bring an entourage, Murnane?" Charles stared across the sea while the captain pulled a spyglass from his coat. A fishing boat approached, bobbing in the choppy sea. He grabbed the telescope from his friend's hand.

Thorn Hayden clung to the mast with one arm and waved the other, continuing to shout "Ahoy." After the initial shock, Charles ignored him, his eyes fixed on the bow of the boat.

Zambak stood tall at the bow, facing forward with her hair billowing about her face like a cloud of light.

How in God's name did they manage this? He didn't care. He just gave thanks.

~ ~ ~

The cheers and catcalls still echoed when Charles stopped kissing her. She didn't care. She grinned and gave the crew a snappy salute, setting them off again. Filipe danced from foot to foot, Thorn frowned, and an austere-looking navy captain had a suspiciously pink face.

"If I may suggest, my lady, perhaps we can continue this reunion—and clarify what has happened—in my cabin?"

She knew as soon as Elliot told her Charles had transferred to the *Reliance* that Julia had died, or he wouldn't be there, and her brother—pleased to be in command of the rickety vessel—had directed the fisherman to continue on.

She clung to Charles and would have made love to him on the deck or followed him to the moon. No disapproving military man would stand in her way. Charles, however, appeared a bit sheepish. He laced his fingers with hers and tugged her toward the cabin. *Silly man. Have it your way.*

On their way, she heard the captain give orders to set sail for Madras. In answer to Charles's question, he explained they had come only to deliver arms and supplies. "We've no dog in this fight, more's the pity," he said. "We'll leave the nonsense to Elliot and the others." Her Majesty's navy apparently thought two additional ships sufficient to subdue the situation for the time being. They were probably right. It wouldn't be long before the shooting started.

Zambak considered the journals she and Charles so carefully kept and knew they were too late. She thought fleetingly of Lin and his honor, of the girls in the Ladies' Seminary, and of Temperance. She could do nothing for any of them when it did. She could only move forward and hope to influence the future.

McGuffin sat them around his table while Zambak's brother monopolized the conversation, and Charles simply caressed her with his eyes in ways that caused her nether parts to quiver and heat to radiate up from her chest.

"I just asked myself the worst place she could go and headed that way," Thorn explained. "I knew she couldn't stay away from Lin's big show up by the temples. After I got away from Hugo—"

That caught Charles's attention. He pulled his eyes from hers and grabbed her hand instead, small consolation. "When did you leave Jarratt? I thought you were hell bent on sinking into the opium tar."

Thorn grimaced. "Sorry, Charles. You wouldn't be wrong. Hugo kept talking about the poppy, that deep peace, and the elation when—well. Like he knew." His hands shook, and Zambak wondered how close he had come.

Her brother addressed her directly then, as if he read her thoughts. "He wanted to pull me into it, and I wanted to go—oh God how I wanted to go—but when we got there, I saw something. The door to the opium den opened, and they threw a man out. Threw him into the street! I bent over to check on him, and Hugo pulled on my coat. When I told him we couldn't just leave him in the street, do you know what he said?"

She reached over and took one of his hands while he swallowed convulsively. She waited for him to go on.

"Hugo said, 'The damned fool let the poppy kill him. Deserves to die in the gutter.'" Thorn's misery tore at her heart as words poured out of him. "I remembered the family at Peters' clinic, Zamb, and thought it could have been me lying there and you not even knowing I died. And I remembered what Charles said about you being in danger. Went to Elliots', but you were missing, and I had to find you. My responsibility wasn't it?"

"Thank God you did," she said, "I never could have convinced those fishermen to get us out of Macao."

He managed the shadow of a smile, swiftly gone. "I hate opium—and I love it. I may always. But you did your best to free me from it, and I owed you my protection. Charles called it duty, and it is, but family, Zamb, it's more than that, isn't it?"

Her heart turned over, and moisture prickled her eyes. She pulled her brother into an embrace. "I love you, Thorn. I'm proud of you. Father will be proud too," she told him over the thickness in her throat.

"Maybe. Maybe eventually," he said. When she let him go, he stared at his lap, shame in the droop of his shoulders.

McGuffin handed her a cup of tea, and she sat back down next to Charles. She sniffed it gratefully and took a sip.

"Different," she said and took another. "I like it. What is it?"

"Grows wild in Assam—Northern India."

Charles leaned over and kissed the side of her head, drawing a glare from Thorn. "You made a spectacle of my sister out there, Charles. Should I call you out? What are your intentions?" he demanded.

"Entirely honorable," Charles said with a gentle smile. "And I'm free to say so, so you can withhold the challenge."

The three men sat in self-satisfied agreement a moment too long. An interminable, chaste—frustrating—voyage loomed in front of Zambak.

She looked at McGuffin. "Tell me, Captain, is it true you can marry people?" Charles rewarded her with a smile so intimate she wished the others to the devil at that moment.

The captain cleared his throat. "I can my lady, but let me be clear. I am the law on this ship. Whether a marriage I perform meets muster with the Church of England on land is another matter. You would have to consult them in Madras. Your mother may not be best pleased with a havy-cavy marriage."

"Let *me* be clear, Captain. I intend to share a cabin with the Duke of Murnane. I don't give a fig how legal your marriage might be on shore as long as it satisfies His Grace's sense of honor for the length of the voyage." His fingers squeezed hers, and joy bubbled up.

And so it was. They married before the mast in front of a crew of strangers with the setting sun at their backs while Macao disappeared over the horizon. Her brother beamed at them, and Filipe danced a jig. He danced late into the night, learning a hornpipe and listening to seaman sing. The entire ship celebrated their joy.

The Duke and Duchess of Murnane, snug in the captain's cabin, didn't join in. They didn't sleep either.

~ ~ ~

A very private and long-awaited celebration went on past dawn in the narrow confines of McGuffin's cabin. Zambak, spent and boneless, lay sleeping in her husband's arms when the first pale light shown through the window. Tranquil and vulnerable, the treasure in his arms filled the empty spaces in Charles's heart and healed his soul.

He had worshiped her with his body through the night as his vows commanded. His fears that the first rush of passion long denied might cause her discomfort or pain vanished in her enthusiastic response, giving love even as he poured his into her. Now, his breathing moved with hers, and his heart matched the gentle beating he could feel against his chest.

A movement, almost imperceptible, alerted him that she began to awaken. He kissed her hair and felt her return a kiss against his shoulder. "Morning?" she asked.

"Yes. The first of many like this," he replied, causing her to go up on one elbow and smile at him.

She closed her eyes and took a long breath before opening them again to peer at him. He loved the way she seemed to see his deepest thoughts and desires. "What now?" she asked.

"More?" he suggested hopefully, moving his burgeoning body against hers.

"Yes, oh yes, but I meant after. Shall we go home or linger in India."

He lay back, wondering what had engaged the unrelenting machine that was her brain the morning after their wedding. "I hadn't given it any thought," he said dryly. "I had other things in mind." Still on her elbow, her hair slipped down over one bare shoulder, distracting him, but he tried to listen, genuinely curious about her complicated thought processes.

"We could stay in India for a while," she said. He waited for more. "Our report is too late to stop the conflict."

"Very true," he said, tweaking one lock of hair.

"Tea may be the answer in the end."

"Tea?" He rose, impatient, forcing her to lay back flat and looming over her for a kiss.

She responded in kind, but all too soon she went on. "We should visit Assam and see about this Indian tea. We might undermine—"

He pushed her idea to the back of his mind. There would be time to think about it later. He kissed her again and let his eager hands roam.

She tipped her head back to give him access to the tender spot where her neck met her shoulder. "Besides . . ."

That penetrated his lust. He pulled up on an elbow. "Besides what?"

"Presenting them with a grandchild would squash any objections my parents might make, don't you think?" She grinned up at him.

He smiled back and lowered his head. "I am happy to oblige your plan, my love," he murmured against her skin.

Epilogue

The Earl of Chadbourn and the Duke of Sudbury saw their wives to bed, promising to join them shortly.

Andrew McGuffin had arrived at Sudbury House that morning, complaining of shore duty and carrying a collection of fascinating journals the duke put aside for study. He also brought a report to Her Majesty the queen and news that filled the duke and duchess with so much joy they hastened to share it with their friends. Even now it called for one more glass of the earl's fine whisky, gleaned from his sources in Scotland. The two men drank with the contentment of those who have arranged the world to their own satisfaction.

"India, though, Richard. You would think they would come on home in easy stages," the earl said at last.

"I suspect, Will, my first grandson will be born in India," the duke answered. He waved the letter that had arrived with McGuffin that morning.

"They didn't say that," Will responded.

"They didn't have to. She says they wanted to see Thorn settled in a business venture—this tea plantation business—but I suspect there is more. They probably think presenting us with a grandchild will smooth over any parental disapproval."

Will snorted. "As if there is any. He's perfect for her, and you know it." He mulled the duke's supposition for a few minutes. "You may be right, though. Charles wouldn't waste time." After another moment, he gave his lifelong friend a sly smile. "Could be a granddaughter, though."

The duke choked on his drink. Will grinned. It wasn't often he could get Richard to lower the façade he showed the world.

Soon the duke doubled over with laughter. "A girl! Oh God, I hope so. It would serve Charles right."

He sobered eventually, and they sipped in companionable silence.

"What do you think about the tea business?" Will asked eventually.

"She thinks it may grow well in Assam, in the mountains in the north of India. She thinks we should bypass the whole mess in China. They plan to leave Thorn in charge. Good idea, that. He needs purpose."

Will eyed his lifelong friend with sympathy. "I hope so, Richard. Perhaps some success will make a difference."

"She wrote that he's building riverboats for transport."

"There's nothing wrong with a duke's heir building with his own hands."

"If it gives him peace, I applaud it. It won't prepare him for the duties that will fall to him, though," Richard replied grimly.

"Time enough for that later. For tonight, we have happy news."

"We do indeed," Zambak's father answered.

They drank in silent camaraderie for a long time, until Richard remembered something else.

"Did I mention that she included a note for my nephew Archie about the tea?" the duke asked.

"The botanist? Archimedes Mallet? Isn't he still at Cambridge?"

"Yes, but one suspects not for long, what with his brother unearthing Egypt. Can't let him have all the adventure, I suspect," Richard said.

Will grinned and sat back in his chair. "Those boys do seem ready to seek their fortune."

"Boys?" Richard raised a ducal eyebrow. "Tell that to your Emma."

Will Landrum, Earl of Chadbourn, choked on his whisky and vowed to have a word with his wife.

Historical Note

On September 4, 1839, ships under the command of Charles Elliot opened fire on Chinese war junks attempting to prevent them from supplying the floating community from Kowloon, now part of Hong Kong. It was at best a skirmish, but it represented the opening fight of the First Opium War.

Charles Elliot and Lin Zexu are historical figures. I have done my best to keep their actions in 1838 and 1839 as accurate as possible in the context of the story, which is, after all, fiction. Timing of events, however, may be compressed by weeks or months. I moved the letter to Queen Victoria, for example, from fall to spring 1839. Scenes of their interactions with my fictional characters are, of course, entirely my creation. The Elliots, to my knowledge, did not host a duke's daughter while in Macao, nor did Lin Zexu ever confront a foreign woman.

Jarratt, Oliver, and other merchants are fictional characters loosely based on actual China traders of the era. I leave it to my readers' research to determine which ones influenced me, if they have an interest. There is one small exception. James Innes is real, and he actually was expelled from Canton and Macao in December 1838.

Lin did indeed write an open letter to Queen Victoria and request assistance of the American missionary, Doctor Peter Parker, with the English. My fictional Doctor Peters is, you might guess, based loosely on Parker, an ophthalmologist who ran a clinic at Zion's Corner (not Quarter). Lin also sought the missionaries' advice about what we now call *withdrawal*. Parker founded an ophthalmic hospital in Canton that still exists; it is now the Canton Pok Tsai Hospital.

A word about language: I have chosen to use names common in the English language newspapers of the era rather than the modern names for places. Thus, Canton and not Guangzhou, for example. I chose Macao over Macau for the same reason. Words related to drug addiction gave me greater problems. The word "drug" generally applied to herbal substances and not to narcotics until the late 1800s. "Narcotic" did exist but was not in general use. "Addiction" referred to a compulsion but did not have the narrow meaning we now ascribe to it. "Withdrawal" as it relates to drug use is a 20th-century term. If my construction seems clumsy to a reader in places as a result, I apologize.

Whole libraries have been written and causes debated for the war that followed Charles and Zambak's departure from Macao. Those books drone on about "opening China," "free trade," and "extraterritoriality." In the end, however, one bit of justice emerges. The First Opium War and the second one that followed it retain at least in name what really fueled the conflict, opium—the desire of China to free its people from the drug's curse and the drive of the merchants to grow rich by forcing it on them. It was a time eerily like our own. After all, it was only business.

Acknowledgments

No book comes to fruition by efforts of an author alone. This one owes an enormous debt to the readers of the previous two books in the series. Their comments, questions, and affection for Charles helped me craft his story.

Any polish the final version displays owes much to my beta readers: Jude Knight and Sherry Ewing, who also patiently listened to my woes and let me bounce ideas off them; Dee Deacon Foster, who gave me Mrs. Josie; and particularly to Cathy Rackowski, whose insight into the emotional dynamic of addiction on the sufferer and family helped more than I can repay.

Finally, my eternal gratitude goes to Debby Gilbert and the good people at Soul Mate Publishing, especially to Tamus Bairen, the best editor a writer could hope for.

Also from **Soul Mate Publishing**
and **Caroline Warfield**:

DANGEROUS WORKS

A little Greek is one thing; the art of love is another. Only one man has ever tried to teach Lady Georgiana Hayden both. She learned very young to keep her heart safe. She learned to keep loneliness at bay through work. If it takes a scandalous affair to teach her what she needs to complete her work, she will risk it. If the man in question chooses not to teach her, she will use any means at her disposal to change his mind. She is determined to give voice to the ancient women whose poetry has long been neglected.

Some scars cut deeper than others. Major Andrew Mallet returns to Cambridge a battle-scarred hero. He dared to love Georgiana once and suffered swift retribution from her powerful family. The encounter cost him eleven years of his life. Determined to avoid her, he seeks work to heal his soul and make his scholarly father proud. The work she offers risks his career, his peace of mind, and (worst of all) his heart. Can he protect himself from a woman who almost destroyed him? Does he want to?

Even poetry is dangerous when you partner with the love of your life. In Regency, Cambridge, it can lead a lady quickly past improper to positively scandalous.

Available now on Amazon: <u>DANGEROUS WORKS</u>

DANGEROUS SECRETS

When a little brown wren of an Englishwoman bursts into Jamie Heyworth's private Hell and asks for help he mistakes her for the black crow of death. Why not? He fled to Rome and sits in despair with nothing left to sell and no reason to get up in the morning. Behind him lie disgrace, shame, and secrets he is desperate to keep.

Nora Haley comes to Rome at the bidding of her dying brother who has an unexpected legacy. Never in her sunniest dreams did Nora expect Robert to leave her a treasure, a tiny black-eyed niece with curly hair and warm hugs. Nora will do anything to keep her, even hire a shabby, drunken major as an interpreter.

Jamie can't let Nora know the secrets he has hidden from everyone, even his closest friends. Nora can't trust any man who drinks. She had enough of that in her marriage. Either one, however, will dare anything for the little imp that keeps them together, even enter a sham marriage to protect her.

And don't miss *Dangerous Works*, where Jamie first appeared.

Available now on Amazon: <u>DANGEROUS SECRETS</u>

DANGEROUS WEAKNESS

If women were as easily managed as the affairs of state—or the recalcitrant Ottoman Empire—Richard Hayden, Marquess of Glenaire, would be a happier man. As it was, the creatures—one woman in particular—made hash of his well-laid plans and bedeviled him on all sides.

Lily Thornton came home from Saint Petersburg in pursuit of marriage. She wants a husband and a partner, not an overbearing, managing man. She may be "the least likely candidate to be Marchioness of Glenaire," but her problems are her own to fix, even if those problems include both a Russian villain and an interfering Ottoman official.

Given enough facts, Richard can fix anything. But protecting that impossible woman is proving almost as hard as protecting his heart, especially when Lily's problems bring her dangerously close to an Ottoman revolution. As Lily's personal problems entangle with Richard's professional ones, and she pits her will against his, he chases her across the pirate-infested Mediterranean. Will she discover surrender isn't defeat? That it might even have its own sweet reward.

Available now on Amazon: **DANGEROUS WEAKNESS**

THE RENEGADE WIFE

The Renegade Wife kicks off the new **Children of the Empire** series, companion stories to award-winning author Caroline Warfield's **Dangerous** series. Raised with all the privilege of the English aristocracy, forged on the edges of the British Empire, men and woman of the early Victorian age seek their own destiny and make their mark on history. *The Renegade Wife* is the story of healing and a journey home, of choices and the freedom to make them, set in 1832 in Upper Canada and in England.

Two hearts betrayed by love…

Desperate and afraid, Meggy Blair will do whatever it takes to protect her children. She'd hoped to find sanctuary from her abusive husband with her Ojibwa grandmother, but can't locate her. When her children fall ill, she finds shelter in an isolated cabin in Upper Canada. But when the owner unexpectedly returns, he's furious to find squatters disrupting his self-imposed solitude.

Reclusive businessman Rand Wheatly had good reason to put an ocean between himself and the family that deceived him. He just wants the intrusive woman gone, but it isn't long before Meggy and the children start breaking down the defensive walls he's built. But their fragile interlude is shattered when Meggy's husband appears to claim his children, threatening to have Rand jailed.

The only way for Meggy to protect Rand is to leave him. But when her husband takes her and the children to England, Meggy discovers he's far more than an abuser; what he's involved in endangers all their lives. To rescue the woman who has stolen his heart, Rand must follow her and do what he swore he'd never do: reconcile with his aristocratic family and finally uncover the truth behind all the lies. But time is running out for them all.

Available now on Amazon: THE RENEGADE WIFE

THE RELUCTANT WIFE

Captain Fred Wheatly's comfortable life on the fringes of Bengal comes crashing down around him when his mistress dies, leaving him with two children he never expected to have to raise. When he chooses justice over army regulations, he's forced to resign his position, leaving him with no way to support his unexpected family. He's already had enough failures in his life. The last thing he needs is an attractive, interfering woman bedeviling his steps, reminding him of his duties.

All widowed Clare Armbruster needs is her brother's signature on a legal document to be free of her past. After a failed marriage, and still mourning the loss of a child, she's had it up to her ears with the great lout of a captain who can't figure out what to do with his daughters and the assumptions she doesn't know how to take care of herself and what she needs is a husband. If only the frightened little girls didn't need her help so badly.

Clare has made mistakes in the past. Can she trust Fred now? Can she trust herself? Captain Wheatly doesn't need his aristocratic family; they've certainly never needed him. But with no more military career and two half-caste daughters to support, Fred must turn once more—as a failure—to the family he failed so often in the past. Can two hearts rise above past failures to forge a future together?

Available now on Amazon: **THE RELUCTANT WIFE**